Praise for Book 1 (*A*
Henrietta and Inspec...

"Michelle Cox masterfully recreates 1930s Chicago, bringing to life its diverse neighborhoods and eclectic residents, as well as its seedy side. Henrietta and Inspector Howard are the best pair of sleuths I've come across in ages—Cox makes us care not just about the case, but about her characters. A fantastic start to what is sure to be a long-running series."

—Tasha Alexander, *New York Times* best-selling author of *The Adventuress*

"Fans of spunky, historical heroines will love Henrietta Von Harmon."

—*Booklist* starred review

"Flavored with 1930s slang and fashion, this first volume in what one hopes will be a long series is absorbing. Henrietta and Clive are a sexy, endearing, and downright fun pair of sleuths. Readers will not see the final twist coming."

—*Library Journal* starred review

A Ring of Truth

A Ring of Truth

A HENRIETTA AND INSPECTOR HOWARD NOVEL

MICHELLE COX

SHE WRITES PRESS

Published 2016
Printed in the United States of America
ISBN: 978-1-63152-196-6 pbk
ISBN: 978-1-63152-197-3 ebk
Library of Congress Control Number: 2016957316

For information, address:
She Writes Press
1563 Solano Ave #546
Berkeley, CA 94707

She Writes Press is a division of SparkPoint Studio, LLC.

To my children, Nathaniel, Owen, and Eleanor.
You must know that all of the stories, read through all
the years, have been a poor attempt to express the aching,
extraordinary love I have for each of you.
I hope you will feel it always.

Chapter 1

Henrietta shifted uncomfortably as she stood next to Clive outside the massive oak double doors of the Howard family home—Highbury, he called it—in Winnetka. Though he had assured her all the way here that his parents would love her, and despite his quick, reassuring wink as they had walked up the flagstone pathway, she still felt uneasy, and her breath caught in her throat when a *servant* opened the door for them and welcomed Mister Clive home. Clive smiled at him and casually handed him his hat and motoring coat, but Henrietta felt sure the servant was sizing her up all the while, and was convinced that he was not impressed with what he saw.

As Clive exchanged pleasantries with the man—Billings, he called him—mostly about the weather and the drive up, Henrietta smoothed her dress and wished to God she had chosen her plain blue paisley. Instead, she was wearing the emerald green dress she had borrowed from Polly to audition in at the Marlowe. It showed off her figure beautifully, hugging her curves and accentuating her bosom, but she felt certain now as she stood there awkwardly that it was all wrong. She had intended to impress Clive's parents, but with a deepening sense of dread, she began to suspect that she should have chosen something more modest. She attempted to console herself with the fact that she had at least had the sense to elaborately pin up her long auburn hair in a somewhat old-fashioned style.

It was times like this that she missed Polly the most. Polly would have known the proper attire to wear when meeting the parents of one's new fiancé. But Polly had not returned from her grandmother's in Missouri where she had fled after Mama Leone had been murdered at the Promenade, and Henrietta didn't really blame her. Since then, Henrietta had received a few brief letters from her, but they hadn't been of any substance. Henrietta had also considered asking Lucy for advice, but she had unfortunately only seen her once since the Marlowe.

They had met for coffee one afternoon and found themselves predictably discussing all of the sordid particulars of their attempt to uncover the "secret" behind the green door at the Marlowe (the burlesque theater where they had both, until very recently, been employed) and how it had all culminated in that terrible night in which Henrietta had been captured by Neptune and his cronies, that is, before Lucy had rescued her—and Clive as well.

Eventually, however, their conversation had moved to lighter subjects, Lucy remarking how much she and the other girls missed her. Leaning forward across the stained table, Lucy had urged Henrietta to join her and Gwen and Rose at the Melody Mill, where they had all picked up jobs as cocktail waitresses, the Marlowe obviously having since been shut down by the police. "It would be just like old times," Lucy had urged. Henrietta had politely declined, a smile she could not contain creeping across her face, then, as she bashfully announced that there would be no need of that now that she had agreed to become Mrs. Clive Howard!

Lucy laughed with delight at the news and begged for all the particulars of the happy event. Henrietta was excitedly able to relate, in great detail, how the proposal had come about, but when Lucy then naturally asked about the wedding itself, Henrietta realized distressingly that she knew very little about the details. They didn't have a date yet, nor did she yet have a ring, Henrietta admitted with a forced little laugh of her own. Lucy suggested with a shrug and a certain provocation in her eyes that perhaps the inspector was just too busy at the moment with his cases, or some such police thing, to worry about these obviously minor details for now. Doubtless he would get around to it eventually, she had teased. Henrietta knew that Lucy had meant her words to be playful and teasing, but they hadn't sat very well just the same.

Not long after this exchange, Lucy had stood up and said she had to run and wished Henrietta the very best of luck. After kisses and promises to keep in touch, Lucy dashed off down Clark, and Henrietta had wondered as she watched her go, not for the first time, about the wedding, and, more importantly, just what her role as a policeman's wife would be—if Clive would expect her to keep on working—at something respectable, of course—or if he would want her to stay home and keep house for him. Either way, she assumed working as a cocktail waitress at the Melody Mill would be out of the question, so she let the idea go as she watched Lucy disappear into the crowd before she had herself distractedly made her way to the trolley.

It was an assumption she felt even more certain of now as she stood apprehensively beside Clive in the marble foyer of the Howards' home, which he had somehow failed to mention resembled a castle, or very nearly so.

She knew that Winnetka was north of the city, but she had of course never been here. The drive seemed to stretch forever, her disquietude growing by the minute, especially when they had finally arrived in the quaint town itself and had zipped past the more modest houses. Sheridan Road curved closer to Lake Michigan now to reveal larger houses—mansions, really—with huge acreage surrounding them, set back from the road, half hidden, if not by symmetrical smatterings of trees, then by privets or brick walls, though Henrietta was able to glance at enough of them to be left speechless.

Many of the estates backed up to the lake itself, making them surely worth thousands—probably millions!—Henrietta calculated, as she fretfully pulled at her gloves as though by pulling them on tighter, she could somehow make them more presentable. Henrietta had never seen anything like this, except perhaps in the movies, of which she had seen very few, actually, and she couldn't pull her eyes away, so mesmerized was she, despite her new betrothed sitting beside her, his fedora hat placed firmly on his head and a pipe gripped loosely between his teeth.

Every once in a while on the drive, between strands of conversation, he had taken his eyes from the road to look over at her, and each time, she felt her stomach churn. She was wildly attracted to him, and she thought him so dreadfully handsome with his hazel eyes and chestnut hair, though some of it was already beginning to gray. She had asked him several times since he had proposed to tell her about his family, but he had each time replied that he wanted to surprise her.

When they had finally turned into a majestic tree-lined lane, complete with an iron gate and two massive lion statues atop brick pedestals at the entrance, she was filled with dread and hoped this was a joke rather than the surprise he had alluded to. Surely this wasn't his parents' home, was it? Henrietta had glanced over at him with more than a little confusion, and, truth be told, a bit of consternation as he had indeed sped down the lane toward the house. Where was the impenetrable Inspector Howard of the Chicago police that she had fallen in love with? Surely he didn't belong here, did he?

"Tea is to be served in the morning room, Mister Clive," said Billings, whose thick jowls did not move an inch when he spoke, as if he were wearing a fleshy mask. Only his droopy eyes moved, and even then, not excessively. "I'm to show you through, if that's agreeable, sir."

"I'll show myself in, Billings, in just a moment," Clive said, looking down at Henrietta now.

"Very good, sir," Billings said with a slight bow of his head and disappeared noiselessly down the hallway.

"Ready?" Clive asked her with a smile, his eyebrow arched. "Not nervous, are you?"

How could she not be? she thought, her heart racing, but she couldn't help but smile at his penchant for reading her mind. "Of course I'm nervous!" she whispered, her eyes darting round the formal entryway and up the grand staircase, lined with larger-than-life portraits climbing the steps to the upper floors beyond. Henrietta had never seen paintings that large before or in such a quantity. Above her hung a gold-and-crystal chandelier that sparkled in the early afternoon sunlight coming through the stained glass of the windows set above the entryway. "Why didn't you tell me it would be like this?" she chastised. "I . . . I don't think I'm dressed right." Again, she looked down woefully at her dress.

Clive grinned. "Of course you're dressed appropriately! You look a dream," he said and bent closer to kiss her softly on the cheek. Despite the welcomeness of his kiss, it did not slip her attention that he had inadvertently changed her phrasing. Her employment as a curler girl at Marshall Fields had brought her into contact with a decidedly more elite clientele than she normally dealt with at Poor Pete's, and she had striven almost immediately to imitate their more eloquent speech. It was something that Clive had commented on, actually, when he had first met her—that she didn't sound like a taxi dancer. In truth, she did pride herself on being able to learn so quickly, but she still made mistakes sometimes, as Clive had just subtly implied.

At the touch of his lips, though, she felt herself melt a little, and she leaned into him, feeling safe, if only for a moment, against his chest. She wished she could stay this way, tucked into him. Clive reached for her hand. "Come on, then. They're really not so bad. Besides, we've done this once already, remember? Surely we can do it again."

Henrietta took his hand and blushed at the memory of how just a few weeks ago, they had made their way up the creaking stairs of Henrietta's apartment building to tell Ma that they were engaged to be married. Henrietta would never forget as long as she lived the look of shock on Ma's face when she haltingly explained that not only was the man standing beside her in the cramped, shabby apartment not her foreman at the electrics as Ma had been led to believe, though Ma had never actually met him, having only heard his *name* mentioned and only once at that, but that he was in fact a detective inspector with the Chicago police. That they had been on a case together and, well, had fallen in love in the process. It was not lost on Henrietta that as Clive respectfully removed his hat and shook Ma's hand, his eyes never wandered once to the miserable surroundings but had instead remained locked on each person's face with a cordial, genuine smile.

Elsie, of course, had rushed to Henrietta's side when the initial shock had been absorbed by all in the room. Stanley, who had only recently, almost begrudgingly, shifted his affections from Henrietta to her sister, Elsie (at Henrietta's insistence), had likewise jumped to his feet with surprising alacrity, muttering, "Oh, Hen!"

Clive's attempt at polite introductions had little effect on Ma, who merely stood with her hands on her hips, eyeing both of them carefully. "Aren't you a bit old for her?" were Ma's first words to the happy couple, delivered bluntly after a few painful moments of silence.

Clive had tilted his head to the side and gave a slight nod in recognition of the question's appropriateness. "Yes, Mrs. Von Harmon, I *am* older than Henrietta. I'm thirty-six, to be exact, nearly twice her age, and I feel at this juncture I should also mention that I was previously married"—here Stan let out a low whistle—"but she died while I was away at the war. Childbirth. The baby, too."

Henrietta heard Elsie, still standing at her side, let out a sad little noise, and she thought she detected a slight ripple of compassion cross Ma's face.

Clive cleared his throat. "That being said," he continued, "I'm very much in love with Henrietta, and I wish to marry her." Here he looked at Henrietta lovingly and took her hand, causing Henrietta to blush slightly and Stan to turn momentarily toward the window, Elsie keenly watching him as he did so.

Ma stared at them for a moment or two longer and then let out a bitter sigh. "Well, if that's what you want," she said with an apathetic shrug, looking intensely at Henrietta and ignoring Clive. "Police don't usually last too long. Don't expect me to cry at the funeral."

"Ma!" Henrietta cried out, looking as though she were about to say something more, but Clive motioned her to stop.

"I understand your feelings perfectly, Mrs. Von Harmon. My own parents felt exactly the same when I joined the force after the war. But, you see, I felt I had to try to do some good in the world when I came back, and this seemed to be . . ."

Ma cut him off with a disgusted sniff and even had the boldness to roll her eyes. Such "highfalutin" concepts of integrity and justice were lost on Ma, Henrietta knew, but she was furious with Ma's response just the same. How could she be so rude? What must Clive think! In shock, Henrietta stared at the floor before gathering enough courage to glance up at him now and was surprised to find his face not one of annoyance or judgment, but one of placid patience.

"If it's any consolation, Mrs. Von Harmon," he continued calmly, "I'm usually not in harm's way. It's only after the crime that I'm called in to investigate."

Ma sighed again as if defeated. "Well, I suppose I don't have any say in it, anyway. One less mouth to feed. Though I don't know what we're supposed to do now, without your wages," she said irritably.

"Oh, Ma! Can't you ever be happy? I won't leave you destitute!" Henrietta chimed in, no longer able to keep still. In truth, however, she wasn't sure how she was quite going to manage that. "And anyway, one minute you're trying to marry me off to . . . to Stan," she sputtered, "and the next minute you act like I'm deserting you when I finally do find someone . . . someone that I love. Very much." It was all coming out badly, and Henrietta didn't know how to fix it in the heat of the moment. She felt Clive give her hand a small squeeze before he released it.

"Not to worry, Mrs. Von Harmon," he said, his hat still in his other hand, "I'm quite able and happy to provide for all of you."

Ma sniffed again. "On a policeman's salary? I think not! We'll find a way. We don't need charity, you know!"

"Oh, I don't know about that, Ma," Eugene chimed in smoothly from his perch in the corner. Henrietta hadn't noticed him sitting on the low stool by the fireplace, his hands folded between his legs. He had been staring at the floor, but he now looked sideways at Henrietta. "If Hen's beau is willing to help us, maybe we should let him, seein' as he's gonna be one of the family now."

"Eugene!" said Ma angrily.

"Have you no shame, Eugene?" Henrietta blurted out. "It's time you grew up and got a job!"

"I *am* only sixteen, Henrietta!" he said with a scowl.

"What difference does that make?" she retorted. "Elsie and I have been working since we were thirteen! Scrubbing toilets or ironing . . . anything! I know you like school, but surely you could find something at night! My God!"

"As a matter of fact," Stan interrupted them, "I was just telling Eugene earlier about trying Olson's. My cousin's neighbor works there, and he might just know of a position on the delivery trucks, riding in the back, jumpin' on and off. Right, Eugene?"

Eugene looked over at Stan now, an odd expression on his face, before he nodded and looked back at the floor.

"That or I'm always hoping something will turn up at the electrics," Stan offered encouragingly.

Ma sank into a chair and put her head in her hands. "That's another thing! I can't believe you lied to us all this time, Henrietta," she said morosely. "All this time I've been bragging to the neighbors about you getting a place at the electrics, and all this time you've been playing me! I must look a fool to the whole neighborhood. I even baked a cake for you!" she cried, suddenly slamming her fist onto the table. "Well, don't expect any favors this time," she said, her voice heavy with disgust.

"Ma!" Henrietta's voice quivered as if she were either angry or trying not to cry. "What would you have me do? We needed the money . . . Poor Pete's wasn't paying me nearly enough, especially after Herbert and Eddie got the flu and the charge bill at Schneider's got so high. I heard of the taxi dancer job at the Promenade, and I . . . well, I went for it . . ."

"A taxi dancer!" Ma cried.

"See? I knew you'd never approve! That's why I had to . . ."

"Lie?" Ma put in angrily.

"Yes, if you want to put it that way. Sometimes lying is necessary, Ma!" Henrietta said loudly, bitterly reflecting as she said it that she was ironically lying now simply to spare Ma's feelings. All of them were in a sense guilty of lying, of continuing the falsehood that all of their woes had to do with their father's actions and that Ma's depressed mental state was not at least in part equally responsible for their current sad existence. They had all become very good at pretending. Henrietta longed to accuse her of wallowing in her own apathetic state and making all their lives harder than they had to be. The truth, as far as she saw it, was that if Ma hadn't become so insular, so retreating from the world since her father's suicide, she would be able to work to help support them as well. Instead, she took in a bit of washing here and there, but otherwise she remained at home, relying on Henrietta and Elsie to bring in money, while her bitterness and anger continued to cloud her mind. Henrietta knew, however, that she could never say these things—the truth—especially now, that it would make things infinitely worse, so, with extreme effort, she forced herself to remain silent.

"That's not the whole story, though, is it, Henrietta?" Eugene asked slyly from the corner.

Henrietta wanted to slap the smug smile from his face. Sometimes she just didn't know about Eugene. He was her younger brother, and though they had been close as children, she found it hard to trust him now. He had always been a quiet child, but he had changed somehow after their father's death. It was as if he had derailed and couldn't quite get back on the tracks again. Henrietta shot him a hateful look, secretly wondering how he had found out.

"No, Eugene, it's not," Henrietta said in a measured voice, knowing it was useless at this point to try to hide her past activities. "If you must know," she said to Ma, with a toss of her hair, "I went from there to being an usherette at the Marlowe."

"What's the Marlowe?" asked Ma in a scared, mystified voice, clearly unsettled that she didn't understand the weight of Henrietta's revelation.

"It's a burlesque theater downtown, Ma," Eugene answered coolly, enjoying Henrietta's angry glare.

"God in heaven!" Ma wailed. "Oh, Henrietta! Not another scandal! I always knew this was bound to happen with you! This is all your father's fault, you know!"

"Scandal? There's been no scandal, Ma!" Henrietta retorted, trembling now. How dare she continually blame everything, including this, on her father. It was taking every ounce of her self-control not to blurt out her belief that her father's death was in part caused by Ma's relentless nagging! Elsie was noiselessly crying now, and Stan had moved to her side and put his arm protectively around her.

"This has gone far enough now," Clive finally put in, firmly but not unkindly. "Mrs. Von Harmon, please. Let me explain. Henrietta only took the position at the Marlowe as a favor to me. It was quite wrong of me, and I regret it now, except, of course, that it brought me closer to her. I asked Henrietta to go undercover for me, as an usherette, to get information on a case. I . . . I misjudged her age . . . and her experience," he said tacitly. "If anyone is to blame, it would be me." He paused to clear his throat. "It should likewise be stated here, though it is by no means necessary, that Henrietta behaved quite admirably. More than that, really." He glanced at her briefly. "She was everything you might be proud of, Mrs. Von Harmon, a model of decency and virtue. She stands before you quite without reason for reproach. On *any* account," he said evenly, looking pointedly at Eugene as he did so. "So much so that I have quite fallen in love with her and have asked her just this evening to be my wife."

He turned his attention now back to Henrietta and continued as if they were alone in the room, looking directly into her eyes. "I'm very much in her debt, not just for her help on the case, which was extraordinary"—he smiled—"but for teaching me to love again. And she has quite unexpectedly accepted me, for which I shall ever be grateful."

Henrietta thought she heard a scoff come from the corner where Eugene was still perched, but she ignored it. Clive did as well and instead addressed Ma and the little group before him. "I earnestly hope that we have your blessing and that you will wish us well. If not for me, then certainly for your daughter's sake," he said, looking at Ma before turning his attention to Eugene specifically. "And your sister's," he added with a certain finality.

There was silence in the room for several seconds before Elsie finally broke it. "Well, I'll say it," she said, grasping hold of Henrietta's hands and then releasing them to embrace her tightly. "Congratulations!" Shyly, then, she moved to embrace Clive as well.

Stan, too, approached and held out his hand to Clive.

"No hard feelings?" Clive asked him with a wink.

"Nah!" Stan answered, though no one noticed, except perhaps Henrietta, that he trembled a bit as he bent to briefly kiss her cheek in congratulations and that he did not exactly meet her eyes.

All of the smaller Von Harmons, who had up to this point been standing in the back of the room along the wall, silently watching the drama unfold, now looked to Ma to see what her reaction would be. Slowly she stood up from the chair by the table, a look of sad resignation on her face. Clive took a step toward her, and Henrietta held her breath.

"Mrs. Von Harmon," he asked forthrightly. "Do we have your blessing?"

"I suppose so," Ma said stiffly with an absent wave of her hand. "I don't see what it matters, anyway." Clive's quiet, commanding presence seemed to have oddly calmed her, or perhaps it had merely deflated her. "You lot," she said, turning toward the little ones. "Get over there and congratulate Henrietta and then get off to bed." At this signal of encouragement, the five of them ran to Henrietta and hugged her, causing her to laugh and kiss each of them affectionately on the head.

"Does this mean you're going to be my uncle?" Jimmy asked Clive with a wispy sweetness, his blanket to his nose.

Clive laughed. "Something like that."

Henrietta glanced at the corner where Eugene, the only one to have not offered his congratulations, had been sitting, but he was already gone, having presumably slunk off to the bedroom. She looked at Clive, whom she saw had noticed as well, and shrugged. In response, he gave her the quickest of winks and smiled at her, causing her heart to explode with love for him all over again. He had been wonderful with them.

Ma shuffled toward the kitchen. "I suppose I should offer you some coffee. I don't think we have any tea."

"Coffee would be lovely, actually. Thank you," Clive answered.

Ma turned back toward him. "You don't exactly sound like a policeman," she said suspiciously. "What did you say your surname is?"

"Howard. Clive Howard," he answered respectfully.

"Howard?" Her face took on a blanched tone and her eyes narrowed. "Where did you say you're from?"

Clive cleared his throat slightly. "I live downtown just now, but as it happens I grew up in Winnetka."

"The Howards of Winnetka?" Ma asked faintly.

Clive did not hide his surprise. "Why, yes! Do you know them?"

Ma looked horribly shaken, almost limp, as she turned slowly back toward the kitchen. "Now how would I know them?" she asked as she went with what sounded like a tremor of worry, or was it outright fear in her voice? "Must of read it somewhere is all," she mumbled.

"I'll help you, Ma" Elsie had volunteered, following her mother to the kitchen.

As soon as the swinging door had shut behind them, Elsie went straight for the cupboard to gather some mugs, saying as she did so, "I can't believe it, Ma! Can you? Henrietta engaged! It's a shame we don't have anything else to celebrate with!"

"Well, we don't!" Ma said bitterly, leaning tiredly against the deep sink after the unexpected turn of events of the evening. "Coffee will have to do, though I'm sure that one out there's been used to much finer. Oh, Elsie!" Ma cried suddenly, holding her hand up to her mouth, as a mystified Elsie looked on. "What are we going to do?"

"I suppose you're right," Henrietta said, trying to push away the memories of that embarrassing evening when her family had eventually toasted her and Clive's engagement with mugs of coffee, though Ma remained subdued through it all until Clive had taken his leave shortly after.

Clive had the good manners not to refer again to that evening's events, more specifically to her family's reaction to him, as a topic of discussion, but Henrietta had longed to try to explain it all to him. She didn't know where to even begin, though, how to describe Ma or even how to bring it up again, so it had remained untouched between them. Now, as she stood in this grandiose house with chandeliers and paintings and servants, of all things, she couldn't help but blush all over again at the mean surroundings she had introduced him to that night.

"I love you, remember?" Clive whispered to her as she gripped his arm tightly. He led her, then, across the massive foyer to a set of closed pocket doors made of thick walnut. Henrietta smiled up at him gratefully and took a deep breath as he rapped a couple of times with his knuckles before sliding one of the doors open just wide enough for them to pass through side by side.

Henrietta tried not to gasp as they entered the large, bright room. Everywhere she looked was luxury and beauty like she had never seen before. The walls themselves were covered with gold damask wallpaper, and everywhere sat neat little groupings of white painted furniture with royal blue upholstery. She imagined that this was what a room in a palace might look like, as her eyes darted from a large urn overflowing with roses on a blue silk-covered table in front of a huge bay window, itself draped with thick blue curtains with gold trim, to the intricately patterned Oriental rug underfoot. Above them hung more paintings in thick gold frames, and along one wall was a large fireplace with low bookshelves on either side that held what looked like small curiosities and trinkets along with various books. A small fire was burning in the grate despite the fact that it was late June, but it somehow did not seem out of place, nor was it too warm.

On one chair in front of the fire sat a woman, presumably Clive's mother, with ramrod-straight posture. She was wearing a fitted silk dress of navy blue, belted at the waist with flared sleeves, matching heels, and, of course, a small pert silk hat perched on the side of her head, her hair perfectly pulled up in the latest style. Near her, next to the fire, stood a man whom Henrietta naturally assumed was Clive's father, wearing a jacket and tie and holding a small pipe in his right hand. Except for a slight paunch to him, he still cut a dignified, elegant figure. There was no doubt he had been very handsome in his day, and still was, Henrietta thought generously.

She could feel both pairs of eyes on her as they made their way into the room.

"Hello, Mother," Clive said, dutifully bending to kiss the woman seated before them. "Good morning, Father," Clive then said deferentially.

"Hello, Clive, darling," his mother responded with muted emotion.

Clive took a deep breath and turned to Henrietta, smiling. "Mother, Father, I'd like you to finally meet my fiancée, Henrietta."

Henrietta's face burned as she felt Clive's mother carefully assess her and saw the slight frown that resulted when her eyes lingered on her dress. Henrietta forced herself, however, to meet her gaze before turning to look at Clive's father.

Mr. Howard gave a little cough, then, and stepped forward briskly.

"Hello, my dear," he said with a distinct English accent, taking her hand and grasping it delicately. "Alcott Howard. Very pleased to meet you." He looked up briefly at Clive, though Henrietta couldn't read what was in his face. Clive's mother then rose and embraced her in the very loosest definition of the word. "You're very lovely, my dear. I can see why Clive is so taken with you." She produced the briefest of smiles, which seemed to Henrietta to be decidedly false.

"Thank you," Henrietta said quietly, not sure what else to say.

"Shall we sit down?" Mrs. Howard motioned stiffly toward a small settee opposite her chair. "Tea is on its way."

"Wonderful. Just what's needed after a long drive," Clive said, clapping his hands together enthusiastically as he sat down next to Henrietta, casually crossing his legs while Mr. Howard made his way to the armchair next to his wife. "I hope Mary's prepared some of her strawberry scones," Clive said cheerfully. Henrietta thought him not nervous exactly, but he did seem a little on edge. But perhaps she was only imagining it.

"Yes, I made sure of it," Mrs. Howard said with what Henrietta thought was her first genuine smile. "I know they're your favorite."

"I say, how *was* the drive, anyway?" Mr. Howard said, leaning back in his chair as he took a deep puff of his pipe, startling Henrietta in his sudden resemblance to Clive. Without waiting for an answer, Mr. Howard went on. "You took Sheridan, I presume? Did you happen to observe what they're doing outside the club? A disgrace, that's what it is!"

"I can't say that I did, Father." Clive turned to Henrietta and smiled. "My mind was rather on other things, you see." He seemed to be relaxing now, and Henrietta only wished she could.

"Putting up a sign, that's what they're doing," his father continued, seemingly unaware of Clive's comment. "A bloody big sign, as if all the world need know the whereabouts of the entrance. It's members-only, anyway, so I don't quite see the point. Damned regrettable. Whatever was wrong with the little stone sign we had previously? Served its purpose. Gaudy as hell this one is."

"Alcott," Mrs. Howard put in warningly. She was a thin woman with a long oval face and high cheekbones. She had a relatively small tight mouth, and when she smiled, Henrietta did not fail to notice her perfect teeth. Her hair was still very dark and thick despite her age, and she had small dark eyes. She was not what one would call beautiful, but she was not unattractive either. In her stylish dress, adorned only with a single strand of pearls and a matching pearl brooch, she exuded a discreet, classic sense of beauty and elegance. Her face was very serious, but it held what Henrietta hoped was at least a hint of kindness.

"Sorry, my dear," he said respectfully. "I get carried away, you know."

"Yes, but I'm sure we have other things to discuss with Clive and his . . . *fiancée*," Mrs. Howard said the word almost with difficulty, "than the club's new signage."

"Quite right," he said agreeably. "Quite right."

There was a faint knock on the door, then, and another servant, a younger one this time, came in carrying an enormous silver tea tray. He set it expertly on the low table between them and stood back.

"Will there be anything else, Madam?" he said stiffly, not looking at anyone in particular but instead straight out the window.

"No, James. Thank you. That will be all for now."

Before he could depart, however, Henrietta spoke to him. "That's funny, I have a brother James, though we call him Jimmy," she said, looking first at Mrs. Howard and then over at Mr. Howard. She was mortified when neither of them, nor the footman either, for that matter, reacted except for perhaps a small attempt of a smile from Mr. Howard, though it really resembled more of a polite grimace. The footman bowed slightly and retreated from the room.

"Yes, you must tell us all about your family," Mrs. Howard said almost with a frown as she leaned forward and began to pour out steaming cups of tea. "Sugar?" she asked Henrietta.

"A little, I suppose," she answered meekly.

"One, then?"

"One?"

"One cube? Or two?"

"Oh. Just one, thank you." Henrietta felt her face flush again. She rarely had tea and certainly never had a sugar *cube*. The stuff they got from the Armory was always loose in a two-pound brown bag.

"Milk?"

Henrietta wasn't sure whether she liked milk in her tea or not, so she answered, "No, thank you," to appear less a nuisance and in case it would require answering more questions. Mrs. Howard handed her the delicate china cup and saucer, then, and went on to arrange the rest of the cups, obviously already knowing how everyone else preferred theirs. Clive reached down and handed her a china plate and a pale blue cloth napkin, for which she was grateful, as it provided a sort of makeshift shield. He seemed to sense her unease, though it probably wasn't too difficult to deduce.

"You must try one of Mary's scones," he said to her. "They're simply delightful. Here, allow me." He reached across and put one on her plate for her with a pair of silver tongs. Henrietta smiled her thanks, but she didn't try it right away. She wasn't sure what to do. Should she just pick it up with her fingers? Or should she use a fork? She looked at the tray and saw four forks stacked neatly to the side, but no one was reaching for them. Surely if she were supposed to use a fork, Clive would have handed her one, wouldn't he have?

In truth, Henrietta was amazed at the amount as well as the beauty of the food displayed on the tray. Not only was there the basket of scones wrapped up in a crisp, linen cloth, but there was a three-tiered tray holding tiny sandwiches cut into triangles, pastries, and even fresh strawberries. Beside the teapot was a large pot of jam and a huge block of what looked like *real* butter. It was all too lovely to eat, and Henrietta wished Elsie could see it. Mr. and Mrs. Howard were busily arranging things on their plates, though Henrietta observed that they only took a few items. She must exercise restraint, she wistfully noted, though she could have easily polished off the whole of the tray's contents herself.

"Well, aren't you going to try it?" Clive asked.

There was no way around it. She would have to just pick it up and hope it was the correct way of doing it. She shot him a look of despair and then tentatively lifted the scone to her mouth with her fingers and took a small bite. It was quite good, she thought, but dry.

Clive laughed a little. "Don't you want any butter or jam on it?"

Henrietta shook her head, not wanting to admit her faux pas. "No, I like it plain," she fibbed and took a sip of her hot tea.

"So, Henrietta," Mrs. Howard said, peering over her cup, "as I was saying. You must tell us about your family. Clive's been positively silent on the matter. Saying we must meet you first. And so, here we are," she said, sitting up very straight. "What did you say your surname is?" she asked.

"Von Harmon."

Clive retained his relaxed air, Henrietta noted, his arm now stretched out casually on the settee behind her. He seemed unaffected by his mother's line of questioning, almost as if he didn't hear it, but instead sat looking at Henrietta, a slightly amused, slightly disbelieving look to his face, as if he couldn't get enough of her, as if he couldn't believe she was his.

"Von Harmon?" Mrs. Howard seemed puzzled. "That rings a bell, does it not, Alcott?"

"Can't say that it does, my dear," Mr. Howard said lazily, stirring his tea as he reached for another pastry.

"I'm sure it does," Mrs. Howard mused. "I'm sure you're related, Alcott, to the Von Harmons somehow. Cousins, I believe, on your mother's side. You know, the ones in France? Or is it Germany these days?"

"Perhaps, my dear. I'm not really sure." He looked up and gave a general smile to the company assembled, his eyes crinkling at the corners.

"Are you French?" Mrs. Howard asked Henrietta.

"I don't know," Henrietta said nervously. "My father used to tell us stories about how the family was originally from somewhere called Alsace-Lorraine, I think."

"There! I was right! She must be a Von Harmon!" Mrs. Howard said approvingly. "How extraordinary! It's a wonder I didn't make the connection before," she said, looking at Clive. "What does your father do, dear?" she asked in a decidedly more friendly tone.

"He . . . he's gone. Passed away several years ago." Henrietta glanced up anxiously at Clive, who smiled at her reassuringly.

"Oh, I'm very sorry to hear that," Mrs. Howard said sincerely. "So much tragedy these days, is there not?" She paused for a moment as if out of sympathy and then continued. "But what *did* he do, when he was alive, that is?"

"He worked at the Schwinn motorcycle factory. On Courtland?" Henrietta explained eagerly, glad to be able to share something about her father, whom she still missed terribly.

"Ah, in business," Mrs. Howard said understandingly. "A vice president, perhaps?" she asked, not being able to keep the hope from her voice and meanwhile chancing a glance at Alcott, who did not appear to reciprocate any interest beyond that of the pastries laid before him.

"Oh, no!" Henrietta smiled. "He was on the line! He was an assembler, I think he used to call it."

"A laborer?" Mrs. Howard said incredulously.

"Well, yes, I suppose you could call him that," Henrietta answered, realizing now that she had said something wrong again.

"Nothing wrong with an honest day's work, is there, Father?" Clive chimed in, coming to her rescue.

"Not at all, my boy. Not at all. But not always nice to get one's hands dirty, though, eh? Not nice at all!"

Clive merely sat back, giving Henrietta a wink as he did so.

Mrs. Howard cleared her throat. "And your mother? What of her family?" she asked weakly.

Henrietta sighed. "Well, I'm not sure, really. She never speaks of them. Her maiden name was Exley, I believe. Martha Exley."

Mrs. Howard stopped stirring her tea and remained motionless now as she stared at Henrietta. Even Mr. Howard paused in his efforts. The silence in the room was deafening until Clive broke it with a noise that oddly resembled a chuckle.

"That can't be," Mrs. Howard said finally, ignoring Clive and setting down her teacup with deliberation. "It simply can't!" she added, still mystified.

"Exley, did you say?" Mr. Howard butted in, finally interested, it would seem, in the conversation.

"Yes, I think so," Henrietta said nervously again, wondering what horrors the Exleys must have committed in the past, judging from the Howards' initial reaction. She looked at Clive for an explanation.

"The Exleys are part of their set," he explained languidly, with a noticeable lack of the drama that had just come before. "They go way back. John Exley and Father are quite good friends. Both at Cambridge together and all that."

"Well, surely it must be a different Exley," said Henrietta delicately. Her mother never spoke about her family, always saying it didn't matter, and Henrietta had assumed they were either dead or far away. On more than one occasion, however, she now remembered disconcertedly, she had sometimes suspected that her mother had come from a well-to-do family simply by the way she often spoke or how she sometimes held herself.

"Exley is not a very common name," Mrs. Howard pointed out slowly. "Where is she from?"

"I'm . . . I'm not really sure. She never speaks about them."

"I'm *sure* John's sister was named Martha," Mrs. Howard continued, turning to her husband after musing a few moments. "Think, Alcott! You must have met her at some point."

"Hmmm . . . Martha . . . Could have been her name. I think I may have met her at a dinner or a Christmas party, some such thing. Very quiet. If I did meet her, didn't say two words to her. Ran off and got married, I think John said once. Not very forthcoming about the whole thing was John. Bit of a hush-hush, you know. Not really the thing one asks about now, is it?"

Mrs. Howard allowed herself to absorb this information before she took up her teacup again. "Well, really!" she said almost to herself, managing a smile before turning back to Clive and Henrietta. "What a morning this has turned out to be!" she continued cheerfully. "To think we may have a Von Harmon *and* an Exley sitting before us! Who would have known you would be so clever, Clive? We thoroughly approve, don't we, Alcott?"

"What? Oh, yes, of course, dear. Course we do, old boy. Any more tea in the pot?"

"I think there's been some mistake, Mrs. Howard," Henrietta offered feebly, unable to accept the past they so clearly wanted her to claim. "I really don't think I'm who you suppose I am. I'm sure my mother isn't this John Exley's sister." Henrietta couldn't imagine her mother growing up in a place similar to this and leaving it all for her father. But then again, could this perhaps have been the reason for her bitterness all these years? she wondered. Had she regretted her decision? And what about all of her father's stories about how their family back in Alsace were part of the "ruling class," as he had called them? She had assumed as she had gotten older that they were just stories he had made up for their entertainment, something to help their meager dinners to go down easier and hopefully last a bit longer, but suppose they had been true? They couldn't be, though, could they?

"Nonsense! I'm sure of it, my dear," Mrs. Howard countered. "Your mother must have had her reasons for keeping quiet on the subject. At any rate, perhaps we'll find out." She paused, but only for a moment. "I know! We must have a party! An engagement party! It's the only sensible thing to do; get the families together again. I'm sure your mother would be happy to be reunited with her long-lost family, would she not? How perfectly splendid!"

"Oh, no!" Henrietta exclaimed before she could catch herself. "Oh, please! I don't think that's a good idea! Do you, Clive?" She looked at him desperately.

"But why ever not, my dear?" Mrs. Howard asked, puzzled. "Surely you want to meet Clive's friends and relatives? They'll be positively thrilled to meet you; they've quite given up hope for Clive, you see, poor thing. And such a beautiful choice he's made."

Henrietta blushed and looked at Clive again. He was absently tracing the fabric on the knee of his trousers. For once she wished he would read her mind. Finally she detected what she thought was the smallest smile on his face as he looked up at Mrs. Howard.

"Mother, we don't want a fuss. Surely we can avoid all this?"

"Well, the families *do* have to meet each other eventually, Clive. Don't worry; it will be modest. Just a few friends."

"I've seen your 'modest' before, Mother," Clive grinned. "All right, then," he sighed. "Very small. We don't want to frighten Henrietta away, you know."

"But . . . she's . . . she's not been well!" Henrietta sputtered. "I don't know if she could make it!" Henrietta felt panicked. Why had Clive so readily given in?

"Why, it won't be right away, dear," she smiled sweetly. "We'll need some time to plan it, and of course, the wedding itself. Have you set a date?"

"Not yet, no," Clive answered. "We haven't gotten that far, have we, darling?" he asked, lightly touching her hand.

Darling? He had never called her that before, and she wasn't sure if she liked it or not.

"I've got it! I've a simply marvelous idea!" Mrs. Howard looked excitedly from one to the other. "You must come and stay with us for a time, my dear, if your mother can spare you, that is. That way we can get to know each other better and plan it all out! It will be splendid. Just the thing, I'm sure. Don't you agree, Alcott?"

"What, what? Oh, yes! Yes, of course, my dear. Enchanted to have you."

"Oh, no! I couldn't possibly . . . I've . . . I'm very needed at home, you see."

"Clive! Surely you can convince her . . ." Mrs. Howard pleaded.

Clive put his hand on top of Henrietta's. "It might not be such a bad idea, you know," he said, looking at her now.

"Clive!"

Clive sighed and stood up. "Perhaps I should show Henrietta the rose garden. It's quite lovely this time of year."

Mrs. Howard peered at him in confusion before a look of understanding then crossed her face. "Yes, dear. Of course. Splendid," Mrs. Howard agreed, leaning back in her armchair now.

Clive reached out his hand to Henrietta. "Shall we?"

Henrietta's suspicions were aroused by this abrupt suggestion, but she desperately wanted to get out of the room, and fresh air sounded heavenly. "Yes, let's," she said eagerly and took his hand, Mr. Howard politely standing as she rose.

Henrietta followed behind Clive to a set of French doors which, when opened, led out onto a wide terrace. Clive led her across the huge slate slabs and down two stone steps to the formal rose gardens that lay beyond. Any other time, Henrietta would have been enthralled by the sight of the maze of shrubbery and roses before her, but she felt too peevish now and a bit nauseous, if truth be told.

Expertly, Clive led her into the maze, and as soon as they were far enough into the garden to be out of sight of the morning room windows, he stopped and pulled her to him, kissing her deeply, entwining his fingers gently with hers. She was shocked at first, completely taken off guard, but after a few moments she felt herself giving in to him, felt herself melting at his touch as his hands traveled down her back. She could not help responding in kind, breathing in the scent of him and wanting it to last forever. After what seemed only a few minutes, however, he pulled away, breathing hard.

"Oh, Clive! What are we going to do?" Henrietta moaned, her heart still racing from his kisses.

"Go through with the party, I suppose," he grinned, still holding one of her hands.

"That's not exactly what I meant," she said and wondered what she *had* meant. "I can't stay here!" she went on, choosing to address the most obvious problem first. "Surely you can see why?"

"Well, when Mother's got an idea fixed in her head, it's very difficult to unfix it," he sighed.

"Clive!" she said evenly, "you know I can't possibly leave them all."

He lifted her hand to his lips and kissed it as he looked into her eyes. "But you're going to have to sooner or later, dearest . . . when we marry. Is that not so? You weren't still planning on living with them afterward, were you?" he said, his accompanying smile kind.

Henrietta closed her eyes in defeat. He was right, of course, but she hadn't had much time to think about it all. "Clive . . . I . . . they need my wages," she said as she stared at the ground, her face burning.

"I know," he said tenderly. "I'll take care of that." He lifted her chin with his finger so that he could look into her eyes. "Say you'll come and stay. Just for a little while? Get to know Mother and Father and all of this," he said, glancing around the huge property. "Please? It would make them so happy. And me."

Henrietta felt herself weaken before the warmth of his gaze upon her. She wanted to please him, to be near him. "I suppose," she sighed. "But not for very long. And I don't know what I'm going to tell Ma."

"Just tell her the truth. Always the best policy, don't you think?"

"I'll try," she said, though she still felt unsure about this whole idea.

"Thank you, darling," he said, bending to kiss her again, and Henrietta, the "darling" still ringing unnaturally in her ears, fervently hoped she wasn't making a dreadful mistake.

Chapter 2

"How are you settling in, my dear?" Mrs. Howard asked Henrietta from across the breakfast table where she sat with Mr. Howard, who was absently munching toast and reading the paper.

"Fine, thank you, Mrs. Howard," said Henrietta, nervously stirring her coffee.

"Did you sleep well?" she asked in a clipped tone.

Henrietta merely nodded, wishing, again, that Clive were there and tried not to feel so horribly out of place, but so much was happening so quickly.

It wasn't long after their stroll in the garden that Clive had proposed to drive Henrietta back to the city to collect her things. Mrs. Howard was visibly upset by this abrupt change of plans, saying that she had assumed they would be staying for dinner, as they saw so little of Clive these days as it was. Clive had responded by kissing his mother on the cheek, which, Henrietta observed, caused that venerable woman's shoulders to sag just a bit, a clear signal of defeat. Mrs. Howard could not seem to refrain, however, from making several—at least three—disparaging comments about how Mary was going to be put out after all the preparations that she had gone through in anticipation of Mister Clive coming home. Clive had responded by saying that he would have a word with Mary in the morning to make it up to her.

Unusually buoyant, as if the some inner sanctum had been breached and thereby conquered, Clive peppered the drive back to the highway with amusing stories of his boyhood at Highbury and the antics he had gotten up to with his sister, Julia, until their voices were drowned out by the roar of the engine straining on the highway, intent on doing its job of returning them to the city from which they had come.

Henrietta instead took to looking out the window at the silhouettes of the trees as they whipped by, though Clive held her hand tight. Here in the farthest reaches of Chicago's shadow, she had become privy to a side of Clive that she hadn't known existed, and she was, frankly, confused. When she fell in love with him, she had known him as the aloof, cool Inspector whom, as she herself had witnessed, could be as hard-edged and violent as the next cop. She had assumed that he was one like herself, living in the grit of the city, trying to struggle through. Now, however, he had revealed what was almost a secret identity, and his was a very different existence altogether. Why hadn't he told her about this other life of his? Maybe he hadn't had a chance? she wondered, trying to be fair, though, if she were honest, she wasn't convinced.

When they finally arrived in front of her apartment building, she was awash with a mounting sense of dread at having to face Ma and tell her the truth about Clive and what it would mean for them all, though, admittedly, she didn't really know herself. Clive gallantly offered to come up with her, but Henrietta knew that that would make things worse, so he agreed to leave her for an hour or so while he stopped off at the station to confer with the chief on certain matters before he would return to collect her. As he walked her to the door, though, Clive carefully placed an envelope in her handbag, the contents of which, to her great embarrassment, she was pretty sure she knew. He instantly dispelled her discomfort, however, by quietly telling her that what was his was hers, or soon would be.

Once inside the dark entryway of the building, Henrietta paused to collect herself before mounting the dirty, worn stairs, silently rehearsing what she would say to Ma and feeling a spark of irritation growing in her chest. Why should she be so hesitant to tell Ma that her husband-to-be was rich beyond their wildest imaginings? Shouldn't she be rushing up the stairs to tell them all that their fortunes had changed? But no, thought Henrietta, disgusted. Ma would find a way to sour even this, and Henrietta could predict that it was going to have something to do with her having to leave them and go so far away—and sooner rather than later it seemed, if Mrs. Howard had her way. And, Henrietta sighed, reluctantly beginning to climb the steps now, there was obviously some dark secret to unearth regarding Ma's connection to that world, and Henrietta did not think it a good one, or wouldn't Ma have mentioned it before now?

With her stomach clenched in a knot, Henrietta entered the dingy apartment, shutting the door behind her with a bit of a shove, as was required these days because it sometimes stuck, and was surprised to find Ma sitting in the ratty armchair by the fire as if she had never left.

As there was nothing else for it, she bravely proceeded to relate to Ma the whole of the truth about Clive, still in a bit of a state of disbelief herself. She was completely thrown off, however, when Ma's first reaction was one of, of all things, tears, as she buried her face in her hands, mumbling, "So it's true, then."

When Henrietta then tried carefully to explain about going to stay with them for an undetermined time, Ma's tears and odd silence turned predictably to irritation.

"But why?" Ma demanded, more than once. "Have you stopped to think what we're supposed to do here without you?"

"This is really just about the money, isn't it, Ma?" Henrietta had retorted.

"Yes, Henrietta, it's always about the money. You'd know that if you had any brains in that head," Ma hissed.

Henrietta felt her fingers grip the envelope filled with Clive's money in her handbag. Part of her was tempted not to give it to Ma at all—she didn't deserve it—but part of her wanted to use it to shame her with the Howards' obvious generosity. To prove Clive's integrity and that something good could come of this strange situation, that she hadn't done so badly after all. Before she could change her mind, she quickly drew out the envelope and handed it to Ma, not being able to hold back a bit of flourish as she did so.

"What's that?" Ma asked, her eyes narrowed.

"Just take it!" Henrietta exclaimed, thrusting it closer to Ma until she finally reached out and grasped it. Ma let her eyes travel briefly over the contents before she tossed it with disgust onto the table, a look of weariness crossing her face now.

"We can't take that money, Henrietta, and you know it."

Henrietta exhaled deeply. "Why not, Ma?"

"Can't you see what he's trying to do?"

"Help us?" Henrietta offered.

"He's paying us off. Buying you, you might say."

"Ma! Don't be ridiculous! He's merely trying to help us. He knows you need my wages, and I . . . I can't work just now."

"Why not? That's what I don't understand. Why can't you be working?"

"Because I . . . I told you . . . I have to stay with them for a while. Clive wants me to . . . well . . . to get to know them and plan the wedding and everything. There's a lot to do . . ." she trailed off here, unsure herself of what was actually going to be required of her to plan what she feared was in danger of becoming a rather elaborate event. "And besides, Ma, I'm going to have to leave soon, anyway . . ." she said, echoing Clive's words to her, "you know . . . when I am married to him. I can't keep living here, giving you my paycheck."

"We can't take charity, Henrietta," Ma said through gritted teeth. "I can't take money from that family."

"Why? It's not charity!" Henrietta insisted, though she rather thought it very nearly was. "Anyway, don't you think you're being a hypocrite? We take charity food from the Armory all the time!"

“That’s different! That’s government food. Everyone does that!” Ma countered savagely, but Henrietta knew she had hit a sore point.

“Then why don’t you ever go down and get it? Why do you always have to send me or Elsie?”

“Oh, why did you have to get mixed up with them, Henrietta!” Ma moaned, ignoring her question. “Why couldn’t you have just met some average man from the neighborhood and settled down? But, no! You always did aim too high!” Ma said angrily, her voice rising.

“I am *not* aiming too high!” Henrietta exclaimed. “How was I to know he’s from a wealthy family? It’s not exactly his fault, you know, any more than . . .” she let her voice trail off.

“Any more than what?” Ma asked angrily. When Henrietta didn’t respond, Ma went on. “Oh, Henrietta, how can you be so stupid?” she groaned. “Doesn’t it worry you in the slightest? He wasn’t exactly honest with you, you know. You don’t even really know him, and now he wants you to stay in his parents’ home while he’s gallivanting around the city? Doesn’t sound right to me,” she grunted, regaining some composure. “You’ll be nothing more than a kept woman from what I can see!”

“Asking me to be his wife and introducing me to his parents does not sound like a ‘kept woman’ to me, Ma!” Henrietta retorted, trying to ignore the fact that Ma’s words had a distressing ring of truth to them, at least regarding Clive’s honesty.

“Well, you do what you like, Henrietta. You always do. Anything I say isn’t going to make a blind bit of difference,” Ma said bitterly as she heavily got to her feet. “Still sounds like they’re buying you to me, though” she added under her breath.

“Why can’t you ever be happy for me?” Henrietta asked in a steely voice.

“Why can’t you ever see things the way they really are?” Ma said bitingly.

Henrietta stood quivering with anger, wanting to say more but not daring to. Finally, she muttered, “Well, the money’s there. Do what you like.”

She stormed off to the bedroom, then, to pack her belongings. She despaired that she didn't have a decent case to put everything in and, for a brief second, considered running over to Stanley's to ask if he had one she could borrow, but she had no desire to face what would surely be his disapproval as well. In the end, she finally settled on the old carpetbag she had once taken from the Promenade, dragging it out from under the bed, and carefully placed a pitifully few items in it. She had been hoping that she would be able to ask Ma about her possible connection to the Howards, but she didn't have the strength for it at the moment; and, anyway, Ma was certainly not in the mood. It was a question that would just have to wait.

The sun was just starting to set with soft pinks and oranges staining the sky when Clive had reappeared to collect her. Ma had not even said goodbye to her, just shuffled past her to the bedroom where she shut herself up, claiming a headache, before Clive reached the top of the stairs, so that the large bouquet of flowers he had brought for her were laid to the side on the kitchen table with the envelope of money placed under it.

Both Henrietta and Clive were silent as they started out on the way back to Winnetka, Clive's cheerful demeanor from before having shifted to one of pensiveness and Henrietta still being upset by the heated exchange with Ma. Henrietta chanced a glance at him now and worried that perhaps his more somber attitude had something to do with her, or was it because of Ma's rudeness? Or maybe it was something entirely different, like perhaps an unsolved case. Annoyingly, her mind kept wandering back to what Ma had said about him, about him buying her and not being honest, but she angrily pushed it aside, determined to rekindle their earlier mood. She tried to draw him into conversation by asking him questions about his car, or about what the chief had said, or, as a last resort, about the neighborhoods they were passing through. Clive responded appropriately, but not enthusiastically, she noted, her heart sinking a little bit more with each of his laconic answers. Finally she took to looking out the window again, though there was nothing much to see in the darkness, and was surprised when he turned off the highway at a place she was pretty sure was not Winnetka. In fact it seemed like they had only gone half the distance.

"Is this Winnetka?" she asked, puzzled.

"No, it's Evanston," Clive said, pulling the car abruptly over to the side of the road and stopping it.

"Why have we stopped?" she asked, concerned. "Do you need gasoline?"

"This is no good, Henrietta," he said, looking at her steadily now. Immediately, her stomach clenched. She should have expected this. She knew it was too good to be true. She had been right all along—and so had Ma. What would a man like Clive possibly want with a girl like her?

"Let's not go back just yet," Clive said slowly. "Let's stop and have dinner first." He looked at her hopefully. "I know a place here. It's very good. Nothing fancy, but decent. And anyway, it seems I owe you a dinner. Remember?" he said with a smile.

"What . . . what do you mean?"

"Don't you remember Polly's apartment? I promised you a dinner?"

"That's what this is about?"

"What did you think this was about?" he asked, concerned, his head tilted to the side. When she didn't answer, the lump in her throat preventing it, he leaned closer to her and tucked a stray lock of her hair behind her ear. "I simply want to get to know my bride-to-be better. I want to know everything about you, Henrietta. To cherish you in the way that you should be. Doesn't that make sense?"

All Henrietta could do was nod, desperately fighting a sudden urge to cry.

"And God knows we won't be left alone for a minute once we get back to Highbury," he said wryly. "So, what do you say? Phillipe's Italian restaurant, just about a mile ahead? Or Mary's cold cuts and cheese in the drawing room?"

Henrietta could not help but smile. "Won't your mother be worried?" she managed to ask.

"I'll telephone them from the restaurant. They'll just have to get over it," he said, putting the car into gear again.

The next couple of hours passed uneventfully as the two of them sat in a dimly lit alcove in the back of the restaurant, though a new intimacy was perhaps born by their honest conversation. Henrietta, at Clive's' prompting, told him more about the death of her father, her mother's subsequent despair, and the true state of their poverty. Clive listened attentively as she told him how she still missed her father terribly but that she was forbidden to speak of him at home, and she read, not for the first time, the deep compassion in his eyes as he took her hand across the table. And while she was grateful for his attentiveness, she grew self-conscious, then, feeling that perhaps she had talked too much about herself. Slowly she pulled her hand from his and took a drink of her wine. She wanted to ask him about Catherine, his first wife who had died in childbirth, or why he lived and worked as a detective when he so obviously didn't need to. Was he trying to escape as well? His parents seemed pleasant enough—his mother a bit designing, maybe, but weren't most mothers? What could he be trying to run from? She was so confused. She could feel Clive's eyes on her, so she finally looked up and met his gaze.

"What were you thinking just now?" he asked.

"Oh, I don't know!" Henrietta answered. "A lot of things, I suppose."

"Such as?"

Henrietta caught his eye. "Something like why you . . . why you didn't tell me everything about yourself."

Clive sighed. "It's a long story."

"But shouldn't I know it?"

"Yes, of course. You're quite right. But maybe we should continue this conversation at home. Would you mind?"

Calling a place like Highbury "home" sounded strange to Henrietta's ears, but she let it pass without comment and merely nodded. Clive signaled the waiter for the bill, and while they waited, Henrietta rested her chin in the palm of one hand and looked at him.

"Do you really have to go back to the city tomorrow?" she asked.

"I'm afraid I do, darling," he answered grimly. "Duty calls. The chief gave me today off, but I need to get back."

She watched as he signed the bill, his signature enough of a promise of payment. "Is this some sort of test?" she asked, suddenly feeling a little woozy.

"A test? Of what sort?" he asked, eyebrows raised.

"You know. Me staying with your family," she suggested.

"Of course it's not a test!" he laughed. "As it happens, Mother very much wants to know you and discover what charms you've managed to work on me, seeing as I've cleverly evaded her matrimonial attempts for years now."

Henrietta could not help but laugh, too. "But what am I supposed to do all day? I'm used to working!"

"I don't know. Explore," Clive said, standing up now and coming around to hold her chair for her. "There's a row boat down by the lake. And I'm sure Mother will keep you busy with plans and all of that."

As Clive led her back through the restaurant, then, squeezing their way through the groupings of red-and-white-checked tables lit only by candles, Henrietta tried to take it all in and commit it to memory. It wasn't a fancy restaurant by any stretch; in fact it was rather plain, and Henrietta suspected that if all of the lights were switched on, some of the corners may have revealed a bit more dust and grime than they should have. Clive's face held a puzzled look as he held the door for her, as she had not immediately gone through but had instead turned to look behind her one more time.

"Coming?" he asked, confused.

She faced him, then, and placed a hand on his arm.

"Thank you for dinner, Clive. It was my first time in a restaurant. A real restaurant, that is. The counter at Woolworths doesn't count."

She smiled and looked around one last time. "Everything was so lovely. I want to remember it."

Clive looked at her at first as if she were in jest, but when he saw that she was in earnest, his bemused face changed to one of unmitigated love and almost worship. Despite them being in a public place, he quickly bent to kiss her and then whispered in her ear, "I'm the one to thank you, my darling. Come, let's go."

In contrast to the drive up thus far, Henrietta had sat very close to Clive as they continued on to Winnetka, content to just be near him without need of conversation. It was only when Clive turned the car into the lane and Highbury came into view that she began to feel nervous all over again. To Henrietta's eye, it resembled a castle of sorts, complete with a turret and buttresses and thick stonework entwined with ivy. To calm her nerves, she began to count the chimneys rising up from the heavy slate roof and stopped at seven before she gave up and took a deep breath for courage.

Having deposited their wraps with the austere Billings, Clive had led Henrietta to the drawing room in search of some cognac, Henrietta hoping to continue the conversation they had started at the restaurant. Instead, they were surprised to discover the Howards, still very much awake and waiting for them. Mrs. Howard had greeted them warmly, but did not then refrain from mentioning, several times, her disappointment in their getting back so late, as she had hoped they might at least have had a game of bridge before retiring.

Seeing as cards were happily, for his part, now out of the question, Mr. Howard declared instead that champagne was in order, despite the lateness of the hour, as they had not yet toasted the happy couple, and the bell was forthwith rung.

Billings eventually appeared with the requested bottle, and the toast was dutifully and unceremoniously made, after which they all sat down politely and small talk had ensued. And though Mr. Howard had been the one to suggest the bottle be opened in the first place, he was regrettably the first to begin nodding in his armchair, perched dangerously near the fire. In the end, Mrs. Howard was forced to come to his rescue before he either burned himself or embarrassingly began to snore and accordingly urged him upstairs with her.

Before leaving the room, Mrs. Howard gave Henrietta a somewhat restrained embrace, saying as she did so, "We're so very glad you're here, my dear. I hope you'll be quite comfortable. Billings will get you anything you need." Henrietta mumbled a thank-you, and, with that, Mr. and Mrs. Howard finally made their way upstairs.

Henrietta watched them go and, feeling tired herself, had expected to follow them. Stifling a yawn, she was surprised, then, when Clive had suggested that they have a quick nightcap on the terrace as they had originally planned. Realizing that it might be a whole week or more before she saw him again, Henrietta willingly accepted, despite the fact that she felt she had already drank a bit too much.

The air was warm as they stepped out, Clive carrying two cognacs. Though most of the property was bathed in darkness, Henrietta could hear the lap of the water off Lake Michigan, which the back of the property gradually sloped down toward. In the distance, she could see the flicker of heat lightning occasionally lighting up the sky under the false pretense of heralding a genuine storm. Henrietta traced the low stone fence with her finger and glanced up at the house, still lit up in places, and was overcome by its sheer magnitude.

"Here you are, darling," Clive said, coming over and handing her a crystal glass.

Hesitantly she took a drink and gasped at the burn as the liquid traveled down her throat.

Clive smiled. "Just sip it."

Henrietta nodded, staring at the cognac and then back up at the house. Neither of them spoke for some minutes until Henrietta, unable to hold it in any longer, burst out morosely, "Oh, Clive, I'm not sure about all of this. . . . I'm not sure I belong here," she added, gesturing widely. "You've seen where I'm from. You have always been kind enough not to comment, but . . ."

"Henrietta," he said calmly. "I don't care about any of that. Frankly, I don't care about any of *this*," he said, nodding up at the house.

"Does it matter to you that I'm an Exley or a Von Harmon cousin, or some such thing? That I apparently have *two* disgraced parents now?"

Clive laughed. "Believe me, being an Exley *and* a Von Harmon is hardly disgraceful. Mother's quite over the moon. I haven't seen her this happy in some time, probably since Julia got married."

Henrietta looked doubtful. "How can you tell?"

Clive smiled.

"Did you make the Von Harmon connection when you met me?" Henrietta asked suspiciously.

Clive arched an eyebrow. "Do you think I did?"

Henrietta thought back to their dance and the Promenade and then later how he had cornered her in the back room after Mama Leone had been killed. She smiled to think how she had been afraid of him then.

"Given the circumstances, I suppose not."

"No, I did not. I don't really think about things like that." He paused and took a long, thoughtful drink of his cognac. "It's me that is the disgrace, really. The black sheep, as it were," he confided, smiling wryly.

"A black sheep?" Henrietta said incredulously. "They adore you from what I can see."

Clive laughed. "True enough. But it doesn't sit well that I spend my days as a cop in Chicago."

"A cop! I remember very distinctly that you told me, not too long ago, actually, and in a rather snobbish way, I might add, that you were *not* a cop, but rather a detective inspector; so there!" she said, raising her eyebrows.

Clive smiled and looked out at the invisible lake. "Tell that to Mother."

Henrietta followed his gaze and asked more seriously, "But why, Clive? Why didn't you tell me about all of this?"

"Would it have made a difference?"

Henrietta paused to consider. "I don't know. Maybe."

"See?"

Henrietta let this sink in. "But why me, then, Clive? You could have any woman."

"Hmm. I seem to remember you asking me this once before," he said, turning toward her now, a smile lurking behind his eyes.

"But now it's even more relevant! Why not some woman more suited to this life? I don't know how to play bridge! I'm a 26 girl, for God's sake! Worse yet, a taxi dancer and an usherette!—though that was your doing. Something tells me I won't be needing my fishnet stockings for any occasions here with your mother! Imagine if they knew that," she said, nodding her head toward the house.

Clive had to laugh. "Well, first of all, as I've corrected you before, I'm not sure I could have *any* woman, though it's kind of you to say." He paused as if collecting his thoughts before continuing and sighed.

"Henrietta, I don't want a society woman, and God knows they threw enough of them in my path after Catherine died. But I'm not interested in all of that. I know it doesn't make sense, but I suppose I was just . . . well, waiting, maybe . . . for something different. I don't know . . . someone good, someone untainted by all of this." He looked at her now, and the intensity of his gaze made her pulse quicken. "I love you, Henrietta. You remind me of a younger, happier time . . . a time before so much sadness came over the world." He reached out and stroked her cheek, and she closed her eyes momentarily at his touch. "Something about you unsettles me, makes my heart beat faster . . . which is quite extraordinary, really, because before I met you, I hadn't discerned that it had nearly stopped altogether." He continued to gaze at her. "There's something different about you, something constant . . . something untouched."

Henrietta gave a little laugh. "I'm hardly untouched, Inspector," she said, daring to trace the stubble along the edge of his jaw.

"You can't fool me, Henrietta," firmly grasping the hand that gingerly touched his face. "For all of your seedy jobs and your get-ups, you're still very innocent, very trusting. I see that now."

Henrietta couldn't help but smile, not just at his words, but at the fact that he had assessed her so completely. It was as if he really knew her, the real her, and it gave her confidence to continue. "Are you forgetting that you've seen me in very compromising situations?" she asked shyly, referring to the case they had been on together, though much of that night was still blurred in her memory either from shock or the drug she had been given by Mrs. Jenkins. Only vaguely did she remember that she had been wearing something quite revealing when Clive had eventually discovered her.

"How could I?" he smiled wryly. "I must confess, however, that though I tried to look away, you quite took my breath away."

Henrietta felt herself unexpectedly blush.

"But in all seriousness, the lengths you were willing to go to help Libby and Iris . . . to help *me*. What you were willing to sacrifice. I couldn't help falling in love with you."

Henrietta turned her head away and shifted uneasily, feeling guilty about the night they had spent locked up together because her motives had not been entirely as Clive imagined them. It was true that she had wanted to help find the missing girls, but her real motive in helping Clive, if she was honest, was because she had wanted to impress this man whom she had fallen for, someone who despite his aloof edge had seemed genuine and true, like her father had once been before he had lost his way, someone different from the nameless crowd of men who sought only to ogle her or touch her. She had wanted desperately to be needed by him, to mean something to him, to be in his life for even just a little bit, and had taken the job for that purpose. She smiled up at him now as she thought about how lucky she was to be here with him, to have won him in the end, though at a very nearly fatal price.

"I just hope I don't prove to be a disappointment," she said wistfully, her nagging thoughts fighting their way back into her consciousness again.

"A girl like you?" he said, tilting his head to the side, allowing his gaze to linger. "Never." He lifted her chin with his finger and softly brushed his lips across hers. Henrietta felt her body responding immediately and before she could stop herself, she put her free hand behind his head and pulled him to her, kissing him deeply, his resulting excitement palpable. When she felt him part her lips with the tip of his tongue, she felt weak and her breath quickened. She couldn't explain the intense passion she felt for him. It was unlike anything she had ever experienced before, and it left her powerless. She had stopped him from going too far that night in the park when he had proposed to her, but she was finding her resolve harder and harder to maintain.

Suddenly, however, it was maintained for her when they heard a noise at the other end of the terrace. Henrietta froze, but Clive very casually straightened, somehow seeming to have already guessed the source, and turned tiredly to see none other than Billings standing in the doorway.

"I'm very sorry to disturb you, sir," the servant said dully. "I saw a light on and came to investigate. I presumed the house to all be in bed already. I do apologize," he said, bowing slightly. "Might I get you anything more this evening?"

"No, Billings," said Clive resignedly, though he was looking at Henrietta as he said it. "We're coming up now, too."

"Very good, sir," he said and disappeared back into the house, but the moment between the lovers was irrevocably broken.

Clive smiled at her regretfully and ran his fingers down her shoulder before he held his arm out to her. "Ready?" he asked. With a sigh, Henrietta took it, and he led her back inside, where they parted for the night with just a quick kiss at the top of the stairs.

Alone in her room, however, Henrietta lay awake for a very long time. She felt unsettled and unusually warm as she tossed and turned, unable to stop thinking about Clive kissing her, of him reaching gently between her legs that night in the park before she had stopped him, or of the whisper of a touch as he had once grazed her breast . . . Irritated and restless, she kicked back the covers and tried to think of home instead, wondering if they were all okay there. It was the first time she had ever slept in a bed by herself, and while she had been delighted by the prospect when she had first been shown to her room, she was finding it difficult now to actually sleep. As the hours ticked on, she had found it hard to drift off without Elsie next to her and Ma's light snoring on the other side, not to mention the twins on their pallet on the floor next to them.

"Did you sleep well?" Mrs. Howard repeated, concerned.

Henrietta startled and pulled her mind away from the memory of Clive's kisses to answer his mother. She would have to pay attention if she wanted to succeed here. Clive was gone for who knew how long, and she would just have to make the best of it.

"Yes. Very well, thank you," she answered politely.

"I have a few things to do this morning," Mrs. Howard was saying, "so I thought I'd leave you to find your way about. I know Clive showed you most of the house yesterday, but you might want to explore the grounds. There's a lovely path that runs along the lake, if you're so inclined. That or I'm sure you have a long correspondence list you'll be wanting to attend to. You're very welcome to use the desk in the morning room, if you'd like. You'll be quite undisturbed. But should you want anything, just ring for one of the servants." She took a sip of her coffee. "Then after luncheon, perhaps we can sit down together and start on the list for the party."

Henrietta smiled weakly. "Yes, of course."

There was a cough in the direction of Mr. Howard. He rose slowly from his chair. He was dressed impeccably today in a suit of the latest cut, though, like his wife, he exuded an air of elegant restraint. His thick, wavy hair was a fine shade of gray and was held in place by some sort of hair cream. He had Clive's kind eyes, and Henrietta could not help think of Mr. Hennessy whenever she looked at him, despite the difference in their stations in life.

Mr. Hennessey was not of the upper classes, but he was a kind of gentleman just the same. He had been her boss at Poor Pete's, the corner tap she had been employed at since she was thirteen when she had turned up looking for work after her father's suicide. Mr. Hennessey had taken pity on her and had allowed her to come in and clean, and she had gradually become a waitress as well as a 26 girl, keeping score for Poor Pete's regulars before she had been lured away by Polly to become a taxi dancer. Still, Mr. Hennessey had been like a surrogate father to her, watching over her and giving her all sorts of advice over the years, as had his wife, Alice. And it was to Mr. Hennessey that Henrietta had directed Clive to officially ask for her hand in marriage. Clive had accordingly made his way to Poor Pete's the very next day after his proposal to Henrietta and, with hat in hand and in all seriousness, had explained his desire to marry Henrietta and had promised to love and cherish her and to provide for her. Henrietta was perhaps the only one to have seen Mr. Hennessey wipe a quick tear from his eye before he had robustly shook Clive's hand and had broken out his best bottle of bourbon for them all to toast the happy couple.

"I must go, my dear," Mr. Howard said absently as he checked his pocket watch for the time. "I'll never make the 9:04 at this rate, dash it! Billings, tell . . . what's his name again?"

"Fletcher, sir. *Jack*," Billings said the name as if it were distasteful, "is what he calls himself."

"He's the new chauffer," Mrs. Howard explained to Henrietta.

"Tell Fletcher, then, to bring the car around immediately, double quick."

"Very good, sir," answered Billings with a bow and promptly disappeared.

"Goodbye, my dear," Mr. Howard said, perfunctorily kissing his wife on the forehead, which she had dutifully tilted toward him. "And goodbye, Henrietta," he said with a little wink, as he hurried across the room. "Enjoy the wedding plans."

"Yes, thank you," Henrietta responded, turning in her seat to answer him, but he was already gone.

Mrs. Howard had excused herself shortly thereafter, leaving Henrietta to stare absently around the room they called the breakfast room, which was different than the long, opulent dining room Clive had shown her yesterday, as well as the morning room, which was not really for eating in, Clive had explained in answer to her questions, except for tea. Henrietta sighed as she took another sip of her coffee, now lukewarm. She had a feeling she was expected to spend part of the morning writing letters, but to whom she couldn't fathom. She supposed she should write to Ma and Elsie, but she had nothing yet to write, having just left home yesterday, and as that hadn't gone particularly well, Henrietta thought a couple of days of silence between them might be for the best.

"Oh, I'm sorry, Miss!" said a voice in the doorway, and for a confused moment, Henrietta thought that it was Elsie. Startled, she hastily looked over to find not Elsie, of course, but a young woman just the same, almost a girl, dressed plainly in a maid's uniform that looked a little too big for her and holding a large silver tray. "I thought everyone was finished. I'll come back later!" she said, making a slight curtsey.

Henrietta hurriedly stood up. "Oh, no! Don't go. I'm finished. I've just been sitting here daydreaming. Here, let me give you a hand," Henrietta said, cheerfully gathering up the plates.

"Oh, no, Miss! I couldn't do that. Please don't do that. Mistress wouldn't like it."

"Why not? I don't mind. And anyway, I'm used to working." Henrietta was about to add that she had had countless jobs as a waitress, but then thought better of it, guessing that it was probably not a thing she was supposed to mention.

"Not you! You're elegant, you are," the girl responded almost worshipfully.

Henrietta laughed. "Hardly that. I'm Henrietta. What's your name?"

"Edna, Miss. Edna Moore. I'm one of the junior maids," she explained. "Used to be in the kitchens, but I got moved up."

"Well, pleased to meet you, Edna," Henrietta said, walking over to where the young maid had set her tray and stacking some dishes on it for her.

"Thank you, Miss, but I really can manage," Edna said timidly.

"Yes, I'm sure you can, but I want to. I need something to do, you see." Henrietta continued moving around the table helping Edna to stack as much as possible onto the tray. "Have you been here long?" Henrietta asked, picking up the napkins.

"Just about two years now, Miss," Edna said without looking up.

"You don't have to call me 'Miss,' you know," Henrietta said with a smile.

"Oh, but I do, Miss," Edna said nervously. "Mrs. Caldwell wouldn't like it if I didn't."

"Who's Mrs. Caldwell?"

"She's the housekeeper here, Miss."

"Well, when she's not around, you don't have to," Henrietta said, giving her an obvious wink. "How about that?"

"Oh, no, Miss! She and Mr. Billings know everything that goes on around here. They'd surely find out," Edna said fretfully, picking up the heavy tray.

Henrietta made a move to follow her, but just then Billings himself appeared in the doorway.

"I *thought* I heard voices in here," he said stiffly. "Edna, get back to your work. I'll deal with you later." Edna's tiny smile had vanished, and she gave Henrietta a deferential nod before hurrying out under the load of the tray.

"Oh, please, Mr. Billings . . ." Henrietta began.

"It's just Billings to you, Miss."

"Billings, then," Henrietta corrected herself. "Don't blame Edna! It was my fault. I was delaying her, asking questions, you see."

"Questions? Asking Edna to provide an intelligent answer to any question of note is rather a waste of time, if I may say so without offense to present company. Should you have inquiries, I hope *I* might be of service in the future. Mrs. Howard does not approve of fraternization with the servants, especially the junior staff," he said sternly.

"I see," Henrietta said, taken aback by his rude dismissal of poor Edna. "Well, I'm very sorry," she said briskly. "I shall try to avoid any further transgressions in the future."

"Very good, Miss." He seemed unaffected by her attempt at coldness. "And now . . . might I help you?"

"Help me?"

"The inquiry you referred to as the reason you were conversing with Edna just now?"

"Oh, yes. I . . . I was . . ." Desperately, she tried to think of a legitimate question. "I . . . Mrs. Howard mentioned a path by the lake, and I was . . . I was just wondering where I might find it."

At this, Billings gave a slight nod of approval, his eyes ever so slightly belying a flicker of surprise, as if he had expected Henrietta's answer to be of a more ridiculous, possibly unseemly nature.

"Very good, Miss. I would be happy to escort you to the East Doors. From there you simply walk through the kitchen gardens until you reach a small gate in the brick wall running along at the back. Just open that—it's never locked—and beyond lies a pretty path, if I may say so, down to the beach. There's a boathouse there and a dock, and the path Mrs. Howard is referring to lies just beyond it. You can't miss it."

"Thank you, Billings. It sounds . . . delightful," Henrietta said, trying to imitate the Howards' speech as much as possible.

"If you're quite ready, then, I'll show you now, Miss. Just this way," Billings said, gesturing toward the door. Henrietta hesitated, as she had not really wanted to go walking just now, but she saw no choice but to follow him. As he silently led her through the house to the East Doors, Henrietta tried to take in the lovely splendors she saw displayed everywhere, her tour with Clive the night before having been somewhat rushed. Beautiful paintings lined the wide hallway as well as statues on pedestals in little alcoves, and there was an enormous arrangement of flowers on a table near the foot of the elaborately carved grand staircase. The bouquet was so large and splendid that Henrietta was tempted to reach out and touch them, to prove that they really existed, but she refrained lest Billings chastise her. By the time they reached the East Doors, which were also made of elaborately carved wood, but of a lighter tone, Henrietta was relieved at the prospect of fresh air and to escape what had begun to seem a bit of a claustrophobic situation. The doors held large leaded-glass windows, which, from where she now stood, cut the gardens beyond into diamonds. A little wooden overhang was perched protectively over the few stone steps that led down to the walks immediately surrounding the house. Henrietta spied a bird's nest in its eaves but did not call attention to it, somehow guessing that if she did, Billings might have it ripped down for its unsightliness.

"Would you like someone to accompany you, Miss?" Billings said as he held open one of the doors for her.

"Oh, no, Billings! Thanks just the same. I'd like to go alone."

"As you wish," he said, bowing slightly and retreating back into the house with what Henrietta perceived to be a decidedly relieved air about him, a feeling she happened to share at this moment, though she wasn't sure if his relief stemmed from not having to assign anyone to assist her or if he were simply glad to have her out of the house, as if she were a odorous contaminant or perhaps a stray pet.

Henrietta felt the crunch of the pea gravel underfoot as she made her way toward the gardens that lay straight ahead, just as Billings had said. She turned slowly around in a complete circle, trying to get her bearings, but she was confused as to exactly where she was. The kitchen gardens lay slightly to the left and were laid out in perfectly neat rows, made up almost entirely of vegetables and herbs, though there were some flowers as well. She walked along, surprised by the warmth of the day—the air inside the house seemed permanently cool—and headed for the brick wall she saw running along the back as well as the gate Billings had mentioned. No one seemed in sight, but as she got closer to the end, however, she saw what she assumed was one of the gardeners bent over some early peas, attempting to tie them up. He looked up briefly and, surprised to see her, rose slowly, unabashedly sizing her up as he did so. Henrietta, however, was used to men looking at her and ignored it.

"Can I help you, Miss?" he asked, a permanent sort of sneer on his face. He was tall and thin with greasy blond hair that hung down, partially concealed one eye. His nose and mouth protruded unnaturally, giving him the appearance of a tall rodent. His dull gray eyes seemed to pierce her.

"I'm looking for the path by the lake. Is it this way?" she said, pointing beyond the gate she already had her hand on.

"Yeah, that's right," he said curtly and bent back over the peas.

"Thank you," Henrietta said deliberately, unsure of what else to say. The man continued working as if she were no longer there, so Henrietta pushed through the gate, a quiet screech escaping from it as she did so, and let it bang behind her. The gardener did not look up at the sound, and Henrietta, deciding not to say anything more to him, continued on her way down the immaculately terraced lawn to where Lake Michigan lay gloriously before her.

At the end of the lawn proper there was a set of stone steps leading down to the beach, which boasted the small dock and boathouse that had been described to her. She made her way toward them, the formal landscaping of the house giving way now to a more wild, irregular array of beach grasses and even a couple of scrub pines. The sheer beauty and peacefulness of it overwhelmed Henrietta, and she suddenly wished someone could see it with her. Her thoughts went immediately to Clive, but he had seen it all before, hadn't he? she realized with a certain wistfulness. This was nothing new to him. Then Elsie, perhaps. Elsie would love it here! But she didn't want to think about Elsie or Jimmy or any of them just now and tried to push them to the back of her mind as she continued on toward the narrow beach. She was too old to be homesick, she told herself, but it was strange being away from them.

She paused for a moment to look out over the lake and let the cool wind whip round her face before she forced herself to move again, stepping down onto the small dock where a boat was tied up with the oars tucked neatly inside. In some ways, it felt good to be alone—it was a luxury she very rarely enjoyed—but she felt a little apprehensive, too, though of what she wasn't sure. She took a deep breath, wondering if she deserved to be here at Highbury, even if she deserved this moment in this solitary place when she knew Ma and Elsie were toiling away back in the noisy, crowded city. She hoped Ma had taken the money. Suddenly she had an overwhelming longing, then, for Clive to be here and hoped she deserved him, too.

Rousing herself from her thoughts, she pulled herself away from the beauty of the view before her and retreated. She stepped back off the dock and walked around the boathouse, peering through one of the cloudy windows. She couldn't see much, however, just a variety of what looked like sail boats. Behind the boathouse she could see the beginnings of a path that ran along the sandy beach and wound its way between the scrub trees that were growing haphazardly along the shore. Henrietta decided to follow it, though she wasn't really wearing the right shoes, but both her curiosity and her unwillingness to go back to the house propelled her forward. She was not normally one for nature, but she found the path very peaceful as it wound through birch trees and alongside an occasional willow.

Eventually a less-worn path opened up to the left, leading up a slight incline, while the main path seemed to continue along the lake. Curious as to where this side path to the left would lead, and thinking it was possibly a route leading back to the house from a different direction, she decided to follow it for a few steps to see what she could see. The ground was less sandy here and more solid as she climbed the little hill. The trees neighboring the path grew thicker, and she could see only patches of the lake now, though she could still hear it. She was beginning to wonder if she should perhaps turn back when she saw a tiny structure just ahead, more like a cottage than a proper house. Smoke was rising from the chimney, and as she drew nearer, she could see washing hanging out on the lines, so it was obviously inhabited. She was about to turn around and go back when she saw an old woman come out of the house, who, upon seeing her, raised a dishtowel in greeting, shouting, "Is tha' you, Daphne?"

Henrietta saw no choice but to approach the woman and introduce herself. Before she could speak, however, the woman began again. "Oo, Daphne! You'll never guess wha's 'appened!" Henrietta thought she detected some sort of foreign accent. Scottish maybe? The woman was hobbling toward her now.

"I'm . . . I'm sorry," Henrietta said, confused. "But, I'm not . . . Daphne. I'm Henrietta. Henrietta Von Harmon."

The woman's face remained a blank.

"I'm staying with the Howards," Henrietta said, gesturing awkwardly back toward the house, the roof of which was just visible over the trees.

The woman peered closely at her, though her eyes were cloudy, which might explain her mistaking her for this Daphne person. She obviously couldn't see very well.

"Ach! Yer na Daphne!" the woman finally exclaimed.

"No, I'm not Daphne," Henrietta repeated slowly. "I'm Henrietta."

The two stood looking at each other, Henrietta feeling suddenly very self-conscious while the old woman tried to place her. Finally she shook her head, as if giving up.

"Well, mebbe ya could 'elp me anyway, like," the woman said, laying her hand on Henrietta's arm and looking around at the ground fretfully. "Please," she said desperately. "I've lost me ring! Me eyes ain wha' they once were. 'Tis gone, me ring is, an I jis' knows 'e took it!"

Henrietta considered the bent figure before her dressed in a long old-fashioned gown with old black boots and an apron tied round her plump middle. Her face was a mask of wrinkles and her hair, beneath a babushka of sorts, was white and wispy. She very much resembled what Henrietta imagined a gypsy to look like. The woman's murky eyes peered up at her.

"You've lost your ring, you say?" Henrietta asked kindly, feeling sorry for her and not knowing what else to say. A missing ring could be anywhere. She had probably just misplaced it, Henrietta surmised.

"Please 'elp me look, won' ya?" the old woman begged. "I were 'opin' ya were Daphne, but I don' see 'er," the woman said, gazing down the path as if expecting someone to appear any minute.

Henrietta looked reactively down the path and then back up toward the house. No one, of course, was in sight. "Are you expecting her?"

"Ach, Daphne will be along pretta soon, though ya never kin tell wit 'er."

Henrietta remained silent, not knowing what else to say.

"You'll coom in an wait, won' ya?"

"Well, I'm supposed to be back at the house for lunch in a bit," Henrietta said tentatively.

The woman's face fell, and she looked as though she were about to cry.

"But I guess I could come in for just a little while, though," Henrietta acquiesced slowly.

"Oo, bless ya!" the woman said, taking her by the arm, then, and leading her back, her limp obvious now, toward the cottage. "I'm in a righ' state, I am. Kinna fine it nowheres. I jis' knows it were 'im. Greedy fingers, is wha' 'e is . . ." She continued to mumble these and similar phrases over and over as Henrietta followed her, causing her to wonder who "he" was and if the old woman was even in her right mind.

The cottage when they reached it was low and small with a cedar shake roof and ivy almost completely covering it, as if the wood beyond were trying to annex it and claim it for itself. Henrietta paused for a moment to regard the structure more closely, lifting her hand to shield her eyes from the sun. It seemed like something out of a fairy tale, and it struck her, just for a moment, that if that were true, she was inadvertently playing the part of the distressed damsel, Gretel or Red Riding Hood perhaps. She smiled to herself at the thought of it.

The old woman turned now to see why she had stopped.

"I'm coming!" Henrietta called to her. She gave Highbury one last hesitant look before she hurried the rest of the way, trying to shake off her wild imaginings, and bent, cautiously, to follow the hunched old woman through the tiny front door.

Chapter 3

Henrietta blinked as her eyes grew accustomed to the dark interior of the cottage and looked curiously around her, relieved that, upon first impression anyway, the interior did not resemble a witch's hovel, an image she admitted to having momentarily conjured up, but rather a quaint, cozy dwelling. A fire was burning in a big stone fireplace that seemed, judging from the pot hanging above it, to be used for some of the woman's cooking, though an old-fashioned wood-burning stove sat in the corner as well. Along one wall was a rustic hutch of sorts that held plates and mugs and a wide variety of pottery and crocks. There were two windows, one above the copper sink and a larger one on the wall opposite by the door, both framed in gingham curtains that blew gently in the breeze coming in off the lake. A small wooden table and chairs sat in front of the fire, atop what looked like a hand-braided rug. At the sight of the kerosene lamp on the table, Henrietta looked around and noted that there didn't seem to be any electricity. It felt strange to go from such luxury but a few moments ago to something that was so rustic and seemed almost of another era.

"This is lovely," Henrietta said, looking around and inhaling the comforting scent of the wood crackling in the fireplace. The woman seemed not to hear her, but stood near the stove, wringing her hands. "Do you live here alone?" Henrietta asked a bit louder.

"Wha'? Alone? Aye, alone, tha' I am," she said, still wringing her hands absently. "'cepting Daphne, tha' is."

"Who *is* Daphne?" Henrietta asked with strained politeness.

"Why, Daphne's me daughta,'" the woman answered incredulously. "She comes an goes, she does."

"Oh, that's nice." Henrietta wasn't sure how to proceed. "So, what does this ring look like?"

"Oo, aye," the woman exclaimed as if suddenly remembering why they were standing there. She took up her dishcloth and began wringing that now in place of her hands and gazed around the cottage with her nearly sightless eyes, as if the ring might suddenly appear. "'Tis a gold ring, it is, wit a big pearl in the middle of it, an next ta it is loads a tiny purple stones," she said, holding up her thumb and forefinger to show its size. "Don' rightly knows the name a the purple ones. But it's gone, it is."

"Well . . . where did you last see it? Can you remember?" Henrietta asked patiently, still trying in her mind to decide if it might not be best to leave the matter to Daphne.

"Ach. It were where it always is. 'Ere, I'll show ya, like." She hobbled past Henrietta toward the room at the back.

Henrietta followed her into what appeared to be the woman's bedroom. It held only a small bed covered with a quilt that looked like it had been made from a variety of material scraps, a little stool by the bed whose purpose seemed to be that of a table, and a tall dresser upon which Henrietta noticed a single photograph in a cheap burnished frame, set atop a small dresser scarf stitched with neat embroidery. The woman shuffled toward the dresser and bent to open the bottom drawer. While she did so, Henrietta stole a glance at the photo in the frame. If she wasn't mistaken, it was of the old woman, apparently taken of her as a young mother, holding a baby. A man, presumably her husband, was standing next to them.

"Is that Daphne?" Henrietta asked.

At the sound of Daphne's name, the old woman stood up straight, looking around eagerly as if Daphne had appeared and seemed all the more disappointed when she saw that it was merely the photograph to which Henrietta was referring. The woman looked at it as if to confirm her answer. "Aye, tha's Daphne," she said blankly. "Tha's 'er as a wee bairn," she added and went back to rummaging through the drawer. A moment later, she pulled out a tiny box covered in faded navy blue felt. Her hands shook slightly as she held it out to Henrietta.

Henrietta took it and saw upon opening it that it was indeed empty. The woman offered no further explanation, so Henrietta felt obliged to continue the inquiry herself. "So this is where you last saw it? You're sure?"

"Aye. Course I am."

"You didn't maybe take it out?" Henrietta asked. "Wear it or show someone, maybe?"

"Ach, noo! Never! Noo . . . 'e took it, I knows it fer certain."

Henrietta snapped the lid back shut, ignoring the strange accusation at least for the moment.

"Perhaps it fell out," Henrietta suggested tentatively. "Should I look around?" she offered.

"Oo, aye . . . ifin ya don' mind. I'd be ever sa grateful. I don' mind fer meself, like, but I'm sa afeared wha' Daphne migh' say. Migh' think I weren' mindin' it sa well, ya see."

"Well, I'm sure there's a simple explanation," Henrietta said, as she began to sift through the contents of the drawer, which seemed to consist mainly of stockings, undergarments, and old-fashioned petticoats. When she was satisfied that it was not there, Henrietta straightened up and opened the top drawer, and then the second and the third, not finding it anywhere. Determined, now, she got down on her hands and knees and looked under the bed and the dresser but found nothing but a lot of dust and cobwebs. The cottage as a whole seemed clean and tidy enough, but it was obvious that the woman's poor eyesight prevented her from getting into the nooks and crannies. Henrietta brushed off her hands as she stood up, surveying the room one more time. "Hmmm . . . I don't see it," she said finally.

"Told ya!" the woman said, wringing the towel again.

"Maybe it's out here somewhere," Henrietta said, going back into the main room.

"Wouldn' be out dare!" the woman said desperately.

"Well, mind if I have a little look?"

"Course ya kin, luv. Ach, why did 'e go an do it?" she said to no one in particular and began pacing now.

Henrietta looked on the shelves of the hutch and in all of the little cupboards, which mostly held jars of canned vegetables and fruits, linens, candles, a ball of twine, a stack of used envelopes with nothing apparently in them, and various antiquated utensils. Henrietta got down on the floor again to look, but to no avail. Slowly she stood up and looked around again, her hands on her hips. "Well, you're right. I can't find it, either."

"Oo, Lord!" the old woman exclaimed. "Wha' am I gonna do?"

The woman seemed to be working herself up more and more, and Henrietta wasn't sure what to do next, especially as she didn't even know who this woman was. Surely living so close to the Howards, she must be known to them. She was reluctant to stay, as she felt she could do no more in what was obviously some sort of innocent mix-up, but she felt she couldn't just leave this poor woman in such a state of despair. She glanced at the clock ticking on the stone mantelpiece. It was just eleven o'clock, so she still had a bit of time before luncheon, as Mrs. Howard called it.

"Tell you what," Henrietta said calmly. "Why don't you make us some tea, and you can tell me all about it. We'll try to figure it out together," Henrietta tried to say soothingly.

"Wha'?" the woman said as if coming out of a daze. "'Tis tea ya wan'? Aye, a cup a tea. Tha's it. Jis' the thing." She turned toward the stove to put the kettle on.

"Do you need any help?" Henrietta asked, looking around again.

"Get two plates off the 'utch," she said, "an two cups. That's it, aye," she said as Henrietta, glad to be allowed to do something, brought them to the table. The old woman carried a plate covered with another dishtowel to the table and pulled it back to reveal what looked like little cakes.

"These is me raspberry buns. Jis' made 'em fer when Daphne comes, ya see. 'Ere! Take one! Noo, please!" she exclaimed when Henrietta tried to desist.

"Are you sure?" Henrietta asked, not wanting to rob Daphne of her treat.

"Aye. Course I am! I kin always make more, like. Dare's loads a raspberries out back. Kinna pick 'em all, tha's 'ow many dare is. 'Elp yerself if yer ever in a mind ta do it," she said, nodding toward what Henrietta assumed was the back of the cottage. "Might take some up ta the big hoose a little later, I migh'."

"Do you mean to the Howards? I could take them if you like. I'm staying there," Henrietta repeated.

"Are ya now?" the woman said, limping over with the kettle and pouring hot water into what looked to be a very old teapot. "Ya moost be a friend a Miss Julia's, then," she said sitting down heavily. "Didna she come wit ya?" she asked, looking toward the door.

Henrietta wasn't sure how to answer this. Clive had told her that his older sister was married and living nearby in Glencoe, but the old woman seemed not to remember this. She wondered who this woman was and how she fit into the Howard family. Perhaps she was a former servant, allowed to stay on in this strange cottage, which appeared to be on their property.

"No, I believe Julia lives in Glencoe now," Henrietta suggested slowly.

"Ach, sa she does! I firget sometimes . . ." The woman seemed to think hard. "She's a Cunningham now, ain' she? Aye, tha's it!" she said and stood up to pour out the tea. "Who are ya, then?"

Henrietta smiled. "I'm . . . I'm Clive Howard's fiancée, actually."

"Mister Clive? Never!" she said, incredulous, pausing to stare at her in a new way. "We'd all but given up 'ope, we did. Took it 'ard when Miss Cathy died. We all fell sa sorry fer 'im up at the hoose. 'Im na long 'ome from the war. Everyone thought in time 'e'd get over it, but, well, nothin' stuck. Ran off ta the city ta become a bobby, 'e did. Nearly killed Mr. 'oward wit the shock of it. I blame the war, I do. Nothin's been righ' since then." She grew oddly silent, now, lost in her own thoughts, staring into her mug of tea.

Henrietta wasn't sure what to say. She longed to ask so many questions, but she wasn't sure how sane this woman really was. She shifted uncomfortably and finally managed, "So, Miss Catherine . . . she was liked, was she?" Henrietta took a tentative sip of tea.

"Miss Cathy?! Course she were liked! But then again, we all knowed 'er from a little lass. She were always running about 'ere wit Miss Julia and Mister Clive when they were wee ones. Everyone were over the moon, they were, when they decided ta marry. It were like a fairy tale, it were. Jis' a quiet ceremony, Mister Clive insistin' on going off ta war, ya see, an, well, tha' were tha'," she mused sadly.

Henrietta felt an odd jolt of jealousy, then, though she immediately chastised herself for envying a dead person. Shouldn't she be happy that Clive had been happy once upon a time?

"Still! Tha' were a long time ago," the old woman smiled. "I'm glad 'e's found another one. Yer wery pretty; I'll give ya tha," she said, peering at her closely as if examining an antique for its authenticity. "An ya seem a nice lass, ya do. Na like tha' other one 'e took up wit fer a time. She were a nasty piece a work. None of us could fathom wha' 'e saw in 'er. We were all afeared 'e would marry 'er. Mrs. 'oward woulda been 'appy enough, though, Miss Sophia's da being sich a big un in politics, like, but it fizzled out in the end. I think tha's why young Mister Clive stays away sa mooch, ya see. Too many bad memories now. 'Appy enough 'e is livin' in filth in the city. Blessed shame, tha' is. But wha' am I sayin?" she suddenly stopped herself and smiled at Henrietta. "Don' matter, does it? Seems 'e's come ta 'is senses now, an tha's all tha' matters." She reached out and patted Henrietta's hand. "They're desperate up dare, like, fer a grandson. Need ta carry on the name, ya see. Terrible rows dare were in the past. You'll 'ave yer work cut out fer ya, tha's fer sure, ta 'and Mister Clive a boy bairn," she said with a mischievous cackle.

Henrietta wasn't sure what to think of all of this. Who was "the other one," this "Sophia," and why hadn't Clive ever mentioned her? And what was all this about carrying on the name, producing an heir? She felt an urgent need to speak to Clive just now, but, in truth, what would she say? How could she bring up such subjects? Though her mind was whirling now with this new information, she realized that the old woman was looking at her curiously, presumably waiting for some sort of response. "Thank you," Henrietta said finally, for lack of anything else to say, and with a weak smile, took another sip of tea.

The woman continued to study her. "Ya look a wee bit young, though, ta keep Mister Clive in 'and."

"I'll try my best." Henrietta smiled unconvincingly. She had no desire to hear any more at the moment of the lovely Catherine or this other love interest of Clive's and wanted desperately to change the subject. "Did you . . . did you used to work at the house?" she eventually managed to ask.

"At the hoose?" The woman seemed flabbergasted by the question. "Aye. Course I did! I were the cook, I were! Then me eyes got bad an I had ta step down. Aboot ten years gone now. Mary's the cook now. I still 'elp from time ta time, like. Big parties an sich, then I goes up an lends a 'and." She reached for the teapot to top up their mugs. "Didna start out tha' way, mind ya. Started out as a pot scrubber."

"Really? How old were you?" Henrietta asked, delighted the conversation was taking a turn away from herself and Clive and nursed it along accordingly.

"Jis' fourteen I were. Coom over from Scotland, ya see. 'Ad a friend who worked fer a big family in New York, the Hewitt's. Tha' were Mrs. 'oward's family afore she married. She were a Hewitt, like. Me friend wrote me a letter saying tha Mrs. Hewitt, tha's Mrs. 'oward's mother, said I could coom an work in the kitchens. Meant everythin' ta me, tha' letter did, though I 'ad ta 'ave someone read it ta me, like. I packed me bags tha' nigh' an left."

"Just like that? Weren't you sad to leave everyone behind?" Henrietta asked.

"Ach, noo! It were terrible dare fer me. Me da were a sailor. 'Amish Boyd were 'is name. But 'e died at sea when I were jis' a bairn, sa me ma took up wit another man, an they married. 'E had noo use fer me, though. Said I 'minded 'im too much a me da, an 'e couldn' stand it, like. Took ta beatin' me whenever 'e got the chance. Me ma tried defendin' me at first, but then more and more bairns started coomin', an it went easier fer 'er if she didna say anythin' when 'e took 'is belt ta me. I ran away once, but 'e found me jis' the same. I won' say wha' 'e did, but it were terrible fer me after tha'. I didn' go ta school, like; they kept me at 'ome ta do the work. I 'ad this friend, though, tha went ta America. She promised ta try an find a place fer me as well. So when I got 'er letter, I decided straigh' away I were leavin'. Got a place on a ship coomin' over as a cook's 'elper, an, well, 'eres I am."

"Didn't you ever tell them at home where you went?" Henrietta asked pointedly. "Even your mother?"

"Aye. I did. Weren' goin' ta, like, but she 'eard me gets up in the night ta sneak oout. She knew I were goin'. Didna ask me ta stay; she knew it were noo use. She told me ta go far this time. Na ta get caugh' again. Then she poot the ring in me 'and. Said ta sell it if I needed it. Tha' it were me father's ring an tha' it 'ad once belonged ta 'is mother." The woman stopped abruptly, now, having somehow brought herself back around to the ring. She put her hand feebly up to her forehead. "Ach! Wha' am I gonna do? 'Ow my gonna get it back?" she said, looking back up at Henrietta.

"*That's* the ring you lost?" Henrietta asked.

"Aye. Course it is! Oo, wha' am I gonna do? Tha' belongs ta Daphne now."

Henrietta had been thoroughly enjoying their talk, but the woman was back to being distracted and cloudy. Henrietta reached out and patted her on the hand. "Don't worry, Mrs. . . ." Henrietta faltered. "Forgive me, I don't even know your name."

"Schuyler. Helen Schuyler," she answered sadly.

"Don't worry, Mrs. Schuyler. I promise I'll help you to find it. I'm sure it's here somewhere."

Mrs. Schuyler seemed to take no comfort in her words but sat looking distraught.

"Why don't you tell me the rest of the story?" Henrietta urged, hoping to take her mind from her distress.

"The res' a the story?" Mrs. Schuyler seemed baffled. "Dare ain' noo more!"

"Well, you obviously got married . . ." Henrietta tried to lead her.

"Oo, aye. Neils. 'E were me 'usband. 'E died a long time ago, though."

"How did you meet?" Henrietta asked, though she surreptitiously glanced up at the mantel clock. She would have to be leaving soon.

"'E were a gardener at the Hewitt's. 'E coom from 'olland. Studied at a big school dare ta learn ta be a master gardener, ya see. Then 'e coom 'ere ta work. 'E worked first fer the Hewitt's, and then when young Antonia married into the 'oward's, they moved 'ere an built 'ighbury—wanted it to look like all the ole estates in New York, see? An me an Neils came wit 'em. 'E were wery gentle were Neils. Then we 'ad Daphne."

"Where does Daphne live now?" Henrietta asked.

"Oo, she's near enough, she is," Mrs. Schuyler answered absently, wringing her hands again.

Henrietta took this as her cue to leave. It was getting late, and she didn't want to keep Mrs. Howard waiting. "Well, Mrs. Schuyler, I should be going. Thank you for the tea and cake," she said, standing up and carrying her mug and plate to the sink. "They were delicious."

"Please, don' call me tha'. Please call me 'elen," she pleaded. "I don' like ta be called Mrs. Schuyler."

Henrietta hesitated. "Well . . . if you're sure . . ." she said, walking toward the little door. "Did you want me to take those raspberries?"

"Raspberries? Oo, aye . . . well, I don' 'ave 'em picked yet, ya see."

"Well, maybe I can stop by another time and help."

"Oo, would ya? I'd be ever sa glad."

Henrietta pushed open the door and stepped out into the bright sunshine, shielding her eyes with her hand again. She hadn't realized how dim it had been in there. Helen followed her out.

"Well, goodbye, then," Henrietta tried to say cheerfully.

Helen put her hand on Henrietta's arm. "Na quite one a 'em, though, are ya?" she said, squinting up at her. "Noo, indeed. Tha' I kin tell, but tha's na sich a bad thing, is it? Migh' be good an all." She paused to look around and added in a quieter voice, "Ya seem a nice lass, ya do. Jis' be careful up at the big hoose."

"Careful?" Henrietta tried not to smile. "Of what?" she asked and wondered if she were going to say of Mrs. Howard.

"Of 'im, a course!"

"Who's him?" she asked, thoroughly surprised by Helen's cryptic answer.

"The tall one. In the garden. 'E's the one who took the ring!" Helen whispered furtively.

"Why do you think that?" Henrietta asked, thinking immediately of the greasy gardener she had met by the back gate. This was the third time Helen had referred to someone stealing the ring, and Henrietta didn't think she could ignore it any longer.

"Cause I seen 'im, I did. Creepin' round me hoose. Coom evenin' time, dare 'e is, creepin' round. I see 'im oot the window, I did. Terrified I am some nigh's. Those are the nigh's I wish ta God Daphne were wit me!"

Henrietta's mind tried to make sense of what the old woman was saying. Could there be any truth to what Helen was telling her? Admittedly the gardener had not impressed Henrietta with his charm, but a thief? And how could Helen with her bad eyesight be so sure she had really seen him, if anyone? But what about the missing ring? It was nowhere to be found, so maybe it *had* been stolen . . .

"Have you told anyone? Anyone at the house, that is? About the gardener?"

"Ach, noo, na as yet. I'm afeared ta, ya see, case they're in league."

Henrietta didn't know what to say to this, but she was becoming anxious that time was ticking ever closer to her lunch with Mrs. Howard. "Well, I'll certainly keep my eyes open, Helen," Henrietta said patronizingly. "But I really must be going now."

"Do ya 'ave ta, like?" Helen said morosely, and Henrietta's heart went out to this poor, lonely soul.

"I'll come again soon," she said apologetically. "I promise. Really I do. But I really must go now," she said eagerly, backing away and giving what she hoped was a cheerful wave.

Helen didn't wave back, but merely stood near the cottage, wringing her hands and watching her go.

With Helen and the cottage behind her now, Henrietta hurried back down the path as fast as she could, but it was difficult the closer she got to the beach and the more the soil gave way to sand. She was perspiring a bit from hurrying as well as from anxiety, desperate to get back in time and confused about all that Helen had told her. She wondered if the old woman was possibly a bit paranoid—the whole business of the ring seemed strange and unreal—and yet when she had spoke about her own life and that of the Howards, she seemed clear as a bell. Perhaps she should take her story about the ring more seriously, she determined, and wondered who she could ask about it as she raced up the terraces, hoping she wouldn't come upon the tall gardener and, more importantly, that Mrs. Howard wouldn't see her running up the lawn in what was obviously a very unladylike manner.

Chapter 4

Antonia Howard looked up expectantly at the breakfast room door, having recognized Billings's footsteps and what must be those of Henrietta following closely behind. Billings prided himself on being as quiet as a mouse, but Antonia always knew when he was close by. She had the good sense not to mention this, however, as it would have hurt his pride immeasurably, and, as she had learned over the years, it was good not to reveal too much of what one knew, or at least of what one suspected.

Take this Henrietta Von Harmon, for example. There was quite a bit she suspected there, but she had had the foresight not to completely give her hand away, though she had hinted, if only to Alcott. Mr. Howard, however, had not been interested in her theories and had warned her about what had happened the last time she had interfered too much. Antonia had dismissed him as she sat at her dressing table brushing her hair the night they had met Henrietta, but she had to admit that his words had a ring of truth to them. She would have to tread lightly this time. Clive was getting older and even more stubborn, if that were possible, and time was running out on their chances for a grandson. But was this really his choice of a wife? Was this impoverished slip of a girl to be the next Mrs. Howard sitting on the board of the Women's League next to the Cunninghams, the

Pullmans, the Fields and the Armours? Was this girl really to inherit Highbury? It seemed unthinkable, and yet, Alcott did have a point. They would have to accept whomever Clive brought home, within reason, of course, or he might not bother altogether. When he had refused to take up with her own chosen replacement for Catherine, the fashionable and extremely eligible Sophia Lewis, daughter of the respected senator, they had out-and-out pleaded with him to settle down and produce children before the whole of the Howard fortune fell into the hands of the Cunninghams through Julia. His reply had been one of shocking disinterest. He had merely said bitterly that there were worse things in life.

Since then they had tried to be hands-off, accepting his "job" on the police force and his miserable lodgings in the city, both of which he stubbornly clung to. The war had indeed changed him. He could still don tails and sip cognac and converse intelligently at a dinner party if called upon to do so, but he seemed to have lost the passion for it. Antonia put it down to a phase, the aftereffects of the war, and was patiently waiting for it to be over, but so far there was no sign of that. He had some silly notion about truth and justice and would go on about it endlessly if encouraged, but couldn't justice be served just as easily on the board of Alcott's firm, Linley Standard? she had often argued. Clive had merely laughed at her, and she had bit her tongue in response.

Alcott, to her great annoyance, took a different approach. He believed Clive would come around in the end, that he merely needed time to see what was really important in life. "Give him some time without the finer things in life, and he'll soon change his tune," had been Alcott's prediction, but so far there was no sign of it coming true. In the meantime it was embarrassing to have a son working in so common a profession. The police force, of all things! In Antonia's mind it was little better than a street sweeper. Perhaps if he were the chief . . . now *that* would be a bit of a different story. At least he had risen to the rank of detective inspector, she had consoled herself with often enough, but it still rankled, and she tried to exaggerate his role if it ever came up in polite conversation at the club.

And now he had somehow met this woman, this *girl*! Yes, that's what Antonia saw her as, barely old enough to marry! And it revealed a side of Clive she wasn't particularly proud of and didn't wish to dwell on for too long. Surely in his base life in the city he had plenty of opportunity to fulfill any lustful urges. What else could he possibly be interested in this girl for? What on earth did they have in common? She admitted to herself that she and Alcott had never really had much in common to talk about, but that hadn't mattered so much in the end. They had at least come from the same social strata, and that was commonality enough. Clive had been purposely vague in describing exactly how he had come to know this girl, Antonia mused, bringing her thoughts back around to the current crisis. She wasn't sure she even wanted to know how he had found her. Surely it must have had something to do with his sordid role as an inspector; he had almost said as much. She would have liked to believe that he had chosen Henrietta because of her possible connections to the Exleys, but he had seemed as surprised as they were when the girl had inadvertently revealed this.

Before he had left for the city this morning, Clive had implored her to get to know Henrietta. He had admitted to her that Henrietta's family was extremely poor. He would explain all that later, he had said, but he insisted that Henrietta was something rather extraordinary. Someone quite wonderful.

She had chastised him for being sentimental, and his face had grown serious then.

"Mother," he had said steadily, "I'm far from being sentimental in this. I *love* Henrietta. She's utterly unselfish and good. Honest, pure. All the qualities that seem remarkably scarce in these parts," he had said bitterly.

"What about Augusta Fields, maybe? She's back from Dartmouth, if you like them that young."

"I take exception to that, Mother," Clive said in a measured voice.

Antonia knew she had overstepped the mark. "All right, forgive me. But you can't really believe there aren't any good, honest women on the North Shore. What about Catherine?"

Clive sighed. "Catherine was different. She was more like a chum. Anyway," he said, drawing his hand through the waves of his hair. "Yes, I'm sure there are some very nice girls . . . *women* . . . but it doesn't matter. I've found the one I want."

Antonia paused briefly to collect her thoughts. She would have to be careful. "I'm sure Henrietta is a very nice girl," she began. "And she's very beautiful, I'll at least give you that. But, Clive, dearest, think for a moment. Whether or not you want to face it, Highbury will be yours someday. And you need to think very seriously about who's going to share the role of running the estate. Do you honestly think Henrietta is the right person for that? Dealing with the servants? Entertaining? The club committees?" She saw his face twist up. "Just listen!" she said hastily. "I'm not saying she's not . . . something very special . . . I'm just saying, you need to think. Very carefully."

Clive sighed again and looked out the window of the morning room where their conversation was unfolding. He was silent for a few moments and then, without turning around, he spoke lowly, "I know she's young and perhaps a bit awkward, Mother, and unsuited for Highbury in some ways. But I love her," he said quietly. "I can't explain it, but I haven't felt this way in so very long. Perhaps ever," he said, turning slowly now to face her. "Please don't take that away from me."

His face had looked so drawn, so sad, then, and she was reminded of how he had looked when he had come back from the war, how his face had held a permanently pained expression.

"She can learn. If you'd help her. Please," he pleaded. "Don't make a judgment quite yet."

Antonia sighed and knew she was beaten, at least for now. "Oh, all right, Clive. I'll try to help her, even like her, but you must promise you'll think about what I've said."

"Yes, of course I will," he promised, and his face had brightened, reminding her suddenly of when he was a boy, and her heart went out to him. He gave her his thanks with a quick kiss on the cheek and had left shortly thereafter, saying that he would try to be back at the weekend if not next week sometime.

Antonia sighed and braced herself now as Henrietta came bursting into the room on Billings's heels. What was she to do with her? Where should she start? She was absolutely beautiful, she admitted, and she seemed deferential, so that was good, but she was still dressed in the simple blue paisley dress (blue paisley, for heaven's sake! It was horribly out of fashion!) that she had appeared in for breakfast, and her hair was all askew, hanging about her shoulders in a mad fashion. Not only that, but she looked flushed and perspiring, as though she had been exerting herself out in the sun.

"Thank you, Billings," she said, as Henrietta sat down gingerly across from her. "Tell Mary that we're ready now."

"Very good, madam."

"I hope I'm not late, Mrs. Howard, I . . ." Henrietta began.

"Not to worry, my dear. And you must call me Antonia."

"Oh, no! I couldn't do that."

"But you must, my dear. I mean for us to get to know each other better. You don't mind if I call you Henrietta, do you?"

"No, of course not," Henrietta said haltingly and then gave her a reluctant smile.

Antonia admitted that the girl was lovely, charming even. Yes, she could see what Clive saw in her. She could forgive him a dalliance with her, but marriage? What was he thinking? Surely even he could see her utter unsuitability. She sighed, not sure where to begin.

"Might I ask how old you are, my dear?" Antonia asked politely as she poured some coffee.

"Nineteen," Henrietta answered, barely above a whisper, which, in and of itself, told Antonia much. So young! What could Clive possibly have in common with her? It was infuriating, considering how many respectable war widows could be easily had these days. "Why, you've not recently finished school then, haven't you?" she said, setting her cup down carefully.

"Well, actually," Henrietta said, shifting uneasily, "I left school a long time ago, Mrs. Howard. Antonia," she put in quickly.

"I see," she said crisply.

My god! It was going to take a lot of spinning to come up with a presentable package before they officially announced the engagement to the glittering, powerful society in which they dwelt. She was going to have to rely heavily on Henrietta's supposed connections, however far back they went. She considered Henrietta closely. Could she really be John Exley's niece? It seemed unlikely; she looked nothing like the Exleys, but how could it be otherwise? It was too remarkable to be a coincidence.

As soon as Henrietta and Clive had departed yesterday to collect her things from the city, Antonia had lost no time in telephoning Victoria Braithewaite from the Club to inquire if she remembered the name of the man young Martha Exley had run off with. After a few minutes musing, Victoria had very satisfactorily (or was it unsatisfactorily?) replied that she believed it was a Leslie Von Harmon, if she wasn't mistaken, why? Antonia had pooh-poohed it, putting it down to a rambling thought that had just that moment popped into her head and that there was nothing in it. Victoria had commented then that it was funny she didn't simply ask John and Agatha herself since she was so intimate with them, but when Antonia had replied that it wasn't quite the thing, you know, Victoria had solemnly responded, in her querulous voice, "Quite so, my dear. Quite so." Antonia had hung up the telephone and felt rather convinced, but still . . .

"May I be frank, my dear?" Antonia asked Henrietta now, in an even tone.

"Yes, I suppose that would be the best," Henrietta answered thinly.

"I realize that you're used to your old ways, but as Clive's wife . . . as the next Mrs. Howard . . . there are certain, shall we say, responsibilities, certain standards which you must uphold and live under . . ."

"And you find me lacking in these?"

Antonia was surprised by the girl's directness.

Before she could respond, however, Henrietta continued. "I'm well aware of my deficiencies, Mrs. . . . Antonia. I've tried to tell this to Clive, but he won't listen. I . . . I know I'm unsuited to be his wife, no one can feel that more than me, but I do love him. Surely that counts for something?" she said earnestly.

Mrs. Howard felt herself wavering a bit. She was pleased with Henrietta's humility and honesty, but still, she must not let sentiment come into it, as it so obviously had between the two of them.

"Of course it does, my dear! I only meant that I mean to help you, if you'll let me."

"You mean instructing me in how to be a lady of society?"

Antonia noticed the blush on Henrietta's cheek. "That's one way of putting it, yes," she said. "I must say," she continued. "I'm rather surprised that Clive didn't explain these things to you. He's been tremendously remiss if he hasn't been forthcoming with what's required of you . . ."

She was interrupted then by James, who came in carrying a large platter that he noiselessly set on the sideboard. Efficiently, he lifted off the heavy silver-domed lid covering it and removed the two waiting plates.

"Thank you, James," Mrs. Howard said as he placed a plate in front of each of them, both of which contained a chicken quarter with mushroom gravy and sprigs of thyme adorning it and very thinly sliced carrots and beans arranged neatly on the side. Antonia looked across to Henrietta, who seemed to be staring at it in an unnatural manner. "Is anything amiss, my dear?" Antonia asked her, genuinely concerned.

"Just that it's too beautiful to eat!" Henrietta said with real feeling. "And so much! Please tell Mary that it looks divine," she said eagerly to James, who uncomfortably bowed but not before giving

Mrs. Howard a sort of hesitant look, which she dually noted and approved of. At least James understood his place.

"That will be all, James," Mrs. Howard said.

James disappeared, and Henrietta eagerly took up her knife and fork.

"A few things, my dear," Antonia said, taking a deep breath. "One should never begin eating until the hostess has started."

"Oh," Henrietta responded and clumsily put her fork down, though it had already speared a piece of chicken. "Sorry," she mumbled softly.

"Quite all right," Mrs. Howard said, picking up her own fork, stiffly signaling Henrietta to begin again. "Also, as long as we are talking about luncheon etiquette, one should never appear to luncheon in what one wore to breakfast or what one wore on an outdoor excursion, especially if we were dining out, which, luckily today we are not. A cotton dress for luncheon is just marginally acceptable. Preferable would be an afternoon dress or a knit suit, and usually a hat. Gloves, of course, if we were out." She watched Henrietta carefully. She had slowed eating considerably as she absorbed this advice, looking down at her clothes as she did so. "Likewise, not to be completely beastly, but a lady never perspires and always keeps her hair tidy for an engagement."

Antonia satisfyingly observed Henrietta stiffen, but there seemed to be a glint in her eye now. "I'm sorry, Mrs. Howard," the girl said steadily, "but my wardrobe is not very extensive. I don't have much with me, but then again, I don't really own very much. If I'm being frank, that is."

Henrietta's icy tone was not lost on Mrs. Howard. "Yes, I rather gathered as much based on the smallness of your . . . case," she said, referring to the abysmal carpetbag Henrietta had arrived with.

There was an unmistakable flicker of defiance in Henrietta's eyes as she took a sip of water and said, "I've just the few cheap dresses I bought when I was a taxi dancer, you see, at the Promenade."

Mrs. Howard drew in a sharp breath, though she immediately then tried to disguise it as something else, perhaps an unfortunate burp, and held her napkin to her lips. Was this girl trying to shock her? She wasn't exactly sure what a taxi dancer was, but she could guess. Oh, Clive! Is this how they had met? The shame of it! If Henrietta's aim had indeed been to ruffle her, Antonia was determined that she wouldn't give her the satisfaction. Carefully she wiped the corner of her mouth with her napkin, thinking quickly.

"Well, then we must go shopping, my dear!" she exclaimed and forced a smile. "Just the thing!"

"But I . . ."

"Now, now. No buts! My treat. No, really, I insist. Indulge me, darling. You'll be doing me such a favor; I haven't had the pleasure of buying a lovely girl some things since before Julia got married. No! I won't hear of it. I insist!" she said whenever Henrietta opened her mouth to protest. "We'll surprise Clive with some pretty new things," she said suggestively. "Won't he be pleased?" At the mention of Clive, she thought she saw a softening in Henrietta's previously defiant eyes, which were dissolving now into reluctant defeat.

"That's very kind, Mrs. Howard. Antonia," she added hastily. "But didn't you hear what I said? I was a taxi dancer," she said guiltily. "Don't you want to know about my past? I . . . I feel like I'm here under false pretenses. I'm not sure how much Clive told you."

Again, Antonia was impressed with what one might call her honesty, but it wasn't enough to squash the rising agitation she was now experiencing at the prospect of Henrietta confiding to her what might be some dark secret. She couldn't bear to hear any revelations just now; she would talk to Clive later, as there was obviously much he had left out. "Nonsense, darling! No need to go into all that just now. We must look forward rather than back. Shall we say tomorrow morning? Ten o'clock? Fletcher can take us into town." She knew that the shops would be virtually empty so early in the day, and she was hoping to avoid running into anyone she knew, especially anyone from the club.

"All right, then. Thank you," Henrietta said submissively. "If you really think it will please Clive," she added. "And you, of course."

"Of course it will," she replied smoothly, noting that her eagerness to please Clive could prove useful at some point.

James entered then and began removing the plates, but not before Henrietta turned to him, saying, "Oh, James! That was marvelous! Please tell Mary that it was so very delicious!" Again, Antonia noted with approval James's obvious discomfort as he tried to bow.

"Very good, Miss," he replied stoically and noiselessly disappeared.

Antonia cleared her throat. "A lady does not generally converse with the staff, Henrietta," she said reprovingly once James had left. "And while we're on the subject, verbal exuberance of any sort is not looked upon favorably in polite society. One contains one's feelings and opinions, you see, unless specifically asked to share them, and even then, a lady is not thought to possess strong opinions either way, as her proper place is to always find herself in support of her *husband's* opinions."

"Oh," Henrietta said plainly, and Antonia once more noticed the flush in her cheek and the spark in her very blue eyes. "I'm rather a disappointment, I suppose," she added, her voice holding the smallest breath of a challenge.

"Nonsense. You will learn. It's only a matter of time," Antonia said lightly, hoping that it was actually true. "And, anyway, Clive seems rather taken with you," she added, James conveniently interrupting them, again, now with two small dishes of lemon sherbet and sprigs of mint, which he placed perfectly before each of them. Antonia noted that Henrietta did not say anything at all this time to James, but still annoyingly tried to imbue her thanks to him with raised eyebrows and a smile. Antonia studied her. She seemed pliable enough, but there was a certain strength to this girl as well, which Antonia could not at the moment decide whether it was a good thing or not.

"Perhaps we should move on to the party, shall we?" Antonia suggested, feeling that now would be a good time to change subjects. "We really should start putting together a guest list."

Henrietta's previously mutinous face sank now, and she gave a little cough as she listlessly picked up her spoon and shaved off a little of the sherbet. Finally she spoke. "It's no use pretending, Mrs. Howard," she said sadly, still looking at the dish in front of her. "There aren't many people for me to invite, and I'm almost positive my mother won't come."

"But she must, my dear! This is one of the reasons we're having the party, to get to know each other's families better," she said, "that and to introduce you into society."

"She's . . . she's quite ill these days. It's difficult for her to get out."

This didn't shock Antonia as much as it perhaps should have. Still, however, she played the part. "I'm sorry to hear that. Perhaps if Fletcher would go to collect her? Or if you think the journey might be too much for her, she could simply stay with us for a time," she attempted to say kindly and thought about what it would be like to have John Exley's long-lost sister—if she *was* his sister—as a guest in her home. It was almost too delicious to imagine.

It was curious that the wayward Martha had apparently kept silent all these years about her true identity, living in some hovel, no doubt, with what must be an errant branch of the Von Harmons, if indeed there was any real link at all to the French or Prussian aristocracy. That one still needed more inquiry, but Antonia had not been idle in that department, either, and had written just this morning to Alcott's family in Derbyshire, England, inquiring more deeply than she ever had previously about the family line.

"Oh, no!" Henrietta responded. "That would be . . . quite out of the question . . . for her to stay here, I mean. She couldn't possibly leave the twins . . ."

"I see," Antonia said. "Well of course you would all be invited. How many of you are there, did you say?"

"There are eight of us," Henrietta answered as if ashamed. "The twins are almost five now. So do you see how it would be awkward?" Henrietta almost begged.

Eight children! What would John and Agatha make of that? she wondered. Or, better yet, what would old Mr. Exley say when he learned that he had eight additional grandchildren? John's mother had died years ago, but his father was still alive and living with another of his sons in Lake Forest. Antonia would have been almost gleeful at the prospect of unearthing the missing Martha if it didn't so disgracefully involved Clive, and thus themselves, in so intimate a fashion. Still, it would have to be dealt with. "Surely you asked your mother about her past when you went back to collect your things? I don't mean to be indelicate, but this really should be resolved, Henrietta."

"I . . ." she faltered. "I meant to, but I . . . other subjects came up."

"Happy, was she? About your engagement?" Mrs. Howard asked skillfully over her cup of coffee.

"Not particularly, no," Henrietta answered with that trace of defiance which was becoming all too familiar already. "She says that Clive is beyond my reach, is how she generally put it, I think. That I've aimed too high, was what she said exactly." Henrietta's gaze did not falter now.

Quite so, Antonia thought in agreement, but she kept silent. Though, surely if Henrietta's mother really was Martha Exley, she would have recognized the Howard name, wouldn't she have? Why, then, would Clive be out of reach? Had it merely been a ruse to further avoid telling Henrietta the truth? But why? It was obviously going to come out sooner than later.

"I hope you don't mind, my dear, but I've made a few inquiries . . . discreet, I can assure you . . . and it seems that the Exleys *did* have a younger sister named Martha and that she ran off with a young man by the name of Leslie Von Harmon, whom you have already said was your father. So you see, there really is very little room for doubt." She watched Henrietta's face as she absorbed this.

"But why?" she finally asked.

"Why what?" Antonia asked, confused.

"Why would she have run off? And why did her family, these Exleys, never come to find her, to find us?"

Antonia sighed. "You must understand, my dear. Things have always been done a certain way, and having the only daughter of the family run off with a penniless boy was even more scandalous then than it would be now," she said, narrowing her eyes and hating the fact that she was now practically faced with the same dilemma, only in reverse. "Who knows why she did it; perhaps he told her he was a Von Harmon and lured her away under false pretenses?"

She paused here to take a sip of coffee before continuing.

"The Exleys are a very old family, very rich, very proud. I'm sure they had great hopes for your mother to marry into another equally splendid family, so when she ran off, the shame of it was just too great, I suppose. Perhaps there is more to the story. John has been Alcott's closest friend these many years, and though I see a great deal of Agatha, the subject has never come up. Quite an inappropriate topic of conversation. Maybe they never meant there to be such a severe separation; perhaps they tried to find their daughter after a time. But perhaps she didn't want to be reconciled; perhaps she didn't want to be found," Mrs. Howard suggested. "Has she really never spoken of her family?"

Henrietta sadly shook her head. Antonia could have been mistaken, but she thought her eyes looked glassy, as if she were holding back tears, and strangely felt a surge of compassion for this young girl sitting in front of her, who, despite all of the obstacles stacked against her, so obviously wanted to please them. None of this, after all, was her fault, and yet . . . she had somehow beguiled Clive. But Clive should have known better! She was tempted to begin blaming Clive all over again when Henrietta finally spoke.

"I . . . I thought they were all dead, or perhaps far away, I suppose. She's very proud," Henrietta said looking up at her, "very stubborn. She won't come."

Antonia sat thinking. Surely Henrietta was wrong here. If her mother was indeed Martha Exley, wouldn't this be the perfect revenge of all, to have her daughter be brought back into the glittering society that she herself had either fled or been expelled from? Why would she not revel in the chance to right the wrongs of the past?

"Perhaps if you wrote to her," Antonia suggested. "Sometimes things are easier to ask in writing than aloud. It seems to me that the answers you seek might be found with her. You might be surprised, you know; events such as an engagement sometimes prove to be excellent opportunities for old wounds to be mended. We can only hope, can't we?" she said, trying to lift Henrietta's now-depressed spirits. Henrietta did not respond, so Antonia rang the bell. James appeared within moments.

"I think we'll retire to the study, James," she said crisply. "We'll have our sherry there while we begin our task.

"Very good, madam," he said, coming over to her chair and holding it for her as she rose. He then went around the table to where Henrietta still sat as if dazed.

"Coming, my dear?" Antonia finally asked her.

Henrietta started. "Actually . . . Antonia . . . I . . . I have a slight headache," she said, looking up at her. "Might I be excused? I think I should lie down for a bit."

"Certainly, my dear. I'll carry on without you. Perhaps after a rest, you could compile your own list and we could compare notes. I must say, this is what comes from walking out of doors without a hat," she could not resist saying as she studied her. She did look rather pale just now, she noticed. It must all be too much, she concluded, and wondered with not a little shameful hope if perhaps Henrietta was having second thoughts.

Chapter 5

Henrietta flung herself on her enormous bed and tried to fight back tears. She did not have a headache as she had told Mrs. Howard, or rather *Antonia*, as she was supposed to call her now, but she did feel distraught nonetheless. Oh, how had all of this happened? It was extraordinary that a little over two months ago she was working as an usherette in a burlesque theater downtown, and now she was being lectured on her upcoming duties as the future mistress of an estate on the North Shore, not the least being to uphold her future husband's wishes and opinions, neither of which she really had a firm grasp of, actually. Could all of this really be happening? She felt as though she were in some sort of dream world, surrounded by shocking stories of her mother belonging to a wealthy family; her father's possible connections with some aristocratic, European cousins; not to mention the strange, fairytale-esque adventure she had had with Helen Schuyler, which she had completely forgotten to ask Mrs. Howard about, so stunned had she been by that formidable woman's criticisms, or, rather, *instructions*, to her on how to be a lady of society. If only she could talk to Clive—or someone who seemed *real*—Elsie, perhaps, or even Stan, she thought with a sad smile. She was overcome with a feeling that she didn't belong here in this large house with its many exquisite, fragile treasures, and yet . . .

what choice did she have if she really wanted to be with Clive? Is that how her mother had felt once upon a time? Trapped? But by whom or what? Her wealthy family's expectations or the poverty she had descended into?

She contemplated telephoning Clive—he had left his number both at the station and at his place—but in the end she thought better of it. She was loath to involve Billings, which she would surely have to in order to place a call, and, anyway, supposing she *could* secure Clive on the telephone without too much incident, what was she to say? That an old woman on the estate had told her she was meant to produce a grandson, that his mother had chastised her for having her hair down or for talking too much to the servants, or, more disturbingly, that she had discovered that he had had another love, maybe *lover*, besides Catherine? No, she would not bother him, and yet her mind drifted to what his apartment might look like, what he did alone there in the evenings, and what he had once told her about taking a woman to his bed who was not his wife. Was that true?

So lost in thought was she that she didn't hear the small figure as it silently entered the room. It was only when the figure noiselessly approached the bed that she noticed and bolted upright in alarm.

"Oh, Miss, I didn't see you there!" said Edna in response to Henrietta's exclamation of surprise. "I've gone and scared you again. I'm ever so sorry!" she said, backing away toward the door, carrying a large stack of what looked like bedding, behind which she had been, up until this point, partially obscured.

"Don't go!" Henrietta said, a slight vestige of desperation in her voice. "Please, don't go on my account. I shouldn't be up here, really. I'm sure you assumed I would be below."

"I did, Miss. Sorry," Edna said. "But not to worry; I've got lots of other rooms to tend to, so you lie yourself back down," she said, deftly managing to open the door despite her heavy load.

"Nonsense!" Henrietta said, sliding off the bed and coming over to where Edna stood. "Here, let me help you with those," she said, taking some of the sheets from the top of the stack. Edna carefully placed the rest on the thick pink-cushioned bench that ran along the foot of the bed.

"What are you doing with those, anyway?" Henrietta asked, glancing at her already-made bed with its exquisite rose damask spread and plump pillows, just one of which was thicker than all of the ones at home put together.

"Changing the sheets, of course, Miss!" she answered, slightly confused.

"But the bed's already made up!"

"Mistress's orders, Miss," she explained with a quick shrug. "Every Monday all the beds in this wing gets changed. We make 'em up quick in the morning while people is washing up so that it's not untidy while anyone's dressing. Then when everyone's off for the day, we come back and change them all, proper like, right down to the mattress."

Henrietta could not help but laugh, startling Edna by doing so. "I'm sorry . . . it's Edna, right? . . . I . . . I guess I'm not used to this," she said, thinking of how back at home they sometimes piled their coats on top of their thin blankets in the frigid depths of winter in a desperate attempt to keep warm.

"Well, I'm sure each house does it their own way, Miss," Edna said somewhat defensively.

"Here, I'll give you a hand," Henrietta said, carefully pulling back the beautiful bedspread.

"Oh, no, Miss!" Edna exclaimed, horrified, and rushed over to try to take claim to the current bedding. "Mrs. Caldwell would be awfully angry at me, and then I'd really get it. Please!"

"Don't be silly. She won't find out!" Henrietta tried to smile reassuringly. "And anyway, it's not a crime to help change a bed, is it?"

Edna gave a shy smile, and Henrietta could see she was wavering.

"Come on, we'll be done in a jiffy!" Henrietta said as she began peeling off the layers of soft, woolen blankets, thinking about how much the boys at home would love even *one* of these.

"You're sure, Miss?" Edna said reluctantly, joining in now.

"Course I'm sure! I'm not so high and mighty, you know. I used to be a waitress not so very long ago," she said confidingly, deciding on the spur of the moment to reveal one of her less risqué jobs.

"Never!" Edna said, almost in awe. "But you're Mister Clive's fiancée, Miss."

"Yes, that's true," Henrietta answered, a smile erupting across her face—an involuntary reaction whenever she was called Clive's *fiancée*; it was still so new. "But I'll tell you a secret . . . I'm really quite poor."

"You don't say!" Edna said, fluffing the pillows now.

"It's true. I live back in the city with my mother and seven brothers and sisters. And we all share two beds between us!" Henrietta felt oddly flushed and excited to be dangerously telling someone the truth, to not play the role assigned to her if even for a few minutes.

"Well, I'd never have believed it, Miss! You sure do *look* like a lady, and most times you sound like one, too."

Henrietta laughed as she considered this, feeling that it was a fair assessment. "I'll take that as a compliment, Edna," she said cheerily. "But I'm having a harder time fooling the Howards, I think."

"Oh, Miss! You shouldn't say such thing," Edna urged. "You're a regular Cinderella, that's what you are."

Henrietta gave an obligatory smile, then, and the two went back to making the bed, tucking the heavy spread neatly into place. As if on cue, they both stood back for a moment, admiring their work, before Edna then moved to pick up the remaining stack of bedding from the bench. "Thank you, Miss, but I've got to be getting on now, and so should you, I suspect."

"Don't be silly. I'll help you. I need something to do, and I need someone to talk to! I'm not used to being on my own so much."

"Well, if you're sure, though if Mrs. Caldwell spots you, we'll both get it. Me worse than you, I'd say . . ."

The two of them spent the next hour making up the beds, and then Edna asked her shyly if she fancied a cup of tea before she had to move on to her next task, which involved scrubbing the scullery and the butler's pantry. When Henrietta accepted, Edna offered to bring her a cup in the morning room or the study, the proposal of which had caused Henrietta to laugh. "No, of course not!" she said and then insisted that she accompany Edna to the kitchen, that is, if she wouldn't get into trouble. Edna replied that she wasn't sure Mary would allow it, but Henrietta followed her down the narrow dull servant stairs at the back of the house just the same. As they entered the big bright kitchen, Mary had her back to them as she stood stirring something on the stove, and Fletcher, the chauffer, was just stepping in through the back door at the same time.

Henrietta felt his eyes travel over her body as he tipped his hat back and said with a smile, "Who's this, then? New maid?" He continued to look her over appreciatively. "Some people have all the luck," he said to no one in particular. "Pretty soon there'll be so many house lackeys, there'll be nothing left for you all to do." He took up a chair at the rough table where a basket of biscuits sat, still basking from the heat of the oven from which they had just come. "Better get a uniform on before the old duffer sees you," he went on, addressing Henrietta directly now. "Might confuse you with one of the swells if you're not careful!"

"Jack!" Edna said, looking nervously at Henrietta for her reaction. Mary, likewise, turned to see who Fletcher was speaking to and upon seeing Henrietta let out a little squeal.

"Lord! Miss!" she said, giving a little curtsey and wiping her hands on her apron. "Can I help you, Miss?" she said deferentially, scowling at Jack, who also hastily stood up now, his hat in hand.

Henrietta suppressed a smile as her eyes alighted first on the now-unsettled Jack and then on Mary. "I was hoping to have a cup of tea with Edna, if that's allowed," she said hopefully. "If I'm not in the way, that is," she added quickly.

"You should have rung, Miss! We'd have brought it to you. Edna! Have you no sense, girl?"

Henrietta's breath caught as she heard Edna being called *girl*; it had been Mr. Hennessey's name for her, and she suddenly wished with all her heart that she could talk to him. "Might I sit down?" Henrietta asked, a bit overcome suddenly by the strain of it all, as she gripped the back of one of the chairs. "Just for a moment?"

"Of course, Miss!" Mary said, bustling over.

"Allow me," Jack said, getting there first and pulling out the chair for her.

"Thank you," Henrietta smiled, "but there's no need for a fuss. Honestly. I . . ." she looked at Edna confidentially, "I happened upon Edna upstairs, and I asked her if I might have some tea. Down here, with all of you, that is. I wanted some company, you see."

"Course you can!" Mary said, carrying over a steaming cup. "Don't think Mrs. Caldwell or Mrs. Howard would approve, though," she added. "Would you like a biscuit?" she said, picking up the basket and handing it toward her.

"No! Thank you," Henrietta said, taking a sip of the tea. "I'm still quite full from lunch, which was simply delic . . ." she was interrupted then by the sound of heels clicking along the hallway.

"Mrs. Howard!" Edna whispered frantically. "You'd best go, Miss!"

Henrietta jumped up accordingly and hurried across the big kitchen to the back door. "Thanks for the tea!" she whispered with a quick smile.

"I should go, too," she heard Jack say. "I'm not supposed to be in here this time of day."

The two of them escaped out the back, which Henrietta saw was very near the kitchen gardens she had just walked through this morning. The bright morning sun had been replaced by clouds now, and a slight breeze had picked up. Henrietta looked around, trying to get her bearings. Off to the left, where the pea gravel drive swept past the house, stood a long low building, which Henrietta guessed was perhaps the garage, or maybe the former stables.

"I'm sorry I mistook you for a servant," said Jack, catching up to her.

"Oh, that's all right," Henrietta smiled. "Until very recently I *was* a sort of servant, so I can understand the confusion."

"No, it's not that . . . not like you look like a servant. Just that, well, I didn't expect a lady of the house to be coming down the back stairs with Edna is all."

"Sounds like something I heard just this morning," Henrietta said ruefully.

"But I can see my mistake," he said, looking her up and down. "No, sir. You're definitely not a servant."

Henrietta arched her eyebrow at what sounded awfully like flirtation and held her hand out to him. "I'm Henrietta Von Harmon, Clive Howard's fiancée."

Jack let out a low whistle as he took her hand. "Now I *am* confused," he said, a smile crossing the rough skin of his face.

"Why's that?" Henrietta asked, genuinely curious. "Is it my clothes?" she said, brushing the skirt of her dress with her free hand.

"No," Jack laughed. "It's because a lady doesn't offer her hand to a lowly servant."

Henrietta released his hand, an awkwardness overcoming her then suddenly, and began walking slowly toward the kitchen gardens, Jack following closely behind. She could see the tall thin gardener, raking now, and she could just make out the scratch, scratch, scratch as he worked, seemingly oblivious to all around him.

"Who's that?" Henrietta asked, pointing to him.

"Him?" Jack said, looking in the direction of the scratching. "That would be Virgil. Why? Has he bothered you?" he asked, concerned.

"No . . . he . . . I'm just . . . trying to learn everyone's name," she fibbed.

"Virgil's one of the gardeners under the head, Mr. McCreanney. They all live above the old stables. I'm there, too," he said, nodding toward the long low building. "Bit of an odd duck is Virgil," he continued. "He's sweet on Edna. But, then, I'm sweet on Edna, too," he smiled.

Henrietta felt a strange pang at this information, though she wasn't sure why. It couldn't possibly be jealousy, she knew, though there was something about Jack that was instantly likeable. He was a good height with thick blond hair and very blue eyes. His smile, she admitted, was very charming, but nothing could alter how she felt about Clive. That was something else altogether.

Perhaps it was more a restlessness than a pang. A feeling of being on the outside, adrift, wishing that she still had the simple intrigues of the servants' world much like those she had been a part of at the Promenade or the Marlowe. She was no longer a part of those lowly worlds, but she didn't seem a part of Highbury, either. But that was silly, Henrietta countered with herself. Of course she was. And this new world had drama and intrigues of its own to unravel, like Ma's secret past or Clive's supposed old flame, Sophia, she reminded herself miserably. Somehow, though, those were different, more serious and weighty than the innocent love triangle Jack hinted at now. Perhaps it was just Jack's openness that was throwing her off. After all, what type of man after talking with him for five minutes reveals who his secret love is?

Henrietta smiled at the thought. "You're quite forthcoming," she commented.

"'Spose I am," he grinned, casually lighting a cigarette now. "But what's the harm there?" he said, blowing smoke out of the corner of his mouth.

Henrietta supposed he had a point and thought of Clive, trying to weigh up whether she thought he was forthcoming. He was at times, she decided, but she sensed there were still secrets there, old wounds he was perhaps hiding.

"Well, I'll put in a good word for you," Henrietta smiled at him, "with Edna, that is."

"Course you will," he said, giving her a little wink. "I can see you're that type of girl. Kind, I mean. I've got to go now, though," he said, smoothly extracting his pocket watch from inside his dark green uniform and casually flipping it open with one hand. "Almost time for me to drive back to the station and pick up Mr. Howard."

"It's that late already?" Henrietta asked worriedly.

"Yes, almost time for tea, *Miss Von Harmon*," he said, lifting his hat to her with a sly grin and hurried off to the stables, Henrietta watching him as he went. When he had disappeared into the stables, she looked back toward the house and then the gardens. She knew she couldn't creep back into the kitchen; she would have to go around to the East Doors and hopefully let herself in without running into Billings. She was unwilling to get closer to Virgil, however, so she stood, contemplating whether she should instead walk all the way around the house and enter through the front doors, when she saw the figure of what looked like Helen Schuyler hobbling up the path that led up from the beach. She could see that she was headed right for Virgil, so she decided to mercifully intercept her.

"Helen!" she said, waving her hand and walking quickly toward her, causing Virgil to turn and notice her now. He stared at her for a few moments, scowling, as she approached but then looked away and went back to his raking.

"Helen!" she called again, giving Virgil a wide berth. This time the old woman looked up, puzzled at first, but then her face relaxed in recognition. She was breathing heavily when Henrietta finally met her.

"Here, let me take those," Henrietta said, taking the wooden box of berries from her. "I would have helped, you know."

"Ta, Daphne," Helen said, squinting up at her.

"It's Henrietta, remember?" she reminded her gently.

"Oo, aye! Tha's wha' I meant, like. 'Enrietta," she wheezed, her hands on her lower back as if to support it.

Henrietta began walking slowly toward the house with her now, and she wondered how much help this woman really was to Mary, even during big parties when extra hands were needed. She noticed that Helen kept her head bent slightly away from the direction of Virgil, who stood motionless now, watching them.

"Jis' keep walkin', dearie, an 'e migh' na pay us any attention," Helen muttered, almost to herself.

"Are you afraid of him?" Henrietta asked softly.

"Aye! Course I am! 'E's the one tha' stole me ring."

Henrietta sighed. The woman seemed obsessed. "But how can you be sure?" Henrietta asked, still not convinced that Helen hadn't simply misplaced it.

"Cause I *seen* 'im, creepin' 'round me place the day it wen' missin'. I thought I told ya all this afore," she said, slightly irritated, or perhaps just confused. "Almost dusk it were. I were bringin' in the washin' when I sees 'im. 'Idin' dare in the bushes, jis' watchin' me. Gave me the creeps it did, an I 'urried inside. I almos' forgot aboot it, but then later on tha nigh' I . . . I were in me bed an then I starts 'earin' a terrible scratch, scratch, scratchin' on the side a the cottage, like claws it were. Like some kind a beast tryin' ta get in. But na wild scratchin, noo, na frantic, like," she whispered, her shoulders hunched at the memory. "This were slow and steady. Careful like." Her eyes darted quickly to where Virgil stood working, but she looked away just as quickly.

"Maybe it was a branch scratching the side of the house?" Henrietta suggested.

"It weren' noo branch!" Helen said with feeling. "Twas tha' evil man. I lay dare all a tremblin' until I guess I moost 'ave slipped off ta sleep. But then I 'eard 'im again . . . this time inside the hoose!" she whispered, and Henrietta, despite the fantastical nature of the story, felt goose bumps appear on her arms and the back of her neck. "'Eard 'im shuffle all around, footsteps comin' closer . . . and then dare were some sor' a noise ootside an 'e moosta got spooked an run off then."

"So you didn't hear him take the ring? Go through your chest of drawers?"

"Ach, noo, but 'e coulda snuck in some time when I were oot. Easy enough. The cottage doesn' lock. Caugh' 'im several times creepin' in the woods down by the lake. Don' know wha' 'e's lookin' fer or why 'e's always dare, but 'e is, like."

Henrietta shivered. "Have you told Daphne?"

"I wrote 'er a couple a letters. Neils taught me 'ow ta write a bit, but she 'asn't written back or coom round," she said despairingly. "I 'ope nothin's wrong, I do," she said, looking fearfully up at Henrietta.

"Do you want me to have a word with the Howards, Mr. Clive perhaps?"

"Ach, noo! I wouldn' bother 'em wit me troubles, na fer the wurld," she said, wringing her hands now.

"Well, something should be done, surely!" Henrietta exclaimed. "Perhaps Mrs. Caldwell or Billings?" she suggested.

"Aye, mebbe Mr. Billings," she stammered after a moment's consideration. "'E an Mr. McCreanney go way back, they do. An Mr. McCreanney, bein' a Scot, too, like, mebbe . . . mebbe 'e'll 'ave a word. Ya don' mind?" she said, peering up at her. "Ya bein' a lady a the hoose, like?"

"Course I don't mind!" Henrietta smiled reassuringly. "It would give me something useful to do. And besides, we can't have you terrified in your own home, now, can we?"

By this time, they had reached the back door of the kitchen, and through the thin, dented screen, Henrietta could see Mary bustling toward them, having spotted them approaching.

"I'll say goodbye, then, Helen," she said. "Leave it to me."

Helen laid a hand on her arm. "Jis' be careful, lass. Dare's somethin' not righ' aboot 'im," she said just as Mary opened the door. Henrietta handed her the box of berries as she held the door for Helen to pass through.

"You're all right," Mary said confidentially to Henrietta as Helen shuffled past her, sweating profusely now. "Mrs. Howard didn't see you before."

"Thanks, Mary," Henrietta smiled. "I'd better get back."

Mary nodded and turned then to talk to Helen, who had heavily seated herself in one of the kitchen chairs.

Henrietta slowly made her way to the front of the house, wondering as she walked what she should say to Billings about the whole affair. She looked cautiously around for Virgil as she rounded one of the corners and past a large viburnum, but he was nowhere in sight now. Still, she felt a cold shudder just the same.

Chapter 6

As promised, or rather, as expected, Mrs. Howard took Henrietta shopping the next day and almost every day after, generously lavishing her with a new wardrobe, including a variety of shoes, hats, and gloves as well. At first, Henrietta was resistant to accepting so many expensive new things, but Mrs. Howard convinced her that she was doing her a favor by letting her indulge her in this way and that she would most certainly surprise, not to mention delight, Clive. As the second week wore on, Henrietta actually found herself if not completely enamored with Mrs. Howard's company, then at least enjoying it somewhat. She could be a rather pleasant companion, as it turned out, as long as Henrietta did as she was instructed.

Their luncheons were divided up between going out to various restaurants or tearooms and staying in, both of which became instructional in nature. The skills and advice learned at both were then put into practice during the evening meal in which Mr. Howard was present, though he seemed not always fully cognizant of what was playing out before him, so lost in his own musings, presumably respecting his firm, was he. They enjoyed a pleasant two weeks, all things considered, the Howards attempting to teach her various card games that she would be expected to know. Mrs. Howard despaired that Henrietta could neither play the piano nor sing. Granted these were becoming quite old-fashioned requirements amongst young ladies, but any accomplishment would have helped Henrietta's cause immeasurably.

Meanwhile, Henrietta noted with pleasure, Mrs. Howard seemed less and less cross with her as time went on and corrected her less often, especially regarding which outfit was to be worn on which occasion. Henrietta's main transgression, if there was one, seemed to be her continued fraternization, as Mrs. Howard called it, with the servants. She was always getting caught chatting with them in the kitchen or, worse yet, helping them with their chores upstairs! Indeed, Mrs. Howard had found it necessary to call her into the study one afternoon to lecture her on the importance of keeping her distance from her inferiors.

Henrietta stood awkwardly in front of her now, dressed in a long navy blue silk skirt with blue oxfords and a sailor-style white blouse with a large bow at the side of the neck, and felt rather like a recalcitrant schoolgirl being chastised for some infraction of the school rules. Mrs. Howard, conversely, sat at her leisure at her elaborate Queen Anne desk, where she went every morning to write her letters.

"Henrietta, my dear," she sighed, putting her pen down. "I'm afraid I really must be rather severe with you. You simply cannot continue to treat the servants as if they were your close friends. Don't think I don't see what goes on around here, and it is really very tiresome."

Henrietta rather thought that Mrs. Howard did not know *all* that went on around the estate, but she did not say so.

"Understandably you are lonely, but soon, after the engagement party, a whole new set of friends will open up to you. Indeed, they will be people you will *need* to form relationships with in order to properly uphold Clive's place in society. Your bosom friend simply cannot be one of the junior maids."

Henrietta bit back a smile and mentally relinquished some credit to Mrs. Howard's wherewithal. In truth, after the Howards retired each evening, she had been sneaking to the kitchen where she could usually enjoy a game of rummy and cocoa with the servants before they all turned in for the night. She couldn't help it, really; she was so used to keeping late hours, and they all seemed to welcome her immensely. It had been awkward at first until she had told them her stories about her own poverty and her long string of jobs to support her family, though she wisely left off the fact that she had been a taxi dancer and an usherette. Still, it was enough for them to accept her as almost one of them, and they were happy for her Cinderella-esque story of becoming engaged to the prince of the house. Most of them, that is. James tended to still snub her, as did Kitty, another of the junior maids whose dismissive behavior toward her, Henrietta attributed to an obvious attempt to impress the unsuspecting James. Mrs. Caldwell tolerated her presence in the kitchen, though she did not, or pretended not to, know that she sometimes helped them in their work. Billings, however, did not approve and had said so publically on more than one occasion.

In fact, Henrietta was pretty sure it was him who had gone directly to Mrs. Howard to snitch on her, thus the current interview. Him or James, Henrietta felt certain. Henrietta's lowly background and socialization with the servants did not impress Mr. Billings, but rather they had the opposite effect they seemed to have had on the others. It was as if he needed the family he so astutely served to be above him, to be his superiors; otherwise, they seemed somehow not worthy of his devotion. Henrietta's common roots and, worse, her desperate clinging to them vexed him to no end, and he had no qualms about complaining to Mrs. Howard with reference to her questionable comportment. Henrietta herself could feel his disapproval and tried to avoid him as much as possible. She had kept her promise to Helen, however, and not long after she had seen her that day behind the house, she had worked up her courage and approached Billings in his private office next to the butler's pantry.

"That's preposterous!" Billings had thundered, after she had explained Helen's story of woe. "Virgil is quite a hard worker. Doesn't give us one minute of trouble! He no more stole that ring than I did. Helen Schuyler served this house faithfully for over fifty years, I'll give her that. But she's a bit touched now," he said, momentarily tapping his temple with an index finger. "She's become paranoid, always assuming someone's after her. Next week it'll be some other thing. She still knows her way about the kitchen, and it's good of her to still help out from time to time, but it's more out of sympathy we ask her up to help than for what she really contributes, and that includes whatever comes out of her mouth. Pay no more mind to what she tells you."

"But, Billings, I've looked for the ring myself, and it's nowhere! Honestly. Something had to have happened to it . . ."

"Yes, something like she dropped it somewhere or lost it down a hole. Who knows? Now, please, don't waste any more of anyone's time."

"But couldn't you have a word with him? Or Mr. McCreanney?"

"Certainly not! I know for certain Virgil is in bed every night, early. Not creeping around in the woods or down by the cottage, that's for sure. Now, really, Miss Von Harmon, I must get back to work, if you'll excuse me." He stood up from his desk where he had been sitting to reinforce that he wanted her to leave.

"Well, perhaps I should discuss this with Mrs. Howard," Henrietta said, trying her hand at a parry.

"That is as you think best, Miss Von Harmon," he countered expertly. "All I can say on the matter is that Mrs. Howard most certainly does not like to be bothered with trivial matters pertaining to the servants."

"But this isn't trivial!" Henrietta had protested. "Helen's terrified!"

"That is as it may be. As I said, Miss Von Harmon, you must do as you feel best," he added as his final thrust.

In the end, Henrietta had had no choice but to accept defeat where Billings was concerned and had instead turned to interrogating those below stairs who were more receptive to her. Mary, however, when asked about Virgil, had nothing concrete to say about him either way; that was Mr. McCreanney's department, she had said. Didn't know much about young Virgil, just that he was a good eater, despite his thinness, and that he didn't say all that much. Thought he might be sweet on Edna, but that was just a guess.

Edna, on the other hand, had blushed when Henrietta mentioned Virgil and said she didn't understand why everyone thought he was sweet on her. Jack, who had been sitting at the table with the two of them as Edna sat mending, pointed out that perhaps it had something to do with the bouquets of flowers he was always picking out of the gardens for her.

"Those are for the house, not me!" she had exclaimed.

"Then why is there always a rose by your bedside?" Jack asked, grinning.

"How would you know what's by my bedside?" she had exclaimed.

"I make it my business to know," he said smoothly, "'Specially where my girl is concerned."

"I'm not your girl, Jack Fletcher!"

"Really now? So you're Virgil's, then?"

"It's none of your business who I fancy! Not saying I fancy anyone, actually."

"Well, if you're not sweet on him, then why'd you dance with him this past May Day at the servants' picnic?"

"Because I felt sorry for him, if you must know!" she said hotly. "No one else asked me." She looked at him with narrowed eyes.

"He's always starin' at you," Jack added.

"He stares at everyone!" she said, abruptly standing now. "I've got to take this upstairs," she mumbled, holding up the trousers she had been mending for Mr. Howard. "I'll leave you two to figure it out yourselves!"

Jack had laughed as Edna hurried out, but his laugh had died down once she was out of earshot, as if he had not been quite sincere in it.

"You're a terrible flirt, you are," Henrietta said to him.

"Well, he does fancy her," he said, taking a final drag from the stump of the cigarette he was holding. "He actually told me once. A queer one he is, though," he said, rubbing it out now.

"Why do you say that? Aren't you just being jealous?"

"Jealous? Of him? As if he'd ever stand a chance with a girl like Edna."

"Well, what's so queer about him?" she asked, a spark of hope igniting.

"Just that he's always creepin' around in the woods, always goin' off alone, down by the lake, I think."

Henrietta shuddered. "He gives me the willies. I can't stand his staring."

They were silent then for a few moments, each lost in their own thoughts, before Henrietta roused herself and stood up. "I suppose I should go up now. It's getting late."

"Henrietta," Jack said deferentially, standing up as well.

"Yes?" she said with a smile as she turned back toward him.

"We're having a party. This Saturday. For Edna. It's her birthday, and we wanted to surprise her, give her a bit of a rub. Do you think you might come?" he asked earnestly. "She'd be honored, I'm sure. She really likes you."

"Oh, Jack! I'd love to. Honestly. But Clive is supposed to be coming back from the city that night, so I don't think I'll be able to."

"Sure," he said, clearly disappointed. "I get it. I just thought you might like to be included, have a bit of fun, but I'm sure Mister Clive will provide that in his own way." She could have been mistaken, but Henrietta thought she detected what might have passed for a hint of suggestiveness in his tone.

"You know I would if I could, though, right?" she added, deciding to ignore it.

"Sure," he said again with what seemed a forced smile. "Good night."

"Good night," she had said lightly and had slowly gone upstairs, but not without perhaps more regret than she should have felt.

Now, standing corrected in front of Mrs. Howard, she wondered exactly how much Antonia really knew about her activities, how much Billings had reported. She felt relatively certain that he would not have mentioned her relationship with Helen, as he was loath to take her story seriously in the first place. She tried to decide if perhaps now would be a good time to broach the subject, as she stood, her hands folded politely in front of her as she had previously been instructed. The decision was made for her, however, as Mrs. Howard went on now, apparently not finished with her lecture.

"This simply must end, Henrietta; do you understand? You cannot continue to cavort with your inferiors!"

"My inferiors?" Henrietta asked, forgetting Helen for the moment and suddenly feeling an angry flush travel up her neck. She longed to untie the silky bow at her throat, despite it being all the rage right now. "They're not my inferiors!"

"Perhaps not as people, not as Christians," Mrs. Howard explained matter-of-factly, "but in station, in employment, then yes. They are. And the sooner you realize that, the better off you'll be."

Henrietta sputtered for a retort but was so incensed she was at a loss for words.

"My dear," Mrs. Howard went on as if she was not aware of Henrietta's obvious indignation, "you must consider. Someday, probably very soon, you will be their employer, the head of this house. Surely you can see that that is a precarious position. You must have their respect and their fear for them to obey you. Can you imagine Kitty, for example, taking orders from you to dust the library after you've spent months playing rummy and drinking cocoa with the staff below stairs?"

Henrietta drew in a sharp breath. So she did know.

"It is much more difficult to hire and retain good staff than you might imagine. Compensation and fairness, even kindness at times, are important, of course, but so is a strong hand. Why, not more than a month or so ago, we had to let Fritz, the old chauffer, go for theft. Terrible business it was. We were lucky to get Fletcher at such short notice." Mrs. Howard sighed. "I know it must be difficult for you, my dear, but you really must try. For Clive," she added suggestively.

There was a knock, then, on the door, and Billings silently stepped in. "There is a telephone call, Madam. It is Mister Clive."

At this announcement, Henrietta felt her heart quicken, especially in light of this irritating conversation in which she currently found herself, if it could even be called that, as it really more resembled a monologue on Mrs. Howard's part. In the nearly two weeks that she had been at Highbury now, she had not spoken to Clive once on the telephone, nor had she received any letter or note from him, which she had convinced herself was because he was terribly busy on his case and which she had tried very hard not to take personally. Happily, now, she made a move toward the far desk belonging to Mr. Howard, upon which the telephone sat, when Billings interrupted. "He wishes to speak to you, Madam," he said, bowing his head deferentially, but not without first shooting Henrietta the briefest look of triumph.

"Thank you, Billings," Mrs. Howard said, pretending she hadn't caught the slight, as she stood up elegantly and walked slowly to the telephone while Henrietta endeavored to recover from the sting.

"Hello? Clive? Is that you?" Mrs. Howard said, speaking more loudly than was necessary. "Oh, yes, hello, darling!"

Henrietta remained where she was, anxiously waiting to hear what his news might be and hoping she might be allowed a chance to talk to him, too.

"Why, everything's going splendidly," Mrs. Howard said, glancing over at Henrietta and smiling falsely. "Of course we're getting along, darling. You needn't even ask that. Yes? Oh, no! Why that's terrible news, darling; we were so hoping we would see you tonight."

Henrietta felt her hopes wither, guessing the purpose of the call now. Involuntarily, she took a step toward the phone, hoping for a moment to talk to him.

"Wretched business, that. Yes, I understand. Tomorrow, then. Yes, I'll tell Henrietta. Yes, of course. Goodbye, darling," she said and briskly placed the receiver back in its cradle.

Henrietta expected her to share the news with her immediately, but instead Mrs. Howard turned directly to Billings, who was still hovering near. "There's been a change of plans, Billings," Mrs. Howard said without emotion. "Mr. Clive has been unavoidably detained in the city tonight and won't arrive until tomorrow morning. Would you inform Mary?"

"Very good, Madam," Billings said with a bow and exited a trifle faster than was usual for him.

Only then did Mrs. Howard turn her attention toward Henrietta.

"It seems he's caught up in some sort of problem with his case," she said languidly. "Something about a stakeout, or some such thing."

"But . . . didn't he want to talk to me?" Henrietta said, slightly stunned.

"Yes, of course he did, dear," she said, almost as an afterthought. "He wanted you to come on the line, but then something happened on his end and he had to go. He asked me to give you his love and said that he'll try to call in a bit to speak to you."

"I see," Henrietta said, feeling embarrassed and deeply disappointed. Suddenly she realized how much she missed him, how alone she really felt. She wished Ma had a telephone so that she might call and talk to all of them at home. "I think I'll go up to my room now and lie down until dinner. Would you excuse me, Antonia?"

"Of course, my dear. A very good idea," she said sagaciously, sitting back down at her desk. "It will afford you an opportunity to think about what I have said," she added, giving her another false smile and turning back to her correspondence.

Henrietta merely nodded and absently stepped outside the study, utterly deflated, and was surprised to see Jack standing there. Despite herself, she smiled. "What are you doing in here?" she whispered, looking around.

"I heard Mister Clive isn't coming back tonight . . ."

"How did you hear that?" she asked, mystified. "I've only just found out myself!"

Jack grinned. "I have my ways," he said mysteriously, but when she continued to look at him, puzzled, he dropped the pretense of mystery and said plainly, "I heard Billings tell Mary so she could adjust tonight's dinner."

"Oh!" she said, "News travels fast, I see."

"So that means you can come!" he said excitedly.

"Come where?"

"To Edna's party. It's tonight, remember?"

The conversation they had had in the kitchen a few days ago came back to her then. She hesitated. She knew she shouldn't go; this would be a terrible example of fraternization, much worse than having a cup of cocoa in the kitchen with the maids, but she still burned with anger regarding Mrs. Howard's horrible self-righteousness. Henrietta knew her judgment was skewed at the moment by her disappointment with Clive and her exasperation with Mrs. Howard and her silly lectures, but she didn't care. How dare Mrs. Howard say they were inferior! It was as if she were calling her own family inferior. And, anyway, she longed to have some fun. Life at Highbury in the company of Mr. and Mrs. Howard, and especially without Clive, hadn't been exactly exciting.

"I'll try," she smiled at him. "If I can slip away."

They both jumped when they heard Billings coming down the hallway.

"Best go," Jack whispered. "Tonight, then. At the stables. Nine o'clock!" he said and ran the opposite way.

"I'll try!" she whispered and hurried up the stairs.

Chapter 7

All that evening, Henrietta moped around the study, hoping for Clive to call back as he said he might, but he did not. After dinner, the three of them accordingly went through to the drawing room, Mr. Howard taking his glass of port and joining them, as was his wont lately, seeing as they had not, in the whole time that Henrietta had been with them, had any male guests with whom he might indulge in cigars and perhaps a conversation of a more political nature than was appropriate with the ladies.

As it was, the conversation consisted of Mrs. Howard again reviewing the proposed menu for the engagement party one last time. Henrietta had never heard of most of the items suggested by Mrs. Howard, and she therefore listlessly agreed to them, having lost interest in the party long ago. She had quickly realized that the whole thing was quite out of her control, and despite her early protests about a having such a large formal affair, especially since she would not be contributing many to the guest list, indeed probably a mere five if she didn't include Ma, Mrs. Howard was having none of it. Consequently, Henrietta had given up and had allowed Mrs. Howard her own way in everything. It might have been different if Clive had been there to support her, but she found she did not have the strength to battle Mrs. Howard alone, especially when it was over something as esoteric and unknown to her as to whether the shrimp should be potted or simply boiled.

Henrietta glanced at the large grandfather clock in the corner for what seemed the hundredth time, and, finally, at the first yawn from Mr. Howard, she fabricated a matching one and begged to be excused for the evening.

"Are you quite well?" Mrs. Howard asked her, looking up at the clock herself. "It's still quite early, you know! Perhaps Clive might yet telephone."

"I . . . I'm rather tired," Henrietta tried to say in an exhausted tone of voice. "I'd like to be fresh for Clive tomorrow," she fibbed. "If he does ring through, have Billings come for me," she said, thinking that her superior tone regarding one of the servants would please Mrs. Howard.

Mrs. Howard did indeed incline her head in approval. "Very well, my dear. We won't keep you."

Mr. Howard stood as she made her way across the room to him and kissed him politely on the cheek. "We make a poor substitute for a fiancé, don't we, my dear? Heh, heh. Well, soon enough, soon enough. Good night, then."

Henrietta, her heart racing, tried hard not to hurry up the stairs. After all, she would still have to wait a bit until the Howards went to bed themselves. Perhaps she should have stayed down there longer and forced a game of cards. Perhaps that would have tired them out sooner! She chastised herself for her lack of foresight as she shut her bedroom door behind her, leaning against it. Ah, well, it couldn't be helped now. She would simply have to wait and decided to focus on her clothes to pass the time. She unbuttoned the long rose evening dress she was wearing and carefully hung it up, still amazed that something so exquisite belonged to her. She felt almost as if she were merely borrowing these lovely items. She knew that hanging her clothes was most definitely Edna's job, but Henrietta refused to leave them draped at the end of the bed for the poor girl to tidy in the morning when she could so easily do it herself.

Carefully she looked in the armoire, wondering which of her new outfits would be most appropriate for a servants' party above a stables-turned-auto-garage. She wished she could find her old clothes, but Mrs. Howard had ordered them to be washed and mended, and they had as yet to be returned to her. She had probably had them burned, Henrietta thought wryly. Besides her simple house dresses that she had worn at home, all of her other dresses, bought on the sly with Polly in her taxi dancer days, were quite revealing, as these, Polly had intimated at the time, would surely bring in bigger tips.

She finally decided upon a long tweed skirt and a plain white blouse and black cardigan. Though nothing Mrs. Howard had bought her could remotely be considered racy, this outfit was particularly unassuming. She had no desire to look extravagant tonight amongst the servants, wanting to blend in as much as possible. Her hair had been done up for dinner, as it was every day now by Mrs. Howard's own maid, Andrews, and after observing it at her dressing table mirror, Henrietta decided to leave it that way. Carefully, however, she replaced the mother-of-pearl pins in the shape of lilies of the valley that Mrs. Howard had bought her just yesterday with plain ones. Satisfied that she looked modest enough, she went to the door and opened it slightly, listening, and shut it again quickly when she heard the Howards on the stairs. She would still have to wait a bit.

She went to the window, but the stables were on the other side of the house from where her bedroom was, so when she peered out through the leaded glass, there was nothing to see but the dark lawns and formal gardens lit by moonlight. Listlessly, she sat down in a chair to wait, thinking about the party and wondering what Clive would make of it when she told him. Suddenly it came to her that she did not have a gift for Edna.

Her eyes traveled around the room searching for something she could use for a gift, but she couldn't see anything that would do. For one thing, nothing her eyes alighted on really seemed like hers. She still felt as though she were borrowing everything. And even if she did have her own old things about her, there would have been nothing suitable to give from amongst that meager collection, either. A scuffed handbag? An old hankie? Her eyes rested on the dressing table, then, and the hairpins. She got up and held one in her hand, deliberating. It would be inappropriate to give a servant any of the jewelry Mrs. Howard had given her, some of which had come from Mrs. Howard's own collection (with a suggestion of more to come), but she wondered if she could possibly give her one of these little pins, as these had been bought specifically for her. She knew they had been expensive, and yet there was a simple innocence to them, which is probably why Mrs. Howard had selected them in the first place. Surely it would be okay to give Edna *one* of them, wouldn't it?

Yes, Henrietta decided, she would and felt excited at the prospect of giving it to her, happy to be able to share the wealth she so recently found herself enjoying. She would have loved to lavish her new good fortune on Ma and the kids, but this, so far, was the next best thing. Edna was probably about the same age as Elsie, she mused. Carefully she wrapped the pin up in a hanky and found a ribbon to tie it with and slipped it into her skirt pocket.

Again she opened the door to her room, and this time heard nothing below. She paused for a few minutes, waiting, and then, heart pounding, she slipped out. She didn't dare go down the servants' stairs, having no desire to run into Billings or Mrs. Caldwell or any of the senior staff, so she slipped down the main staircase as quietly as she could. The front doors were too heavy and loud to open, and she couldn't go out the back kitchen door, as Mary and some of the kitchen staff were surely still in there. Her best bet seemed to be the East Doors, so she made her way toward them accordingly. The hallways were dark, and, luckily, she did not run into any servants. Once she thought she heard Billings and hurried into the study to avoid being seen, but it was only Andrews passing by with what looked like some freshly ironed blouses of Mrs. Howard's. When she finally got to the East Doors, they were locked, of course, but Henrietta was able to unlatch them easily and, wincing as they creaked open, slipped out into the warm July air.

She followed the gravel path around the back of the house until it connected with the main drive and wished that the moon were more full and bright, as it was quite dark here in the back of the property. She could see the old garage, however, part of which was lit up, a beacon in the vast darkness surrounding the estate.

She was surprised, as she got closer, to hear music. She paused for a moment just outside the door, collecting herself, and took a deep breath. She was having second thoughts now, her earlier anger and disappointment giving way to reason and sound judgment. Mrs. Howard would be furious if she found out. But before she could completely change her mind, though, the door opened promptly, and Henrietta laughed to see Jack's surprised face.

"You came!"

"Yes," she said, looking over her shoulder at the house. "I hope I'm not too late . . ."

"No, no! Come in," he said, holding the door open for her. "Edna! Come see who's here," he called out as Henrietta stepped inside, an odd fusion of smells made up of motor oil, cigarette smoke, and a lingering remnant of old straw hitting her as she did so and reminding her, rather unexpectedly, of when she had sometimes gone to see her father at the Schwinn factory and how he had been elbow-deep in grease in the maintenance shed, giving her a little wave to shoo her home before anyone noticed her.

Edna looked up expectantly and, seeing Henrietta, burst into a smile even as a blush crept up her face.

"Oh, Miss!" she exclaimed. "You're here, too?"

"Yes," Henrietta said, coming over to her. "I hope you're not bothered. Jack invited me," she said, looking back at Jack, who had followed her over. "Anyway, happy birthday!"

"Of course I'm not bothered! I'm flattered, Miss. We . . . we don't have much to offer, I'm afraid," she said, looking around with an air of distress.

"Don't think Mr. Billings would approve, though, do you? Or Mrs. Caldwell, for that matter," came a nearby voice. Henrietta turned in the direction it was coming from and saw that it was Virgil. He had been standing behind Edna in the shadows.

"Well, good thing they won't find out now, isn't it?" Jack said, giving him a meaningful look.

Virgil merely shrugged.

"Would you like a drop of cherry wine, Miss?" Edna asked. "Mary gave it to us. Said she had no more need of it in the kitchens, but I think she was fibbing. Mary's awfully good, you know. I think she meant it as a present," she said, holding up the bottle for Henrietta.

It was clear to Henrietta that Edna had already more than sampled Mary's wares, and she smiled, happy that Edna was having a chance to enjoy herself. "Of course, I'll have some," Henrietta said politely, and Jack obliged her by filling up a glass. As she took a sip, she looked around and was surprised that there were so many people here, most of them junior staff that she didn't even recognize, surmising that they must be under Mr. McCreanney's outdoor wing. Jack had pulled two of the cars out, the Daimler and the Bentley, so that they had room at least on one side of the garage. The Mercedes Benz Roadster and the real prize, the red-and-white Isotta Fraschini Tipo, were still locked up tight on the other side. Mr. Howard, it was said, had a penchant for collecting cars.

Henrietta was glad there were a lot of people, hoping that her presence would be less a focus of attention this way. With Mrs. Howard's words still buzzing annoyingly in her mind, she did not wish to socialize with the staff as a whole; she had really just come for Edna and Jack, she told herself. She hadn't expected Virgil to be there, but of course that made sense. Why would he be excluded? She glanced over at him now, and though he looked a bit dirty and greasy and was staring at Edna, he seemed innocent enough. He was perhaps just one of those people unfortunate enough to be born with a permanent frown. Perhaps Helen was mistaken about him, after all.

"Aren't you going to introduce me?" Henrietta said to Jack and let her eyes dart to Virgil. Maybe she should try to get to know him and judge for herself, she decided.

Jack gave her a puzzled look. "Sure," he said confusedly as he jammed the stump of his cigarette into the corner of his mouth. "Where are my manners?" he said, squinting slightly from the smoke. He stepped toward Virgil and two other men standing near him. "Miss Von Harmon," he said, nodding toward Henrietta, "this is Virgil, one of the gardeners here. And this is Clem and Bernie. They're gardeners, too."

Both Clem and Bernie nodded shyly, Clem managing to mumble, "Pleased to meet you," for them both.

"Please call me Henrietta," she said, looking at Clem and Bernie rather than Virgil. She attempted a smile.

Virgil merely stared at her. "You're Master Clive's woman, aren't you?"

"Virgil!" Edna exclaimed. "This is his fiancée!"

"That's what I said."

"No, you didn't!" Edna said. "Don't pay him no mind, Miss," Edna said to her. "He . . . he doesn't mean to be impertinent."

"That's all right," Henrietta said reassuringly. "And, yes, Virgil," Henrietta said, looking at him squarely. "I *am* recently engaged to Mr. Howard." It felt strange to call him "Mr. Howard," as, in her mind, that title implied Clive's father and because she had known Clive as *Inspector* Howard for so long.

"You're very pretty," he said, matter-of-factly, almost like a child.

"Thank you, Virgil," Henrietta responded with forced politeness, and Edna could not help but turn her face away in shame. "I meant to tell you that the gardens are very beautiful," Henrietta continued, still addressing Virgil. "I admire them very much," she said, trying to look at all of them now in turn.

Clem and Bernie broke into smiles and looked at the ground, pleased with the compliment, but Virgil remained silent. Finally, Clem said, "Thank you, Miss. I'll tell Mr. McCreanney. He'll be pleased, he will."

Henrietta smiled at him and then looked around uncomfortably, not sure what to do next. She felt it was unfair to judge Virgil because of his abrupt boorishness, and yet she couldn't shake the feeling that he somehow reminded her of Larry, or Neptune, as he was called in the underworld, the man who had nearly killed her. She shivered and turned slightly away.

"Music and everything!" she said brightly to Jack and Edna, searching for something to say. "I haven't heard any for an age . . . and I adore this song!" she said, hearing Fred Astaire sing "Night and Day" and spotting the phonograph in the corner. "Where did you get it?"

"It's Jack's," Edna said, looking up at him, admiringly, and visibly grateful for the change of subject. "He brought it with him when he came."

"Ah . . . an uncle gave it to me," he said quickly. "Always givin' me things," he added. "Be right back!" he said and slipped over to the corner to whisper something to the young boy Henrietta had seen doing odd jobs around the estate and who now sat happily on a stool near the phonograph changing the records.

"It's a lovely party, Edna," Henrietta said.

"Thanks, Miss! It is, isn't it?" Edna said, a permanent smile on her flushed face.

Jack strode up to them again. Paul Whiteman's "Something Had to Happen" was playing now, apparently a result of his whispered direction to the boy. "Come on, Edna, let's us dance!"

"Well, I'm not sure," Edna said, looking at Henrietta as if for approval. With a smile, Henrietta shooed her away with her free hand while she took a sip of her cherry wine. It was nothing like the aged wines she had had since meeting Clive but pleasant just the same. Hesitantly, Edna took Jack's hand, and he led her to the center of the floor. Other couples joined in, then, including Clem and Bernie, who made a beeline for Kitty and another maid, Bridget, both of whom had been standing in a corner, laughing and whispering.

Left alone now, Henrietta wanted to turn and see Virgil's reaction to Edna dancing with Jack, but she didn't dare. She was surprised then when Virgil suddenly pushed his way past her and tapped Jack on the shoulder just as the song was finishing and "Blue Moon" by

Dick Robertson was starting up. Henrietta saw Jack give him an irritated look before reluctantly handing Edna over to him. For her part, Edna gave Jack a fleeting look as he walked toward the corner where James stood drinking from a flask, before giving her polite attention to the hungry Virgil. Edna was clearly not repulsed by him and seemed, according to some of her comments in the kitchen, to feel almost sorry for him. Or was there something more there? Henrietta wondered. Perhaps she couldn't decide whom she liked better, though Henrietta thought it an easy choice. She stood trying to study Edna's face for a clue as Virgil awkwardly danced with her, all the while staring at her as if he wanted to devour her. Again, an image of Larry came into her mind, and she shuddered and turned away.

"Would you like to dance, Miss?" came a voice beside her, causing her to jump. She turned and was surprised to see that it was Jack; he had somehow made his way over to her without her even noticing. "Or is that wrong of me? To ask you, I mean. I just thought you might feel left out, is all."

Henrietta smiled. It had been a long time since she had danced, and she admitted that she felt like it. But should she?

"I can see you think it's wrong. Sorry," Jack said genuinely.

"No, I . . . I was just thinking. No, I'd like to dance. Why not?" she said, smiling, not wanting to hurt his feelings or to appear too superior. A polka was playing now as he led her out to the makeshift dance floor by the side of the parked Mercedes. She held out her arms to him, careful to keep a distance between them as they stepped into the rhythm.

"Say, you're pretty good!" Jack said smoothly. "You could be a dancer, you could."

Henrietta laughed. "Think so?"

"Where'd you learn?"

"Oh, here and there. Let's just say, I had a lot of practice."

There was a moment of silence then before he asked, "Having a good time?"

"I am. Thank you. It's just what I needed." She smiled gratefully. "Edna seems happy," Henrietta said, nodding toward the spot where she was now dancing with Clem. Virgil, she noticed, was back to sulking in the shadows.

"She's swell, isn't she?" Jack said, but it seemed to Henrietta that it lacked any real feeling.

"She's very pretty," Henrietta tried to encourage him.

"That she is! Sweet, too."

"Do you think she enjoys Virgil's attentions?" Henrietta asked coyly.

"I certainly hope not, but I mean to find out."

Henrietta didn't know what to make of his comments, so she remained silent until the dance ended. The polka had been very fast, and Jack had really spun her. He was flushed now, and as they stopped, his face was very close to hers and Henrietta thought she saw what she had seen so many times in men's eyes. His growing attraction was obvious to her, and she offered up a silent prayer of thanks that her own feelings did not match his. "Thank you, Mr. Fletcher," she said smiling falsely at him and feeling an actual ache in her stomach for Clive as she took a step back. She regretted coming now. It had been a mistake.

"Perhaps we should have presents now!" she said loudly in Edna's direction, who had meanwhile been standing off to the side, watching wide-eyed the exchange between her and Jack, as had several of the other servants. Henrietta was aware of many eyes on her and hated the fact that Mrs. Howard's words were ringing in her ear again about the dangers of familiarity.

"Yes!" said Jack, following suit, and a little crowd gathered around Edna as she shyly faced the little pile of gifts that had been placed randomly on one of the oil-stained workbenches. Bashfully, Edna reached for one and proceeded to open it and then the next one, everyone exclaiming over each one as she worked her way through them all. Kitty and Bridget had gone together and gotten her new handkerchiefs, and the scullery maids had gotten her a small box of chocolate. Clem and Bernie had brought some flowers from the garden, with Mr. McCreanney's permission, they assured her, and Jack had given her a new hair ribbon. Edna had been delighted with all of the gifts and had shyly thanked each person. Though Henrietta had been the one to divert attention to the gifts, she decided on the spur of the moment not to give her the pin in front of everyone, as it would make everyone else's seem mean in comparison. As she stood thinking of how she could give it to her without anyone else noticing, Virgil made his way forward and thrust a tiny box into Edna's hands.

"Here you are," he said sullenly.

Edna blushed and smiled. "Thank you, Virgil," she murmured. She fumbled a bit, nervous, before she finally got the tiny box opened. Carefully she peered inside and let out a gasp. "Oh, Virgil! It's beautiful! Oh, my! I'm sure this cost a fortune! You shouldn't have!"

Everyone was straining to see what the box contained, and when Henrietta finally got to look, she let out a gasp of horror. Inside the box lay what looked to be a very old ring with a large pearl surrounded by a spray of amethysts. It was Helen's ring! She was sure of it.

"What's this mean, ole Virg?" snickered Clem. "Weddin' bells, is it?" he said, poking Virgil with his elbow, but Virgil, irritated, gave him a little shove.

"Ooh!" giggled Bridget, standing near Edna, now. "Maybe it is!"

Edna ignored them and seemed only focused on Henrietta's strained features, as she, too, stared at the ring. "What is it, Miss?" Edna asked fearfully.

Henrietta did not answer at first and merely looked at Virgil, who was still looking at Edna, apparently unaware that anything was wrong. "Virgil, where . . . where did you get this?" Henrietta asked him.

"That's only for me to know," he said surlily. "Don't much matter where I got it from, just that I did, like."

"For shame, Virgil!" one of the scullery maids gasped. "Speaking to Miss that way!"

"What's wrong, Miss?" Edna asked again.

Henrietta looked from Edna to Jack and realized that everyone was waiting for her answer. She couldn't possibly explain it in front of them all. "I . . . it's nothing. I . . . it looked like something else, something someone had . . ." she was about to say "lost" but thought better of it. "I . . . I think I just need some air. I'll just slip out for a moment," she smiled, not wanting to ruin the party. "Put another song on!" she suggested, though her voice was strained. Thankfully the odd-jobs boy obliged, and after only a few moments of hesitation as he quickly looked through the stack, he put on Al Bowlly's "The Very Thought of You."

Gingerly Henrietta squeezed past the servants who were standing near Edna now, admiring her new things. She glared at Virgil as she passed him, but he seemed unaware of her scrutiny. She opened the door of the garage and was relieved that the air had cooled a bit, bringing some much-needed relief after the stuffy, smoky air in the garage. She leaned against the side of the Daimler, wondering what she should do. It couldn't be a coincidence, could it? So Helen had been right all along . . . Virgil *had* taken it, and now she had proof! But what should she do about it?

She felt vulnerable suddenly and wanted very much to return to the safety of the house. It must be well past eleven by now, and, looking up at the big house, she saw that it was mostly dark. She decided not to go back in to say goodbye as she felt it might be a signal to them to disperse, and she had no wish to interrupt their festivities.

"Are you all right?" said a voice nearby. She jumped and saw that Jack had magically appeared yet again. "Can I get you anything?"

"No, I think I'm going to go back up to the house." She tried to smile. "You know . . . before I'm found out," she said, smoothing down her skirt. As she did so, she felt her present for Edna in her pocket. She took it out and held it tightly in her hand.

"Are you sure? We have more to drink than the cherry wine, if that's the issue."

Henrietta smiled. "No. Thanks, though. I'm quite all right."

"Well, come say goodbye, then . . ." he said, gesturing back toward the door, seeming almost desperate to get her back in.

"No, honestly. I don't want them to think they have to leave, too. I really am just very tired. Would you see that Edna gets this?" she asked, placing the wrapped hairpin in his hand. As she did so, he held her hand for a few more moments than seemed to be necessary.

"Course I will," he said quietly.

Henrietta gently pulled her hand from his. "Good night, then." She smiled feebly.

"Let me . . . let me walk you back to the house. It's awfully dark," he urged.

Henrietta hated to admit it, but ever since her ordeal with Neptune and his thugs, she was actually still jumpy to be out alone after dark, the fact of which irritated her, as she had never been afraid before. It was something Neptune had taken from her, and she resented it. "Well, maybe part of the way," she said reluctantly. She was glad to have someone to walk with, but she wondered if it was wise to be alone with him after what she had recognized in his eyes as they danced. "Are you sure you want to leave the party? You might miss your chance with Edna, you know," she said and couldn't help a tiny smile from escaping.

"You mean because of Virgil?" he scoffed as he held out his arm to her, and she took it. They began walking up the drive. "Though I will say he's more serious than I imagined," Jack said after a thoughtful pause. "What do you make of that fancy piece he got her? You seemed upset . . . is it because you think it too much?"

"Well, no, not that exactly," Henrietta said, wondering if she should confide in him. He was so easy to talk to . . . "It's just that it looks very similar to a ring that Helen . . . do you know Helen? Helen Schuyler?" she asked, looking up at him questioningly. "She lives in that little cottage down along the beach path? She helps in the kitchens sometimes, I understand."

"Oh, yeah . . . her? I've heard of her. Never met her yet, though. They say she's crazy."

"Well, confused perhaps, but I don't think she's *crazy*. She lost a ring, and she's terribly upset about it. I was passing by the first day I arrived, and I helped her look for it."

"Maybe she lost it, and Virgil found it. That would explain how he could give her something so expensive on his pittance of a wage . . . no offense, like, Miss."

"Maybe," Henrietta mused, choosing to ignore his disgruntled comment. "But that's not the only thing," she said more eagerly now, glad to have someone to work her theory out with. "Helen swears that Virgil *stole* it!" she whispered.

"Stole it? How does she know?" He seemed intrigued.

"She says she's seen him lurking around her place and that she's heard him scratching at the walls of her cottage at night."

"Scratching? That's odd."

"That's what I thought." She shivered again. "It gives me the creeps!"

"Hmmm. Well, that's a strange tale. Think we should tell anyone?"

"I tried telling Billings, but he wouldn't listen."

"You told Billings?"

"Well, part of it, but he all but threw me out of his little pantry."

"You've got guts, I'll give you that!" he said, looking at her approvingly. "Even I'd be scared to tell Billings that!"

Henrietta laughed outright and was surprised by how good it felt. It seemed like she hadn't done so in a long, long time.

"You should have seen your face when she opened it!" Jack smiled, encouraged by her laugh. "I thought you were going to keel over right there in the garage!"

"Yes, I suppose I did look rather silly." She laughed again, partially embarrassed now by the evening's antics.

"What was silly?" asked a deep, resonant voice. Startled, Henrietta looked up and saw none other than Clive standing in the drive right in front of them! His eyes were trained on Jack, who quickly withdrew his arm from Henrietta's grasp.

"Clive!" Henrietta said, giving a squeal of delight and throwing her arms around him. "Why didn't you say you were coming after all? I would have waited up for you!" She was so thrilled to see him that tears formed in the corners of her eyes, and she couldn't stop smiling.

"But you *are* up, darling, aren't you?" he said pointedly, his voice oddly quiet.

Confused, Henrietta released him and took a step back.

"You have a previous engagement, it would seem," he said, his eyes traveling to the stables and quickly back to Jack. "And you are?"

"Fletcher, sir. Jack Fletcher. I'm the new chauffer."

His eyes lingered on Jack as if he were trying to place him. "Have I met you before?" he finally asked.

"No, sir. I don't think so, sir," he said, looking away.

"I'll take it from here, Fletcher," he said icily. "Thank you for seeing Miss Von Harmon safely home."

"Yes, sir. Good night, sir," Jack said and turned quickly back toward the stables.

"Thanks, Jack!" Henrietta called out as he hurried off. "Oh, Clive!" she said excitedly, turning toward him now, "I'm so happy you're here! I . . ." The stony look on his face, however, gave her pause.

"Jack, is it?" he said evenly.

"I mean Fletcher," she said gingerly, the thought dawning on her that perhaps he shared his mother's opinion regarding the servants. If that were the case, he would certainly not approve of the party she had just been to, she reasoned, though she had originally thought he would find it amusing to hear about. She saw by his face that she was probably mistaken.

"May I ask what you were doing in the stables?" he asked, his eyes searching hers.

"Well, I was . . . just that . . . I was at a birthday party, if you must know," she said with an air of defiance.

"A birthday party? Fletcher's?"

"No! It's Edna's birthday, one of the junior maids. Just a little gathering . . ." she said, looking back wistfully at the stables. "No harm done, really," she tried to say cheerfully, hoping this was true.

His eyes lingered on her. "What was it you were discussing

with Fletcher so animatedly as you came up the drive? Might I know?"

"Well, it was all about the stolen ring that Edna got," she said, confused by the point of his question.

"Stolen ring?" he asked, tipping his hat back, as if surprised by her answer.

"Yes, I've been wanting to tell you all about it!" she said eagerly. "I . . . I think I've stumbled onto something. A case, that is. It was Helen's ring, but now Virgil's gone and given it to Edna . . . just tonight . . ."

The words were tumbling out haphazardly, and Henrietta broke off abruptly now, feeling like it was coming out all wrong. This isn't how she had imagined telling Clive about the "strange case of the missing ring," as she had begun to call it in her mind. She had envisioned herself telling Clive about it while they sat side by side on a sofa with a cognac and a fire blazing in front of them as rain pelted the windows. She had likewise naively (she saw that now with a hot flush of realization) imagined his praise at her new-found sleuthing abilities as they tried to solve the case together and him saying that by all means she should join him in cracking some of the city's more interesting cases once they were married. No, telling Clive in this awkward way as they stood in the dark on the gravel drive, immediately after her humiliation at being caught with the servants, was not what she had in mind, and somehow it wasn't coming out as neat and logically as it had just minutes ago with Jack.

"Who's Helen? Not Helen Schuyler?" he asked, rubbing his brow, his other hand on his hip.

"Yes, her! She's lost a very valuable ring. Well, not lost. It's been stolen. But tonight it turned up with Virgil. I'm sure it's the same one!"

"Who's Virgil?"

"One of the gardeners! Tall? Blond hair? Scowl?"

Clive's face did not register any recognition.

"Really, Clive, don't you even know your own staff? Well, anyway . . .

he gave it to Edna tonight! The very same ring that Helen described to me as having lost!"

Clive looked doubtful.

"I asked him where he got it," she went on hurriedly, "and he rudely said it was his own business. There! That's suspicious, isn't it?"

Clive rubbed his hand through his hair. "Henrietta, theft is a very serious accusation, and Helen Schuyler is not a reliable person."

"Yes, so everyone says, but she seems all right enough to me. She really did lose the ring somehow. She showed me the empty box. And Clive . . . she said she's heard *scratching* noises at night, and she's seen Virgil with her own eyes sneaking around the cottage!" Henrietta hissed.

"Helen Schuyler is as blind as a bat," Clive sighed.

Henrietta paused for a moment to think. "Well, if Virgil did come by it legitimately, where did he get the money?" she asked triumphantly.

"Maybe he saved up; maybe he found it; maybe it's a cheap copy," Clive reeled off.

"You don't believe me, do you?" she asked quietly, searching his face for the truth.

Clive stared at her for what seemed an eternity before he unexpectedly reached out and stroked the side of her face. "Henrietta, this issue aside, do you really think it wise to spend your evenings with the servants?" he asked gently. "Especially the male servants?"

The touch of his hand was so very welcome, and yet his question cut her to the quick. Not only was he obviously of the same opinion as his mother, but, she slowly realized as she took a step back, there was a deeper accusation here, a more serious one.

"Don't you trust me?" she asked steadily.

Clive looked away, irritated, and then back at her. "Of course I trust you."

"Is this about cavorting with the servants or about Jack Fletcher?" she asked, the truth dawning on her.

"Henrietta, you're being ridiculous now."

"Am I? Well, what did you expect me to do, night after night here?" she asked, diverting the real issue. "Play bridge with your parents and go to bed at nine? Not one call from you. Not one note! I know I'm supposed to be planning an engagement party with your mother, which I don't even want, but I've done precious little of that, believe me! She doesn't really want or need my help." Her voice was elevated now, but she couldn't help it.

"What am I supposed to think when I return and find you outside in the dark, arm in arm with a young servant?"

Henrietta's indignation was on fire now. She knew she was guilty of fraternizing with the servants, but to be even mildly accused of giving her affections to Jack Fletcher incensed her, even though the memory of her dance with him and the look in his eyes distressfully nagged her now as she tried to defend herself. Deep down she knew she was not completely innocent.

"Forgive me," Clive said thinly. "I thought you might enjoy Highbury. I can see now that I was wrong."

"Oh, it's a beautiful place," Henrietta answered, her voice still elevated. "And yes, I'm grateful, if that's what you want me to say. I'm grateful your mother has taken me shopping and lavished me with new outfits and beautiful things," she said, gesturing at her skirt, "but was it really for me or was it so that I wouldn't be an embarrassment to her?"

"Henrietta . . ."

"When you asked me to marry you," she said, interrupting him, "I said yes to Inspector Clive Howard of the Chicago police, not Mr. Clive Howard, esquire, of the Highbury estate. And when you asked me to be your wife, I thought you asked Henrietta Von Harmon—26 girl, taxi dancer, usherette—not Miss Von Harmon of the society pages. This isn't who I am," she said, gesturing at the house, "and just asking me to marry you doesn't make me one of you, does it?" she whispered angrily. "I don't think I belong here, and I'm not sure you do either. You say that Highbury and this life doesn't matter to you, that you don't want a society woman, and yet you leave me here to become part of it while you run off to the city to be the inspector. If you despise Highbury so very much, why do you want me to be a part of it?"

"This is exactly why I didn't tell you who I really was," he said bitterly. "For the same reason you didn't want me to meet your family," he argued, thrusting his hands into his pockets.

"That's not true," she countered. "I didn't want you to meet them because of how rude Ma can be, that and I didn't want to have to explain to her what my job really was. You knew from the beginning that I was poor."

"And it obviously didn't matter to me in the slightest, did it? Not the way my situation seems to ruffle you."

"It doesn't 'ruffle' me! The difference is that I didn't hide anything from you."

He stared at her intensely as if he wanted to say more, but didn't. Finally he looked away from her. "Perhaps we should call it a night," he said grimly, gesturing toward the house.

"Yes, I rather think we should."

They walked in silence toward the house, Henrietta burning with indignation but sickened as well by how the evening had gone. When they finally reached the East Doors after what seemed an eternity, Henrietta paused before going in and turned to him. "What are you going to do about Helen's ring?" she asked, her lips pulled tight.

"I don't intend to do anything."

"I see," she said evenly.

Silently and perfectly erect, she climbed the main staircase, overcome by an awful ache in her throat as she forced her tears to remain inside of her. Not until she had shut the door of her room did they burst from her as she curled up on the bed, fearing as she sobbed that she had lost him after all.

Chapter 8

Clive sighed as he made his way into the billiard room and headed for the sideboard where the whiskey was kept. He poured himself a large tumbler full and took a deep drink, topping it up again immediately and rubbing his eyes with his free hand. What had he done?

"So you're back then, old boy?" came a voice in the direction of the fireplace. The coals were dying down, but Clive could discern his father's outline sitting in his worn leather chair and felt an unusual gladness at finding him still up.

Clive went over and slumped into the chair opposite. "Yes, I'm back, Father, for any good it's done." He took another large drink of whiskey.

"Oh?"

Clive rubbed his forehead. "I've just seen Henrietta, and I rather think I've made a mess of it."

"Found her down at the stables, eh?"

Clive looked up, his brow furrowed. "You knew?"

"Billings keeps me informed," he said with a wry smile. "Is it that bad?" he asked, taking a sip of his own cognac.

"I suppose not, but I stupidly overreacted and now I've bungled it." He was silent for a few moments before continuing. "Do you think I've made a mistake?" he asked quietly, still looking at the fire.

His father took his time in answering. "About overreacting or about asking Henrietta to be your wife?"

"About Henrietta," Clive replied noncommittally.

"Do you love her?"

"Very much," he said hoarsely.

"Then, no. You haven't made a mistake. For all the flibber-flabber your mother goes on about regarding society and who's who, I've learned one thing, my boy, and that is that it's only love that matters in the end. That might sound like the musings of an old man, but there it is. Time's damned short; no use wasting it on things that don't matter."

Clive groaned. "Oh, Father, I really have made a mess of it."

"No doubt, old boy, no doubt. But not so much that it can't be fixed, I suspect." He paused for a few moments, looking into the fire. "Give her time, Clive," he said gently. "She's not Catherine, and she can't just slip into this role on a sixpence. What's more, she's very young. You should take her in hand more and not leave her so much alone. It isn't good for her. Or for you."

There was a silence between them, then, as Clive mulled over his words, feeling that his father had the right of it. After a time, Alcott stood up and patted Clive on the shoulder as he passed him. "Good night, old boy," he said in a low tone. Clive, still staring into the fire, patted his father's hand in reciprocal fashion and nodded his thanks before his father pulled away and made his way slowly across the room.

"One more thing, Father," Clive asked without turning around. "Who hired Fletcher?"

"The chauffer? Why, Billings takes care of all that, my boy. Runs it by me, of course, but he dirties his hands with all that," he said as he continued on his way out. "Good night."

Clive sat gazing into the fire, wanting another drink but too tired to stand up and get one. He had been foolish, that he knew. He had let his emotions get the better of him. The problem was that he wasn't used to these types of feelings anymore, especially jealousy. It was new to him, and he wasn't sure what to do with it. He hadn't had enough time with Catherine to ever be jealous, really, and truth be told, hers was a more quiet demeanor that did not lend itself to attention, not the type of vivaciousness that Henrietta possessed. Henrietta's beauty was uncommon, perfect actually, though she seemed at times not to realize its full potential. She was always the object of men's eyes—he himself had witnessed it on several occasions—and she instantly lit up any room she entered without saying a word, even the smoky, dim interior of the Promenade where he had first set eyes on her. He realized with a sigh that he was going to have to come to terms with the fact that men would forever be ogling her, that there was an endless stream of Fletchers on the horizon for him to navigate. On Henrietta's part, he had seen her flirtations in the past as well. She knew at least partially how to use her charms—he himself had been the object of them—but she had retained an innocence of sorts even so. If he were honest, he believed entirely in her trustworthiness, her utter faithfulness to him, and he cringed with shame at how he had looked at her tonight. Though he believed he had accurately read the desire in Fletcher's eyes, he knew there had been only innocence in Henrietta's as she had walked up the drive with Fletcher, and it stung him now to remember the hurt in her face when he had all but accused her of unfaithfulness. Damn it! Why had he been so stupid?

He stood up restlessly now and walked to the sideboard to pour himself another whiskey. He picked up the heavy crystal decanter, gazing at it absently as he poured. He set it down carelessly and forced himself to think about Henrietta's parting words. That she didn't belong here. Was it true? The better question, as Henrietta had so astutely asked, was, *did he*? He walked back to the fireplace and stoked it, causing the flames to rise up, a fleeting brightness momentarily filling the dark space around him.

He had grown up in luxury, educated at Cambridge, taught to sail and to ride, and had indeed been groomed in every way to take over his father's dynasty when he came of age. His summers had been divided between time at his father's family estate in England and his mother's relatives on Long Island and in Newport, his father having thus provided a whisper of aristocracy, his mother the dripping wealth. The war had blasted that world for him, however, and though he had risen to the rank of captain in the army, he had had a difficult time embracing the old order of things once he had returned, wounded and crippled with grief over the death of Catherine and the baby he had never seen, not to mention the atrocities of the war. He had accordingly taken up a life in the refuse of the city, solving crimes—often brutal ones—which he had claimed, at least initially, was his way of making the world a better place. But now, as he stared at the fire, he asked himself if that had been entirely true. Had he just been running from the shards of his former life? His parents had gone on bravely with the facade, but he (he had prided himself often enough) had chosen a more truthful life. Or was it really a more cowardly way? he now mused. When he had come back from the war he had found it impossible to go on where he had left off as if nothing had happened, and, yet, now . . . now that he had met Henrietta, he wasn't sure how he felt anymore. Could he really just abandon Highbury and the work of generations of his family before him, simply because he felt it to be wrong somehow? He wasn't sure he had the courage for it, for whichever path he might choose, actually, though Henrietta's presence in his life did fill him with renewed vigor and, more importantly, hope.

One thing was for sure: he had been stunned by Henrietta's insight earlier this evening. She was right. How could he expect her to accept and adapt to this world when he had himself so deliberately fled from it and even at times ridiculed it? This, he realized, turning it over and over in his mind, was the crux of the problem. If he were really planning to reject Highbury and everything it stood for, why abandon Henrietta here with his parents for his mother to mold into an acceptable socialite? Why even have a wedding; why not just elope? Did Highbury mean more to him than he was willing to admit? Clearly he was going to have to figure it out. When he had asked Henrietta to marry him, he had been sincere, and he still was, but he hadn't wanted to think of the practicalities at that moment, nor did he now, really, but he saw, with a deep sigh, that he must. Where did he intend to bring his new bride to live? His small apartment in the city near the police station, No. 124? If there had ever been a vision of this in his mind, it had been fleeting and romantic but not very realistic, he saw that now. Would he feel safe having Henrietta and, hopefully, his children alone there at all hours of the night and day while he was out tracking criminals? And yet, neither could he quite see them taking the helm at Highbury once his parents passed away, or sooner, if they no doubt had their way. His father had mentioned more than once his desire to return to England for a protracted stay. Clive was loath to sit in an office all day listening to stock reports and accounts payable, and yet he wasn't sure how he was going to escape it, for wasn't one linked to the other? Even if he wanted to be master of Highbury, he knew it was impossible without taking the reins of the firm as well.

He flopped back into the leather armchair, sighing deeply. Unfortunately, he was running out of time. He would have to make a decision by tomorrow. That was the real reason he had come back this weekend, though he could barely afford the time. Seeing Henrietta had been an added bonus to the plan. The board of Linley Standard had called a special session for tomorrow afternoon. His father was apparently thinking of stepping down as chairman sometime in the near future. "Not to worry about a date, old boy," he had told Clive. "Just an idea." The board was eager to name a successor for when that time came, though, hopefully, they had all uttered respectfully, that would not be for quite some time. Naturally, Clive was the forerunner for the position, and they wanted him there for the vote, as a surety of his commitment, or something like that, they had said. He had not told Henrietta yet; he had been hoping to discuss it with her before he made a decision, but the evening had instead taken a very different turn.

He had been hoping to ask her about their future life together, how she liked Highbury, if she could see herself as its mistress someday. Instead he had stupidly quarreled with her over a servant and a missing ring! Idiot! She had said she didn't feel she belonged here, so wasn't that his answer? But had she really had enough time to know for sure? His father was right; it had been unwise to leave her here alone with just the two of them as company, especially his mother. Clive knew how she could be, and yet he had left Henrietta anyway. But what choice had he had? The chief had been insistent, and so had his mother. It had seemed like a good idea at the time, and, perhaps if only sub-consciously, he had wanted to keep her safe here from Neptune's clutches. He was bothered that while Neptune was in jail, his lieutenants were still at large, and who knew what their instructions were? Clive rubbed his brow at the thought of Neptune's insane obsession with Henrietta and took another drink of whiskey. He supposed he had been hoping that his parents would fall in love with Henrietta just as he had, but he saw now that it would take more time.

He had laughed when his mother had telephoned him at his apartment early on during the first week of Henrietta's stay, furiously whispering how she was quite at her wit's end with Henrietta in her insistence on helping the maids make the beds, trading recipes regularly with the cook (and writing them down to send to her sister!), and staying up to all hours playing rummy and drinking cocoa in the kitchen with the junior staff, causing them to be found constantly yawning the next day and in need of reprimanding! Clive had bit back a smile as she continued her whispered report, no doubt locked in the study away from Father's and Billings's ears. "She has a defiant streak to her, Clive," Mrs. Howard had warned with exasperation, "which will need some handling, and she has no idea how to dress for dinner!" Ah, yes, thought Clive, the ultimate sin.

"Well, happily that won't be a problem here, as she'll have no use for gowns and such, seeing as there's only the policeman's ball, and that's just once a year," he had answered flippantly.

"Stop being ridiculous, Clive! You can't seriously be considering living in that hovel with her! We've indulged your whims long enough, but sooner or later you're going to have to face your responsibilities," she had hissed. "It's your duty to take over Highbury, and, as much as I do not wish to cause you pain, darling, you're going to have to do it and you just might regret having Henrietta as its mistress!"

"You surprise me, mother," he said with affected disinterest. "And all along I thought you merely wanted a grandchild. You're becoming an awful snob in your later years."

"Don't be glib, Clive; it doesn't become you."

"Just be patient, Mother," he had said wearily. "She'll learn; I'm sure of it. I have every faith in you. And in her."

Despite his mother's (and Henrietta's, for that matter) reservations as to her suitability, Clive, on his part, had none. In fact, he loved her because she was so . . . on the surface, anyway . . . so *utterly* unsuitable. He loved the fact that she had been willing to sacrifice her whole life to support all of those brothers and sisters of hers, how she stood in line for government-issued food, how she had not been too proud to scrub toilets at the corner tavern at thirteen. And, yes, he loved the image of her helping Edna with the bedding as they perhaps laughed and shared secrets, completely inappropriate as it was, something he could never imagine his mother doing in a hundred years. Yes, there was a defiance of sorts to Henrietta, a fiery pluck, but there was a sweet willingness to please as well, a combination he found irresistible. And though he was embarrassed to admit it, he loved that she made him feel desperately young again. She brought out a part of him that had existed long before the war, a part of himself that he had assumed had died. She had chosen *him* to bestow her love upon out of all the men he knew she could have easily had. She had helped him in countless ways, and she trusted and felt safe with him, the thought of which caused a nagging guilt to well up, though he tried valiantly to repress it. No, she was more than suitable—she was perfect. He longed to rescue her from her miserable poverty, to share all that he had of himself, whatever that might be, if she would only let him. He had found his Cinderella and had the ability to give her anything she desired—a beautiful wedding, beautiful clothes, money for her family, a place in society—but to his surprise, she appeared to be uninterested in all that, if tonight's quarrel was any indication. She merely wanted her prince; she wanted *him*. And while his heart swelled at the thought, he wretchedly recalled that it was the inspector she wanted, not the esquire, and wondered grimly which one he really was.

If only she knew, he thought, his mind wandering back over the cases of the past year, many of them vicious and terrible, what his life as an inspector was really like. Though they had been through a horrible ordeal together with Neptune, no harm had miraculously come to them in the end, and he could see by the way she talked about old Helen Schuyler and her silly missing ring that she saw detective work merely as exciting, jolly good fun. He admitted that her young eyes had seen a lot of this world already, but nothing compared to the evils he had witnessed in the city's darkened streets.

The case he was on at the moment, for example, was particularly grisly, and some part of it haunted him even now as he tried endlessly to work it out. A young girl, just seventeen, savagely assaulted by what appeared to be more than one man. At first it had looked like a random crime, but there were things about this case that made Clive wonder if it was somehow linked to a bigger conspiracy. He had a strange feeling about this one; something wasn't adding up. He was missing something. He and Charlie and Kelly, recovered now from the last case and out of the hospital, had planned a stakeout for tonight at an abandoned warehouse on Goose Island, which is why he had telephoned Highbury to say he wouldn't be coming until tomorrow morning. At the last minute, though, the gang was tipped off and fled before Clive and his men could get there.

The case was weighing heavily on his mind as it had all the markings of being a repeat crime, a string of murdered women having been found recently in the city's alleyways. Worse yet, he was realizing slowly, he was having a hard time maintaining an emotional distance.

His feelings for Henrietta were interfering with his perception of the case, he could tell. It had happened last time with Neptune. He had missed certain clues, and Henrietta had almost been killed as a result. This time, she wasn't anywhere near the case, he had made sure of that, but he still wondered if his judgment was off. Was he losing his touch? One thing was for sure: he was becoming too vulnerable, and he couldn't seem to stop it.

He held up his glass to the fire and peered through it, watching the soft glow of the embers illuminate the caramel-colored whiskey. Was escape to Highbury the answer? If they took up a life here, Henrietta would be shielded and protected from the brutality and grime of the city, but would she love the esquire as much as the inspector? Would it make him less of a man, not only in her eyes but in his own?

The old grandfather clock in the corner dully chimed out the hour of two, and Clive, tired of being alone with his swirling thoughts, achingly stood up, finally, and went to bed, having come to no particular conclusion of note, except perhaps the certainty of his own foolishness.

Chapter 9

When Henrietta awoke it was later than usual. She had been awake most of the night and had only fallen into an irregular sort of sleep in the last few hours. The intruding sun, shimmering hopefully through the lace curtains at her windows, unfortunately did not have the power to dispel her dark mood. Last night had been all her fault, she decided, as she pushed aside the heavy coverlet and pulled herself out of bed. Clive had every right to be upset. She was always too flirtatious; hadn't Ma been telling her that forever? And why hadn't she listened to Mrs. Howard? She should never have danced with Jack, she fumed, and worse, all the servants had seen! What if it got back to Clive? she worried. She hadn't meant anything by it; she had only done it to blend in, to not spoil the party, but a nagging voice kept reminding her that she had rather liked it. Not Jack necessarily, but the music and the dancing, the drinking of cheap cherry wine rather than fine cognac or brandy. There were aspects of her old life, she confessed, that she missed, and the party had shown her that.

And yet, if she were honest, she conceded, staring at herself in the mirror of her dressing table as she brushed her long auburn hair, being in a place as beautiful as Highbury had astonished her. She had not known that places like this even existed. She felt it was unreal, somehow, as if she would wake up soon from this dream to find herself back in the dingy apartment, the charge bill at Schneider's staring her in the face.

But why hadn't Clive told her about his life? She could not help continually circling back to this. She supposed he hadn't had a chance, not really, but, still, she felt more than a little bit—if not betrayed, exactly—then certainly misled. He had said that night on the terrace after the Italian restaurant that none of this mattered to him and that he didn't want a "society" woman, but she wasn't so sure that that was true. His mother was clearly of the opinion that they were to someday take over Highbury (however laughable that seemed to Henrietta) and was constantly instructing her regarding what would be required of her when she was head of the house here. Surely Clive must have an inkling of his mother's expectations; did he share them? She couldn't tell exactly; he seemed full of contradiction. And what if he did? Is this what *she* wanted?

Part of her imagined how heavenly it would be to live at a place like Highbury, but at the same time she saw how impossible it would be for any number of reasons. For one thing, what would she do about her family? She couldn't see abandoning them to make their own way in the city, but neither could she see bringing them here. She cringed when she fleetingly imagined Ma and her dirty apron shuffling bitterly through the halls of Highbury, making disparaging comments whenever one happened to occur to her, which undoubtedly would be every few minutes or so. On the other hand, was Clive just going to send them money every month to make up for her lost wages? Given Ma's less-than-grateful reaction already, Henrietta was pretty sure that that arrangement wouldn't work, either.

The problem of what to do with her family aside, the more important issue, it seemed to Henrietta, was whether she was actually worthy of this role, whether she was even up to the task. Originally, whenever she had thought about being with Clive, being married to him, her mind always drifted back to the short evening they had spent at Polly's apartment when she had sat mending the usherette costume while he had contentedly looked on, smoking his pipe, presumably musing about his cases. That had been her quaint idea of marital bliss, not hosting dinner parties with the Howard "set"—whatever that meant—or playing rounds of golf or attending gala balls, however momentarily exciting that might sound. She had told him once that she didn't want to be a disappointment to him, and she couldn't see how, especially after last night, that she wasn't. He deserved someone equal to . . . well, to him, someone better than her.

The inescapable truth, however, was that she loved Clive, more than she thought possible. She ached to be held by him, loved by him. He possessed the ability to make her feel safe and protected, all the while causing her pulse to quicken whenever he was near. There had been an emptiness in her, one that she was barely even aware of, since her father died, and there existed from that point onward a low, persistent urgency to fill it. Flirting, she had found, sometimes made it disappear for a little while, but it always came back, restless and painful. Clive was the only man, the only person, really, who abated and calmed it. She wanted, no *needed*, desperately to be with him, to make him happy . . . to give him a child, she blushed to herself. She thought she might know how to do that, how to be all those things for him in the city, with its straight, gridded streets, but here, in this strange dream landscape with its multitude of undulating, unwritten rules hidden just beneath the glittering surface, she doubted her ability. Though she had been making obvious progress in the short time Clive had been away and was even gaining confidence under Mrs. Howard's tutelage, albeit begrudgingly at times, this morning it seemed as if it had all been undone by one evening's antics, leaving her doubtful as to her capacity to ever successfully navigate this labyrinth.

But she wanted to be with Clive, she groaned, to please him . . . make him happy, and if this was what he wanted, she would have to try. She saw no choice, as she sat staring at the mirror in front of her, but to have to sacrifice her family, her life in the city. She would endeavor to play the hand she had been dealt and only prayed she wouldn't shame him in the process. She would try to fill the role he obviously wanted her to fill, and she would have to figure out what to do about her family later.

But perhaps it was already too late, she worried. She had made a bad start of it, hadn't she? Angrily she put down her brush and rested her forehead against one hand. Going to a servant's birthday party and dancing with the chauffer—what had she been thinking? Maybe Clive would never find out, she grasped. But did she really want to keep a secret from him? Already he didn't trust her, and she could see why. Perhaps it was time to go home. Helping Mrs. Howard with the engagement party plans had obviously been a sham; she wasn't really needed here at all. Maybe it really had been a test all along, and she had clearly failed. Yes, she would go home, she decided, convinced suddenly of the wisdom of this new idea. But what about Helen? she remembered abruptly. She couldn't just abandon her, especially now that the ring had surfaced. But what could she do, really? No one seemed to take her seriously, except Jack, of course. Maybe she could see Helen before she left?

Henrietta shook herself. There was nothing for it now but to go downstairs and face them all. Steeling herself, she took a deep breath and a last look in the mirror before slipping out of her room and descending the grand staircase.

She was surprised, then, when she found the breakfast room deserted, except for Clive, who sat languidly at the table. He of course rose when she entered, and their eyes met, Henrietta searching his for any indication of his mood. His face broke into a wary smile, then, and he strode across the room to her. He did not embrace her, but merely took one of her hands and held it for a moment before speaking.

"Henrietta, can you forgive me?" he asked earnestly.

This was hardly the greeting she had expected, and an embarrassing little gasp escaped her lips as a rush of feeling came over her. Two hot tears formed in the corners of her eyes, blurring her vision a little as she looked up eagerly now at him.

"Oh, Clive, there's nothing to forgive," she said in a low tone and was about to launch into her own apology when he went on speaking.

"I've been a fool," he went on hurriedly. "I know you've been faithful to me, and I had no right to call your virtue into question."

She looked down at the floor in shame at the memory of her dance with Jack, but he mistook it for sadness. With just one finger, he lifted her chin and kissed her softly, tenderly, sending shivers rippling through her, but she made herself pull away.

"No, Clive. It's me. I . . . it was my fault. I'm the fool. I knew it was wrong to go and spend time . . . fraternize, as your mother calls it . . . with the servants, but I went anyway. She has warned me repeatedly that it might cause complications later, when . . . *if* . . . ," she added hastily, "we live here, but I didn't want to listen." She let go of his hand and walked over to the windows. She knew she should tell him now about the dance, but she couldn't muster up the courage. "I know it's no excuse," she said instead, "but I suppose I thought it would be a bit of fun. Nothing else."

Clive followed her and gently turned her to him again. "Henrietta, listen. I've been remiss; I see that now. I didn't mean for your stay here to be so long; it's just that the case is getting more complicated now, and we are so close. But I was wrong. You're absolutely right; I should have telephoned or written. I guess I'm not used to having someone wait for me."

A small, tingling sliver of hope began traveling through her at the prospect of their rather serious quarrel being smoothed over so easily. "I forgive you," she said quietly. "And I'm sorry, too," she added, then, hoping that this would be enough to alleviate the strand of guilt that still nagged.

"Don't be," he said, smiling at her so benevolently she thought her heart would break.

"But why *did* you come back last night?" she asked distractedly. "I thought you were tied up with the case."

"We were planning a stakeout," Clive sighed, "but the guy we are tracking was tipped off somehow. The chief told me to go home for a while. At least for a night, anyway. Turns out he has a heart after all," he grinned. "That, and I have some business with Father . . ."

"I wish you'd let me help you!" she interrupted. "Like I did with Neptune," she said brightly, laying a hand on his arm.

A shadow passed across Clive's face. "It's not a nice one, Henrietta. Very dark."

"And the last one wasn't?" she murmured, removing her hand. She turned back toward the windows and gazed out at the lake. In the distance she could see the smoke rising from what must be Helen's chimney. An idea occurred to her, then, and she slowly turned back around. "Then help me with mine, Clive," she suggested tentatively.

"Yours?"

"My case," she smiled. "'The case of the missing ring.'"

"Oh, Henrietta, I'm sure that's just a simple misunderstanding," he moaned.

"You don't believe me, do you?"

"Of course I believe *you*, darling, it's just that Helen . . . Oh, all right," he agreed, remembering his father's words of advice to him. He was eager to erase the events of last evening and to make up for his absence these past two weeks. Actually, he found her fascination with Helen a bit amusing. "Come on, let's have breakfast, and then we'll go investigate."

"Do you mean it?" she said, her face lighting up in delight. "Oh, Clive, Helen will be so grateful. You've no idea how troubled she is."

"Oh, I think I do. You do realize she's a bit touched in the head, don't you? That's why Father allows her live out the rest of her days in the cottage."

"Isn't that all the more reason to check on her? Don't we owe it to her to put her fears at ease?" Henrietta reasoned.

Clive sighed. "You're right, of course," he said, smiling patiently, the thought inconveniently dawning on him that she sounded very much like what the mistress of Highbury should sound like. "We'll go directly, but then we need to talk."

"That sounds awfully serious."

"It is, Henrietta. You said some strong things last night."

"Yes, I did, rather. But . . ."

"Well, I'd like to talk about them, about Highbury, about us. Agreed?"

"Yes," she sighed, "agreed." Though Clive's manner was congenial now and accommodating, Henrietta couldn't shake the feeling that he was still tense and preoccupied, and a part of her worried what he might yet have to say.

Henrietta hurriedly drank some coffee and ate a piece of cold toast before they began their walk to the cottage, which was surprisingly pleasant despite the somewhat-serious undertone that still existed between them. Alone, now, in the crisp air away from the confines of the house, they became almost giddy and walked hand-in-hand along the path by the beach, Clive leading, with his arm stretched behind him, pulling a laughing Henrietta along, as the path was too arrow to allow them to walk side by side. Before long, the cottage came into view.

When they finally reached it, Clive paused outside the little front door to pull his jacket down into place and straighten his tie. He gave Henrietta a quick wink, thrilling her, as he knocked loudly. When no one came, Clive knocked again, louder this time, and called out, "Mrs. Schuyler?"

Clive waited a few moments, poised, but then relaxed his stance when still no one came. Again he knocked.

"She must be in there!" Henrietta said under her breath. "Where else could she be?"

Just then a face appeared from behind the gingham curtains at the window, and a moment later the door opened and a frightened-looking Helen stood before them.

"Oo, Mister Clive!" she said enthusiastically after she took a moment to deduce who it was. "Wha' are ya doin' 'ere an all?!" She glanced back at the interior of the cottage. "I'm in a bit of a state. I'm jis' doin' the ironin', like. Kin I 'elp ya wit somethin'?" she asked, peering up at him.

"Hello, Mrs. Schuyler," Clive said, removing his hat. "I'm sorry to intrude, but Miss Von Harmon tells me you've lost a rather precious ring," he said inclining his head slightly toward Henrietta. "I thought I might look in and inquire about it."

"Oo, aye! Course ya kin!"

Helen looked over Henrietta now as if seeing her for the first time. Yer 'ere as well, are ya?" she said, a partially toothless grin appearing on her face. "Come in, come in!" she muttered, hobbling out of the way for them to get past.

Clive and Henrietta stooped to get through the tiny front door and stepped inside.

"'Tis true enough wha' she tells ya," Helen said, wringing her hands. "But I didn' mean to bother ya wit me troubles, tha' I didn', sir," she said meekly.

"Nonsense, Helen! Mr. Clive wants to help, don't you?" Henrietta said, nudging him.

"Yes, of course I do," Clive smiled politely. "Now then. Mind if I ask you a few questions?"

"Na a tall, Mister Clive. Na a tall!"

Clive opened his mouth to speak, then, but before he could utter any words, Helen interrupted him, "Would ya like a spot a tea, mebbe?"

"No, thank you, I've just had my breakfast."

"Jis' 'ad breakfas'! Lord, Mister Clive! But then, again, all ya up at the big hoose always did rise late, like."

"It *is* rather shameful, isn't it?" Clive smiled patiently.

"Ach, noo, me lord, 'tisn't. I didn' mean anythin' by it," Helen said, her nerves getting the better of her now. Henrietta tried valiantly not to smile.

"I'm not a lord, Mrs. Schuyler. Remember? Just 'Mister Clive' is fine."

"Tha's right. Sorry, sir," she mumbled, her face flushed with embarrassment.

"Perhaps you could tell me about the ring. Can you describe it?" Clive asked.

"Describe it?"

"What did it look like?" Clive asked, biting his lip.

"Oo, aye! Well," Helen said, shuffling over to the table so she could lean against it. "It's aboot sa big," she said, gesturing with her thumb and forefinger. "Dare's a big pearl in the center wit purple stones all around it, ya see."

"And it's very old, right, Helen?" put in Henrietta.

"Oo, aye! 'Tis old. It belong ta me grandmother, ya see. An who knows afore tha'?"

"When did you last see it?" Clive asked.

"Well, 'spose it were a couple a weeks ago. I don' rightly remember," Helen said, wringing her hands.

"And you searched the house with her?" Clive asked Henrietta, who nodded eagerly. She was pleased that he was at least pretending to play the part of the detective.

"Ach, Mister Clive, I've searched nigh' an day, I 'ave. I jis' knows 'e took it!"

"Tell him about the scratching, Helen."

"Oo, aye, Mister Clive," Helen agreed, her voice suddenly dropping to just above a whisper. She glanced fearfully toward her bedroom window. "Terrible scratchin' noises I 'ear, Mister Clive. They frighten the life out a me, they do! Like some kin' a beast, 'tis."

Henrietta felt a chill just listening to her.

"Scratching?" Clive asked. "What sort of scratching?"

"Almos' ever nigh' I 'ear the scratchin' ooutside the cottage, all differen' places, but usually jis' by me window. Like an animal in soome ways, but na wild, na frantic, jis' slow an steady, like. Na animal would scratch tha' way, Mister Clive!" she said, and to their surprise, she burst into tears. "'Tis somethin' evil!"

Henrietta hurried over and put her arm around Helen. "It's all right, Helen. Mr. Clive will figure it out; I'm sure of it. He's very clever, you know."

Helen eventually wiped her eyes with the corner of her apron. "Well, I'll give ya tha', Miss Sophia. Or are ya Daphne?" she said, peering at her. "Noo, yer na Daphne," she said after a moment. "Yer na

Sophia, though, are ya?" Not waiting for an answer, as if it no longer mattered who Henrietta was exactly, she went on, "Aye, Mister Clive's always been a clever one an all."

"Want to tell me about Sophia?" Henrietta asked, her eyebrow arched as she looked pointedly at Clive.

Clive gave an uneasy, halfhearted shrug. "She's just someone that I used to know. It doesn't matter now." He turned his attention back to Helen. "I'll just have a look outside, shall I?" he asked with what might be construed as excessive eagerness.

As Clive ducked through the little door, Henrietta followed close behind, trying to decide if she should pursue the Sophia conversation. Her attention was diverted, however, when Clive stopped just outside of Helen's bedroom window. Henrietta watched him as he stood a few paces back, looking at the woods and then back at the window.

"There's an awful lot of footprints," Henrietta said, pointing toward the ground just below the window and moved toward them. Clive gently grasped her arm to hold her back.

"Not just yet," he said, still observing. He made a complete circle around the cottage and then came back to the bedroom window.

"There's a lot of footprints everywhere," he said, putting his own shoe next to one of them to gauge their length. "About my size," he said, almost to himself. He walked closer to the window ledge now and observed what indeed looked like deep gouges just under the sill. After looking closely at them for a few moments, he ran his finger along one of them as if to feel their depth. "Strange," he said. He pulled back some tall grass growing along the base of the house and revealed what looked like a burrow just under the house, with crumbled bits of earth near it. "Looks like an animal's been digging," he mused. "That would explain the scratching and the marks."

"But they wouldn't be up by the sill," countered Henrietta. "And what about the footprints?"

"Well, that *is* strange, I'll give you that. But there has to be some explanation." He turned to Helen, who had been standing off at a distance as if she didn't want to get too close. "Mrs. Schuyler, you say you think someone took the ring. Why do you say that?"

"Ach! 'Cause I sees 'im all the time, creepin' roun'. An it were jis' after tha' tha' me ring went missin', like."

"Who's *he*?"

"Why, tha' lad from the gardens. Tall, 'e is. Thin. Blond hair. I sees 'im all a time when I goes up ta the big hoose ta 'elp. Always in the garden, 'e is."

"She's talking about Virgil," Henrietta explained.

"And Virgil's the one who gave Edna the ring, correct?" he asked Henrietta.

"Yes, exactly."

"Wha's this?" Helen asked. "'E's gone an given it away? Ta young Edna, ya say?"

"We think he may have done," Henrietta answered tentatively.

"Ach, tha' swine!" Helen despaired.

Clive rubbed his brow. "It's quite easy to clear this up. Mrs. Schuyler, do you feel up to a walk to the house?"

"Wha'? Now?" she asked fretfully. "Wha' about me ironing?"

"You'll have to come back to that later," Clive said, a shade of impatience registering in his voice.

"Well, I suppose I could. Why? Wha' are we doin' up dare? I'm not in trouble, am I, Mister Clive?" she said, wringing her hands.

"No, Mrs. Schuyler," Clive said in a softer tone. "Of course you're not in any trouble. I'd just like you to take a look at Edna's new ring and see if it's yours."

"Oo, aye! I see. Well, if ya think it best, Mister Clive," she said hesitantly. "Let me jis' get this pinny off," she said, reaching behind her to undo her apron strings as she walked back toward the cottage.

"Do you lock the cottage, Mrs. Schuyler?" Clive called after her, almost as an afterthought.

"Lord, noo, Mister Clive! The cottage don' lock. Never 'ad a need of it afore," she said, coming back out now and giving the door a good tug.

"I see," Clive mused and led the two women back to the house.

As fate would have it, Edna was seated in the kitchen helping Mary to shell peas when the three of them arrived back at the house, having gone straight to the kitchen's back door. Both Edna and Mary stood up when Clive entered.

"Mister Clive, sir!" Mary exclaimed. "Is there something wrong? We didn't hear the bell."

"I didn't ring, Mary. I'm sorry to interrupt you. It's Edna I'd like to talk to."

"Me, Mister Clive?" Edna said nervously and glanced at Henrietta in despair.

"What's she done?" Mary asked, exasperated.

"No, no," Clive smiled. "It's nothing like that. Miss Von Harmon, here," he said, gesturing with his hat, "has told me what a lovely ring Edna received for her birthday." Edna turned a deep shade of red and looked at the ground. "And it just so happens that this ring seems extraordinarily similar to the one Mrs. Schuyler misplaced not some two weeks ago."

"Oh, Helen! It's yours?" Edna asked, confused.

"Don' rightly know," Helen said, the hurt in her voice clear. "Tha's wha these two lords and ladies is sayin'."

"I'm not a lord, Mrs. Schuyler," Clive reminded her, giving Henrietta an exasperated look.

"Ach! Sa yer na, Mister Clive. I firgit sometimes, like. Don' pay me na mind."

"Perhaps you would show us the ring, Edna?" Clive asked her kindly.

"Certainly, Mister Clive," Edna said, putting down the bowl of peas she was still holding with an unusually tight grip. "I keep it in my pocket, if you must know," she said, blushing again. She slipped her small hand into the front pocket of her uniform and pulled out a small object wrapped in a handkerchief. Silently she walked over and handed it shyly to Clive. "Here you are, sir," she said, curtseying slightly.

Clive carefully unwrapped the bundle in his hand, Henrietta and Helen looking on anxiously beside him. Helen gasped when she saw the ring. "Tha's it! 'Tis mine, it is!" she nearly shouted.

"Here," Clive said, placing it in her hand. "Look closely. Make sure it really is yours."

Helen eagerly grabbed it and held it up before her dim eyes, feeling it carefully with her fingers as she did so. "Oo, aye! 'Tis it! Yuv found it, Mister Clive! God bless ya!"

"Wait a moment, Mrs. Schuyler," Clive said, laying a hand gently on her arm. "I need to hold on to that for a bit." When Mrs. Schuyler seemed to hesitate, Clive added, "No need to worry. But we haven't quite gotten to the bottom of this. For example, how exactly did this Virgil come to be in the possession of such a piece?"

Edna blushed a deep red. "I'm sure he didn't mean any harm, Mister Clive," she said pleadingly.

"No doubt there's a simple explanation," Clive said, though his face, Henrietta noticed, was drawn tight. "Mary, perhaps you'd give Mrs. Schuyler a cup of tea while I look for Virgil."

"Yes, Mister Clive!" Mary said, bustling over to the stove where the kettle stood, and Edna pulled out a chair, helping Helen into it. "He'll be out in the gardens this time of day," Mary offered.

"Thanks, Mary," Clive said and looked at Henrietta, inclining his head toward the door.

"Won't be a moment," Clive said to the little group at the table and strode out the door, Henrietta following him.

"See what I mean?" Henrietta said breathlessly, trying to keep up with Clive's determined strides across the grounds. Clive didn't speak, however, until they came around the side of the house to where the kitchen gardens lay, various workers bent over the crops.

"Which one is he?" Clive asked impatiently.

Henrietta furtively looked out over the gardens. "I don't see him," she said, finally. "He must be here somewhere, though," she put in eagerly, not wanting to give up the chase now. "He always is."

Together they walked closer to the gardens until they spotted Mr. McCreanney attending a small fire, burning twigs and garden refuse. He was leaning on a rake, smoking a cigarette, but he stood up straight when he spotted Clive striding toward him. He quickly took off his cap.

"Mister Clive, sir! I didna know ya were home, sir. Wery good ta see ya, it is, sir."

"Thanks, Edward."

"How kin I 'elp, sir?"

"I'm looking for one of your men, actually. Virgil is his name. I'm not sure what his surname is."

"Aye, Virgil, sir. Virgil Higgins. 'E's feelin' poorly t'day, sir. Toll 'im ta 'ave a lie down fer the morn. 'E's not in any trouble is 'e, sir? Can't imagine it of that lad, though. Good as gold, 'e is. 'Ard worker; never a moment's trouble, 'e is."

Clive studied Mr. McCreanney's face. "No, he's not in any trouble necessarily. I just need to ask him a few questions. I daresay your word goes a long way toward my opinion of his character, though, Mr. McCreanney."

"Thank ya, sir," Mr. McCreanney answered, genuinely pleased. He slipped his cap back on. "I best be gettin' back ta work, then, sir. You'll find Virgil in 'is room above the garage," he said, crushing his cigarette underfoot now as he picked up the rake he had set aside.

Clive nodded his thanks and turned back toward the stables, shoving his hands in his pockets.

"I don't like this one bit, Henrietta," he said, irritated, looking at the ground as they hurried toward the stables. The wind had picked up now, and Henrietta strained to hear his words as they walked. "McCreanney's a good man. He's probably the most honest man on the estate, and his word means a lot."

"Well, there has to be some explanation, Clive," Henrietta said, frustrated herself. "How did Virgil come by the ring, then?"

"I don't know. I just hope this isn't a waste of time. Well, it *is* a waste of time, actually. We have some rather important things to discuss, but instead I'm chasing after a two-bit piece of jewelry."

"So . . . so you don't think it has any value? The ring, that is," she asked, choosing to ignore his reference to what was surely to be the uncomfortable conversation he alluded to.

"Well, of course it doesn't have any value!"

"Clive! I'm surprised at you," Henrietta said sternly, but deep down she felt guilty that she had ruined his plans. But if Clive were going back to the city soon, as well as herself . . . perhaps . . . she didn't see any other option but to get to the bottom of Helen's anxiety right now. They might not have another chance.

"Well I'm no expert, but I don't see how it can," he added grimly.

They had reached the stables, and Clive looked up at the dark windows above the garage.

"Perhaps I should let you lead the way, since you apparently know your way around," he said, gesturing with his hand.

"That was uncalled for, Clive," Henrietta said hotly, surprisingly stung by his words.

Clive rubbed his eyes. "Forgive me. You're right, of course. I didn't mean that. It's just that I am not really up to a confrontation just now, with Virgil or with Fletcher, actually," he said, his eyes roaming the garage and beyond. "Fletcher doesn't seem to be here, though, so let's just find Virgil and get this over with."

Henrietta decided to let his comment go as they climbed the outside stairs leading to a small balcony of sorts that ran the length of the building, several doors to what were presumably bedrooms leading off of that.

"Mr. Higgins?" Clive said loudly as they stood on the balcony, looking at the row of doors and wondering which was his. "Virgil?" he called again, louder this time. "This is Mr. Howard. I need to speak with you, please!"

They heard a squeak, then, as one of the doors toward the end of the row slowly opened. A pale blond man in a thin plaid bathrobe stood in the doorway.

"Mr. Higgins?" Clive asked, walking toward him, Henrietta following closely.

"Yeah?" he asked dourly.

"I'm Clive Howard," he said respectfully. "You are employed by my parents, Mr. and Mrs. Howard."

"Yeah?" Virgil asked again, his jaw slack and unshaven. "Heard of you. Seen her," he nodded toward Henrietta.

"Yes. Indeed," Clive said stiffly. "This is my fiancée, Miss Von Harmon," he added briskly, inclining his head toward her.

"She said call her Henrietta," Virgil said, staring at her.

"Look, might we come in?" Clive said, his polite tone vanishing by the minute.

"Why?"

"Because I need to ask you some questions," Clive said firmly.

Virgil hesitated for a moment and then stepped aside, halfheartedly waving them into his room. Henrietta gingerly followed Clive inside and almost gagged at the smell of unwashed flesh and urine in the musty, dark room. She was tempted to put her hand over her nose, but she managed to refrain. She looked around and saw a small cook plate in the corner, near which sat a kettle and a few dirty mugs. Clothes were scattered about on the floor alongside two dirty mattresses. Henrietta tried to modestly avert her eyes from the unmade beds, one of which had clearly just been inhabited by Virgil, and looked instead at the peeling paint on the ceiling.

"Good God, man," Clive exclaimed. "This is a bit below the belt."

"Not my fault, *sir*," he said sullenly. "They're all like this. I reckon they haven't seen a lick of paint in twenty years."

"This is a disgrace. I'll have to speak to McCreanney about this. This is unsanitary."

"Won't do no good. He says for us to keep our heads down and get on with our jobs. Says the big house don't want to know about it."

"Well, he's wrong, there. I'll speak to Father directly," he said, looking around one more time. "Who sleeps there?" he asked, nodding at the other mattress.

"Jack. Why?"

"Of course it would be Fletcher," he said, looking up at the ceiling, annoyed. "Where is he?"

Virgil shrugged. "Don't know. Always about, here and there, that one is. Always using the telephone in the garage," he mumbled.

"Listen," Clive said, looking at him steadily, "I believe you gave one of the maids a ring for her birthday."

"What if I did?"

"Where did you get it?"

"None of your business!"

"Now listen, Higgins," Clive said, taking a step closer to him. "We can do this the hard way or we can do it the easy way."

Virgil swallowed visibly and tied his bathrobe more tightly around himself. He glanced over at Henrietta. "I don't need to tell you nothin'," he said with his characteristic sneer, though Henrietta thought she caught an element of wariness in his speech.

"Just tell me where you got the ring," Clive said, his voice rising along with his exasperation.

"No."

Clive sighed and waited a moment. "Right," he said resignedly and with a sudden burst of energy, grabbed him and threw him up against the wall. Virgil's face was one of terrified shock as Clive pinned him with his forearm. "Tell me."

Virgil's eyes darted back to Henrietta. "There's a lady present," he bleated. "You wouldn't thrash me in front of a lady, would you?"

"She's seen worse," Clive muttered, but he relaxed his grip a fraction as he said it.

"You're probably right, and she's no lady, anyways," Virgil said with a grin, erroneously assuming he was out of imminent danger.

Within seconds Clive struck him heavily across the upper right cheek with his fist, Henrietta stifling a scream as he did so.

"You watch your mouth, you little shit. Now, one more time. Where'd you get the ring?"

Virgil was crouched over now, holding the side of his face with his hand. The look he gave Clive was a mix of hatred and fear. "In town," he snarled. "At a pawnshop, if you must know."

"Not from Helen Schuyler's cottage?"

"Who?"

Clive grabbed him again and pinned him up against the wall once more.

"I don't know any Helen!" he squealed. "Honest. Unless you mean that ole bat down by the lake?"

"You're sure? You didn't just slip in there one day and take the ring? Give her a bit of a scare while you're at it?" Clive said, his face close to Virgil's.

"No. I bought it! I never go near her place . . ."

"Liar!" Clive shouted, shaking him.

"Clive!" Henrietta called out. She had not expected things to get this out of hand.

"I'm not lying! I . . . I have a slip," Virgil said desperately. "Let me show you . . ."

Clive released him with a shove, and Virgil, stumbling at first, scrambled to his mattress, where a tattered copy of the Bible, its cover torn off, but a cross visible on the front page, lay beside it. Trembling a bit, he flipped through it until he found several pieces of paper and drew one of them out, shakily handing it to Clive. Henrietta saw that the side of his face was beginning to bruise now.

Clive examined it carefully and showed it to Henrietta. It was indeed a receipt from a pawnshop in Winnetka dated last week with a full description of Helen's ring and the price paid: Nine dollars and forty-five cents. Clive whistled. "Expensive." He handed it back to Virgil, then, who stuffed it into the pocket of his robe.

"Happy now?" Virgil asked, his contemptuousness returning.

"Why didn't you just say so from the beginning?" Clive asked, irritated.

"I was ashamed," he snarled, looking at the floor, his anger still hovering near. "Not respectable to buy a gift for someone from a pawnshop, is it? Now she'll go and tell it to Edna," he said, looking up at Henrietta with disgust in his eyes.

"Show some respect, Higgins," Clive said evenly, "or I'll thrash you again. Or dismiss you. She's to be my wife and *your* future mistress someday."

Henrietta was stunned by this announcement, the revelation of Clive's true feelings on the subject surprising her. So he did see her as Highbury's mistress . . . She quickly looked from one to the other.

Virgil gave Clive an antagonistic, unbelieving look and said with a little cough, "If you say so."

Clive reacted by shoving him against the wall again. "Bastard!"

"Clive!" Henrietta shouted. "Stop! Come, let's go. We found out what we needed to," she said, putting her hand on his arm.

Slowly Clive released him with another little shove and walked to the door. "Get back to work," he grunted. "You're little sojourn in bed is over," he added and angrily slipped out the still-open door.

As Henrietta followed Clive across the balcony and down the stairs, her heart racing from the altercation she had just witnessed, she wasn't sure what to think. Her mind was divided between the new information they had gotten from Virgil regarding the ring and Clive's violent outburst. She had seen this side of him before, one that only seemed to surface while in the role of the inspector. Or was there something more to it this time? Did it have something to do with her honor? But if he himself was convinced of her virtue, as he had stated not an hour ago in the breakfast room, would he really feel the need to defend it so rashly? Perhaps he wasn't so convinced after all. If that *was* the case, she thought, nettled, it was all her own fault, the result of her ill-conceived amusements, in particular her dance with Jack.

Henrietta hurried to match Clive's determined pace. He was a strange combination of gentleness and consideration on one hand

and powerful, even violent, authority on the other, which, she had to admit, she felt uncontrollably attracted to.

"Damn it," Clive uttered under his breath as they walked back to the house along the pea-gravel drive. "I lost my temper with the servants. Rule number one," he said, piqued.

"Well, it was a different sort of matter," Henrietta said soothingly. "And besides, he *was* rather impertinent."

"But now I look a brute, Henrietta! Don't you see that? The man had a perfectly good excuse for the ring! He certainly has McCreanney fooled, though, I'll say that."

"But . . . but it still doesn't explain how the ring got there, does it?" Henrietta asked hesitantly. "Perhaps we should go into town and find this shop. Ask the shopkeeper if he remembers who brought it in. That seems the next logical step. Maybe Virgil *is* innocent in all this after all, but *someone* had to bring it in."

"It was probably Helen herself and she's simply forgotten," Clive said disgustedly.

"That can't be true! It's her most prized possession! Granted, her memory is a bit off at times, but she wouldn't have done something like that, surely!"

"Well, whatever it is, I can't worry about it any longer," Clive said tiredly.

"What do you mean?" Henrietta asked, confused. "We can't just give up now!"

They had reached the East Doors, and Clive paused to look at his pocket watch. "Henrietta," he said sternly, "we'd best let the servants get on with their work."

"But what should we tell Helen, who's sitting in the kitchen, waiting? Or Edna, for that matter!"

Clive ran his hand through his wavy hair. "Hmmm. Yes, there's the question of who actually owns the ring. Tell them I need to hold on to it until I have time to investigate it further," he said as he held the door open for her.

Henrietta paused, however, not wanting to go in just yet, as a new idea had suddenly come to her. "I know!" she said excitedly. "We could ask her daughter, Daphne! She lives somewhere near here, Helen said. Maybe Daphne took it, or found it, and brought it to the pawnshop, not realizing its sentimental value. Or maybe she did, but didn't care! Maybe she needed the money . . ."

"Henrietta," Clive said wearily.

"Yes?"

"Daphne's been dead for twenty years."

Henrietta felt the blood drain from her face. Goose bumps formed on her arms and on the back of her neck. No! Helen couldn't be that unhinged, could she? "That can't be . . ." she murmured.

"I'm afraid it is," he sighed. "Now do you understand?" As he stood, still holding the door open and gesturing for her to go in, big drops of rain from the storm that had been threatening all morning finally hit the dusty ground.

Henrietta stepped inside as if in a trance. "But . . ." Her mind was reeling as she walked with Clive down the thickly carpeted hallway. She thought about how Helen had called her Daphne so many times . . . "I don't understand," she murmured. Could Helen simply have misplaced the ring after all? But how had it turned up in a pawnshop? Surely she hadn't taken it there herself, had she? How could Daphne be dead?

"The mind can do strange things, as you and I have both seen," Clive said matter-of-factly, referring to the sordid affair with Neptune. He paused at the padded leather door of the library. "I think I need a drink before lunch," he said, pushing the door open. "Care for one?" he asked her.

Henrietta nodded. She rather thought she did, actually.

As Clive poured two brandies from the sideboard, Henrietta looked around in awe. She had yet to be in this room. It had a vaulted ceiling upon which a beautiful fresco was painted and trimmed in gold. The whole room was surrounded in thick dark bookcases, the only break being a space that had been carved out for the massive fireplace in the center of one wall. High above them was another set of bookcases that circled the room, a tiny balcony of sorts running along in front of them with a movable sort of stairwell to reach them. Henrietta glanced up at the one large window, the rain pelting against it now, making the atmosphere seem abnormally dark and dreary. Scattered throughout the room were leather armchairs and sofas and even a few tables and chairs, presumably for more serious endeavors of study. Henrietta thought it would be a lovely place to play rummy. Clive handed her a brandy and then walked absently toward the fireplace and leaned one arm against it, though no fire was burning.

Had he been merely placating her this whole time, then? Henrietta wondered. Had he known from the beginning how this must be some silly mix-up on Helen's part? Henrietta suddenly felt very foolish and not a little annoyed with Clive. Still, Henrietta countered, if he had really not suspected something, why would he have become violent with Virgil? But did that really have more to do with his feelings regarding her? Or was he taking out his anger with Jack on the poor, unsuspecting Virgil? But was Virgil really so innocent? Something told her that he knew more than he was saying . . .

"Well, it still doesn't explain everything, though, does it?" she said tentatively, walking closer to the fireplace.

"Henrietta! Enough, please," he said, annoyed. "I simply can't afford to spend any more precious time on this," he said, looking at his pocket watch again. "At least not today. I have more pressing matters to attend to that are infinitely more important."

"More important than an old woman who's . . . who's lost something precious . . . and is, well, terrified?" Henrietta sputtered, conscious of the fact that her retort had come out sounding whiny and childish.

"Yes, actually. I'll speak to Billings and have him sort it out."

Billings? she thought, cut to the quick that he so readily dismissed not only himself from the case but her as well. "I could try . . ." she suggested.

"No, Henrietta. I'd rather you not. Remember that we agreed you needed some distance from the servants, at least for a while? I think it best if you left the investigating to me."

Henrietta fumed. She knew he was right, about the servants, anyway, of course, but this was different! This was not a matter of socializing; it was trying to solve the case, something they could do together if he would only take it . . . take *her* . . . seriously. She wanted to be more to him than the dull mistress of Highbury! She was so angry, so hurt, she could not even think of what to say to him.

"Look, Henrietta, this afternoon I have a very important board meeting at Father's firm."

"On a Saturday?"

"Yes, it's quite irregular," he paused. "The truth is that Father is considering stepping down as chairman, and the board wants to vote on who his successor will be."

"And they want you, don't they?" Henrietta said slowly after a moment's pause.

"Yes, I'm afraid they do."

"And that will mean a life here at Highbury," she said, piecing it together. "No more Inspector Howard?"

Clive nodded, his eyes locked apprehensively on hers, impressed by her deduction. "It would appear that way, yes."

"When were you planning on telling me?"

"I tried to this morning! I said we had a lot to talk about, but instead I ended up on a wild-goose chase and hitting one of the servants," he said irritably.

"I'm sorry you thought it was a waste of time," Henrietta said coldly.

Clive sighed. "No, not a waste of time. Just that . . . we have a lot to talk about, Henrietta," he said seriously.

"So it would seem."

The silence between them stretched out uncomfortably as they looked at each other, trying to read the other's thoughts. Finally, Henrietta spoke. "Do you despise it here so very much?"

"Do you?"

"Does it matter what I think?" she asked quietly.

"Of course it does! How can you say that?" he searched her eyes and sighed. "Oh, Henrietta. I . . . I'm not sure what to think anymore," he said, rubbing his shoulder now, the incident with Virgil and now the rain causing his old war wound to ache. "Of course I love Highbury, it's just that I'm not sure this is the life I want."

"You might want to tell your parents that; they seem to have an altogether different vision of the future."

"Yes, yes, I know! But why should one family have all this while there's so much suffering going on in the world? Frankly I find it all a bit obscene. Oh, I don't know. It's not just that . . . it's this place! Set aside like some relic from the past under a glass dome for people to gaze at and comment about its quaintness before setting it back on its shelf to collect dust while they dash out, living a real life. It belongs to a different era, a simpler one." He paused for a moment, collecting his thoughts. "It holds so many memories for me," he said tacitly. "A different lifetime—a way of life that's gone, and every minute spent here agonizingly reminds me of it."

"You mean of Catherine?"

He closed his eyes briefly, and he sighed. "It's more than Catherine. It's my childhood—everything, really. I still remember the carriages we had—grooms and livery boys. Our property was huge back then. All the servants; the vast parties and . . . oh, I don't know . . . it just seemed a more innocent time. Then there was the war . . . ," he said, gripping his glass so tightly that his knuckles appeared white. "Henrietta, there was so much death," he faltered, his voice oddly strained now. "So much blood. No meaning to it." His eyes looked haunted. "I . . ." He broke off here, his brow furrowed.

She stepped closer to him and put her hand softly along the side of his face. "Then let's not live here. It doesn't matter, does it?"

He placed his own hand on top of hers. "But it does, unfortunately. It's not that easy. You've obviously perceived what's expected of me . . . of us. Could you do it?" Clive asked, looking anxiously into her eyes, "if it comes to that?"

Henrietta felt her heart melt despite her misgivings. "If you wanted me to . . . I suppose I could try. But Clive, I'm not sure I'm the right woman, the right wife . . ." She struggled to put her thoughts into words. "Take the servants, for example. It would be hard for me to . . . to distance myself . . . ," she faltered, thinking of Jack and Edna in particular.

"You'd learn. It's not as hard as you think. Distance doesn't have to mean unkindness."

Henrietta wasn't convinced of this, and, though a part of her knew better than to continue, she haphazardly decided to plunge ahead with what had been plaguing her all morning. She didn't think she could go forward in this conversation if she did not. "I danced with Jack last night," she blurted out, wanting to rid herself of her guilt. "Not . . . not because I have any feelings for him, but because I wanted to fit in at the party!" The moment the words burst out, however, she regretted it and wished desperately that she could retrieve them, but it was too late now.

Clive's eyes searched hers, and he did not say anything, which was worse, actually, than if he had shouted. Henrietta held her breath and was cut to the quick when he pulled his eyes away and she saw in them not disgust, but hurt.

"Yes, I'm aware of your indiscretion," he said quietly.

Henrietta bristled. Any repentance she had been feeling was immediately replaced my indignation. "You know? But how? Are you spying on me?" She flashed her blue eyes at him. "Don't you trust me?"

"Don't be tiresome, Henrietta. Of course I'm not spying on you. Father told me, actually."

"Your father?" She was stupefied.

"Billings apparently reported it to him this morning," he said, grimly.

This was intolerable! Billings, too! "Where *are* your parents, anyway?" she said, looking around now and realizing that she hadn't seen them all morning. She had assumed that they had finished breakfast before she came down, having slept in, but surely they should be about by now.

"Father's at the firm, presumably lunching there, waiting for me. And Mother's decided to spend the day at the club."

"Whatever for?"

"I think she wanted to give us some time alone. 'To discuss matters' is how I think she put it."

"You told them we quarreled last night, didn't you?"

"I may have mentioned something to that effect to Father when I came in. He was still up, you see, and I was upset, truth be told."

"I'd rather you didn't discuss our quarrels with your parents," Henrietta retorted. "It paints me in a very bad light, and I don't need any additional help in that department!"

"Actually, I painted myself in a very bad light, if you must know!" he said, annoyed now.

They were interrupted then when Billings entered the room holding a small silver salver in one hand, upon which were two envelopes.

"Pardon the interruption, sir," Billings said staidly, "but there are two letters for Miss Von Harmon. They arrived this morning, while you were . . . *out*," he emphasized, as if they had committed a crime, or at least a serious misdemeanor. Did he already know about Clive's rough handling of Virgil? "They were set aside by young Arthur and only now brought to my attention. I'm very sorry, sir."

Before Clive could answer, Henrietta took the two letters from the tray and examined them. "Thank you, Billings," she said absently, ignoring his accusatory tone. "They're from home," she said to Clive, turning them over. One letter would have been unusual, but two gave her a very definite feeling of foreboding.

"Luncheon will be served soon, sir," Billings said, hovering nearby.

"We'll be in directly, Billings," Clive said, dismissing him.

"Very good, sir," he said, with only a hint of disappointment, as if he had wanted, perhaps, to hear the contents of the missives Henrietta now held.

Henrietta set her snifter down on one of the gleaming tables and carefully opened the first letter, fear filling her heart. It was from Elsie, and she knew she wouldn't write unless something was wrong.

Was it one of the twins? she wondered desperately. But if something were seriously wrong, wouldn't Elsie have run down to Kreske's Drug Store to use the telephone?

Nervously, Henrietta pulled out the single sheet of plain white paper in Elsie's delicate hand. It read:

Dearest Henrietta,

Thank you for your nice letter this week past telling us that you arrived safely. Mr. Howard's home sounds heavenly, and I am sure you will have many interesting stories for us when you come home.

I hope you are well and that you are having a lovely time with Mr. Howard and what I hope are his kind family. I'm sure they were as surprised as we were by the happy news of your engagement. All the neighbors were quite surprised and happy for you when we told them all about it, even Ludmilla, who says she figured a wedding would be sooner than later with you, referring I'm sure to your beauty and your sweet temper and nothing mean, though Ludmilla always has a way of making everything seem sour, even things that are meant to be nice, doesn't she? Mr. Hennessey, by the way, has stopped in several times at Dubala's to ask after you, bless his heart. He sends his love.

We are all well at home, except, of course, Herbert, who had the beginnings of a cold in his ear not but a few days ago, but who has bravely fought it off it seems. There is not much other news, except perhaps that Ma seems a bit out of sorts, more so than usual. I thought she would be happy that you were settling down, as she is always going on about you (you know how she does), but your engagement to Mr. Howard has seemed to have brought her a bit low. I have tried in my own quiet way to ask her about it, but she does not want to talk about it.

Her mood was brought even lower, however, by some

trouble that Eugene has found himself in, and though I would not for the world interrupt your happy time, it is for this reason, really, that I am writing, to ask when you might be thinking of coming home. I wouldn't dream of asking you, except that we were rather expecting you back before now and were wondering if perhaps your plans had changed in any way. I feel terrible for interrupting your time with Mr. Howard, but I do wonder when you might return to offer us your advice and any comfort you might be able to give Ma. Please let us know as soon as possible, for which I am very sorry.

Your loving sister,
Elsie

Henrietta let out a deep breath and glanced over at Clive, who was patiently watching her.

"Everything all right?" he asked quietly.

"It's from Elsie. She wants to know when I'm coming home. Eugene's done something, apparently, and Ma's upset."

"Such as?"

"She doesn't say, which is a bit worrying."

"And the other?"

Henrietta looked down at the other letter and frowned when she saw that the return address was from Stan, of all people. "It's from Stan, I think," she said, opening it slowly.

"Pipsqueak?" Clive asked, intrigued, taking a sip of his brandy.

Dear Hen,

Sorry to bother you and all. Elsie says the inspector's house is very grand, which I'm sure is quite a boon to you, though it's a bit deceptive if you ask me, which you're not, so. Elsie, by the way, doesn't know I'm writing, but I know from her sweet nature that she won't have told you the whole story with Eugene. I myself cannot divulge it, even to you, as I promised Elsie I wouldn't. But I will say that you're quite needed back at home somewhat urgently. No doubt the inspector is dazzling you with delights, but if you can at all cease to be mesmerized by his flashy charm, you might just get back here.

Sorry to be the cause of disappointment, but, in truth, all your old chums round here miss you, not just me, and it would be good to see you. Who knows, maybe this inspector is not all he's cracked up to be. You could be murdered up there, and we would never know! That is not a pleasant thought, I know, and probably not one that should be included in a correspondence, but it is a rather sobering consideration. Still, Elsie says you are old enough to make your own decisions, so I suppose she is right.

Anyway, if you could see fit to come home quick, your ma and Elsie, not to mention me, would be greatly relieved.

Your friend,
Stanley Dubowski

Henrietta folded the letter back up and put her hand to her forehead. "I've got to go home, Clive."

"Anything serious? Is someone ill?"

"Something to do with Eugene, but they won't say what. The fact that Stan wrote as well must mean it's something serious."

"Wouldn't your mother have telephoned?"

"I'm sure she'd rather die than ask for my help. That's why Elsie had to do it. I'm going up to pack."

"Now?" he asked, incredulous.

"Yes, now."

"But I can't possibly drive you this afternoon, not with this meeting."

"Yes, I realize that!" Henrietta was growing irritated now, impatient to get back to her family, waves of guilt washing over her. Wasn't this proof that she was going down the wrong path? God was punishing her for being selfish; it was obvious. Or at least, He was trying to tell her something. What could have possibly happened to Eugene? she thought desperately. Perhaps he had run away? Perhaps he was in the hospital? Panic was filling her heart, and it was obvious that Clive did not share her anxiety. His silly board meeting, which might not produce anything concrete anyway, was clearly more important than her family's problems. "I have to go home, Clive," she said firmly. "Today. Now."

Clive sighed. "Henrietta, see reason. You don't even know what this is about. You're acting like a child! You confess that you've spent the evening dancing with another man just as I'm asking you to decide about our future—your future—and now you want to run off because of some mischief Eugene's found himself in! That's rich! You must have some opinion, Henrietta. This is your life, too!"

She looked at him coldly. "I've already explained about Jack, and if you choose to make an issue of it, then so be it. As to the future, if we have one, I don't think it matters very much what I think," Henrietta said coolly. "I think you've already made up your mind, regardless. And, anyway, what was it you said to me just now? *Distance doesn't have to mean unkindness*. Perhaps there's some truth to that." She knew that a part of her was being unreasonable, but she couldn't help it.

"What do you mean by 'if we have one'?" he asked, confused.

"Just that perhaps we need time to reconsider."

"Reconsider what?"

"Whether we're really suited for each other."

Clive looked at her, stunned.

"Clive," she went on, "we made a promise in the heat of the moment. We weren't really thinking, either of us. Let's both think more carefully about this marriage before you give your father and the board a decision. Take me out of the equation and then decide based on what your heart tells you. And if necessary, I release you," she said quietly, "freely."

"Henrietta, don't . . ." he whispered.

"I have to go, Clive."

"Don't . . ." It seemed hard for him to get the words out. "Don't do this." He looked at her steadily. "Don't be my undoing," he pleaded, just above a whisper.

She did not say anything, but she could feel the tears coming.

Furtively, he searched her face and finding her resolute, altered his expression then to one of sad resignation. "If you really won't wait, I'll have Fletcher take you," he said emotionlessly.

Her brow furrowed. "Jack? You trust me to be alone with Jack in a car all that way?"

"Yes," he said, not taking his eyes off hers, "I do trust you."

Suddenly, then, she felt a flood of emotion, a flood of love for him, such that she couldn't speak.

"Have a safe journey," he said, almost inaudibly, his face hard now.

Henrietta did not know what else to say, stunned by her own stupid volley of words. She had gone too far this time, and she knew it. She longed for him to put his arms around her, but he did not. In fact, he retreated now to his previous place by the fireplace. There was nothing left for her to do but to go upstairs and pack as she had said she would. She had perhaps meant only to test him, but he was taking her at her word, and it pained her more than she had thought possible, and she found it difficult, actually, to breathe. But now she didn't know how to undo it.

"Goodbye, then," she managed to say sadly and slipped out the door. Clive, his outstretched arms braced against the cold fireplace, did not say anything more but continued to stare at the empty grate, his jaw clenched hard.

Chapter 10

Quiet tears spilled down her cheeks as Fletcher pulled away from Highbury not an hour later. Henrietta sat dejectedly in the backseat of the Bentley, her many sorrows blending together into an indiscriminate fog. Not only did she feel that she was possibly losing Clive, but, if she admitted it, she felt the loss of Highbury as well as they drove down the lovely shaded lane flanked with huge oak trees, the enchanted beauty of which increased her present state of misery.

She had managed to hold back her tears as Clive, assuming the role of Billings and donning an umbrella against the steady rain that continued to fall, had rather coldly escorted her to the car and had solemnly wished her luck, offering no further words of endearment. With a face of granite, he gave Jack a nod and a little salute with his forefinger, signally him to pull away. Henrietta had bravely kept her eyes on the road ahead, but at the bottom of the lane, her resolve crumbled, and she gave one last look back. Clive, however, had already gone back in.

She turned back around, then, her throat aching as she fought to hold back her tears. Her distress over Clive mingled with worry about her family to form a hard knot of wretchedness in the pit of her stomach. Guilt in many variations washed over her. She felt guilty for leaving her family in the first place, guilty for being so stupidly involved with the servants, and even guilty now at leaving poor Helen, who seemed to have no one to take her part. Her mind naturally drifted then and lingered on a kindred sorrow, that being Helen's poor lost, dead daughter, and she found she could no longer hold back the tears and cried silently as Jack pulled the car onto the highway now.

In her despair, Henrietta gazed forlornly at the rivulets of water that ran down the window and was determined, if nothing else, not to speak to Jack at all. He had made little comments here and there about the weather or the traffic, all of which she had ignored. She would prove that he meant nothing to her, and, yet, she wondered as the minutes ticked on, who was she trying to prove it to? Herself? Clive would never know of her sacrifice here in the car. It was too late for that. Jack had eventually grown quiet, but when they were finally nearing the city, he ventured to speak again.

"I'm sorry if I got you into trouble last night," he said hesitantly.

Henrietta glanced up at the rearview mirror to look at him for the first time since the journey had begun. He seemed so genuinely concerned and had such a look of contriteness on his face, however, that Henrietta, her tears dried up now and despite her previous, private resolution, gave in and spoke to him.

"It wasn't your fault," she said with a sigh. "I . . . we worked it out."

"Didn't look like it to me," he said, looking at her in the rearview mirror. "Begging your pardon, Miss."

Henrietta avoided his eyes and looked out the window. "You might as well call me Henrietta," she said. What did it matter that the servants were familiar in their address of her now? She was leaving Highbury and going back to her old life; she might as well give up the fatiguing role of distance and superiority that she was supposed to be maintaining. Still, she found she had nothing in particular to say to Jack.

"At least you found out more about poor Helen's ring," he said hopefully into the rearview mirror.

Despite her lethargy, Henrietta looked up at him now, her interest piqued. "How do you know about that?"

"Edna told me."

"Oh," Henrietta said, sinking back down into the seat.

"Wish I could have seen it!" he added.

Henrietta caught a glimpse of his face in the mirror. She could tell he was trying to please her, to win her over.

"It wasn't very pleasant, actually," she said dismissively.

"Glad Mister Clive's still got the ole one-two. Serves Virgil right, the twit."

Henrietta looked out the window again, remembering how Clive had so roughly dealt with Virgil. Fresh images of Clive throwing him up against the wall flooded her mind and made her shift uneasily. "Well, he deserved it," Henrietta found herself saying.

"No doubt!" Jack said, fully encouraged now. "Edna says he managed to produce a receipt from a pawnshop," he ventured, looking in the mirror again. "Probably a fake," he scoffed.

"I saw it, though. It seemed real enough to me. Some shop in Winnetka called Selzers, I think."

"Well, what if he did buy it legit? How'd it get there?"

"That's exactly what I thought!" Henrietta said, enticed into the conversation almost against her will. "And what about the strange scratches at Helen's cottage?"

Jack let out a low whistle. "Edna told me about that. Definitely strange, that is. Creepy, actually."

"Do you think whoever took the ring did that as well?"

"Hard to say, but why?"

"I'm not sure. To scare Helen? Make her more confused?"

"Could be."

Henrietta looked out the window again. "Clive thinks it's an animal."

"Naw! I went down and had a look. Ain't no animal did that."

"No, I didn't think so, either," she said, looking back at him through the mirror.

"All I'm sayin' is that our friend Virgil has got himself a wicked-looking knife. Long and thin, it is, almost like a letter-opener."

Henrietta drew in a breath, picturing Virgil slinking about Helen's cottage at night with such a knife. "He . . . he says he's never been down by the cottage."

"Bull! I've heard him sneak out at night, plenty of times. That's the God's honest truth."

Henrietta felt goose bumps again. She was surprised that Jack shared her exact suspicions and theories, and it was so gratifying to be taken seriously. But then again, was Helen, as Clive had insinuated, really to be believed? "Have you ever heard Helen mention Daphne?" she ventured.

"No, but Mary told me. How she goes around talkin' about her like she's gonna walk in the room any minute."

"Yes! Bizarre, isn't it? Do you think she's crazy?"

"Hard to tell, really. My own grandfather still talks to my grandmother every day, though she's been dead these past fifteen years. And he don't seem crazy to me, but what do I know?"

"That's what I thought! Just because she gets confused about Daphne doesn't mean she's completely insane. She still helps cook at big parties, doesn't she?"

"True enough," he said, turning onto Fullerton now.

Henrietta smiled. "Did you know she calls me Daphne sometimes? It's sad, isn't it? I wish I knew what happened."

"I know a little," he offered. "Mary told us one night in the kitchen before Mrs. Caldwell found us and broke it up as idle gossip." He looked at her in the rearview mirror. "Apparently Daphne was killed by some Doctor McFarlen."

"Killed?"

"On accident, it was. Seems this Daphne was walking on the side of Sheridan road between Highbury and town, Mary says, when the ole Doc comes racing through in his car on an emergency call. Didn't see Daphne and hit her straight on. Mary says the car hit her so hard her boots flew off. They found 'em in the ditch nearby."

"Oh, my!" Henrietta exclaimed, horrified. "Poor Helen!"

"Mary says she never really got over it. Went into some kind of a black depression. The Howards, to give 'em credit, called in all sorts of doctors, trying to help her."

"So what happened?"

"She got a bit better as time went on, went back to workin' in the kitchen, but she was never the same. Mary used to be her undercook, but they eventually sort of just changed places."

"What about the doctor? He must have been devastated, too."

"I 'spose so. Gave up practicin' after that, I think Mary said. That or he moved somewhere else; I forget."

The conversation fizzled out then as Jack needed to concentrate more on navigating the heavier traffic. They had already reached Armitage, and Henrietta felt her stomach clench now that she was almost home, afraid of what awaited her there. The conversation about Helen and Daphne had distracted her from her woes regarding Clive as well as her family's problems, but now that the building loomed in front of her, her anxiety over what might have happened to Eugene rushed to the forefront. Jack pulled the Bentley up to the curb and swiftly came around to open the door for her. The rain had stopped now, and the sky was a strange yellowish green. As she stepped out of the car, a wet mugginess in the air hit her as well as the unmistakable smell of nearly drowned earthworms that had sought refuge on the pavement, having escaped the temporarily flooded patch of mud and weeds surrounding the apartment building. She saw Jack look appraisingly at the building, which seemed all the more dirty and gray for being wet. She could only guess what he was thinking.

"Not exactly Highbury, is it?" she asked ruefully.

"Well, it's home, ain't it?"

"Where are you from, Jack?" she asked, trying to delay having to go up but marginally curious as well.

"Here and there," he grinned. "Don't matter much."

Henrietta reached out and took the carpetbag that he had gotten out of the car for her. "Thanks."

"Want me to carry it up for you?"

"I think I can manage." She smiled.

"Want me to make a few inquiries at Selzers? Couldn't hurt . . ." he suggested.

"You wouldn't mind?" Henrietta asked eagerly. "I wanted to myself, but I . . . I had to come home."

"Family troubles?"

"You could say that." She smiled tiredly.

"I'll keep my eye on ole Virg, too. When you get back I'll give you the lowdown."

"I'm not sure when that will be, actually," Henrietta said sadly, wondering what the future held for her and Clive, if anything.

"I know one thing," he said, his tone changing suddenly. "If you were my girl, I wouldn't let you out of my sight for two minutes." He said this last part almost to himself, and Henrietta was aware of how very close he was standing to her now. She hoped he couldn't hear her swallow hard as she took a step back. She was amazed at how easy it was to talk to Jack, but at the same time, it always made her just a little bit uncomfortable. Perhaps it was his forwardness.

"Thanks, Jack."

"Goodbye, Miss Von Harmon," he said wistfully as he stood back to let her pass.

Henrietta made her way up the dirty stairwell and paused on the landing outside her family's apartment. It felt good in an odd way to be home, but as she climbed the creaky steps, she couldn't help but compare their mean, nicked-up front door as it came in sight with Highbury's grand entrance of thick polished wood and windows of leaded glass, complete with a servant just on the other side to be of service. What had she done? she thought miserably as she noticed, perhaps for the first time, the two broken spindles at the far end of the landing. She took a deep breath and determinedly opened the door.

"You're home, Hen!" came a shout from Jimmy as he looked up in surprise and hurled himself onto her.

Henrietta burst into a smile as she held him tight, Donny and Doris crowding round her now, too. She looked about the room, even as she distributed hugs. Ma was sitting dejectedly on the stool by the fire, not even bothering to look up, and Elsie stood beside her, a relieved smile on her face.

"Where's Eddie and Herbert?" Henrietta asked, looking round.

"Eddie got a job as a message boy," Elsie said eagerly, "and Herbert's burning boxes today on Milwaukee."

"Well! That's encouraging," Henrietta said as she unpinned her hat and hung it up beside the door, setting her nearly empty carpetbag down as well.

She had sought out Edna before she left to ask for her old clothes and to tell her to be patient regarding the ring, that Mr. Clive was going to instruct Billings to investigate further.

"Mr. Billings?" Edna had said, surprised. "He won't do nothin'!" Edna moaned, dejected. "Oh, Miss, I think I'll just give it back to Helen. It's obviously hers, but I feel bad that Virgil's out all that money. Doesn't seem fair, does it?"

"No, it doesn't. But it's out of my hands now."

"When are you coming back, Miss?"

"I'm not sure, Edna," she said sadly.

"You didn't have a fallin' out with Mister Clive, did you?"

Henrietta didn't say anything.

"'Cause I'm sure he loves you. Anyone can see that."

"But maybe not enough," Henrietta said wistfully.

"What do you mean by that, Miss?"

"Oh, it doesn't matter. You wouldn't know where my old clothes are, would you?"

"I believe I do," she said, thinking for a moment. "Mrs. Caldwell put 'em in the laundry, up on the shelf. I'll bring 'em up to you."

She had dressed quickly after Edna had delivered them and had put the few personal items she had brought with her back in her old bag, which she had found sitting forlornly at the bottom of the wardrobe. She ran her hand along the beautiful things Mrs. Howard had bought for her and then quickly closed the wardrobe door. They didn't belong to her, she thought; they belonged to Highbury, and she silently then left the room.

Henrietta sighed now as she looked around the miserable room. The smell of potatoes frying in lard and the pungent odor of cabbage boiling itself into mush floated up from the apartment below, permeating their own apartment as it usually did. She felt close to tears, but then Elsie appeared by her side and embraced her tightly, holding her close. When she finally released her, she herself wiped a tear away and smiled up at Henrietta.

"Oh, Hen! I'm so glad to see you. You look lovely!" she said with sincere admiration. "Jimmy, you take the twins out to play," she said to Jimmy, who was still glued to Henrietta's side.

"But I want to stay and see Hen!"

"You'll see her later; go on!"

"Awwww, gee!" he said glumly, as he grabbed the twins by the hands. "But I'm hungry!"

"Here," Henrietta said, picking up her handbag and opening her coin purse. She put a whole quarter in each of their hands. "Go on and buy some sweets!" she said.

"Oh, Hen! Thanks!" they squealed and dashed off down the stairs, racing and pushing each other in delightful glee to be the first to the bottom.

Henrietta's smile faded as she turned back to Elsie then and took hold of one of her hands. "What is it, Els?" she said, looking from her to her mother. "How come you're not at Dubala's on a Saturday afternoon?"

"Oh, Hen! Eugene's in jail!" Elsie whispered, giving a little cry.

"Jail? What do you mean?" Henrietta said nauseously, making her way over to where her mother sat, forlornly, like the old carpetbag at the bottom of the wardrobe. She had been bracing herself for something bad, but not this!

"Yes! He's in jail!" her mother spit out. "He's been there for three days now, while you're off gallivanting at Highbury!"

"Oh, of course this is somehow my fault," Henrietta said bitterly, surprised by how quickly she and Ma were back to arguing. It was as if she had never left. "Wait a minute . . ." she asked, a thought suddenly occurring to her. "How do you know Clive's home is called Highbury?"

Henrietta studied her mother closely, and within seconds, the hard, bitter lines dissolved into anguish as she buried her face in her hands and began to sob. "Oh, Henrietta! What are we going to do?" Henrietta noted that she didn't answer the question, but she let it go in favor of concentrating on Ma's evident distress, something Henrietta rarely saw.

Elsie went and knelt beside her mother, putting her arms around her. "Don't worry, Ma! We'll think of something . . . won't we, Hen?" she asked, looking back up at Henrietta.

God in heaven! What were they to do? Henrietta thought as she began to pace now around the room. She paused in front of the window and rubbed her forehead. The sun was just beginning its long descent.

"What happened?" she asked, turning back toward Elsie. Her mother still had her face buried.

"He . . . he was staying at the rectory . . ." Elsie said hesitantly.

"The rectory?"

"With Fr. Finnegan . . ."

"Why?" Henrietta asked, incredulous, but a nagging suspicion was forming in her head.

"Because the old fool convinced Eugene that he's got a vocation!" Ma suddenly said, coming up for air. "Told him it's a sin to fight it, that he would be less a burden to us as well."

"A burden! He could be out earning money!" Henrietta exclaimed. "Instead Herbert's out burning boxes all day for a few cents! He's only eight!"

"It's just on Saturdays, Hen," Elsie said cautiously, inclining her head ever so slightly toward Ma as a warning not to say too much.

"So how did he end up in jail, then?"

"We don't know the whole story. Just that he apparently stole some very valuable candlesticks from the rectory," Elsie continued.

"And Fr. Finnegan called the police?" Henrietta asked, disbelieving.

"Apparently so," Elsie said with a sad shrug.

"Has anyone spoken to Eugene?" Henrietta asked, pacing again.

"Stanley went down to see him, but he's not saying much. Says he doesn't want to talk about it."

"Did he ask him if he really did steal them?"

"Henrietta! What a thing to say! Anyway, he didn't need to," she added sadly. "The police found them on him when they picked him up."

"Good God!" Henrietta said and looked over at her mother, who was staring absently into the empty fireplace again, her face blotched and red.

"What are we going to do, Hen?" Elsie asked anxiously, pulling her eyes from Ma to look questioningly at Henrietta.

"I don't know!" she said, annoyed, twisting her hands as she walked up and down.

"Do you . . . it's just that Stanley thought maybe . . . Mr. Howard might . . . you know, being an inspector . . . that he might be able to help is all. What do you think?"

As soon as she had heard what the nature of the trouble actually was, Henrietta had had a sinking feeling that it was going to come to this. But how could she telephone Clive now? After all that was said between them? She moaned loudly and buried her own face in her hands.

"I know it's very shameful, Hen," Elsie said quietly, "but we don't know what else to do."

Henrietta looked up, knowing she had no choice in this matter. She would have to ask for his help; there was no way around it. She had already humiliated herself in front of him countless times, it seemed; why stop at one more? "Yes, of course, I'll telephone him," she said, forcing a smile. "I'll pop down to Kreske's and try him. He was planning to be out for the afternoon, but perhaps he's back now." She walked back toward the door and pinned on her hat. "Is there something you can make for supper?" she asked Elsie.

"I was going to make soup," Elsie suggested.

"I'll buy some bread while I'm out," she said, feeling as though she might be sick, the hard reality of her life at home hitting her full force. Again she had to fight back tears as she realized that her brief respite at Highbury, her time at the ball, as it were, was really over now, and she was back to being Cinderella.

When Clive arrived, it had already gone dark. Henrietta met him at the door and felt a nervous fluttering at the sight of him. Tentatively she tried to read his face. It was set hard, but his eyes looked at her with such love and compassion that she wanted to go to him now and fiercely embrace him. She forced herself to stay where she was, however, and pulled her gaze from his face down to the large, expensive-looking suitcase he was holding.

Without stepping inside, he gently set the case down just inside the door and politely removed his hat. "You forgot your things," he said deliberately, as if he had rehearsed his words. "I thought you might need them."

Henrietta stared at him, trying to decipher his meaning. Did he intend, then, for her to never return to Highbury, giving her the clothes as some sort of goodbye gift? She supposed it wasn't fair to assume this was his intention, but hadn't she herself left them behind for that very same reason? Clive was looking at her now, though, with such longing . . . surely this was not his intent?

"May I come in?" he asked.

"Oh! Of course! I'm sorry! I'm . . . I'm not myself, I suppose," Henrietta said, opening the door wider for him and gesturing for him to enter.

"No, you wouldn't be, I'm sure," he said, stepping in. "Perfectly understandable." Once inside, he glanced quickly at the assemblage in the room.

"Mrs. Von Harmon," he said, addressing Ma, who was sitting stonily at the table now. "Good evening. I'm very sorry to hear the news. I'm sure there's some perfectly good explanation," he said encouragingly.

Ma merely nodded, expressionless. Elsie came over from the corner where she had been standing with Stan, who had annoyingly dashed over after his shift at the electrics to "comfort them in their distress," was how he had put it . . .

"Gee whiz, Hen!" Stan had said when he first saw her upon hurrying up the apartment-building stairs. She had just come in from Schneider's, where she had gone after telephoning Clive from Kreske's, and she and Elsie stood in the kitchen putting away the staples, along with a few luxuries she had bought, Elsie exclaiming every now and again as she examined each thing, saying that this or that would have been particularly enjoyed by poor Eugene. Henrietta had bought as many groceries as she could carry, having absconded Clive's money from Ma, who finally admitted that she had stashed the whole lot in a coffee can in the broom closet. She had wanted to chastise Ma severely for not using it, choosing to nearly starve the lot of them instead, but she knew it was not the time for another argument. They had enough to deal with as it was.

"You look so much older," Stan said as he stared at her, the disappointment in his voice both obvious and irritating.

"I haven't even been gone a full two weeks, Stan!" Henrietta said, her back to him.

"I think it's the hair," Elsie said, smiling. "You've done it a different way."

That must be it, thought Henrietta, though she wasn't about to share that Mrs. Howard's *maid* had taken to doing her hair in the latest fashions each day.

"Well, still," Stan had said. "I'm not sure it suits you," he added with a sniff.

"Stanley!" Elsie had exclaimed.

"Good thing it's not up to you, then," Henrietta retorted and worried that she still saw a tinge of adoration, to put it mildly, in Stan's eye regarding herself.

"Well, I don't know about that," Stan said, puffing out his chest. "With Eugene gone and, well, Elsie and I . . ."

"Stanley!" Elsie blushed, "Not now!"

"Well, anyway, I'm sort of the man of the house for the time being," he said proudly. "You know, to watch over you and all . . ."

Henrietta regarded him for a few moments, contemplating whether she should crush his fantasy or just leave him be. In the end, she had decided to leave him to his delusion, but she did wonder what he had meant by "Elsie and I"? Surely Elsie hadn't engaged herself to him already? she worried, as she slowly tucked the bread into the breadbox.

"Thank you so much for coming, Mr. Howard," Elsie said now to Clive as he stood there among them.

"Not at all, and, please, call me Clive."

"All right," Elsie said, blushing slightly, "Clive."

Stan let out a little cough.

Clive glanced over at him. "I see you're here, too. Stanley, isn't it? Why am I not surprised?" he said, arching his eyebrow. "I believe you spoke to Eugene; is this true?"

"I did," Stan answered with a little nod.

"What's his version?"

"He won't say nothin'. I asked him why he did it, and he just shrugged. Quiet kind of a fella, you see."

"Has he seen a lawyer yet?" Clive asked Henrietta, who was standing near him.

"I'm not sure."

"Right," Clive sighed. "Before I left the house, I telephoned Jones to see what he could dig up. He's being held at precinct fourteen. No one's been assigned to the case yet, so that's good. Fewer toes to step on that way. I'm headed there now, but I just wanted to see if there was anything else you could tell me to shed any light on the situation."

"I can't think of anything, Mr. . . . Clive," Elsie said. "We know very little about it ourselves. Could you . . . could you bring him some things?"

"I don't see why not," he said, "but I should leave as soon as possible."

Elsie hurried to the kitchen to gather a few items together for him.

"Let me come with you," Henrietta said quietly to him. "Please."

Clive studied her face, and she wished she could decipher his thoughts, as he always seemed able to do with her. When she had telephoned him at Highbury, she had been surprised when Billings had said that Mister Clive was indeed in and had promptly delivered the phone to him. She had meant to be calm and collected with him, but she couldn't keep the waver out of her voice as she explained what had happened to Eugene and what she knew. An intense feeling of love had passed over her then as she heard him say across the staticky line that he was on his way even before she had to humble herself to ask for his help. He had spared her that humiliation, and she realized in that moment that she needed to be with this man forever. But she had been so stupid! Saying so many things she hadn't really meant. She only hoped it wasn't too late.

"Don't you think you'd be better here, with your family?" he asked finally, and Henrietta couldn't help but wonder if there was a deeper meaning to the question. He seemed so serious.

"I'd like to help you. And Eugene," she said. "Sometimes he'll talk to me."

Ma snorted, but Henrietta ignored her.

"Please."

"All right, then. Come, if you wish," Clive said with no emotion, though his eyes looked pained.

There was mostly silence between them as they rode side by side in his car to the Logan Square station, Elsie's care package placed carefully between them, the sun completely gone now.

"What . . . what did you tell the board?" Henrietta finally asked tentatively.

"Let's talk about it later," Clive said tonelessly, not looking at her, keeping his eyes on the road. "We need to concentrate on Eugene just now," he said with what seemed to be genuine concern.

Henrietta nodded silently, seeing the reason in this but still a little hurt by his quick dismissal.

"Tell me about this Fr. Finnegan," he said.

"Well, I'm not sure what to say, really," Henrietta said, glad, despite the odiousness of the priest, to have something to talk about. "I don't like him much. Neither does Ma."

"Why?"

"Just the way he is. Like a drill sergeant. The poor altar boys live in fear of him; he's always correcting them. Eugene used to be one, but he quit. Fr. Finnegan came round to the house, then, said he should come back, something about him being his best server. Pa tried to encourage him, but Eugene wouldn't go back. Gene's awfully stubborn, you know."

"Hmmm," was all Clive said.

"Fr. Finnegan's always going on to Eugene that he has a vocation. Trying to get him to become a priest. I don't know why."

"So you don't think Eugene really has a vocation?" Clive asked, glancing over at her for a moment.

"Not particularly. He's good at school, but that's hardly the same thing."

"And what does this Fr. Finnegan think of you?" he said, allowing his glance to linger longer.

"He doesn't like me much. He thinks I'm not virtuous, I suppose, like everyone else," she said, looking out the window.

Clive turned his eyes back to the road and remained silent.

"I have a theory, you know," Henrietta said after a moment.

"Tell me," Clive said, an unexpected trace of emotion hovering near.

"I think I know why Fr. Finnegan let Pa be buried in the churchyard," she said in a low tone, still looking out the window. "By rights, he shouldn't have been, you know," she murmured, turning now to him.

Clive arched his eyebrow. "Go on."

"I think he did it to get Ma on his side. About Eugene, that is. She owes him now, you see, which is why she can't ever speak up."

"I see," he mused. He was silent for a few moments and then spoke again. "Any idea why he was staying at the rectory?"

"None. I was as surprised as anyone."

They had arrived at the station by now, and Clive stopped the car just outside of it. He went around and opened the door for Henrietta, looking at her fully for the first time since they had left the apartment. "Leave the talking to me, okay?" he said sternly.

Henrietta merely nodded and followed him up the stone steps. Once inside, Clive pointed to a bench where she should sit while he spoke privately to the station commander, showing him his badge as he did so and every once in a while looking over at Henrietta and gesturing. Finally Clive came back toward her. "They're setting up a cross-examination room for us to talk to him," he said, inclining his head toward the back of the station. "We'll both go in, and you can give him the package, but then I want you to leave while I question him. Understood?"

"Yes, but . . ." Henrietta started to counter.

"That's the deal. Yes or no?" he asked firmly. He was definitely in the role of the inspector now.

"Yes, all right," Henrietta acquiesced.

They followed a sergeant to the back, where he paused in front of a steel door with a small grilled window. The sergeant unlocked the door, and Henrietta felt she might start to cry when she followed Clive inside and saw a very miserable-looking Eugene sitting at a small table, his head in his hands.

He looked up when they entered and scowled. "Oh, it's you two," he said unpleasantly. "Come to see the fallen, have you?"

"Eugene!" Henrietta exclaimed, her pity quickly evaporating.

The sergeant retired to the dark corner, his hands behind his back, as Clive reached for a chair opposite Eugene and gestured to Henrietta to take the other one. "Watch your mouth!" Clive said, his voice slightly elevated. "I'm here to help you."

Eugene did not reply but sat surlily looking at the table.

"I brought you these things from home, Eugene," Henrietta said, putting the package on the table and passing it over to him. "They're from Elsie."

"I'll need to examine that when you're through," the sergeant said from the background, and Clive nodded his acceptance. Eugene remained silent, not even acknowledging the gift at all.

"Eugene, what happened?" Henrietta asked desperately.

"I don't want to talk about it."

"You didn't really steal those candlesticks, or whatever they were, did you?" she pleaded.

"Maybe," he said, glancing up at Clive briefly. "Listen, Henrietta. This doesn't concern you, so just go back to whatever you were doing with this charmer," he said sulkily. "Stay out of it."

"Right," said Clive authoritatively. "Time for us to have a little talk. Please leave us, Henrietta."

"But I . . ."

"You heard me," he said, not taking his eyes off Eugene.

"Go on, Henrietta! Your ole man told you to get lost!"

Swiftly, Clive reached out and grabbed Eugene by the collar, causing Henrietta to give a little scream.

"Don't you *ever* speak to her that way," he said angrily, his face inches from Eugene's as he stared into his eyes, his breath coming fast, before he finally released him with a shake. Eugene's face had belied genuine fear when Clive grabbed him, but now it relaxed again into a precarious smirk as the sergeant approached to escort Henrietta out to the waiting room.

"Clive, don't hurt him," she begged, but Clive did not answer her, nor did he look back as the sergeant passed her to a waiting officer outside the room and then closed and locked the door.

Chapter 11

Eugene sat looking at him with affected disgust, but Clive could read the fear in his eyes. He had seen it countless times in this profession, sitting in just such a chair before a suspect.

"Can't a guy have a cigarette?" Eugene finally whined.

"Sergeant, do you have a cigarette you could lend this boy?" he asked.

"Yes, sir," the sergeant said, and after fumbling inside his uniform jacket, he stepped forward and handed Eugene a cigarette and matches. Clive waited for him to light it, noting the slight tremor in his hands as he did so. Eugene took a deep drag, holding the smoke in for as long as he could before blowing it out slowly.

"Start talking, kid," Clive said evenly.

"I don't want to," he said, leaning back with feigned confidence, his hands crossed in front of him.

"Look, set aside the dramatics," Clive said angrily. "This isn't my case. So you've got about fifteen minutes to spill your guts while you still have half a chance of me getting you out of this before O'Conner shows up. He's the detective that handles this precinct, and he's not the sharpest wit anymore, shall we say. No disrespect, sergeant," he said without turning around.

"None taken, sir," the sergeant answered dutifully from his post in the corner.

"This looks like a pretty open-and-shut case, on the surface, anyway, and I'm not so sure O'Conner's up to sifting through the shit for the truth. So unless you start talking, you're looking at about ten years in the slammer, kid."

Eugene took another taut drag of his cigarette, hesitating. "I didn't do it," he said finally.

Clive inclined his head. "Go on."

Eugene's eyes flicked to the sergeant in the corner. "It's difficult," he said thinly. "Does he have to be here?"

Clive wished to God he had his own sergeant, Jones, with him. As it was, he would have to do it alone. "Could you leave us, Sergeant?"

"Not really supposed to, sir."

"Just give me five."

"Okay, five minutes," he said begrudgingly and unlocked the heavy door and stepped outside.

"Why were you at the rectory in the first place?" Clive asked, wasting no time.

Eugene hesitated but then haltingly began. "I . . . Fr. Finnegan said I should come stay with him. That we could talk about a way to get me to stay in school and even beyond if I felt I had a vocation. He said I should stay with him for a while and he would tutor me, then I could take the seminary exam. I . . . he can be very persuasive," he said, looking at the ground and then back up at Clive, a challenge in his eyes—the very same challenge, Clive startlingly recognized, that he had seen from time to time in Henrietta's eyes as well. "He convinced Ma, said that there was plenty of food for me and that it would be one less person to feed, specially seeing how we must be strapped now for money with Henrietta off with . . ." he stopped abruptly and looked up at Clive.

"Do you actually want to go into the Church?" Clive asked directly.

"I don't know!" Eugene answered morosely. "That's the honest truth of it. I'm not sure."

"So what happened?"

Eugene was stubbornly silent again now, looking angrily at Clive as if trying to decide whether or not to defy him. Clive could feel the vibration from Eugene rapidly jiggling his leg under the table.

"Clock's ticking, kid. The sergeant will be back in a minute," Clive countered.

Eugene exhaled a thick cloud of smoke. "Nothin' happened at first," he acquiesced bitterly. "It's a nice house. Plenty of room. His cook, or whatever she is, made a big dinner. Later we sat in the front room talking."

"About what?"

"I don't know! I don't remember what . . . stupid things, really. But then it changed . . ." Eugene took another drag.

"Go on."

"He sat next to me . . . said he . . ." Eugene began, looking up furtively at Clive now. There were tears in his eyes, which he angrily wiped away. "Said he knew my secret and that I shouldn't be ashamed of it. That he had the same secret." He looked at the floor.

"Then what happened?" Clive asked calmly.

"He . . . he put his hand on my leg . . ." Eugene whispered. "I . . . I stood up, then. I . . . I didn't know what to think, what to do. I just wanted to leave. I made my way to the door; he tried to stop me, said he hadn't meant to scare me. I tried to get around him, but he said wait, that I'd forgotten my bag. He called for his cook to bring it, so I waited. I should've just left, but I stupidly didn't. It seemed like a long time, but then the cook came in with the bag and handed it to him. He said it felt awfully heavy and was there anything I wanted to tell him. I said no and I went to grab the bag, but he snatched it back first and opened it and then pulls out these two gold candlesticks. 'What have we here, Mrs. Kronovich?' he says to the cook."

"What was the cook's reaction?" Clive interrupted.

"She looked afraid. Afraid of him, I think. I don't even know if she understands English. He told her to go, and then he just looked at me. I told him I didn't take them, but he wouldn't believe me. He said that everyone gives in to temptation once in awhile and that I had just gone astray. Said I was in danger of being a bad seed ever since my father died, and this was just proof of it. He said then that there was no way around it now but to inform the authorities, that he had tried to help me, but it was no use. I begged him not to call the cops, but he just smiled. Said there was only one other way; if I agreed to be counseled by him, he would reconsider." He paused for a moment, the cigarette almost burned down to his fingertips now.

"And?"

"He . . . he put his hand on my shoulder. It seemed like he was going to . . ." he broke off, then.

"To what?"

"I don't know!" he said loudly. "All I know is that I pushed him. I just pushed him away," Eugene said, almost as if he couldn't believe it himself. "I grabbed the bag and ran out. I should have just left it there, but I wasn't thinking."

"And so he really did call the police," Clive said almost to himself. "I wouldn't have expected it."

"Fucking bastard," Eugene said, snuffing out the cigarette now.

"What's the secret, Eugene?" Clive asked steadily. "Answer me truthfully."

"Fuck off," Eugene said and looked at the ground again.

"You just don't do yourself any favors, do you, kid?" Clive said.

A commotion could be heard out in the hall, now, which Clive worriedly attributed to O'Conner's arrival, and he knew all would be lost in a moment. "Listen, Eugene," he said quickly. "O'Connor's going to take over now, but I'll try to get you out on bail in the morning." The voices outside were getting closer now. "Just deny everything," Clive said quietly, standing up and leaning toward him, his hands on the table. "Say you want a lawyer. I'll talk to the chief and see what I can do to get the charges dropped. It's hard with the Church, but he's got a connection."

"Don't leave me here!" Eugene whined.

"It's only one more night. Listen," Clive said, "when you get out of here, I'll arrange a job for you somewhere. You work at it one year, *faithfully*," he said, pointing a finger at him, "and contemplate this vocation of yours. If you're still serious about it, I'll help you."

Eugene nodded despondently, his eyes listless.

The door opened then and O'Conner's big bulk barged in.

"Well, what do we have 'ere?" he boomed out. "Little thief, eh?"

Clive bent close to Eugene and whispered, "One more thing. It's not a sin—your secret; remember that." Eugene did not respond but merely turned his head away. Clive stood up straight then to face Inspector O'Connor and asked respectfully, "Could I have a word, Inspector?"

"Certainly!" O'Connor boomed. "Though I think I can handle this case. Seems pretty straightforward," he said, walking back toward the door, Clive following him out.

"What happened?" Henrietta asked when they were back in the car together heading down California toward the Von Harmons' apartment. Clive had been contemplating how much of Eugene's story to share with her, and he still wasn't sure how forthcoming he should be.

"I don't think he did it," Clive said finally.

Henrietta breathed a sigh of relief. "What happened then?"

"I'm pretty sure this Fr. Finnegan set him up. I think he planted the candlesticks on him. I need to pay him a little visit tomorrow."

"But why would he do that? That doesn't make sense! Eugene's a favorite of his."

Clive let that comment sit for a few moments as he considered what to say next. He wanted to be honest with her, but how much should he reveal? It was a terribly inappropriate subject, one he didn't necessarily want to broach, but he saw no other way around it if Henrietta were to really understand the gravity of the situation and its many gray areas. Perhaps it would be for the best, really, if she knew. "Henrietta . . ." he began unsteadily, "I'm pretty sure Eugene's a deviant . . . a homosexual, that is."

He looked over at her, but she was just staring straight ahead at the road. He was completely unprepared, then, when she said quietly, "Yes, I thought he might be."

"How . . . how did you come to that conclusion?" he asked with narrowed eyes.

"Just a feeling, I suppose," she said, not looking at him. "Behind the bar you see all types. Your start to get a sense of who's who. And don't forget about Lucy," she said, chancing a glance at him now.

Ah, yes, he recalled. Lucy and her gang who had befriended Henrietta at the Marlowe. He had never asked her implicitly about what she had seen there in the dark corners of the dressing rooms, but perhaps he should, he mused. At any rate, he realized, this made Eugene's sticky situation easier to explain.

"What else?" she asked now.

"What do you mean?"

"What else did Eugene say?"

He looked over at her again and decided that he might as well reveal it all. "Well, from what Eugene has told me, it appears Fr. Finnegan suffers from the same affliction. He invited Eugene to the rectory to talk about his 'vocation,' and made an advance of some sort. Eugene pushed him away, apparently, and as he was attempting a quick getaway, Fr. Finnegan conveniently discovers two stolen candlesticks in his bag. Says he'll call the cops unless Eugene agrees to . . . well, you can guess the rest."

"My God! I can't believe it!" Henrietta said, disgusted. "I always knew there was something about Fr. Finnegan I didn't like," she muttered, as she turned to stare out the side window. Clive wished he could study her face, but it was impossible while driving in the dark. He was afraid he had upset her and was about to speak when she spoke first, still looking out at the darkness as she did so.

"Well, at least we know Eugene is innocent. Of the crime, at least," she said practically and turned to face Clive now. "But what are we going to do? No one will believe Eugene over Fr. Finnegan."

"Leave it to me," Clive said, grimly, though a certain relief came over him. He was once again impressed with her fortitude. "I intend to get the charges dropped. I have a few friends in high places, I should say. Meanwhile, I'll get Eugene out on bail in the morning."

"But what about this Inspector O'Connor that I saw going into the room? He looks like a brute!"

"I had a word. Told him I was a friend of the family, so he'll go easy. Just routine, no rough stuff."

"Oh, Clive, how can I ever thank you?"

"There's no need, Henrietta," he said genuinely. He stole another glance at her and was overcome, as he always was. Whenever he looked at her, his pulse maddeningly quickened. What was he to do with her?

When his mother had returned home to find Henrietta abruptly gone due to "troubles at home," as Clive had described it, he had perceived that she could not help but reveal her secret pleasure at the news. It was one thing he was not particularly fond of in his mother, her delight in the downfall of others. Fortunately, he was leaving soon to meet up with his father at the firm, so he was spared from having to listen to any lengthy speculations regarding Henrietta's troubles or to any derogatory comments about Henrietta herself. While his mother's whispered reports on the telephone seemed to have lessened somewhat this past week, he hadn't been sure whether this was due to a lack of examples and incidences of impropriety on Henrietta's part or if it was just that his mother had become more guarded in imparting them. His dreaded attendance at the board meeting today had at least saved him from having to listen to it all yet again from her this afternoon.

He sighed. That was another thing—the result of the meeting. He gave Henrietta another fleeting look.

As if she could read *his* mind now, she spoke just then. "Do you want to talk about the meeting?" she asked hesitantly. "Perhaps we could go somewhere and talk . . . the Lodge maybe? For old times' sake?"

It pained him to see her nervousness, and though he hated to dismiss her, he knew this was not the time or place. "It's late, Henrietta.

Let me take you home. I'm sure your mother and Elsie are still up, quite concerned about tonight's events."

"Yes, you're right, of course," she said, though he saw the disappointment in her face. "But we need to talk about it, Clive," she said, looking up at him tentatively.

"Yes. Agreed. I'm going to work on Eugene's case tomorrow. Then why don't I take you out? Properly." An idea had been forming in his mind since he had gotten her call this afternoon. "How about dinner at the Burgess Club?"

"Oh, Clive! Truly?"

His heart swelled at her sudden excitement.

"Oh," she said, suddenly deflated. "I didn't bring anything to wear."

"Yes, you did. I brought a case for you, remember? I made sure Andrews packed whatever you might need."

"Oh, Clive!" she beamed. "Thank you."

"Not at all," he said as they pulled up in front of the apartment.

A light drizzle had begun. Her excitement from just a moment ago evaporated. "I . . . I think I should go up alone, don't you?"

"Yes, of course." He would have liked to have spent more time with her, but in truth it *was* rather late, and he could sense he was not completely welcome up there, anyway. Slowly he came around to open the door for her. Gracefully she got out and hesitated in front of him. He was acutely aware that she wanted him to kiss her. Her obvious need was painful to him, and it took every ounce of strength not to take her in his arms and kiss her . . . hold her . . . please her in whatever way she desired, but he knew it would cloud the conversation he needed to have with her tomorrow night. He had made his decision.

"Why did you leave your things behind?" he asked, his eyes lingering on her.

She met his gaze. "I suppose because I didn't think they belonged to me."

He nodded slightly, taking this in. "Is that because you don't think you belong to Highbury? Or to me?" he asked quietly.

"There's always going to be a part of me that belongs to you," she said, before she could catch it. "I . . . I thought you would have known that." She paused, as if to say something more, and reached out a hand as if she were going to caress his cheek. But before she could do so, she pulled it slowly back. "Good night, Inspector," she said sadly and turned away.

"Good night, Miss Von Harmon," he said softly, hoping she could not see him trembling. The sight of her before him, so low and uncertain, almost crushed him. "Seven o'clock."

"Yes, I'll be ready," she said and, giving a faltering wave, disappeared into the building.

Chapter 12

When Clive arrived at seven o'clock the next evening, Henrietta was indeed ready for him. She had been delighted to find that Andrews had packed several beautiful things for her. Much too beautiful for the sparse apartment on Armitage, however, which had been another reason that Henrietta had left them behind. She hadn't wanted her family to see the evidence of her luxurious stay at Highbury. She had told them stories, granted, especially the boys, who marveled at her description of Mr. Howard's beautiful cars and the many rooms of the house, but she had purposefully left out much, especially if Ma was within earshot. In whispered moments, she had shared a bit more with Elsie—descriptions of the food, the flowers in every room, the library filled with books, even the gorgeous rose gardens, and Elsie had loved hearing it all, as if it were a story from a book. Naturally, then, when it was finally time for Henrietta to retreat to the bedroom to dress for her date with Clive, Elsie had followed closely behind and sat fingering the leather straps of the expensive case after Henrietta had unceremoniously heaved it onto the bed.

Henrietta had left most of the contents packed inside the case for a number of reasons. Firstly, she had wanted to keep it out of sight; secondly, there wasn't much room in the old armoire in the corner, the only repository for the whole family's clothes put together; and lastly, she supposed that there was some part of her that didn't want her stay here to seem permanent. Now, however, as she dressed for the night ahead, she had no choice but to finally, carefully, remove some of the beautiful things. Elsie watched, nearly spellbound, as Henrietta had pulled out one after another, truly happy for her sister and her obvious good fortune, oblivious to the fact that it could very well be in jeopardy, a feeling Henrietta had not been able to shake all day.

"Oh, Hen, that one's lovely," Elsie said almost worshipfully as she fingered the sleeve of a deep gold Schiaparelli gown. "Have you decided which one you're going to wear tonight with Mister . . . I mean, Clive?"

Henrietta laughed a little. "You sound like one of the maids when you say 'Mister Clive.'"

"What's it like having maids, Hen?" Elsie asked, as if she were asking about some exotic custom in a foreign country.

"Peculiar," Henrietta said as she unpacked several pairs of shoes, all different colors. "I didn't like it, actually. I was always trying to help them work, and I got in loads of trouble."

"Oh, Hen, that sounds like you!" Elsie laughed. "You never do quite fit in, do you?" Henrietta was struck by the truth of those words. She didn't fit in, here or there, now, it seemed.

"You can borrow any of them if you like," Henrietta said, gesturing toward the various skirts and gowns. Exactly how long did Clive expect her to stay away? Or was this a more permanent arrangement? she sadly wondered again. Well, if it was, she had only herself to blame.

"Oh, no, Hen! They wouldn't fit me, I don't think." Elsie was bigger boned than Henrietta, definitely taking more after their mother, while Henrietta had their father's looks. Still, Henrietta noticed since she had come home, Elsie seemed to be taking more of an interest in her appearance these days and guessed it had something to do with her relationship with Stan, which seemed to be intensifying. In the past, Henrietta had offered many times to help Elsie beautify herself, but to no avail. Elsie had never been interested, and, indeed, it was often a cause of strife between them. Now, however, Henrietta observed that Elsie had begun to try to style her hair a bit and had even taken to wearing clips to bed.

"How's it going with Stan, then?" Henrietta asked coyly.

"Oh, Hen!" Elsie blushed, though she couldn't help smiling. "Fine, I suppose."

"Seems more than fine to me," Henrietta teased.

"Well . . . can you keep a secret?"

Henrietta nodded encouragingly.

"Stan says he wants to marry me!" Elsie whispered excitedly.

"Marry you?" Henrietta exclaimed. "That's quite fast!" she said, though as soon as she said it, she realized how hypocritical it was, considering her own situation and her hasty acceptance of Clive. But hadn't their own alacrity perhaps resulted in a certain level of regret that they were currently mired in?

"Yes! Isn't it?" Elsie whispered gleefully, unaware of Henrietta's obvious meaning.

"Does Ma know?"

"No! No one does. It's not official, see. He hasn't *actually* asked me, just said that he's *going* to ask me—*probably*—at the proper time, he says."

"Oh! . . . Well, that's lovely, isn't it?" Henrietta said, thinking about how typical of Stan this particular approach was—slow and sure, covering all the bases.

"Hen? Can I ask you something?" Elsie said hesitantly after a moment's pause.

"Course you can," Henrietta said, slipping out of her cotton dress and stepping gingerly into a long black gown, which she had finally decided upon for this evening's rendezvous. She had already done her hair earlier in the day.

"Have you ever . . . have you ever kissed Clive?" Elsie asked, only looking briefly up at Henrietta before furtively looking away, her face a brilliant shade of red now.

Henrietta tried hard not to smile. "As a matter of fact, I have," she said confidingly.

"Do . . . do you think it's wrong?"

"Wrong? No," Henrietta said after a pause. "Not really. If it doesn't get carried away, that is," she said. She turned from Elsie under the guise of looking for the correct shoes so that Elsie wouldn't see her face. "Have you?" she asked finally, turning back toward her now.

Elsie nodded, still a bright shade of red. "Just the once, though."

"Did you like it?" Henrietta asked, her eyebrow arched. The thought of Stan in an amorous position only made her want to laugh.

"I did, Hen," she whispered. "Is that bad?" she asked, giving her a pleading sort of look as she tightly fingered the case's leather strap.

"No," Henrietta said gently. "It isn't bad. It's supposed to be that way. Just tell ole Stan to be careful."

"Careful?"

"You know, you don't want to end up in the family way."

"Oh, Hen! We would never do that!" Elsie said, genuinely shocked.

Henrietta smiled. "Somehow I believe you. Now, button me up, would you?"

Elsie got up off the creaky bed and helped her. "Oh, Hen! You look gorgeous!" she said when Henrietta turned back toward her. "Wait till Ma sees you!"

"That's what I'm worried about. Come on, better get it over with," she said, lifting the still partially-filled suitcase off the permanently sagging bed and shoving it back into the dusty space underneath.

Henrietta thought she detected at least a hint of admiration in Ma's eyes as she walked out into the front room. She was dressed in a Jeanne Lanvin black linen organdy dress, cut in the current mermaid style so that it hugged her curves beautifully. It was elegantly simple, adorned only with a plaid pattern of paillette embroidery giving way to an underdress of crepe de Chine. At her throat hung a gold-and-diamond pendant given to her by Mrs. Howard during her stay with them and which Andrews had packed securely in a separate pouch in the case. With it, of course, Henrietta wore black heels and black evening gloves. In short, she looked absolutely stunning. "Oh, Hen!" Elsie said, following her out and unable to stop her worshipful praise. "You look like a movie star! Doesn't she, Ma?"

"I suppose so," Ma said begrudgingly, sitting down heavily into the ratty armchair by the fire. "Don't think it's right, though, you going out and your brother just out of jail this morning." Eugene was currently asleep in the other room, having indeed been released just before noon, thanks to Clive's machinations. He had arrived home, sullen, of course, and after brusquely answering a few of Ma's questions, took himself off to bed and hadn't woken up yet.

"I don't see what that matters, Ma! He's in bed."

"All I know is that you're never here, and now that you are, you're off with *him* again. Don't you see enough of him already at Highbury?"

There it was again, Ma's use of the word *Highbury*, strengthening Mrs. Howard's theory that she really was perhaps the long-lost Martha Exley. Since that first luncheon together, Henrietta had wretchedly gone over and over Mrs. Howard's attempt at unraveling the mystery of Ma's past and had tried to come up with her own alternate explanation of things, but her theories had continued to come up empty and inadequate. Instead, what was surfacing was a whole new batch of wounded feelings, demanding her attention at the most inopportune moments, though her exploits with Helen and the missing ring over the last week or so, not to mention her troubles with Clive, had done their best to distract her. In truth, however, it hurt her immensely that not only had Ma kept her true identity hidden from them all these years, but that she had had to discover it through strangers—through the detached and condescending Mrs. Howard rather than from her own mother!

Now it made sense, though, why Ma had always rolled her eyes when Pa had told his stories of their aristocratic roots, which were surely an exaggeration, she still believed, even now. His grand story of their lost wealth was surely no more than a fanciful invention on his part, while Ma's had actually been real! But why had she never shared her story with them? Why not tell how she had given it all up for love? There was at least a romantic element there to be admired, if nothing else.

"Why did you do it, Ma?" Henrietta asked, sinking down onto the small divan opposite her mother. Elsie, intrigued, silently followed and stood behind the divan, watching Ma all the while. "Why did you run away from it all?" Henrietta continued.

"Run away from what?" Elsie asked, curious, but no one answered her.

For just a moment, Ma held Henrietta's gaze before she furtively looked over at Elsie, after which Henrietta perceived Ma's hesitation give way to defeat. It was impossible for her to keep up the pretense any longer. Her faced now revealed a strange mix of guilt and sadness as she looked away from Henrietta toward the window.

"I was very young," Ma said gradually. "When we ran away, I don't think I really understood what I was getting into," she added cryptically. "Not that it makes it any better."

"But why? Why did you run away from that life, from your family? Were you so much in love with Pa? Or was there something horrible there, something you couldn't face?" Henrietta asked, bracing herself for the answer, hoping it wasn't somehow what she herself was running directly into.

"I was pregnant," Ma said, looking back at Henrietta again. "With you."

Henrietta heard Elsie gasp behind her and whisper, "Oh, Ma!"

No one said anything for a few moments as the reality of this revelation sank in. Somehow some part of Henrietta's mind had guessed the truth before now, but she hadn't consciously understood it or believed it. Now that it was out in the open, however, any shock, any surprise or even pity that she might have felt gave way unexpectedly to the beginnings of anger as if the two of them had somehow switched roles and she were now the mother chastising the daughter, her mind flitting back over the years to all the arguments they had had. How dare Ma accuse her all these years about being too flirtatious, too affectionate, constantly doubting Henrietta's virtue, when all the while she had gotten herself pregnant! She simply couldn't tolerate the injustice of it, her hurt, angry feelings welling up inside of her like hot pokers.

"Oh, Ma!" she finally blurted out. "How could you? How could you blame me all these years of being loose, when you . . . you . . ."

"Oh, Hen!" Elsie exclaimed, timorously sitting down beside Henrietta as if she would any moment need to arbitrate.

"I'm sorry, Henrietta!" Ma said in a rare moment of apology, her usual angry facade beginning to crumble away. "I don't know why I am the way I am with you. Why I said all those things. I guess I was afraid the same thing might happen to you. You being so much more beautiful, so much more confident than I ever was . . ." her voice trailed off as she held her head in her hands.

"What happened, Ma?" Elsie asked faintly.

Ma remained silent, her hands covering her face, the two girls just looking at her until she finally looked up at no one in particular, her shoulders hunched. "It's true that I am an Exley, as I'm sure you've heard by now," she said quietly. "As the only daughter, I was supposed to marry well, but no one ever seemed that interested, despite the money they would have received as a dowry. I hated those parties that my parents held to try to foist me off onto some contemptible man who would have me for the money. It just made me feel big and awkward, and I soon began to despise myself and everyone else, too." She glanced up at Elsie, as if it were too painful to look at Henrietta. "The only one that was ever nice to me was Les."

"Who *was* he?" Henrietta asked. "Was he really one of these Von Harmons from Europe that the Howards are going on about?"

"I really don't know. Maybe. He certainly thought he was. That was the thing about Les. Always puffing himself up, always had everyone believing he was more than he really was. He fooled me, anyway," she said despondently.

"How did you meet him?" Henrietta asked, her mind still trying to take it all in.

Ma took a deep breath. "He was the butcher's delivery boy. I used to see him when he came to the back door. I used to spend a lot of time in the kitchen. The cooks were kind to me, kinder than my parents or my awful nanny, actually. Maybe that was why I was always so big." Her eyes looked sad as she said this. "Les always had a smile for me. He was kind, and I started to look forward to seeing him. I started to make sure I was in the kitchen when he came for a delivery. One day he came back later, in the afternoon. Said he forgot something, and, well, one thing led to another . . . and I ended up pregnant," she said sadly.

"Oh, Ma," Elsie repeated. "You must have been terrified."

"I was. I didn't know what to do. I didn't know about such things, really. When they eventually realized what had happened, my parents wanted me to go out East with relatives and give the baby away, but I just couldn't leave Les. I told him, finally, that I was pregnant, and he just laughed. Laughed!" Ma said, her old bitterness creeping back into her voice. "His very words were, 'Well, I suppose we should get ourselves married, then.' That was it. That was my proposal. At the time, though, I just wanted to get away. And he offered a way out. I didn't think what it would mean." Ma shifted in her chair and gestured around the apartment. "Turns out, this is what it meant."

"You regret it, don't you?" Henrietta asked.

"Of course I regret it!" she said angrily, and Henrietta felt herself wince. "The alternative was probably worse, though," Ma said, her tone instantly shifting to one of defeat. "I've tried not to think about it over the years, as it wouldn't change anything. I know I was cruel to him in the end, but he deserved it."

"Deserved it?" Henrietta could not stop herself from asking. "Why?"

"Oh, what would you know about it?" Ma said fiercely and then began to cry.

"It's okay, Ma," Elsie said tenderly as she reached over and rubbed her arm. Ma pulled away from her touch, however, leaving Elsie to awkwardly gather her hands back into her lap.

"Well, didn't you ever try to go back? Or didn't they ever try to find you?" Henrietta asked, a part of her still unbelieving that this could have happened to her mother.

"Oh, yes, they did," Ma said, looking up and wiping the corner of her eyes with her apron. "I was too stubborn, though. Too proud. At first it was exciting to be with Les in our own place, away from all the snobbery of my past life. All the rules and niceties that must be relentlessly observed, but it grew tiresome after a while, the poverty, that is. Les tried his best to provide, I'll give him that, but the babies kept coming, sinking us further and further. My father found me just after you were born," she said, looking at Henrietta. "Came round while Les was at work and saw me in my squalor. He offered to take me back if I would quietly divorce Les, or at least separate from him, but I refused. When he saw that I would not be persuaded, he begged me to at least give him the baby." Ma's eyes flicked back to Henrietta now. "Let them give her all the advantages I couldn't in the life I had chosen, he said. Told me that it would be unfair on the baby to let it live in squalor when they could give her everything. But I couldn't do it. I wouldn't give him the satisfaction." Ma looked utterly defeated now, her proud armor having fallen away completely, and it was painful to see the wrinkled shell that was left. A tear ran down the side of Henrietta's face, and she moved to brush it away. Ma shrugged then and looked up at Henrietta. "Maybe it was wrong. I don't know."

Henrietta grasped her hand. She managed to hold it for a moment before Ma pulled it weakly away. "Of course it wasn't wrong, Ma. I wouldn't have wanted that life, away from all of you," she said soothingly and was immediately struck by the poignancy of her words. As a myriad of thoughts went through her mind, it occurred to her how very old Ma looked now sitting across from her.

"He told me that it was my last chance," Ma went on, apparently not yet finished with her tale. "That he would cut me off if I persisted in my stubbornness, but I wouldn't relent. He left then. I can still remember it. The light was growing dim, and I hadn't yet lit the lamps. He stood in the doorway." She gestured with her hand toward the door as if it were the same one. "He turned back, one last time. 'Please, Martha. See reason' is what he said to me, and he looked at me with such pain . . . but I was angry and I shook my head, like a child, though I suppose I still *was* a child, in a way. Then he turned and left. That was the last time I saw him. My parents kept their word, and I've kept mine."

Ma stood up now, wiping her eyes again, and walked to the window, staring out at nothing in particular. "Do you see now why it's a perverse sort of irony that you're to end up there, anyway? I suppose it was meant to be. Maybe what God wanted all along, and I just stood in the way."

Henrietta longed to go over and embrace her, but she was afraid she would be rebuffed. "Oh, Ma," Henrietta said sadly from where she sat. "I never knew. I'm sorry."

"I couldn't believe it when you told us you were engaged to a Howard," Ma continued as if Henrietta hadn't spoke. "Some sort of justice, I suppose. Now they can all see how low I've been brought," she said, gesturing at her frumpy body. "The prodigal daughter returning."

"Well, Mrs. Howard says that—" Henrietta began, but Ma snipped her off.

"I don't care what Antonia Howard has to say, about anything, really," she barked, looking over at Henrietta, a vestige of her cold, sad bitterness for life momentarily surfacing despite the outpouring of her tale.

"But I . . ."

She was interrupted again by a knock on the door. Both she and Elsie jumped, and Henrietta glanced up at the mantle clock. Five minutes past seven! "That must be Clive!" she said, standing up hurriedly and patting her hair in place. She had meant to meet him downstairs. Ma shuffled toward the bedroom. "I don't want to see *him* right now," she said angrily, wiping her eyes again.

"Ma! Shhh!" Elsie said, fretfully following her. "He'll hear!"

"Ma! Don't you want to thank him for helping Eugene?" Henrietta asked, incredulous, Clive having judiciously not accompanied Eugene up to the apartment earlier today.

"Not now," Ma said, wearily.

"Ma!"

"I'm grateful, Henrietta. I really am, but I can't face anyone just now. Thank him for me, won't you? Please?"

There was another soft knock now.

"Just a minute!" Henrietta called out toward the door. "Well, good-bye then, Ma," she said, clearly upset. She felt a desperate longing then to embrace her mother, but she knew it was futile.

"Just be sure. Sure about your choice," Ma said before disappearing into the bedroom, a lifetime's habit of restraining herself from physical affection impossible to overcome, even now, despite the intimacy just shared.

Elsie paused before following her in. "Don't worry," she whispered to Henrietta. "You have a good time. I'll look after her."

"Thanks, Els,"

"Good luck," she smiled and disappeared with Ma into the bedroom, just as Henrietta opened the front door to greet Clive, brushing back a few stray tears before he could see.

Chapter 13

The members-only Burgess Club sat squarely on Michigan Avenue and had done since 1854, just as the city was becoming truly civilized and a new social elite was emerging with it. It was a gentleman's club of the highest order, though the lounge and dining room were open to mixed company in the evenings. Its staid, quiet interior had an air of old-worldliness to it with its deep wood paneling and heavy beams running across the intricate plastered ceiling. Thick pewter fixtures throughout completed the formalness. Even many of the couples that sat now in the Kensington room seemed to match the stateliness of the surroundings and were indeed of a more mature set, though there was a sprinkling of young couples as well, flaunting martinis and the latest cocktails, despite the concentrated efforts of the powers that be to keep out the nouveau riche. The small orchestra was old-fashioned, too, in its predilection for quiet waltzes, making it unlikely that the latest jazz or big band hits would be heard in these hallowed halls.

As the maître d' held her chair for her, Henrietta sat down carefully across from Clive, trying not to stare too conspicuously at the beautiful tables. Everything was so elegant—the crisp linen, the flickering candles in their crystal settings, gorgeous bouquets of roses everywhere, even the gleaming silver. She nervously glanced over at

Clive, who was perusing the wine list now, as a waiter stood at attention nearby.

He had been quiet on the ride over, as had she, though her thoughts were roiling in on themselves in an endless stew of emotion. When he did speak, Clive mostly talked of Eugene's case and related what details he knew about O'Connor's questioning of him, the terms of his bail, and how Fr. Finnegan had thus far managed to elude his attempts to question him. Clive took her silence as concern for Eugene and rushed on to explain how he had a couple of leads on employment for him and the "deal" he had struck with him at the station last night.

Henrietta had merely nodded and absently thanked him as she tried desperately to sort out her emotions. While she was of course concerned about Eugene and his welfare, she was in truth preoccupied with what Ma had revealed just as Clive had come to fetch her. She had gotten pregnant! With *her*, she thought sadly. Is that why they never seemed to get along? Not only did she remind Ma too much of Pa, but she had been the inadvertent cause of Ma's subsequent descent into misery. No wonder Ma never seemed to like her all that much. She simultaneously represented everything Ma was not and everything she had lost.

As she watched the buildings around them grow taller the closer they got to downtown, Henrietta wondered if she had potentially lost all as well. She stole a glance at Clive, but it was impossible to tell what he was thinking. He had seemed so cold in the car yesterday on the way to and from the police station, and he still wasn't overly attentive, merely cordial, she would say. His eyes had quickly traveled over her body and her exquisite Lanvin dress when she had opened the door of the apartment to him, and she perceived the attraction in his eyes as he stood there. She had also felt the heat from his fingers, briefly grazing her shoulders, as he had politely wrapped her in her borrowed velvet stole.

Even now, seated across from him, she caught his eyes linger on the low-cut bosom of the dress, though he distractedly looked away whenever her eyes caught his. She knew that look, the look of desire in men's eyes, but she knew that desire alone wasn't enough for a man like Clive. Suddenly she was very tired of being in suspense, tired of wondering what had happened at the board meeting, of wondering what his answer to them had been, of wondering what, if any, future they had together. Though if he were really having second thoughts about her or about Highbury, she surmised, why take her to such an exquisite place? Why not just tell her last night in the car? Or was this merely some sort of farewell gesture driven perhaps by guilt? If he didn't speak soon, she would have to! She thought she might crack with the strain of not knowing.

She waited as he ordered for them and instructed the waiter to bring a bottle of Dom Perignon to begin with. He handed the wine list back to the waiter, and rather than look at her, he distractedly looked out at the dance floor, seeming to watch several couples waltz as he absently (or was it irritably?) tapped his fingers on the table. There was nothing for it! She would have to speak, she told herself, and cleared her throat, the sound of which drew his attention back to her.

"Clive . . ." she began.

"Yes?" he asked, leaning forward a bit.

"I . . . I just wanted to say what a beautiful place this is," she faltered.

"Yes, it is, isn't it?" Clive said, a trace of disappointment in his voice. He looked around as if really seeing the club for the first time. "We've been members for time in memoriam," he grinned. "Certainly from its founding, anyway. My great grandfather had a hand in financing it, I believe. On my mother's side, that is. She was a Hewitt—cousins, I think, to the Carnegies."

"Oh, I see." Henrietta didn't know what else to say. "Do they live around here? Your mother's family, that is? Or up by Highbury?" she asked tentatively, as if *Highbury* was a sensitive word between them now.

Clive smiled. "Here? No. They're all on the East Coast. Long Island. Newport."

Henrietta merely nodded, remembering now what Helen had told her.

"I'm very rich," he said, looking at her steadily as he leaned back.

"I gathered," Henrietta said, meeting his eyes.

"I just want you to know . . . know everything."

"I see."

"Henrietta . . ." he said, shifting uncomfortably.

"Yes?" She could feel her palms beginning to perspire through her black gloves.

"I—" but he was interrupted by the waiter, who appeared now and presented the bottle of champagne for Clive's approval. Clive nodded, and the waiter bowed obsequiously before popping the cork and then elaborately pouring a small taste in Clive's glass. When Clive nodded again, the waiter replied, "Very good, sir," and began to delicately fill both their glasses, Henrietta making a study of the roses on the table rather than having to look directly at Clive while he did so. It seemed to take the waiter an insufferably long time to then wrap a linen cloth around the neck of the bottle and adjust it perfectly in a silver bucket of ice near the table before he finally left them in peace.

"To us," Clive said, holding up his glass and clinking it against hers as she held it up, watching her all the while. Henrietta tried to read what is in his eyes, but it was impossible.

"Is there an us?" Henrietta dared to ask with forced casualness, taking a sip of her champagne to steady herself. She saw some emotion cross his face, but she couldn't tell what it was.

Clive cleared his throat as he set his glass down gently. "I suppose that depends on you," he said.

Henrietta did not quite understand his meaning and took in a sharp breath in anticipation of what he might say next.

"Henrietta," he said deliberately, "you told me yesterday that you release me from this engagement." He fingered his glass, looking down at it. "Is that true; do you still hold to that?" he asked, looking up at her now.

Henrietta slowly exhaled. It was as she feared, and she felt a rising sense of panic. As she looked into his hazel eyes, now, though—the first thing she had noticed about him at the Promenade—they seemed large and vulnerable, and she felt an exquisite love for him despite the tearing of her heart. She had no wish in this moment to hold on to him, no wish to hurt him more than she already had. "Yes, I do still hold to that, Clive. I have no wish to hold you where you do not wish to be held. I do release you if . . . if that's what you want." She found it difficult to keep her voice from wavering and took another sip of champagne to steady the slight tremor in her hand.

"I see," he said quietly with a slight tilt of his head. "Then I do accept your release, Miss Von Harmon, as Inspector Clive Howard of the Chicago police."

Henrietta bit her lip, hoping to hold back the flood of tears that were welling up ferociously. She didn't know where to look. She couldn't bear to look at him, so she simply looked down at her blurry hands.

Clive began again, his voice surprisingly wavering a bit, "But I *do* ask you, as Clive Alcott Linley Howard, esquire of Highbury Estate, Winnetka, to be my wife . . . if you will have me, that is."

His words took several moments to register to Henrietta as she sat trying to wipe her tears before they completely ruined her face. She looked up slowly now, as she began to understand his meaning.

"Oh, Henrietta, please don't cry," he said, deftly pulling out his handkerchief and handing it to her.

"Clive," she whispered as she gingerly wiped her eyes. "Are you sure?"

"Quite sure," he said, smiling freely now, lovingly. "But before you answer, you should hear everything I have to say."

Her eyes searched his, waiting.

"When I met with the board yesterday, it was as I suspected. They claim they will not approve of Father's eventual resignation—as if they really have that power," he scoffed. "But leave that for now. They claim they will not accept Father's resignation unless I agree to take his place." He took a long drink of champagne. "I accepted," he said evenly, looking directly at her. "I cannot run away from my duty forever, Henrietta. The police force was a refuge for me, oddly, for a time, a time when I most needed a distraction. I see that now. Sifting through other people's misery to escape my own. But enough is enough. The future . . . our future, I hope . . . is at hand. It's time I took up my real responsibilities. Not right away, of course—Father's still actively running the company—but soon, I should imagine. In the next few years, probably." He looked at her apprehensively and took another drink of his champagne. "So now you know the whole of it. No secrets. No hiding who I really am or who I must eventually be. If you say yes now, you know, at least in part, enough to make a decision about whether you want to spend your life with me, knowing it to be what it is, knowing what you will have to sacrifice. Your family will be provided for, if they will accept help, so do not base your decision on that score, either. It comes down to this, Henrietta, my darling," he said, taking her hand now across the table, "whether you love me, *this* me, enough to accept my hand and all that goes with it."

Hot tears welled up in Henrietta's eyes again. She did not have to deliberate. She already knew that she wanted this man sitting across from her no matter what she had to endure to be with him, that she wanted to share—no, *give* her life to him. She opened her mouth to speak, but no words would come out. She tightened her grasp on his hand and nodded.

"Is that a yes, then?" he almost laughed.

"Yes, I will marry you, Clive Howard of Highbury," she said finally and couldn't help but give a little laugh, too. "Oh, Clive, I love you so. You've no idea how happy you make me," she said, gazing at him, her heart near to bursting. Ma had told her to be sure, and she was. She had never been so sure.

Beaming now, Clive released her hand and removed a small velvet box from the pocket of his dinner jacket. He opened it slowly and took out a ring with a diamond bigger than any she had ever seen, set amongst a nest of emeralds. He held out his hand to her, palm up, and timidly she laid her hand in his. Slowly and with extreme gentleness, he pulled off her glove and grasped her small, naked hand in his. "This is a very old ring that has been passed down through the generations of the Howard family," he explained. "I asked my mother for it yesterday to give to you properly as behooves the future mistress of Highbury. She gave it to me freely, with no hesitation," he said, his eyebrow arched and a knowing look on his face, as if to indicate that there would be no obstacle on that front. "Henrietta Von Harmon," he said now, gently putting pressure on the ring and slowly sliding it down her finger, "with this ring, I ask you to be my wife. I promise to be a faithful husband to you, forsaking all others, and cherishing you with my life."

Two tears escaped Henrietta's eyes despite her best efforts to corral them. "Oh, Clive," she managed to say. "It's simply beautiful," was all she could get out, afraid that if she continued she would begin to openly cry.

"I love you, Henrietta. Make no mistake," Clive said softly, his head tilted to the side in a manner Henrietta had come to love.

Henrietta could find no words to say, but instead sat gazing at him, her mind whirling. So it was true, she thought. He did love her! Loved her enough to marry her despite her obvious unsuitability and her poverty, despite even the shameful actions of her father and now her brother.

"Next week is the engagement party," he went on. "And that's for my mother. But tonight is *our* night. That's why I've brought you here in particular, hoping of course that you would say yes."

"It's very lovely," Henrietta said, wiping her tears and smiling at him gratefully.

"And on that note, a dance is in order. A *real* dance," he added, answering an uncertainty between them that stretched all the way back to the Promenade. "Shall we?" he asked, ignoring the waiter, who had just now brought the first course.

"But what about the food?" Henrietta asked, smiling through her tears.

"It will keep. We won't have this moment again; let's take it," he said, pulling her up and leading her to the dance floor. "Tales from the Vienna Woods" by Strauss was being played, and Clive masterfully led her amidst the few other couples on the floor. He held her very close, his fingers on the small of her back, and she felt she could barely breathe, such was her intoxication for him.

They held each other for the first part of the dance, not needing to speak, happy merely in each other's arms. But at one point, Clive did pull back to look at her. "You do realize what you're getting yourself into, don't you?"

"I have a fair idea," she smiled.

"I need you to stand at my side and be the woman that I know you really are. No more sulking, no more tears. Your role as the petulant child must end," he said, giving her a serious look.

"Am I being scolded?" she asked demurely, running a finger along the side of his face.

"Indeed, you are," he tried to say gravely, but he couldn't help but smile. "No more discussions about whether you're good enough or some such silly notion. I'm the future master of Highbury, and I'm telling you that you are."

"And am I to be ruled by you?"

"In matters such as these, yes, you are to be ruled by me," he said sternly. Before she could react, though, he went on in a much softer tone. "As my wife, however, you are my equal, nay, my superior," he whispered, "in all the ways that matter, that is."

He bent, then, and kissed her despite their public forum, Henrietta's heart beating fast. She was overcome with happiness, much more than when she had hesitantly said yes to his proposal that night in Humboldt Park. She had been attracted to him then, even loved him perhaps, but not so deeply as she did now. She knew now so much more about him, knew his struggles and his burdens, his tenderness and his love for her. And, more importantly, he had perceived that there was more to her than the young girl hiding bravely behind a risqué costume and an accompanying wink and a smile. She knew that he wanted the truest part of her, the part that no man had yet discovered, and she loved him utterly for it. And she had accepted him, accepted his hand and Highbury, and now she must be equal to it, she resolved, as they glided to the last strains of the waltz. There was no more reason to second-guess herself anymore. It fleetingly occurred to her, however, as the dance ended and Clive led her back to their table where their food sat cold, that just as Ma had run from the North Shore for love, she was running to it for the very same reason . . . but she managed to push this thought away.

From there the evening evolved readily, possessing as it did so its own peculiar rhythm of time, moments of it slowing down to the point of solidification to be caught forever in the amber of memory, even as minutes and then hours unnaturally rushed by, expiring before they could catch and hold them all. They were both of them almost giddy in their happiness, barely touching any of the food put before them, preferring to spend most of the night in each other's arms, dancing, or talking in whispers about what the future might hold, feeling perhaps for the first time that they were finally on the same path.

Henrietta never wanted this night to end, so beautiful, so perfect was it, knowing instinctively, despite her young age, that very few such nights come along in a lifetime. Eventually, however, they both sensed it was time to leave, they being one of only three couples left in the whole of the dining room, the staff yawning in the background and the orchestra winding down now. Reluctantly, then, they finally made their way down to the quaint lobby, lit only by candlelight, and waited for the Alfa Romeo to be brought round. Henrietta sighed.

"Thank you, Inspector, for such a lovely evening," she said, slipping her arm through his.

"Still *Inspector*, is it?" he grinned.

"You'll always be the inspector to me," she said. "It will be my special name for you," she smiled up at him, and he held her hand up to his lips to kiss it. "Are you at least a little happy about taking over your father's firm?" she asked wistfully. "I couldn't bear it if you're not as supremely happy as I am at this moment."

"I'll be happy no matter what I'm doing as long as I have you," he said, his eyes heavy with happiness.

"But won't you miss being a detective, even just a little?" she asked.

"Perhaps a bit . . . but, in truth, I—"

"Your car, sir," said one of the doormen, approaching, and whatever Clive was about to say was dropped as they stepped out into the warm July night. One of the valets then opened the car door for Henrietta, and she slid in as Clive came around to the driver's side, lightly slipping the valet some cash as he did so.

"Thank you, my good man," he said.

"Not at all, sir. Have a good evening."

There was barely any traffic on the abandoned streets as Clive slowly pulled away from the Burgess Club. As they picked up speed, they were content in the warm silence that lay between them now, each abandoning themselves to their own thoughts. For the moment, all of Henrietta's problems were comfortably pushed to the side by the largess of happiness that had come upon her, though a part of her ached at the thought of having to separate now. She longed for the night to continue on, not wanting the spell to be broken, and an idea suddenly occurred to her, then.

"Did Catherine live at Highbury?" Henrietta asked hesitantly, breaking the silence.

Clive let out a deep breath as if not expecting this subject. "Yes, she did," he answered dutifully. "It made the most sense, since I was going away to the war," he said, glancing over at her.

"So you didn't have your apartment, then?"

"No, that wasn't until I returned."

"May I see it?"

"What, now?" he asked, surprised, his eyebrow arched with a smile. "Isn't it a bit late?"

"I might not ever have another chance. And anyway, don't you think you should introduce me to Katie?" she asked, referring to his dog.

"Clancy's got her for the night."

"I see."

"Well, perhaps for just a nightcap," he offered. "I can't keep you out too late or your mother's low opinion of me will drop even further," he said with a wry smile and steered the car in the direction of his apartment rather than back north to Logan Square.

Henrietta was surprised at both the sparseness of the place as well as its relative tidiness. It was merely a small apartment above a tobacco shop with just a few rooms, the smell of cedar and tobacco lingering heavily in the air. She had tried to imagine Clive's place many times in her mind, but it was nothing like what she had expected, as she stood just inside the door, looking around as she removed her gloves, one of them catching a bit on the heavy diamond ring now on her finger. As Clive took her stole to hang it, she looked around for any intimation of personality, but there was sadly not much to lend itself to an interior view of Clive's mind or soul. There was a bookcase on one wall with some books, mostly military history, she noted, and a radio nearby. Still, it was clean, but it made her sad to think of him coming back here each night; it seemed a lonely place.

"Champagne or cognac?" Clive called from the kitchen now.

"Do you always have champagne on hand?" she asked, amused.

"I've found it best to be prepared," he called back. "You never know when Clancy might stop over for a nip."

Henrietta laughed.

"Which one?" Clive called again.

"Champagne, please," she answered. "Need any help?"

"I've got it," he said and appeared a few moments later with a bottle in one hand and two glasses held precariously in the other. "Excuse the informality," he said, holding them up slightly with a shrug.

"What, no butler?"

He laughed. "I have an old Irish lady that comes in and cleans, but that's about it, I'm afraid." He handed her a glass and began to pour. "So, what do you think? Not as exciting as you thought, is it?"

"I must admit, no," she smiled, taking a sip. "Have your parents been here?"

"Only once," Clive said, pouring himself a glass. "Mother was appalled, of course. But let's not talk about them; it's frightfully tiresome."

"If you insist," she smiled.

"Please," he said, gesturing toward the worn leather-buttoned divan. "Sit down." He set down his glass on a small side table and went to switch on the radio, Guy Lombardo and his Royal Canadians coming through on *Your Hit Parade.*

Clive loosened his tie and looked over at Henrietta now as he perched himself carefully at the edge of the divan, his heart fluttering. He had done what he had set out to do, and she had accepted him, accepted Highbury. He felt his heart swell in his chest with love for her and was determined to keep her safe. He would never let what happened to Catherine happen to her. He didn't mean to go through that heartache ever again unless he was old and doddering and both of them were ready to leave this world for a different one. He sat back now, praying he could control himself. It was dangerous, he knew, to have brought her here with no chaperone, no servants to inadvertently interrupt them. He would have to be strong.

Henrietta had leaned back as well, letting her eyes delightfully close as she listened to the next song that had come on, "Two Sleepy People" by Hoagy Carmichael. It was one of her favorites. When she opened them again, Clive was staring at her, his head leaning against his fist, his elbow propped against the back of the couch. Her heart began to beat fast just looking at him watch her, though she was conscious of feeling a bit tipsy. Why did Clive not seem to be? she wondered. He was so awfully handsome, she thought. Had she been a fool all these years to keep her virtue intact when her own mother had gotten herself pregnant with a butcher's delivery boy? Had she been wrong not to give in to Clive? He had said just tonight that he needed her to be a *woman*, not a petulant child; isn't that what he had said? She wanted so very much to show him that she could be the woman she knew he desired. She could see it in his eyes. And there was something about giving herself to him here, in this place that belonged only to him.

Her breath was coming fast now as she timidly reached up and cupped his cheek in her hand, surprised by the stiff stubble that was there now. His eyes closed briefly at her touch, and tenderly, he covered her hand with his. Slowly he leaned forward to kiss her then, the scent of him as he neared driving her mad. He was gentle at first, barely caressing her lips with his own, but then he grew more passionate, almost desperate, as if he were abandoning all caution as he kissed her lips, her cheek, the tender place behind her ear.

Henrietta's heart raced as his kisses traveled down her neck now, lingering briefly where the gold-and-diamond pendent nestled in the hollow of her throat, and she trembled when his fingers deftly reached inside the top of her bodice and began to trace the curve of her breast. She murmured faintly as he shifted his weight, pressing her back as he kissed her until she was lying flat. He was on top of her now, and she felt on fire as he continued to cover her neck and bare shoulders with kisses, moving slowly downward until he came to the soft swell between her breasts. He kissed the tops of them, inching lower with each kiss and sending shivers through her. Urgently he fumbled with the folds of her dress, pulling them up and reaching beneath. She felt his hand travel up her leg, and she arched toward him.

Suddenly he stopped, however, breathing hard. "Henrietta, we shouldn't . . ."

"I . . . I want you to . . ." she whispered, though deep down she was terrified.

"Do you trust me?" he said hoarsely, his eyes searching hers deeply.

"Yes," she answered softly.

"Completely?"

Her breath was so rapid now from either fear or desire that she could no longer speak; she could only give a tiny nod.

He searched her eyes again desperately, wildly, and then finally looked away, shuddering painfully. With a heavy groan he slowly sat back, running his hand through his wavy hair. Gently he pulled her up to sit beside him. "I can't take advantage of you, of the trust you've placed in me," he sighed. "Good God," he almost shouted, "but I want you so much, so very badly, Henrietta. I'm afraid of how much I need you," he said, almost in agony, his voice wavering.

"But . . . we're to be married," Henrietta said modestly, adjusting the top of her dress slightly and feeling deeply humiliated.

"All the more reason I should honor you as would be fitting of my wife."

Henrietta wasn't sure what to say and sat despondently looking down at her hands. Clive reached out and took one of them. "It isn't you; you know that, don't you, darling? My God, it isn't you. Just looking at you makes me tremble; the thought of touching you," he whispered, "of being intimate with you is almost too much for me to bear. And yet I must bear it for your sake. I am honor-bound to bring you to the altar unsullied, even by me."

Henrietta was still looking at her lap when he put his fingers lightly to her chin and drew her gaze to him. "But I feel very deeply what you were willing to give," he said and kissed her then. She leaned into him, resting her head against his chest.

"I love you, Clive Howard."

"I love you, too, Henrietta."

Chapter 14

The next week found Henrietta back at Highbury, the big day for the engagement party almost at hand.

At Clive's insistence, though, she had spent a few days at home before returning to Highbury. He hoped, he had said, that it would give the Von Harmons a chance to be together after Eugene's release and time for Henrietta to spend with her mother, whom, he assumed, must feel her absence rather acutely. Perhaps this was so, Henrietta had thought wryly, but she no longer cared that much.

Ma's revelation about her past was having a strange effect on her. Her first reaction, of course, had been a deep sense of pity for this woman and how fate had cruelly used her, but as time went on, Henrietta found that instead of eliciting more sympathy or compassion in her heart, Ma's story was becoming more a source of anger to Henrietta than anything else. She found herself blaming Ma now for almost everything . . . their father's death . . . their miserable poverty . . . even the shame she had felt over the years for her beauty and her attractiveness to men. Ma had made her feel this way, she reasoned, and she had had no right to! And naturally she blamed Ma for losing her virtue with her father; the fact that she herself had attempted to do the very same with Clive in his apartment just a few nights ago made her indignation burn doubly bright with embarrassed guilt.

Her anger took her by surprise, however, and she wasn't particularly proud of it, but try as she might, she just couldn't bring herself to forgive Ma. Not after everything that had happened. It was obvious that all of their problems went back to Ma, and Henrietta found Ma's stupid stubbornness now regarding her engagement to one of the Howards and the subsequent party that was nearly upon them almost too much to bear.

Bitingly she asked Ma what she planned to do when the wedding rolled around, if she would excuse herself from that as well, secretly suspecting that she just might. Ma's tired response was that she would cross that bridge when she came to it. This was a new type of response from Ma, one of abject apathy, and though it annoyed Henrietta just as much, it unsettled her, perhaps because it was unfamiliar and because she therefore had no known tactics in place yet with which to navigate it. Since Ma had confessed her past, the sting seemed to have gone out of her normally acerbic comments. She was becoming less and less a creature of ferocity as the days went on and more a creature of a broken sort, still occasionally lashing out, but with claws much duller and useless now. This in and of itself should have slaked Henrietta's bitterness, but instead it seemed to fuel it.

For the few days she remained at home, Henrietta could not shake her bad mood, the heated, pointless conversations with Eugene not particularly helping. He spent most of his time in the bedroom, Ma and Elsie doting on him, or out walking, he claimed, half the day and night. Henrietta tried to put aside her feelings and her shame regarding Eugene's situation until perhaps after the party, when she hoped to have more time to think about it. He was still not free and clear, though she knew Clive was working on getting the charges dropped.

Something else, however, was nagging Henrietta, but she couldn't quite name it, though it, too, had an aroma of guilt to it. Guilt perhaps that she was taking up the life Ma had abandoned. It felt fundamentally wrong somehow, as if Ma's apparent sacrifice had meant nothing, but what else could she do? She was about to make the same one. She was about to sacrifice her own family for another one, for love, just as Ma had, but it hadn't really turned out for Ma, she kept reminding herself. Ma had abandoned wealth and privilege for her father and her, and now her father was dead at his own hand and she herself was running back to Ma's old life, a different sort of wayward daughter, which seemed to invalidate Ma's painful choice in the space of an instant. Henrietta was sure now of her decision, sure of wanting to be Clive's wife, but being here around Ma, simmering in this emotional stew, made her cross and impatient.

When Clive finally came to pick her up, she was sadly glad to get away. The sight of Jimmy and the twins crying as she got into the car grasped at her heart, but it had to be done. Bravely she waved goodbye to them, the false smile on her lips perhaps just a little too obvious.

She was eternally grateful that it was Clive driving her and not Jack, not wanting to be alone with Jack for that long. It wasn't that Henrietta didn't trust him, or herself for that matter, but she did not wish to mar the new understanding she had with Clive, their new beginning, as it seemed in her mind. The time for childishness was over now, she told herself. No more secret rendezvous with the staff, no nighttime cups of cocoa. No mention was made as to what had occurred between them in Clive's apartment, but Clive seemed all the more tender and loving as they headed north in his car, the crowded buildings of the city giving way to the more open landscape of the little towns beyond, mirroring Henrietta's own drifting thoughts.

The sky was a brilliant blue, with not even one stray cloud, and the farther they got from the city, the more Henrietta's musings on her problems at home gave way to musings about her problems at Highbury. For one thing, she knew she had to put aside her silly feelings of inadequacy. She tried to shore up her confidence by reminding herself that she was, in truth, an Exley and a Von Harmon, whatever that meant exactly, and it was time she started acting as such.

Mr. and Mrs. Howard welcomed her back with open arms, Mr. Howard giving Clive a wink as he shook his hand and clapped him on the back as the happy couple stepped out of the car onto the pea gravel, both of the Howards being there at the doorstep to greet them as they pulled up. Even Mrs. Howard was oddly accommodating and friendly to the extreme, causing Henrietta to wonder if Clive had spoken to them, possibly threatening them. In truth, he had.

He had been drinking a scotch in the library with his father after the fateful board meeting, his father to celebrate and Clive to steady his nerves, when his mother had walked in.

"Clive's done it!" Alcott said proudly to his wife. "It's all settled now! You don't know how happy this makes me, old boy." He went to the sideboard to pour a sherry for Antonia and held it out to her.

"Bravo, darling!" Antonia said warmly to Clive as she took the proffered glass. "I knew you would see sense in the end," she said, taking a sip. "Speaking of sense," she said casually, "it was terribly good of you, darling, to have Fletcher drive Henrietta all the way home. I happened to see him when he returned—quite by accident, really—and he admitted that even he was rather taken aback at the state of, let's just say, their accommodations. I had no idea it was so extreme! Family troubles, didn't you say it was? I do hope it's nothing serious!"

A tremor of irritation passed across Clive's face, but Mrs. Howard didn't seem to notice.

"Such a shame, isn't it?" she continued, almost happily. "But when *is* Henrietta planning on returning, Clive? It's just that with the party next week, I really do need to know. Any change of heart, perhaps?" she asked carefully, taking another sip of her sherry. "Better to change your mind now, darling, than later," she said, glancing at him surreptitiously. "No harm done, you know. No shame in that, darling."

"Antonia," Alcott said warningly.

"I want the ring, Mother," Clive said evenly, as if she hadn't just spoken.

"The ring, dearest?"

"You know what I mean. I want the family ring. I should have done this before, done it properly. I've made a mess of it, but I mean to amend it as best I can."

"He's right, Antonia," said Alcott. "We need to give him the ring."

"Well, if you're quite sure, Clive," Antonia hesitated. "It's just that . . ."

"Mother, stop. Please. I know what you're going to say, and, frankly, I don't care," Clive said animatedly. "You want me to take over the firm. Fine. It's done. You want me to take over Highbury. Fine again. Not my first choices in life, but there you have it. There are worse things, I realize that, and I know my duty. I was a soldier once, remember, and, have no fear, my duty will be faithfully discharged." He took a long pull of his Scotch. "But there is one thing that I *will* choose for myself. And that's my wife. I married Catherine because everyone wanted us to. It made sense. We were happy, yes, in our way, but that's over now. Now it's *my* choice," he said, looking slowly from one to the other. "If she'll still have me, I mean to marry Henrietta Von Harmon, and that's the end of it. So, I'll have not one more word about her inadequacy, her social ignorance, or her poverty, or anything else you can dig up. Do you understand? Those are not the values by which my heart is governed, nor will I teach it to be so. I love her," he said fiercely. "And I mean to make her my wife and the mother of my children, so you'll just have to learn to live with it, or so help me God, I'll walk out of here and the whole bloody place can go to the Cunninghams."

"Quite so, my boy," Alcott said solicitously, coming over to him and patting him on the back. "Quite so. You've misunderstood us, no doubt," he said, shooting Antonia a stern look. "Henrietta is a lovely creature, and we want only your happiness, Clive."

Antonia was not so contrite in her demeanor, however. In fact, quite the opposite. "I was only trying to help, darling, as you asked me to, remember?" she said sulkily.

Clive had seen this maneuver before, however, and kept his face stony.

Finally, Antonia had capitulated with a sigh. "Very well. Of course we want your happiness, dear. I suppose you know best. You have my word: no more uncomfortable comments. We will welcome her with open arms," she had said tiredly, her eyebrows creased and a slight frown forming at the corners of her mouth.

And so they did. Mrs. Howard kissed Henrietta on the cheek now as she stepped out of the car from the long drive up from the city and held her hand, admiring the beautiful family heirloom sparkling now on her finger. Henrietta had not slipped it on until they were in the car, away from Ma's eyes, carefully removing it from its box resting in her handbag. Affectionately, Mrs. Howard put her arm around her and led her in, Clive and Mr. Howard following, while James came out to unload the bags.

Henrietta was glad to be back in her old room. It felt as though she had never left, and she took in a deep breath, looking around at everything as she did so. It seemed familiar now, but for the sheer entertainment of it, she tried to see it all again as if it were the first time, as Elsie would no doubt see it when she arrived in a few days, and felt a jittery fluttering in her stomach as she did so. She longed to help them, even Ma, she begrudgingly admitted, if they would only let her. Well, it might take time, she reasoned.

She looked at her case perched at the end of the bed and resisted the temptation to unpack it all herself. She had to school herself to stop acting like one of the servants! Instead, she shivered with pleasure and sat down on the chaise lounge, trying to find a comfortable position. She looked again at her lovely ring and felt another burst of love for Clive. She knew it was silly, but the ring somehow made her feel more confident, more sure of herself, as if it were a token or a sort of ticket, honestly procured, that allowed her now to walk about freely in this world, to become an inhabitant, not just a spectator.

Unable to settle, Henrietta got up and walked to the window, gingerly pulling the lace curtain back so that she could see the grounds below. The sun caught the jewels on her finger and illuminated them as her eyes travelled to the lake beyond, sparkling as the sun caught it, as if it, too, were layered with diamonds. Though the cottage was not in view from where she stood, her thoughts turned to Helen and her own poor excuse of a ring. A ring kept all these years for a girl who was long-ago dead. The sadness of it overwhelmed her. She wondered what would become of the ring, and of Helen, actually. Would she eventually just die, alone, in the cottage? Hopefully not from fright, she thought, shivering a bit.

In her heart Henrietta felt that the ring rightfully should be returned to Helen. It had been either taken from her by theft or given over in a state of confusion. Either way, it seemed still her possession. As much as she liked Edna, Henrietta wasn't sure it held any real sentimental value for her. It had obviously been given as a love token by Virgil, but Edna these days seemed only to have eyes for Jack. She should do the right thing, Henrietta concluded, and return the ring to Helen. She wondered how Billings had handled the whole mess, if at all, as he seemed to think these petty quarrels amongst the servants beneath his consideration. And she wondered if Jack really had gone to Selzers to investigate. She was dying to ask him, but she had made a promise to Clive, and even more so to herself, to remain aloof, to be the woman he wanted her to be.

She sighed. Poor Helen. Surely it would be considered acceptable to simply visit her and see how she was getting on? Perhaps she could take Clive with her to make it seem more respectable. Wouldn't this sort of thing be their duty some day? But if that were true, she reasoned, why didn't Mr. and Mrs. Howard involve themselves more? She recalled, then, the sad state of the stable bedrooms. Clearly, there was much that could be done.

Unfortunately, however, she did not find a chance to broach the subject with Clive all day, as they were kept busy with a photographer that Mrs. Howard had arranged to be on the estate to take formal engagement pictures of them, and it had gone on longer than anyone had expected. Clive had told her on the drive up that he could only stay one night, but when they parted for the evening after dinner and a round of bridge with his parents, Henrietta found herself disappointed nonetheless that they had had so little time alone. But she was determined to not be a "petulant child" and managed to keep her emotions in check. She hoped she was improving.

"Good night, Henrietta," Clive had said, as they parted outside her bedroom door now.

"I'll miss you," she said longingly.

"I know, darling, but we're so very close on this case, and I'd also like a word with Eugene's Fr. Finnegan. He's cleverly evaded me thus far, but I mean to ferret him out just the same. Anyway, I'd only be underfoot here."

"What do you mean?" Henrietta laughed, "*I'll* be underfoot!"

He spontaneously kissed her then, and after looking down the hallway to see that no one was about, he drew her to him and kissed her again, longer this time.

"When can we get married, Clive?" she asked breathlessly when he finally pulled back. "Please say soon."

"Yes, I agree. Very soon, darling," he said, gently brushing back a strand of her hair that had come loose.

"Why do you call me 'darling'?"

"Because you *are* my darling. You're darling in every way," he said, running his finger along her shoulder now. "Does it bother you?"

"It did at first a bit, but now I quite like it."

"I'm glad," he said and kissed her goodnight, leaving her feeling weak as she shut the door and laid down on her bed, unable to go to sleep for a very long time.

The next few days threw the entire household into a frenzy of excitement. Despite the heightened activity, Henrietta still hoped to find time to slip off to see Helen, but it was not to be. Not only was Clive already gone, but Henrietta herself was kept very busy by Mrs. Howard with last-minute fittings and details, all of which, to her credit, Henrietta tried her hardest to be interested in. Likewise, she attempted to contain her interest in the servants to just that of Helen and successfully avoided conversation with any of them, including Jack. She found it most difficult, however, not to speak to Edna when she came to clean her room each morning, so she began making it a habit to be out of the room by the time Edna appeared.

Finally, however, the long-awaited day of the engagement party arrived, the cool morning air producing a surfeit of dew after mingling with the warm ground. Birds of all varieties could be seen hopping about on the wet grass, devouring the many insects hiding there. Henrietta was a bundle of nerves and scolded herself repeatedly for wanting Clive at her side sooner than this afternoon. She forced herself to dress calmly and sat patiently as Andrews did her hair.

"Thank you, Andrews," Henrietta said politely as the older woman packed up her little case of hair accoutrements.

"Good luck tonight, Miss," the normally silent Andrews ventured. "Be a lovely party," she smiled genuinely, the gap between her front teeth showing momentarily.

Edna came in, then, just as Andrews left, and Henrietta, feeling about to burst from the strain, broke down and grasped Edna by the arms. "Oh, Edna! I'm so nervous!" she burst out, taking one of the pairs of shoes Edna had just polished from her arms.

"Oh, Miss!" responded Edna, appearing to not know what to say. Henrietta thought she saw a hurt look in the girl's eyes and felt ashamed.

"I'm sorry I've been distant, Edna," she said sincerely. "I'm trying to . . . trying to . . ."

"I know, Miss." Edna smiled sadly. "I understand. I figured it would happen sooner or later," she said, which caused a fresh swell of guilt to pass over Henrietta, as well as a fresh irritation at the silly code of propriety that prevented the two of them from being friends.

"Here, let me help you with the bed!" Henrietta said, pulling back the coverlet of the bed as Edna went to set down the other shoes.

"Oh, Miss! No! Not on your big day . . ."

"Please let me help you, Edna. If I don't do something, I think I'll scream!"

Edna, apparently not one to hold grudges, smiled her acquiescence, then, and the two set to work stripping and remaking the bed, the physical act of doing something concrete going far to calm Henrietta's nerves.

"I miss all of you, you know," Henrietta said as she smoothed the coverlet back into place. "I have to force myself not to sneak downstairs at night," she said earnestly. "But I . . . I told Mr. Howard . . . Clive . . . that I would try to be . . . oh, I don't know . . . more proper, I guess you could say."

"Like you're doing now?" Edna couldn't help but say with a teasing smile.

Henrietta threw a pillow at her. "Ungrateful girl!" she said, laughing. "Now!" she urged, plopping another one down on the freshly made bed, "tell me some gossip before you have to move on. I don't dare help you in the other rooms or Mrs. Caldwell will be sure to know somehow. Then it'll get back to Mrs. Howard and then to Clive, and then all is lost, I'm afraid."

"It's Kitty, if you ever want to know," Edna said confidentially. "She's the snitch."

"I see," Henrietta murmured, grasping hold of the bedpost and looking at Edna expectantly. "Well?"

Edna laughed. "There's not much to tell. You've only been gone a few days, really."

"Any news of Helen's ring?"

"Just that Mr. Billings took hold of it. Says he'll get to the bottom of it, but it don't seem like it to me. Meanwhile, Virgil's in a state. Never seen him like this before. Demanding his money back, he says, or the ring itself. Helen's taken herself off to the cottage. Supposed to be up here today, though, to help with the party."

"What about Jack?" Henrietta said tentatively. "Any word from him?"

"About the ring?" Edna asked, puzzled. "What would he care?"

"Just that he said he might inquire at the shop in town and see if they remember who came in to sell it," Henrietta said, trying her best to appear nonchalant in regards to Jack's movements.

"Well, that's not a bad idea!" Edna said. "Why didn't I think of that? Or, better yet, Mr. Billings? He ain't takin' this seriously, that's for sure. But, no, Jack ain't said anything, least not to me, anyways," she shrugged.

"Who do you really fancy, Edna?" Henrietta asked suddenly. "I thought you were sweet on Jack, but maybe it's Virgil after all?" she teased.

Edna blushed a deep red. "I don't know. I thought I was all for Virgil. You probably think that's daft, but Virgil's actually a nice-enough fellow. Just rough around the edges. You just have to get to know him. He's got an awfully good heart, you know, and I guess I feel a little sorry for him. He doesn't really mean half the things he says. He'd never steal; I just know he wouldn't. That's why none of this ring business makes sense."

Henrietta wasn't convinced of this, but she bit her lip rather than say so.

"But then again, Jack's nice, too," Edna went on. "He's very handsome and charming and everything, but I don't know . . . sometimes I'm not so sure he really means it."

Henrietta nodded, having oddly felt that way herself around him, and hoped that she had not inadvertently pulled Jack's attention from Edna, if Edna really cared for him, that is.

"His eyes are lovely, though, ain't they?" Edna went on. "But then again, there was something nice about when I danced with Virgil. And then all the expense he went through for my gift, whatever the truth of all that is. It all got confused that night . . . I can't help wonder if it was meant as a betrothal. But he ain't said anything about it since. Though it does make a girl feel special," she said, her face slightly flushed. She looked up then as if remembering where she was. "I'm sorry, Miss! I'm talkin' nonsense. And on your big day, too!"

"Never mind that. I've got plenty of time to be dawdling," Henrietta laughed. "Anyway," she said, wanting to return to Edna's problem, "sometimes it's fun to have rivals." She gave her an inquisitive look.

"Not for me, Miss. I'd rather know what I'm about. The dilly dallyin' upsets me. And now," she said after a moment's pause, "with both of them in the house tonight . . . I don't know what I'll do!"

"Both of them in the house? A chauffer and a gardener? What do you mean?"

"Haven't you heard? Well, I guess you wouldn't have," she mused. "James is down with the flu, just this morning. Doctor Belden was called in. Mr. Billings had already asked Jack to help out, seeing as it would save him having to get someone temporary in, but now he had to go and ask Virgil to help in the kitchen, too, at this last minute. Provided he can get all the dirt from under his nails out, says Mrs. Caldwell. He's down in the kitchen now with his hands in a soak."

"Well, that's terrible!" Henrietta said. "About James, I mean. I hope it doesn't turn serious. I lost two siblings from the flu. I don't really remember them all that well, I'm sorry to say; I was just little myself."

"Yes . . . I lost my ma that way," Edna added sadly, gathering up the bedding. "Well, Miss," she said, visibly giving herself a little shake, "I'd better get on. Mrs. Caldwell will skin me alive, 'specially on a day like today. And I'm sure you're busy an all," she said, hurrying now toward the door, Henrietta slowly following her.

"Thanks, Edna," she said, leaning against the doorframe.

"Why are you thanking me? I should thank *you*," she whispered, now that she was out in the hallway. "Good luck!" she said with a smile. "It'll be all right. You'll be lovely." And with that, she turned and hurried off.

Henrietta watched her go, and despite Edna's cheerful goodbye, she felt a strange sense of foreboding, one which she could neither explain nor completely eradicate from her mind. She wished again that she had had time to visit Helen. Something was nagging at her there, and she just couldn't put her finger on it. She had been too busy with preparations the last couple of days, and she knew she would be summoned downstairs any minute now. She remembered, then, Edna's comment about Helen coming up tonight to help with the party and felt encouraged. Perhaps she could find time to slip away down to the kitchen to see her at some point. If nothing else, she planned to have a word with Billings. But, she cautioned herself, wouldn't that count as meddling with the servants? But wasn't this to be her future role? she countered with herself. Wasn't this a case of making sure justice was being done? Oh, she was so confused! If nothing else, she thought with a sigh as she took a last glance in the mirror, it could be argued that it was, at the very least, a case of compassion.

Chapter 15

"Are you sure this is the way?" Elsie asked as Stan maneuvered the truck along the narrow lane they had just turned down.

"She said to turn at the sign that says 'Highbury,' so this has got to be it," Stan responded, his tone one of irritability, presumably from the long drive up and now the frustration of having to find the estate itself.

"Fancy having a name for your house . . . and a sign to go with it!" Elsie sighed dreamily.

"I don't see what the big deal is," Stan muttered.

"I agree," Eugene said from behind them where he lay stretched out on the backseat. "Rich bastards that have more money than they know what to do with!" He sat up now and peered down the lane just as the massive Highbury with its turrets and gabled rooflines came into view. "See what I mean? Look at this joint," Eugene said. "Hen's landed the big time here."

"Oh, my!" was all Elsie could say. "Oh, Stanley! Isn't it gorgeous?"

"If you like monstrosities, I suppose," he said absently, still trying to figure out where to go.

Eugene laughed in the back.

"Stanley!" Elsie moaned. "You said you'd be nice."

"Course I'll be nice. What's that supposed to mean? Can't a man have an opinion?" he snapped.

They could make out a man in uniform now, waving them forward and directing them to the circular drive in front of the entrance of the large stone house. Stan, determined to arrive at the party of his own accord, though Henrietta had offered to send a car, slowly drove the delivery truck he had begged and borrowed from Mr. Kreske to the spot indicated, another servant in uniform stepping forward now.

"Look at these monkeys," Eugene said under his breath.

With some difficulty, Stan rolled down the stiff window. "Where should I park this? In back okay?" he asked the servant, who had gingerly bent down toward the half-open window as if not wanting to dirty himself on the truck's dusty exterior.

"That won't be necessary, sir," the servant said, reaching for the door handle and opening the door before Stan could say anything, while another servant moved in a slow, dignified manner to open Elsie's. Stan, not sure what to think, just sat in the car. Elsie quickly descended, however.

"Stanley, come on!" she urged. "You heard them; they'll take care of it."

Reluctantly Stan got out, then, followed by Eugene. Stan walked around to the back, where he began opening the rear doors to get their bags, Henrietta having convinced them of the wisdom of staying the night rather than driving all that way back to the city at what would surely be a late hour. Elsie had never been away from home before, and she was tingling with nervous excitement. The servant who had opened the door for Stan hurried forward.

"Please, sir," he urged condescendingly, "I'll take those. No need to exert yourself."

"Yeah? Well, where will I pick them up at?" Stan asked, his hands on his hips, unconvinced.

"They will be taken directly to your rooms, *sir*," the servant responded distastefully.

Stan looked from him to Eugene. "What do you think, Gene?"

"Stanley!" Elsie finally said, her embarrassment growing. "Come along! More cars are driving up now!" she said, looking down the lane to where a Rolls-Royce had just turned into the drive.

"Oh, all right," Stan said, reluctantly handing the keys to the servant. "But be careful!" he warned him. "This isn't mine, you know. Can't bang it up or anything."

"Of course not, sir. Very good, sir," the servant said, bowing slightly. Elsie thought she detected the smallest grimace of distain on the footman's face and glanced quickly over at Stanley, who, thankfully, she noted, had not observed this small slight to himself. Determinedly, Stan took Elsie's arm, then, and they made their way up the stone steps, Eugene trailing behind them.

Elsie was grateful to have Stanley to hold onto, as she was frightfully nervous at the prospect of the night ahead. *Terrified* was actually a better word to describe her current feelings. She had never been good in social situations. She always felt too big for her clothes and always seemed to say the wrong thing in public. It was mainly for this reason that she preferred going out in Henrietta's company. Henrietta had a natural charm about her and never seemed at a loss of what to say, especially to men, Elsie's own particular downfall. She was so happy to have found Stanley. She had discovered, as time went on, that he was very easy to talk to, almost like a brother, and she grasped his arm now as they went in, grateful that she had him to rely on, as Eugene certainly wouldn't be of any help, she knew. Eugene had been unusually quiet when he first came home from the police station (Elsie couldn't bring herself to say the word *jail* now, even in her mind), but he was back now to his querulous self.

Elsie took a deep breath, trying to calm her nerves, and smoothed down her skirt as she took in the beautiful foyer, her face immediately breaking into a smile of happiness for Hen and what her new life was to be, though she could never imagine herself here. It was far too grand, too beautiful by far. She offered up yet another silent prayer that the evening would go okay, that they wouldn't embarrass themselves somehow. Already they had had a near miss when Stan had arrived at the Von Harmon apartment to fetch her and

Eugene, only for her to observe, in a panic, that his good serge trousers needed letting down! Hadn't his mother noticed? They had been delayed, then, while she had hurriedly fixed them, hoping upon hope that this wasn't a bad start to the evening.

Before she had returned to Highbury last week, Henrietta had taken Eugene to Kaufman's and bought him a jacket and a tie and had insisted on buying a new dress for Elsie as well, as nothing of Henrietta's new wardrobe fit her, and, anyway, upon further consideration, Henrietta was of the opinion that Mrs. Howard might not be too pleased should she so freely lend one of her newly acquired gowns from New York or Paris to her sister, even for just this night. Henrietta had tried to convince Elsie to get an evening gown, but Elsie would not be persuaded, choosing instead a brown wool suit (trimmed with faux fur!), which, she wisely pointed out, she could use for other occasions—perhaps even her wedding, she had said shyly with a bashful smile—whereas an evening gown would be utterly useless to her beyond tonight's extravaganza.

No, Elsie reminded herself, even as she again smoothed down her wool skirt with perhaps just an inkling of regret now, seeing glimpses of women at the top of the staircase passing by in shimmering gowns, she had been wise to choose this one.

A butler (at least that was what Elsie presumed he was) appeared and led them up the grand staircase, Elsie's brown Oxfords sinking a bit with every step she took into the thick red Oriental carpeting, so that she finally resorted to proceeding up the stairs on just her tiptoes. She clung to the immense gleaming banisters, wondering how long it took to polish them to such a high sheen and deducing that Henrietta was certainly quite brave. Elsie knew her limitations, at least she thought she did, and she knew she would never have the courage, Stanley or no, to ever be at home in a place such as this, but she hoped with all her heart that Hen could.

The butler led them to the threshold of a large vaulted room in which hung several crystal chandeliers, all ablaze with candlelight. Elsie's breath caught in her throat, and she felt her stomach seize up yet again as she gazed at the beautiful silk drapes hung at two-story windows on the far wall, the delicate silk-embossed wallpaper, the linens on little tables scattered about, and the huge displays of flowers that seemed to be everywhere. A small ensemble played in the corner, and a host of footmen weaved in and out among the guests, carrying large trays of champagne and hors d'oeuvres to the swelling crowd. Elsie was tempted to pinch herself to make sure it was real, but she felt in danger, actually, of not being able to move at all. Before she could test this theory by trying to enter, however, the butler, still standing beside them, smoothly prevented them with an outstretched arm.

"One moment, if you please," he said, his thick jowls not moving. "Your names?"

"I'm Stanley Dubowski," Stan said proudly, trying to puff out his chest, "and this here's Elsie, that's Henrietta's sister, and this is Eugene, her brother," he said, pointing a thumb at Eugene. "We're invited, you know."

"Just so, sir," said the butler emotionlessly and with the smallest of deferential nods. "If you'll just wait a moment, I'm to announce you," he said and stepped inside the room just in front of them.

Elsie's stomach knotted again, and she looked desperately over at Stanley. Before anything could even be said between them, however, they heard the butler's sonorous voice boom out, "A Miss Elsie Von Harmon, a Mr. Eugene Von Harmon, and a Mr. Stanley Dubowski!" He stepped aside, then, bowing slightly, as they entered the room.

Elsie felt her face flush and then, after a moment of panic, somehow found her legs moving, Stan pulling her slightly. She didn't dare look up but instead concentrated on the parquet floor as they moved across it, allowing herself to be ignominiously led.

When she did finally have the courage to actually look up, she was grateful that no one seemed to be paying them the slightest bit of notice besides perhaps one or two elderly women in the corner who seemed to be whispering something to each other. Bravely now, Elsie looked around a bit more, trying hard to locate Henrietta. She had naively (she saw that now) expected that Henrietta would be right inside the door waiting for her, but that didn't make sense, did it? Stan meanwhile continued to lead them further into the room to an uninhabited space to the left of the main doors, Elsie taking in the little details of the room as they made their way. It was more beautiful than she had imagined, more beautiful even than Henrietta had described it! But then again, she supposed Henrietta had done that on purpose to spare her feelings, and she felt a fresh rush of love for her sister. "Isn't it lovely, Stanley?" she whispered.

"I suppose so," he said with his hands awkwardly in his pockets. "If you go in for all this sort of thing," he added miserably. He looked moodily around the room and knew he could never compete with this. No wonder she had chosen the inspector, when he had all of this to give her. Obviously Howard must have told her early on; why else would she have become so attracted to him so quickly? It was a cruel blow, seeing Henrietta in this new light. He had thought she was good—pure of heart and all that—but he saw now that she had succumbed to temptation after all. Temptation of an easy life. Why else would she want this crotchety old man? He was clearly a snob; anyone could see that. Surely it couldn't have anything to do with real attraction, he had reasoned a hundred times before. In truth he had pondered this many times late into the night and could only come up with pity on Henrietta's part. She must have pitied the inspector, he had concluded, an old war vet. But now! Now he saw it for what it really was. Now it was all becoming clear. She had been lured by the money, not pity! The inspector went down a notch in his opinion as well. Flashing his millions at a young girl. Playing with her the way he had at the Marlowe. It made him sick, it did. If it were up to him, he'd have nothing to do with either of them ever again, but here he was, linked to them through Elsie—his tried-and-true Elsie.

Anyone could see the advantage of choosing Elsie over Henrietta! Now *this* was the girl for him, he repeatedly convinced himself. He had discussed it long and hard with his parents, particularly his mother, and they had all agreed together that marrying Elsie would be the all 'round right thing to do. His father had delicately asked if he really loved her, saying that he didn't like to ask, of course, but, not being able to rightly determine the answer from his own inferior, to be sure, observations, he felt it necessary to ask out loud, to which Stan had become quite incensed, saying that of course he loved Elsie—what a silly question! All that remained was time, he had said, time for him to save up enough for a modest ring. He took Elsie's hand now in a fit of feeling, Elsie turning and smiling at him and returning his gesture with a gentle squeeze of her own.

Where *was* Henrietta, blast it? He looked around for Eugene and saw that he had already drifted toward a passing servant who was balancing what looked like a very heavy tray of champagne. He watched as Eugene slyly took a glass.

"I say! Hello!" came an English voice beside them, and an older, stout man, an elegant woman on his arm, appeared as if out of nowhere. "I'm Alcott Howard," he said pleasantly enough, holding out his hand to them. "Terribly sorry to have not greeted you at the door. Been a bit tied up in the other corner, one might say."

"Stanley Dubowski," Stanley said, firmly grasping his hand.

"And this is my wife, Antonia," Mr. Howard said, gesturing toward the rather stern-looking woman at his side. Mrs. Howard's face held a decidedly false smile, as if it had been painted on, and she limply held out her hand to them.

"You must be Henrietta's sister. Elsie, isn't it?" Mrs. Howard asked with exaggerated politeness, all the while looking her up and down, appalled at what she was wearing. Hadn't Henrietta counseled her? Her attire was more appropriate to a walk on a moor, had there been one nearby, or perhaps the inspection of a school if one were some sort of officiating body employed to do so. Still, there was nothing to be done about it now. Her escort—Stanley, was it?—was just as unsuitably dressed. She had specifically told Henrietta that it was white tie! And here he was in a serge suit! Her eyes darted beyond the pair of them conversing clumsily now with Alcott to what must be the brother, a drink already in his hand, of course, and having the bad manners to openly gape at his surroundings, one of his hands in his trouser pockets! Antonia silently despaired.

She put her hand up to her forehead to steady herself and took a deep breath. She had promised Alcott earlier in her bedroom that she would do her utmost to ensure that Henrietta and her family felt welcome.

"None of your shenanigans, Antonia," Alcott had said with an unmistakable suggestion of firmness.

"I don't know what you mean," Antonia had replied glibly, pulling on her long gloves.

"Yes, you very well do," Alcott said. "This wedding has to come off. This is our last chance; I feel it. It's too late to debate the girl's qualifications. Clive's made up his mind, and that's that. Don't cross him, Antonia," he said warningly. "He's on the edge. At least she's an Exley; that should count for something," he hissed. "Be happy with that. If you won't swallow your silly pride for one night for the sake of your son, then at least do it for Highbury," he had said in a bitter tone and walked out, leaving her to finish dressing alone.

"Are you feeling quite well, my dear?" Alcott was asking now, looking at Mrs. Howard pointedly. "It's all the excitement, you see," he said pleasantly to the two still standing in front of him.

"Yes, of course, darling," Antonia drawled, shooting him a dagger.

"I was just saying, my dear, that Clive and Henrietta should be making their entrance any moment. Miss Von Harmon, here, is naturally most anxious to see her sister."

"Yes, I quite agree. No doubt they'll be along in a moment," she said, managing a smile. "It's too bad your mother couldn't make it," she continued sweetly. "We were so hoping we could meet her. She's ill, Henrietta tells us."

"Yes, she . . . she is," Elsie said shyly, shifting her weight and managing to make eye contact with Mrs. Howard for a few seconds before looking away again.

"Well, next time perhaps. Excuse me, won't you? I had better go and find out what's become of our errant guests of honor. I'll leave you in Alcott's capable hands," she said with barely a smile and made her way out to where the faithful Billings stood at attention.

Expertly predicting her intention, the old servant stepped forward slightly and said inconspicuously, "They're just on their way, Madam," inclining his head slightly toward the back hallway, where she could see them now walking together, holding hands and smiling at each other. It was obvious that Clive was besotted with the girl, and a small part of Antonia was, in truth, glad for him. She knew she had her work cut out for her, however, if she was going to pull this thing off in the eyes of society. At least she had a willing pupil in Henrietta, she would give her that. She observed her now with great approval. The Edward Molyneux gown of deep green velvet with a bias cut that they had chosen for tonight's gala was simply stunning. She had had it shipped from Paris, and Henrietta's hair was beautifully swept up in a fine mesh of pearls holding it delicately in place. At her neck were the family pearls, given to her just this morning by Clive, as his gift to her to officially mark their engagement. And on her finger, of course, sat the family ring, the emeralds catching the color of the dress perfectly. She had to admit, especially after the rather jarring meeting of her sister just now, that Henrietta was indeed coming along nicely. Henrietta had learned much already in her short time with them thus far, and there was much promise. She shuddered to think what she would have done if Clive had stupidly chosen someone like the sister instead. Yes, thought Antonia, there was hope.

"Ah, Mother," said Clive with a smile as they approached. "You look lovely," he said, kissing her lightly on the cheek.

"Thank you, darling, but not as nice as the two of you," she said and genuinely meant it. Clive, with his wavy chestnut hair slicked back and his tails and white tie, looked positively dashing. He had considered wearing his dress uniform, but Antonia had advised him not to, and in the end he had decided against it, hoping to leave that chapter behind. It was 1935, after all. The war had been over for nearly seventeen years.

"You look absolutely divine, Henrietta," Antonia said, patting her hand.

"Thank you, Mrs. Howard, for everything."

"Antonia. Please," she said with a smile and kissed her on the cheek. "Come along now. You are both very late; if you delay any longer, I'll positively have to scold you." With that, she gave a nod to Billings and then slipped inside the ballroom.

"Ready?" Clive whispered to Henrietta now. "Remember, the Burgess Club was for us. This is for them," he said, almost grimly, his eyebrow arched and his face set as if he were going into battle.

Henrietta nodded and couldn't help feel butterflies as she heard Billings's voice boom out, "Miss Henrietta Von Harmon and Mr. Clive Howard!"

Henrietta gripped Clive's arm tightly as they entered the room to a hushed buzz of excitement that then spontaneously erupted into applause. Henrietta could not help smiling, despite her nervousness. She steadied herself, trying to remember that this was just another role to play, like the Dutch girl so long ago at the World's Fair or the burlesque usherette at the Marlowe. Those were supporting roles, though, she realized, and this was finally the lead, the part she had been waiting for; only it wasn't a part in some fantastical production, she thought apprehensively, it was real.

Forcing herself to keep her head up, Henrietta gazed around the room without really being able to see anyone in particular. It was overwhelming, but she was determined to hold up under the spotlight. Through the noise that was roaring in her head, she vaguely heard Mr. Howard speaking now.

"Ladies and gentleman!" he said loudly. "Ladies and gentlemen!" he said, the crowd slowly quieting now. "A toast!" he said, and a hush fell over the room. "To my son, Clive Howard, and his beautiful fiancée, Miss Henrietta Von Harmon. May you have many happy years together!" he said with real feeling and held his glass up to them. He took a drink, then, and the crowd followed suit, shouting out, "Here, here!" and, "Cheers!"

Clive nodded his thanks to the crowd and then bent to kiss Henrietta softly on the cheek, causing the crowd to politely clap again.

"And now!" Mr. Howard boomed out, "Please enjoy yourselves!" The small ensemble began playing then, and the general buzz returned to the room as people drifted back into the groups they had formed previously, Henrietta exhaling a deep breath of relief.

"Thank you, Father," Clive said, approaching the Howards now, Henrietta on his arm, "very much. It means more to me than you know." Clive reached out and shook his father's hand then, as Elsie made her way over to them as well, Stan trailing along behind.

Upon catching sight of Elsie, Henrietta breathed another sigh of relief and hurried forward to embrace her. "Oh, Hen! I mean . . . Henrietta," Elsie was saying now, "You look beautiful! You really do!" she said, enraptured. "Too bad Ma couldn't see you!"

Henrietta winced at Elsie's use of the word "Ma," having been instructed that "mother" or "M'ma" was a more gentile form of address, but she hid any embarrassment from her face and forced herself not to check anyone's reaction, instead keeping her eyes on Elsie's.

"Thank you, Elsie," Henrietta said simply, giving her sister another hug. "You do, too." She felt a sadness, then, that Ma really hadn't come after all. In her heart of hearts, she supposed that she had perhaps hoped that maybe . . .

"Oh!" Elsie said, clearly uncomfortable with the compliment. "Thank you," she said bashfully and looked over at Stan, who, drink in hand, was peering at Henrietta over the rim of it.

"Hello, Stan," Henrietta said coyly. "I'm glad you found it all right."

"Yeah, I found it all right. Long jaunt up here. Nice place you got here, though, I'll give you that," he said, turning to shake Clive's hand. "Must cost you an awful lot to heat it."

"Yes, it does, rather," Clive said congenially, though Henrietta could tell he was trying hard to hold back a smile.

"Where's Eugene?" Henrietta asked. "And Mr. and Mrs. Hennessey?" she said, looking distractedly out over the crowd.

Stan shrugged. "Eugene's here somewhere," he said, looking around absently. "But I haven't seen Mr. and Mrs. Hennessey yet."

"They should be here any time now," Elsie put in. "They said they were leaving the same time as us. Oh, Hen! It's all so gorgeous! Why didn't you tell us how beautiful it all is?" she said, continuing her raptures.

She was interrupted, though, by Mrs. Howard, who came up behind Clive and Henrietta now and laid a hand on each of their arms. "Might I steal these two for just a moment?" she asked sweetly. "There are a few people Henrietta should meet."

"Oh, gosh! Of course!" said Elsie. "No, we musn't take up your time!" she said quickly, giving Henrietta a smile. "I'll find you later. I'll keep an eye out for the Hennesseys!"

"Thanks, Elsie," Henrietta said, as Mrs. Howard led her and Clive to a little group standing closer to where the musicians were playing. Instinctively Henrietta knew this must be the Exleys and took a deep breath, holding her head high and giving it a little toss.

Mrs. Howard was positively brimming with delight now as she put her hand on Henrietta's bare back and gestured toward the man and woman standing in front of them. "Henrietta Von Harmon," she said, "I'd like you to meet Mr. and Mrs. John Exley, your aunt and uncle and our very dear friends. John and Agatha Exley, Henrietta Von Harmon, Martha's daughter."

"Oh, my dear!" Mr. Exley said, taking her hand formally, but then leaning forward to kiss her on the cheek, Mrs. Exley joyfully joining in on the other side as well. "We had no idea! None whatsoever that Martha even *had* a child! We'd lost all contact with her! Oh, you must believe us. It wasn't until just a few days ago that we discovered who

Clive's intended really was. It's all been hush-hush, you know! Still, old boy," John Exley said to Mr. Howard, who was standing near Clive, "you might have let on before this. We've been driven mad with curiosity!"

"I wanted it to be a complete surprise," Antonia said with a cool smile, "but Alcott convinced me it would be too much, too cruel to find out just tonight. This way you had at least a few days to get over the shock of it." She let out a false little laugh.

"The shock!" said John, laughingly. "That's an understatement if I ever heard one. We . . . we thought Martha dead, really, or gone to live in California or some such place," he said quietly now, causing a somber tone to creep in over the jovial, happy conversation. "Father told us . . . well, never mind. It doesn't matter now, does it?"

"Well, I'm very glad to meet you," Henrietta said, happily, trying her best to encourage the pleasant tone they had begun with. "I had no idea Mother had family nearby. She never spoke of it. Still," she said cheerfully, "better late than never, isn't that so?"

"Yes, I quite agree," Clive said, chiming in.

"Isn't it strange, but for the off chance of meeting Clive, none of us would ever have known of the other's existence? It's quite a lot to take in, isn't it?" Henrietta offered.

"Indeed, yes!" Mr. Exley said, recovering. "What a happy occasion all round. Well done, Clive! I must say, your future bride is quite beautiful, despite the family connection," he laughed, giving Henrietta a playful wink.

"Thank you, sir," Clive said, smiling proudly.

"I understand Martha isn't here?" Mr. Exley said, looking out reactively over the crowd. "I was sorely disappointed to find she was too ill to attend."

"Nothing serious, is it, dear?" Mrs. Exley put in.

"No, it's . . . it's more of a nervous condition, really," Henrietta said hesitantly.

"Ah! I see. Martha always was very sensitive," John Exley said, almost to himself. "Still, there's time, I daresay. Perhaps we could come to her at some point?"

Henrietta felt a sense of panic at this suggestion, but she forced herself to not reveal it. "Yes, perhaps," she smiled politely, "when she's quite recovered."

"But of course, of course," he said reassuringly.

"Perhaps you'd like to meet my brother and sister, though?" Henrietta offered. "They're here tonight."

"We'd be delighted, my dear. How many of you are there, did Alcott say? Eight? By Jove! Who would have thought it of Martha!"

"Yes, there are eight. Two others died of the flu, though, when they were quite little."

"Oh, my!" Mrs. Exley put in. "Ten births!"

"And you're the oldest; is that correct?" asked Mr. Exley.

"Yes, that's right."

A servant came through with a tray of champagne, then, and as Henrietta gratefully reached for a glass to calm her nerves, she was surprised to see that it was Jack! He had the insufferable effrontery to wink at her, but she looked away. Clive, however, she was almost certain, had caught it.

"And how old is the youngest?" Mrs. Exley was asking.

"Just turned five. There's two of them; they're twins." This conversation regarding her parents' proliferative history was becoming embarrassing to Henrietta, but she didn't know how to shift it.

"Good heavens! Wait until Father hears this," Mr. Exley said, musingly.

Henrietta saw her chance. "Your father? That would be my grandfather?" she asked, her face lighting up in a smile. "I never knew any of my grandparents. We grew up quite alone, as you can imagine. Is he here?" she asked, looking at Mrs. Howard now.

Before Antonia could say anything, Mr. Exley answered for her. "Yes, he's over there at that first table. He's suffering from gout and walks with a cane at the moment, or I daresay he would have been over here already. In fact, I'm sure he's quite cross that we haven't presented you as yet. Come. Shall we? And then we'll go and meet . . ."

"Henrietta?" said Elsie, very timidly, from behind Henrietta. "I'm sorry to interrupt you, but the—"

"Martha?" said Mr. Exley, who had suddenly gone very visibly pale and was staring at Elsie. "Forgive me," he said then, quickly. "You're obviously not Martha," he added with a flustered chuckle. "You must be Henrietta's sister, isn't that right?"

Elsie nodded and looked to Henrietta for guidance.

"This is my sister, Elsie," Henrietta said formally to Mr. and Mrs. Exley. "These are our aunt and uncle, Elsie. Mother's brother and his wife." Henrietta had instructed Elsie beforehand that they would be here, but her awkwardness was nonetheless obvious.

"Pleased to meet you," Elsie finally said shyly.

"Forgive my outburst, my dear, but you look exactly like Martha," Mr. Exley exclaimed. "Extraordinary!"

Elsie blushed and managed to stammer out, "Thank you." Henrietta rescued her by gesturing toward Eugene, whom she had noticed had shuffled up as well. "And this is Eugene, my brother. Eugene, Mr. and Mrs. Exley, your aunt and uncle."

Eugene shook their hands but didn't smile. "Ma's never spoke about you."

"Quite understandable, really," Mr. Exley said, feigning a smile and clearing his throat.

"I daresay, John, if you're not going to have the decency to bring the girl to me," came a gravelly voice behind the Exleys, "I have no choice but to come to you."

"I'm sorry, Father," Mr. Exley said, making room between himself and his wife for the older gentleman to come through. "We were just coming. Allow me to present your granddaughter, Henrietta Von Harmon. Henrietta, your grandfather, Mr. Oldrich Exley."

Everyone seemed to hold their breath as Mr. Exley, Sr., looked keenly at Henrietta. He was slightly stooped, but he still commanded a presence, despite his snow-white hair and narrow pointed beard and the horn-rimmed glasses he wore at the end of his nose. He peered at her now, and Henrietta bravely held his gaze, though she couldn't read what was in his eyes. He seemed neither judgmental nor overly kind, either. "You have a look of your father to you," is all he said. "Still, that isn't your fault, is it, my dear?" he grunted with a poor excuse for a smile as he took her hand and kissed it. "I'm very glad to meet you after all these years. It's been far too many."

Henrietta breathed a sigh of relief as he released her hand then and turned to Elsie and Eugene.

"And these are my other two grandchildren, are they?" Mr. Exley, Sr., asked, peering at them closely. "Now these two have a look of Martha to them. Same dark hair, same eyes."

Elsie gave a little curtsey, causing Henrietta to squirm internally. Only maids curtsied! "Pleased to meet you, sir," Elsie said deferentially. "It's lovely to have a grandfather, isn't it, Hen? I mean, Henrietta . . ." she added quickly.

"This is Elsie," Henrietta said, forcing her voice to be calm and sure, "and this is my brother, Eugene." Eugene shook his hand weakly and met his eye for only a moment, Mr. Exley, Sr., studying him intently.

"And there are five more of them at home, Father! Can you believe Martha's been living in the city all these years and had such a pack of children? I wouldn't have thought it, would you?" John said, clearly attempting to propel the conversation smoothly forward.

"No, I would not have," the older man said seriously. "But then, Martha was always one for secrets and surprises. However, the fact that she has chosen not to attend tonight is certainly not one," he sniffed.

"Well, I'm delighted," said John Exley. "My brothers will be, too. Martha was our baby sister, you see. I'll write to them directly upon returning home tonight. We have so much catching up to do, perhaps we—"

He was interrupted, then, by Mrs. Howard, having just herself been approached by the silent Billings, who had whispered something in a low tone to her.

"Clive, darling," she said, after dismissing Billings with a nod. "It seems the musicians have been asked to play something more suitable for dancing, but that can't be done until the floor is opened by the two of you. I'm sorry to take you away from this irresistible reunion, but would you be so kind as to oblige?"

"But of course, Mother," Clive said with uncharacteristic alacrity. He looked at Henrietta, then, and held out his arm to her. "Shall we?" Gratefully, she took it. "You'll excuse us," he said, bowing to the assembled Exleys.

"Of course," said John Exley. Mr. Exley, Sr., merely nodded, his eyes following them all the while.

Once on the dance floor in Clive's sturdy arms, Henrietta felt a sense of relief, though she knew all eyes were on them.

"You're doing beautifully, my darling," Clive said, smiling down at her. "If I weren't already so in love with you, I'd be smitten all over again."

She was about to offer an apology for her family, but she bit it back, remembering her resolve. "I should hope so," she teased instead, "or I might have had to approach you myself." She smiled suggestively.

"Brazen!" Clive grinned, his eyebrow arched. "You're not as experienced as you let on, though, you know, Miss Von Harmon. Your secret's out."

"Perhaps," she said, smiling so that her dimples showed. "I need a teacher, however. So far, you're doing admirably, but there are one or two things I may be in need of extra help with," she added with a coy smile.

Clive looked away and held her tighter, a smile of happiness creeping across his face.

"Now that's what I call a happy couple," said Mr. Hennessey to his wife as they stood off to the side amongst the crowd, watching Clive and Henrietta on the dance floor.

"You're quite right, William," said Mrs. Hennessey. "She's like a Cinderella at the ball out there. And to think how she showed up at our doorstep all those years ago; a little waif was what she was back then. Good Lord, all skin and bones, the poor thing! Now look at her!" Mrs. Hennessey said proudly.

"Well, I'm happy for her," Mr. Hennessey said. "Been through a lot has that one," he said, nodding his head approvingly, still staring at Henrietta. "Made something of herself, she has. Can't believe she asked us to come to something like this, though," he said, looking up at the vaulted ceiling and back down again. "Wonder how much all this costs." He clutched the bottle in his hands and looked over at his wife now, who stood contentedly eating the rather large collection of hors d'oeuvres she had managed to amass from the veritable army of passing footmen. In fact, her tiny china plate was positively mounded high.

Alice Hennessey was as rounded as Mr. Hennessey, though a bit shorter, which made them look remarkably similar, like two wooden bowling pins in a child's game. She was in every way a partner in Poor Pete's, their corner tavern in the city, and, admittedly, she had not been happy when William had succumbed to pity that day and given Henrietta a job scrubbing floors. They had had little enough money as it was without him hiring an employee, but she had come to see the wisdom of his decision down the line, as Henrietta's charm and beauty began to bring in more customers and as she herself had grown to love Henrietta just as much as William seemed to. Often, over the years, when she carried William's dinner, wrapped in a dish-towel, down the back steps to him from their apartment over the bar, she would contrive to bring extras for Henrietta, whom she could see was probably not getting enough back at home.

Mr. Hennessey had three children by his first wife, who had died when the children were still very little. He had married Alice not long after, but, despite their young ages, the children had never really warmed to her. Their daughter (Mrs. Hennessey called them *her* children as well from the very first moment of her union with Mr. Hennessey as a kindness not only to him, but to them, though none of the said children had ever seemed remotely grateful for this endearment), Winifred, lived out in New Jersey now with her husband, Roger, and worked as a school teacher. The Hennesseys jointly wrote letters back and forth to her, of course, but Winifred rarely had much of interest to share in her dutiful missives back to them. Mrs. Hennessey had often thought they might someday be filled with the antics of her classroom or the goings-on of the school itself, but alas, that was not to be, as Winifred never veered from relating the briefest of facts, the dry routine of her and Roger's life never seeming to alter from one week to another. Though they had been married these fifteen years, Winifred and Roger had not yet been blessed with any children of their own, though Mrs. Hennessey still lived in hope, never understanding why William said that perhaps it was a blessing given Winifred's rather rigid demeanor. Nonsense, Alice would say in response, all she needs is a couple of babies to soften her up! As it was, the blessing of a child not being something in the Hennesseys' power to give, they instead contented themselves with waiting patiently for Winifred's letters to come each month and learned to be happy with them, sparse though they were, as, they supposed, it was better than nothing.

Their son, Tommy, the youngest, was likewise a bit estranged from them. He had left long ago after a couple of scrapes with the law and after Mr. Hennessey had likewise sadly found a large amount of cash missing from the old black cash register on the bar of Poor Pete's. The last they had heard he was in New Mexico or Arizona, or someplace like that, though they had not received a letter in a long time, which Mrs. Hennessey knew was very heartbreaking for her William. Indeed, Mr. Hennessey had been heard on more than one occasion to say that Tommy had always had a chip on his shoulder, and that nothing anyone did could ever seem to knock it off for him, poor lad.

And then there was Billy, the oldest and their favorite, though neither of them had ever dared to say that out loud. He had been killed in the war, and that had been the end of it, the end of him, and the end of anything that had ever resembled what might be called mirth in the Hennessey household ever again, really. As if by some unspoken agreement, the Hennesseys rarely spoke of him, except on the anniversary of his death, when they would take out the photograph of him in uniform, the medal that had been sent to them, and the letter telling them that he was no more and that he had died bravely.

So it was that when Henrietta had come along, she had naturally become more or less like a daughter to them in more ways than one. At first Mr. Hennessey had taken her on out of guilt that he had let Les Von Harmon nearly drink himself into a state of delirium before he had stumbled out and killed himself. Guilt had haunted him for months after that until Alice had finally brought him round to his senses, telling him that if it hadn't been at Poor Pete's it would have been somewhere else. Les was bound to do it, she said, after it had come out that he had been so terribly in debt, and it wasn't their responsibility what happened when their customers left the premises. Anyway, she had shrugged, at least his last hours were spent happy with a bottle of rum.

But Les hadn't looked happy to him, William knew. His eyes had looked haunted and pained. He could still see them sometimes at night when he couldn't sleep, those eyes, watching him. Watching him when his oldest daughter, Henrietta, had shown up at Poor Pete's, begging for a job. How could he refuse her, especially, he realized immediately upon seeing her, as she was so obviously going to need someone to watch over her? She had been gorgeous even then, and unexplainably, he had felt an almost-immediate desire to protect her, a thing of beauty that one only witnessed perhaps once in a lifetime. While she worked for him, he was able to keep his eye on her, and he eventually made her a 26 girl, hoping that if she made more money she would stay longer. Once or twice a month, he would even resort to stacking her tips despite the watchful eyes of Mrs. Hennessey, though he couldn't afford to do this every time, as profits were pretty slim as it was. The Depression had been hard on them so far, though money, he knew, could always be found in people's pockets for vice.

When Henrietta had announced out of nowhere that she was leaving to become a taxi dancer, he had fretted with worry, but, as Alice had so wisely pointed out, they couldn't keep her forever. He had young Dubowski report in sometimes on how she was doing, as he knew he followed her regularly and carried a torch for her, even now, he surmised, as he looked across the room where Stan stood stiffly next to Elsie, though his eyes, Mr. Hennessey saw, never left Henrietta.

He had spotted Stan and Elsie standing in the corner right after they had themselves arrived, and they had come hurrying over to greet them, eager to exchange comments of shock and surprise at everything they saw around them. At last he and Alice would have something substantial to write to Winifred this week.

Elsie had just a few moments ago gone to get Henrietta, but she hadn't returned with her. Instead, next thing he knew, Mr. Hennessey saw Clive and Henrietta out on the dance floor. Well, he could wait. He enjoyed just watching her shine. He had always known Dubowski wasn't for her; she needed someone better. Not that young Stan wasn't a first-rate sort of chap, the kind of kid one wouldn't mind having for a son, but Henrietta deserved someone truly special, he thought, as he looked again at Clive. Howard seemed a decent sort, had looked him in the eye and shook his hand manfully. He had to admit that he had been touched beyond words that he had come to ask him—him!—for Henrietta's hand. It had meant a lot to him, and he felt this Clive was perhaps someone worthy of his Henrietta. He looked around again at the opulence he saw everywhere and mused that if anyone could pull this off, it would be Henrietta. Yes, she belonged somewhere like this, and he felt somewhere in back of him that Les's watching eyes would approve as well.

"Mr. Hennessey!" Henrietta cried as she came toward them, the dance having ended and other couples taking to the floor now as another song started up. Henrietta's eyes positively glowed, and Mr. Hennessey thought she had never looked more beautiful, more radiant. She hugged him tightly and then, releasing him, held her arms out to Alice, who quickly licked her fingers before embracing her as well, carefully holding onto her plate with one hand as she did so.

"Thank you for coming! I know it was a long journey for you!" Henrietta said, genuinely happy to see them.

"Here you are," Mr. Hennessey said, handing Clive the bottle he had been fretfully gripping since he had arrived. "Little engagement gift for you."

"Oh, Mr. Hennessey!" Henrietta exclaimed, recognizing it as one of the dusty bottles of scotch that always lay tucked away on the top shelf of the bar, unused. "That's one of your good ones!"

"Laphroaig 1890," said Clive, examining it with a low whistle. "Where'd you come across this?" he asked, impressed.

"Billy sent it back when he was over there. Before . . ." He broke off, then.

"Billy was their son who was killed in the war," Henrietta explained gently.

"I didn't realize. I'm very sorry," Clive said genuinely. "What regiment, if I might ask?"

"18th Infantry."

"Brave they were. I was in the Second Calvary."

"You were? I didn't know that . . ."

"I've got the bum shoulder to prove it," Clive said, smiling as he tapped his shoulder. If it were possible for Mr. Hennessey to approve of him any more, it had just occurred.

"Thank you," said Clive, nodding to both of them. "We'll save this for a very special occasion, indeed."

"You're most welcome," Mr. Hennessey said, beaming proudly, glad that his gift had been so favorably received and appreciated.

"You'll make the most beautiful bride!" Mrs. Hennessey exclaimed, leaning excitedly toward Henrietta. "I can't wait to see your dress!"

"Alice!" Mr. Hennessey exclaimed, a look of shock on his face. "We haven't been invited!"

"Well, of course we're going to be invited, good Lord!" Mrs. Hennessey said, finishing off a tiny meatball, the last morsel on her now-empty china plate. "The poor thing's invited us to this," she said to him as if Clive and Henrietta weren't standing right in front of them. "It follows, then, that we would be invited to the wedding; isn't that right, Henrietta?" she asked plainly, turning to her now.

Henrietta smiled at her and nodded. "Of course you're to be invited. In fact," she said more seriously, looking directly at Mr. Hennessey, "there's something I was hoping to ask you." She looked up at Clive for assurance, and he gave a slight nod of encouragement. "Mr. Hennessey, I . . . I was hoping you might give me away. At the wedding, I mean. Would you . . . would you consider it, walking me down the aisle, that is?"

Mr. Hennessey's previously jovial face transfigured then as his brows furrowed and he swallowed hard. "You're sure?" is all he managed to say, looking at Clive.

"Of course I'm sure," she said, slightly puzzled. "If you wouldn't mind. If you do . . ." she went on quickly, "Eugene will do it, I just thought . . ."

"No!" he interrupted sharply. "I'd . . . I'd be honored to," he said, forcing a smile and grasping her hand tightly. "Honored, girl," he said. "If you'll excuse me for just a moment," he muttered rather abruptly and jostled past them, laboriously weaving his way through the crowd.

"Ahh, the poor thing," said Mrs. Hennessey. "Overcome he is, is all. Just give him a minute," she said with a quick smile and a little wink. "Pleased as punch, he is," she said and hurried after him.

"Do you think I've upset him?" Henrietta said to Clive as she watched the Hennesseys leave the room.

"Yes, but in a good way," he said, reaching for her hand and holding it.

They were not to be left alone, however, as Henrietta became aware of a very chic, elegant woman now approaching them. She had been standing nearby with a rather dapper young man, who released her now and stood watching her in a disgruntled sort of way as she made her way over to them.

"Oh, God," she heard Clive groan and felt him brace himself. The woman, while not exactly beautiful, was attractive in her own way, her face being a bit too long and thin, which gave her the odd resemblance to a young horse. Even her eyes were big and brown, her lashes thick with mascara, and she wore bright pink lipstick on her full lips, which, Henrietta observed, were always held slightly open in a decidedly provocative manner. Her gown was exquisite, a salmon silk with a black net overlay that must surely have come from Paris or London, Henrietta guessed. She was utterly elegant and oozed sophisticated confidence.

"Are you not going to introduce me to my rival, you naughty boy?" she drawled at Clive.

Clive took a deep breath. "Miss Sophia Lewis, allow me to present my fiancée, Miss Henrietta Von Harmon," he said, inclining his head toward Henrietta. "Miss Von Harmon, Miss Lewis. Miss Lewis is an old friend," he said obligingly.

"Is that what you call it these days?" she laughed. "Well, call it what you must. I'm an old flame," she said confidentially to Henrietta. "You must ask him sometime. If he'll tell you, that is. He can be rather fierce at times, but I expect you know that by now."

Henrietta wasn't sure what to say, or to think, for that matter. So this was the infamous Sophia she had heard about. "Yes, I'll do that," Henrietta tried to say confidently.

"I can see that I've upset you," she laughed. "Don't worry, darling, I'm not a threat, not a serious one anyway. He tossed me over long ago. Not his type, I can see that now. You like them pretty young," she said, fingering Clive's lapel for a moment before letting it go.

"Not to offend, Sophia, but why exactly are you here? I suspect my mother somehow," he said, looking out over the crowd as if to locate her.

"Did you forget I am a friend of Julia's? I'm here at her invitation, actually."

"Of course," he said with a roll of his eyes.

"Anyway, you needn't worry. I'm here with the dashing Lloyd

Everton, and I'm quite taken with him," she drawled, batting her lashes at Clive.

"Yes, I can tell," he said, sarcastically, looking over at Everton, who was meanwhile feigning indifference.

"Do me a favor, though, would you, Clive? Dance with me. One last time. You don't mind, do you, darling?" she asked Henrietta. "You don't look the jealous type. Why should you be? After all, you managed to snag him."

"I think you're intoxicated, Sophia."

"I'm sure I am! That's the whole idea, is it not? Please, Clive!" she said with a pouty whine.

"Absolutely not," Clive began, but Henrietta interjected.

"Go, Clive. Honestly. There's no harm in it, and, anyway, I'll powder my nose."

Clive looked at her with quiet pause, questioning. "You're sure?"

"Of course I'm sure. Go on. I trust you . . . remember?" she whispered.

"Oh, very well," he sighed, as he gave her a grateful smile and gently rubbed her finger with his thumb before releasing her hand. Stiffly, then, he held his arm out to Sophia to escort her to the dance floor.

For the first time that night, Henrietta found herself momentarily alone, and she looked over the crowd for any sign of Elsie or Stan, or Eugene, for that matter. She glanced over to where she had left them with the Exleys, but they had all since scattered. She spotted Mrs. Howard watching Clive and Sophia on the dance floor with what looked like delight on her face, seeming to confirm that Sophia had indeed been Antonia's first choice for Catherine's replacement. She would have to be careful there, she noted.

She continued looking out over the crowd until she saw Mr. Howard now, talking with none other than the Hennesseys. They seemed fully engaged in a conversation, and Henrietta wondered what they would possibly have in common enough to discuss so enthusiastically. She was about to go rescue one or both of the parties when she suddenly caught a glimpse of Elsie—on the dance floor, no less—with a young officer! She surveyed the room again for any sign of Stan, but he was nowhere to be seen. Moreover, when she looked at Elsie again, she seemed to be positively beaming, causing Henrietta to sigh. Elsie was ever too obvious. She was about to move closer when she heard a low voice near her ear say, "I've finally got you," startling her and causing her to turn and look. It was Jack.

She exhaled loudly, "Jack! You startled me!"

"Sorry," he said. "Didn't mean to." He shifted the empty tray he was carrying. "I've been waitin' for you to come round to the stables, or at least the kitchen," he said a bit too irritably for her liking. "I found out some interesting things about Helen's ring . . . I thought you wanted to know . . ."

Henrietta looked around covertly, hoping no one was noticing her talking now to Jack. She tried to keep her shoulders in line with his so that they remained side by side, making it not so conspicuous that they were indeed having a conversation.

"I do, honestly, Jack, but not now!" she tried to say out of the corner of her mouth.

"When then? You're never around like you used to be. I can't just come up to the house, you know."

"Jack, listen, I . . . I can't do that sort of thing anymore. I promised Clive . . ."

"That what? That you can't talk to whoever you want to? That you'd be his obedient dog and only come when he calls you? Is that it?"

"Jack!" she said, venturing to look at him.

"I'm sorry," he said immediately. "I . . . I didn't mean it . . . just that . . . I thought we were friends."

Henrietta sighed. "I like you, Jack, but I . . . I can't be friends with the servants anymore. Not like that."

"They don't own you, you know," he said bitterly.

"Yes, I know that," she said, exasperated, though she was rather taken aback by his increasingly angry tone, one which, before tonight, she had never heard from him before. "It's my choice," she said after a pause.

"I see. Well, I'll be off, then," he said, obviously upset.

"Jack . . . don't be like that."

"I thought you cared about Helen is all," he said with a shrug.

"I do! I was planning on slipping down to the kitchen to say hello to her, if I can ever get away. That or find Edna to give her a message from me."

"Helen's not down there."

"What do you mean?"

"Just that she's not. The flu, same as James, is what I heard."

"Oh, no!"

Henrietta internally scolded herself for not going down earlier to the cottage. Hadn't she had a bad feeling? Silently she resolved that nothing would stop her from doing so tomorrow morning. "Is Edna around?" she asked, giving the room a searching perusal, but instead of locating Edna, her eyes caught Clive, laughing with Sophia as they talked with the Exleys. Just at that moment, he happened to look her way, and she saw his eyes flicker almost imperceptibly toward Jack then back to her. Sophia put her hand on his arm, then, and he was reluctantly brought back into their conversation. But he had seen, she knew, and she felt a small knot of tension in the pit of her stomach.

Beside her Jack gave a wry laugh. "Maids don't serve above stairs; don't you know that? They're kept below; only men, footmen, that is, can serve in public."

"Jack, please!"

Distraught, now, she was about to say something more when a tall woman in a pale blue dress appeared at her side, causing Jack to instantly stand at attention with his empty tray held dutifully in front of him. The woman eyed him carefully and did not seem fooled by his now-formal stance. "I'd like a sherry, please," she said to him condescendingly. "Not too dry."

"Very good, Madam," Jack said deliberately and gave a slight bow before hurrying away.

"Watch that one," said the woman, her eyes still following him before she turned her attention fully to Henrietta now. "He's an insolent one. I'm a master at reading servants. I'm always right in that department, though no one usually listens to me."

Henrietta wasn't sure what to make of this strange woman. Though she had obviously never met her, she had a familiar look to her, her wavy chestnut hair done up in the latest fashion, her clear, honest hazel eyes. She briefly glanced over again to where Clive stood, but he still had his back to her.

"You must be Miss Von Harmon," the woman said, holding out a gloved hand. "Since no one appears to be even remotely interested in the formalities, at least where I'm concerned, anyway—though, I will say, we *are* dreadfully late—allow me to introduce myself. I'm Julia Cunningham, Clive's sister."

"Oh!" Henrietta said, making the connection now about why she looked familiar. She did indeed look very much like Clive. "I'm so glad to meet you! But how . . . how did you know it was me?" Henrietta asked, curious.

Julia laughed. "Well, I could flatter you and say I recognized your great beauty, which Clive has repeatedly mentioned in his letters to me," she said, her eyebrow uncannily arched just as Clive's was wont to do. "But in truth," she smiled, "it is the ring."

Henrietta glanced down at the marvelous ring on her finger and smiled, holding it up a bit. "It *is* beautiful, isn't it? I feel terribly afraid that I might lose it!"

"Nonsense!" said Julia. "Not with your lover constantly clasping your hand; that will surely keep it in place. However, Clive's not the most affectionate man, is he? Not in public, anyway. Where is the 'old boy'?" she said looking around. "Shouldn't he be permanently at your side, showing you off to everyone?"

"He's . . . he was dancing with Miss Lewis, I believe her name is, but I don't see them now," Henrietta said quietly, looking over to where they had been standing.

Julia laughed outright. "Oh, yes! I quite forgot. She begged me for an invitation, so I finally relented, knowing it was harmless, of course. You've nothing to fear there, my dear. It was very fleeting, if it was anything; more Mother's scheme than anything else. Clive, I think, went along with it to appease her until he'd had enough. Oh, heavens, no!" she said, laughing again, Henrietta's face still displaying a trace of apprehension. "Clive and I are very close, my dear. And I don't think it's a breach of confidence to tell you that he's already written me too, too many letters in which you repeatedly and rather boringly—no offense meant, of course—make up the main theme, telling me over and over of his great love for you. It really becomes rather dull reading." She paused here for a moment before continuing. "But I've not heard him this happy, this excited, in many long years," she said with real sincerity now. "And I have to say, my dear, I love you unabashedly just for that. I hope you know how fragile is the heart you hold," she said, looking into Henrietta's face with great kindness. "Despite his rather gruff exterior, that is. But I expect you know that already, don't you?"

Henrietta looked into Julia's eyes and was again discomfited by how much it seemed like looking into Clive's. "Yes, I . . . I think I do," Henrietta answered quietly. "He's quite different, you're right, when we're alone . . . not that we're alone that often!" she added quickly with a blush.

"I can only imagine," Julia said confidingly, her face breaking into a big smile again. She put her arm through Henrietta's. "I like you!" she said, looking out over the crowd as she did so. "I want us to be the very best of friends; would you mind terribly?" She looked back at her now. "I suppose you have an awful lot of friends already. So do I, come to think of it. But I want you for my especial friend! Please say yes!"

She was so enthusiastic, so cheerfully encouraging, that Henrietta couldn't help but smile and say that, yes, she would be her especial friend. In her heart, she was pleased, actually, because, besides Elsie, she hadn't ever really had time for a real friend. There had been Polly, of course, and Lucy, but they were really just girls from work, not bosom friends. For the whole of the past week, she had tried to mentally prepare herself to simply "get through" tonight; she certainly hadn't expected to come away with a new friend.

"So! How do you find us?" Julia asked, taking a sip of the sherry Jack had just delivered, deliberately not looking at Henrietta as he hurried away. "Not too ferocious, I hope? You musn't mind Mother. She'll come round. She always does, especially where Clive's concerned. She's a terrible snob, it's true, but she actually does have a good heart, when she cares to reveal it, that is."

Henrietta wasn't sure what to say to that and noticed that Elsie was standing off to the side talking still to the young officer. Where was Stan? The one time she needed him, he was nowhere to be found. Any other time he was constantly lurking about, one step behind her . . . And where were the Hennesseys? Perhaps *they* might rescue Elsie . . .

"And what do you make of the Exleys?" Julia said, looking over at them now. "You can't imagine Mother's shock at finding out you're their best friends' niece! It was sheer heaven to have heard her! She wasn't sure what to do! And it's not often Mother is confounded. Still, the Exleys are an okay lot, as families go, snobbish as well, sorry to say, but then again, they all are, really. You might have had a worse time of it, oddly, if your grandmother were still alive, but since she's gone now, Mr. Exley might be more, shall we say, forgiving."

"It's *my* mother I'm worried about," Henrietta ventured to say, deciding to try out her new confidant.

"Yes, I can see how it probably is. I'm guessing that's why she's not here, is that not right?"

"She simply can't face them, I think," Henrietta said apologetically. "Something like that, anyway."

"Hmmm . . . Yes, it will take time, I should imagine. But it's not impossible." She smiled. "That must be your sister," she said then, changing the subject and looking out toward Elsie, "in the brown suit."

"Yes," said Henrietta, clearly embarrassed. "I tried to get her to wear a gown, but she wouldn't. She's not used to this sort of thing, you see. Well, neither am I, really." Henrietta smiled weakly.

"Oh, don't worry! It gives the old biddies something to gossip about! And in the end, it doesn't really matter; you still walk away with the prince, do you not?!"

Henrietta couldn't help but laugh outright. She found Julia's witty ridicule delightfully engaging and amusing, despite the fact that Julia herself obviously adhered to all of the societal conventions expected of her, as evidenced by her appearance, her bearing, and even her manner of speaking. It made it all the easier—if only for this evening, anyway—for Henrietta to endure it all, and she felt instantly endeared to Julia because of it.

"Who is it that Elsie's talking with, do you know?" Henrietta asked.

"The young officer?" Julia asked, peering over at the two of them now, the young man bent very close to Elsie, engaged in what looked like an entertaining conversation. "That's Lieutenant Harrison Barnes-Smith. He's a neighbor, of sorts. His uncle—he'll be around here somewhere . . ." she said absently, looking around and giving up after only a minute. "He was Clive's commanding officer in the war. I don't know why they were invited, really; I think Mother's gotten a bit carried away," she said, looking around the room again, assessing it more critically this time. "But no one ever listens to me."

"Is he nice?"

"Who? Harrison? As far as I know. He's very charming. Bit of a ladies' man, I've heard. Should we be concerned?"

"Well, maybe. Elsie's quite naive, actually, and she's, well, she's almost engaged to someone else. He's here tonight, but he's disappeared somewhere. It's not like him, really. He's usually annoyingly attentive."

"Julia! Here you are!" said a thin, impeccably dressed man striding toward them. At first glance, he might be considered handsome, Henrietta decided, with his dark hair and blue eyes. But upon further inspection, she judged his eyes to be small and cruel, especially when he looked at Julia, and his small mouth formed a permanent sort of grimace beneath his thin mustache. Indeed, at this moment he seemed to be looking at Julia with a combination of irritation and something else, perhaps dislike? Surely not!

"We've been looking for you everywhere, you know! Your mother is very irritated. It seems Clive's betrothed has also disappeared; no surprise there. She's probably . . ."

"Allow me to introduce Miss Henrietta Von Harmon," Julia calmly interrupted him. Henrietta had not failed to perceive a shadow of something darker cross Julia's face as he had approached. Julia gestured toward him now. "Miss Von Harmon, my husband, the honorable Randolph Cunningham," she said acerbically, giving him a venomous look. The whole exchange was quite shocking to Henrietta, who found it hard to believe that someone as lovely and jolly as Julia would be married to someone who seemed so mean and despising and who didn't seem to particularly like his wife all that much. She was at a loss for what to say.

"I beg your pardon, Miss Von Harmon," Randolph said, bowing slightly toward her but without any real remorse in his tone. "I only meant to convey that your presence is very much required and dare I say, *desired*, this way," he said, gesturing back toward where she had last seen Clive standing with Sophia.

"Thank you, Mr. Cunningham," Henrietta said smoothly, allowing herself to be led along with Julia back to the little group of Howards and Exleys. Julia winked at her and smiled, but Henrietta thought it seemed disingenuous now and saw something else in her eyes, possibly fear. Henrietta was grateful to see Clive among the little group, Sophia nowhere in sight, and he made his way over to her and stood by her side, Julia simultaneously leaving her to greet and stiffly embrace her mother, but not before giving Clive's arm a quick pat.

"You've met Julia, then?" Clive whispered to Henrietta, a look of anxious expectation crossing his face.

"Yes, she's wonderful."

"I knew you'd like her."

"Randolph seems a bit . . . strict."

"He's an ass," Clive said bitterly, glaring at him now. "An utter brute, and I hate him. He's absolutely beastly to her."

"But I don't understand. She's so lovely, so cheerful . . ."

"She tries to be, in her own way . . ." He broke off, however, as Henrietta noticed Antonia coming toward them now. Smoothly, Clive managed to turn his back to his mother and say in a low voice in Henrietta's ear, "Come on, let's dance. It's our only chance to be alone."

She smiled and took his hand as he led her to dance to George Gershwin's "Someone to Watch Over Me." To her surprise, they were joined on the dance floor eventually by none other than Elsie and Stan, who was doing his best to keep up. Elsie was smiling beside herself, while Stan's brow was furrowed as he tried to concentrate on his steps. Henrietta bit her lip and looked away, turning her attention back to Clive.

"Did you enjoy your dance with Sophia?" she tried to ask in an innocent tone, looking up into his eyes to read them, but he skillfully kept them blank. "She's very pretty," she added teasingly.

"I wouldn't know," he said.

"I think she still likes you."

"Probably."

"Well!" she said, trying not to laugh.

"How was your conversation with Jack?" he asked, his eyebrow arched.

Henrietta blushed. She wanted to blurt out that the two incidents were not comparable by any means, but she refrained and played along instead. "Uneventful," she said casually.

"I see. I might have to interrogate you later," he said, teasing her now with a smile. "Police business, of course."

"Would it be wrong for you to kiss me right now?"

"Very much so, I'm afraid. Later," he whispered, and she gripped him tighter, a happiness filling her as he spun her around the floor, no more mention of either Jack or Sophia being made between them.

It was the only other dance they were allowed, as it turned out, the rest of the evening being spent making their way around the room, greeting the Howards' guests and fabricating small talk. It was well past midnight when the last of the guests finally said goodnight. Julia, upon leaving, had first taken her hand and then embraced her tightly, promising that she would come round for a visit as soon as she could arrange it. The Hennesseys had also been very ebullient in their goodbyes, thanking the Howards profusely for their hospitality, Mr. Hennessey shaking Clive's hand stiffly, and whispering to him to take care of his girl. The Exleys, too, seemed loath to depart from their long-lost relation and promised to entertain her and Clive, as well as all the Howards, very soon, to which Clive, of course, offered his thanks, Henrietta simply grateful that there was no other mention at present of them traveling into the city to see Ma.

At one point in the night, Henrietta had found herself momentarily alone with old Mr. Exley, during which time he had expressed a desire to talk with her at length and in private on some future date, if that were possible. There was much he would say, he said, about what had happened with her mother. Not all of it had been their fault, he wished her to know, but there would be time enough for that later, he had added in a low voice just as Mr. Howard had joined them then and the conversation had naturally fallen to other subjects.

Indeed, all of the goodbyes seemed to take even longer than the hellos, and by the time Henrietta wearily found herself outside her bedroom door, it was very late indeed, Eugene, Stan, and Elsie having already been accordingly shown to their rooms.

Clive had walked up the long staircase with her, his fingers entwined with hers as they went. Henrietta paused now outside her door to say goodnight to him, as was their routine whenever he was at Highbury. Tonight, however, looking up and down the hallway, he opened the door and led her in, saying in a deep, whispered voice that it was just for a moment, that he wished to hold her for a few blessed minutes in the quiet of her room and to talk, just for a little bit.

Clive was immensely proud of her, the more so because Julia had found a moment to whisper to him that she positively adored

Henrietta and wholeheartedly gave her approval. It was the only person in this world whose opinion really mattered to him, except perhaps his father's, and his heart was full to bursting.

He turned to her now and enveloped her in his arms, resting his cheek against her soft hair, and was sorely tempted to lay her down on the bed there and then, as the whole evening had had the feel of a wedding rather than a party, and it seemed unnatural to not proceed now to a deeper intimacy in a locked room together. He refrained, however, kissing her tenderly instead. When he felt her small hands reach under his suitcoat, touching his chest and then timidly wandering to his back, he thought he might go mad and pulled back with immense effort, breathing heavily, as he gripped her hands and removed them from around him.

"Goodnight, my darling," he said, huskily. "I should go."

"Do you have to?" she asked, looking up at him with such trusting blue eyes that he felt himself waver.

"Yes, it's for the best," he said gently. "I'll see you in the morning. You were wonderful tonight. Everyone is quite taken with you," he said, resting his finger under her chin and kissing her longingly. "Goodnight," he whispered finally, "we'll talk about it all tomorrow." He slipped out, then, the blood coursing through his veins despite his exhaustion.

Henrietta watched him walk down the long hallway to his suite of rooms, her thoughts whirling with all that had happened, trying to keep it all straight in her mind. Overall, she was more than happy with how the evening had turned out, though she had learned later that the Hennesseys had embarrassingly asked Mr. Howard for a tour of the house and that Eugene had slipped off below stairs and had had to be rooted out by Stan, neither of them saying, even when she had asked, exactly what he had been doing down there. It was then that Harrison had apparently made his introduction to Elsie . . .

But at least it had gone well with the Exleys, she felt, as she shut the door and began to undress. Yes, she concluded, her silent prayers had been answered and the evening had gone well, though she had no idea as she slipped, exhausted, into her bed that it was far from being over.

Chapter 16

Henrietta was not quite asleep, the evening's events still whirling round in her head, the many conversations she had been privy to coming back to her in fits and starts, when she heard a faint knock on her door. Not sure if she had heard right, she sat up, listening closely, and, hearing it again, this time a little bit louder, she quickly pulled back the covers and switched on her bedside lamp.

"Who is it?" she asked, reaching for her dressing gown. She hurried to the door, suspecting that it might be Clive, that he had perhaps changed his mind. Her heart began to beat a little faster, the thought of being alone in her room with him again causing her to flush with a strange combination of unease and anticipation. After all, her mother—Ma!—hadn't waited, she reasoned distractedly.

When she reached the door, she paused to collect herself, opening it just a crack, and was surprised to see not Clive, but Elsie huddled there.

"Oh, Hen, can I come in?" Elsie whispered, shivering from being out of bed in the cold hallway.

"Of course you can!" Henrietta said, surprised by the sudden disappointment she felt and drew her in. "What's happened?" she asked, putting her arm around her.

"Oh! Nothing's happened!" Elsie said quickly. "It's just that I can't sleep. The bed's too big."

Henrietta laughed. "I had that problem at first, too. Go on; climb in," she said, gesturing toward her own massive four-poster bed.

"I haven't woken you, have I?" Elsie asked as she perched herself on the bed while Henrietta slid in beside her, the bedside lamp giving off just enough of a soft glow to inspire a confidence. In truth, Henrietta did not like sleeping alone half as much as she always dreamed she would and was glad now that Elsie had come to find her. Sometimes they had talked at home in bed in fragmented whispers, but it was hard with Ma just on the other side of Elsie. She was a light sleeper and often told them to "Go to sleep!" if they got too loud. Just the two of them together now was an unexpected treat.

"Not at all, actually," Henrietta said, snuggling under the covers. Though it was July, the air was cool in the house at night, as it had been an exceptionally mild summer this year. She wished she could light a fire, but she didn't dare. "I was just lying here awake, anyway, thinking about tonight."

"Oh, Hen! Me, too! It was such a lovely party! I wish Ma could have seen it. And Herbert and Eddie, actually. Wouldn't they have had fun?"

Henrietta smiled at the thought. "Yes, Julia said I should have brought them, but I don't think she really meant it. There weren't any other children tonight. She says she has two boys herself, though you wouldn't think it, would you?"

"Heavens, no! She looks so young! How old do you think she is?"

"I'm not sure; I'll have to ask Clive. I know she's older than him, but not by much I should think."

"I like Clive," Elsie said, lying down and looking up at the bed canopy. Abruptly, she raised herself up on one elbow. "He's very kind, actually. He asked me to dance; did you notice? You were talking with Mrs. Howard and some of her friends, I think."

"Yes," Henrietta said with a sly smile. "I noticed. I'm very glad he did; I was worried that you might not enjoy yourself tonight."

"Oh, no, Hen! Not at all! It was perfectly heavenly!"

"Would that have something to do with a certain lieutenant?" Henrietta asked teasingly.

Elsie sat up fully now, clasping her arms around her knees as she drew them up to her chest. "Oh, Hen!" she gushed without any attempt to hide her feelings. "Wasn't he lovely?"

"Well, I never got to meet him properly, really; I just saw him from afar."

"He's so handsome, isn't he? And so polite! I've never seen manners like that before, except for Clive, of course," she added hastily.

"Julia says the lieutenant's very charming, Els, and very popular with the ladies, if you know what I mean," Henrietta said, warningly.

"Oh, I can see why!" Elsie gushed.

"What about Stan?" Henrietta asked, trying a different tactic.

Elsie's brow furrowed momentarily. "Oh, he wasn't too happy, I can tell you that!"

"But, I mean, how do you feel about him?"

Henrietta was about to further ask Elsie if her thoughts about Stan and marriage had changed since they had last talked when she heard another knock at the door. Both girls froze, Elsie ducking down under the covers as if she were a mischievous schoolgirl, stifling a giggle as she did so.

It *must* be Clive this time, thought Henrietta as she slid out of bed and hurried to the thick rosewood door, wondering what she would say to him with Elsie in the room. She would have to cut him off before he could say anything suggestive. And what would Elsie think about Clive coming to her room after hours when he assumed the whole house to be asleep?

She opened the door a crack, trying to think of what she would say, when she gasped again to see not Clive but Jack standing in the hallway, looking ragged and overwrought. She drew her dressing gown around her tighter. She hadn't opened the door any wider, but she saw his eyes try to look past her before he returned his frantic gaze back to her.

"What are you doing?" she whispered.

"Can you help me?" he whispered back. "It's Helen."

"What do you mean?"

"I went down to check on her after the party, her being ill and all," he said, his words tumbling out fast. "She's pretty bad, Miss. She's asking for you. Says she needs to tell you something. I . . . I tried to put her off . . . distract her . . . but she just gets more and more agitated. In the end, I said I'd go and fetch you. Please, Miss. She's in a terrible bad state. I think she might be dyin'."

"Oh, God!" Henrietta said, putting a fist to her mouth. She wasn't sure what to think, what to do. Maybe it was just one of Helen's delusional states. What could Helen possibly have to tell *her*? And anyway, didn't she think she was Daphne half the time? But maybe that's who she actually wanted to talk to . . . Maybe it was something important . . . A deathbed confession to Daphne? Maybe something about the ring?

"Miss, please!" whispered Jack.

"Why haven't you woken Mr. or Mrs. Howard? It sounds like she needs a doctor."

"Do you think I should?" Jack hesitated, looking at her desperately. "I just thought, after the party and all, they probably wouldn't appreciate being woken up in the middle of the night. I thought maybe if you saw her, she'd calm down or *you* could decide if we needed to wake the house up."

Henrietta paused. What he said made sense, and, she had to admit, she was not all that eager to wake the Howards, either. What if it *was* a false alarm? "I suppose you're right," she mused aloud. "But we should tell Clive at least," she said, stepping out slightly and looking down the darkened hallway.

"I tried that, Miss. I can see how he feels about us being alone together," he said with a shade of bitterness creeping back into his voice. "And I didn't want to get you in trouble again, not after the last time. So I went to him first, but he's not there."

"Not there?" she asked, confused, looking down the hallway again.

She was touched, however, by Jack's thoughtful consideration of her situation.

"No, Miss. Not anywhere that I could find him. Not in his usual spots . . . library, billiard room. The house is dark."

"That's odd . . ." Henrietta said, more to herself than anyone, baffled at Clive's possible whereabouts. She had seen him walk down the hallway to his rooms . . . "Isn't Billings about?"

"Not that I could see." He twisted his cap in his hands again. "Miss! I don't think we have much time!"

His face, crumpled in agitation, finally forced her hand.

"Well, I suppose . . ." she murmured and bit her lip, deciding there was nothing for it but to go down to the cottage and see if she could be of any help. She just hoped it wasn't a wild-goose chase created by Helen's jumbled imaginings. "Just a moment," she said to Jack. "Let me get my things on. You wait here."

"Okay, but hurry!" he said, looking up and down the hallway.

Henrietta gingerly closed the door and practically ran to her armoire to find some clothing to put on. Elsie, sitting bolt upright in the bed now, the covers drawn up to her neck at the sound of a male voice in the hallway, of course wanted to know what was happening and was beside herself when Henrietta told her she was going to check on one of the older servants who was ill. Naturally, Elsie wanted to go as well, but Henrietta insisted that she stay and keep an eye out for Clive.

"If he turns up, tell him to come down to the cottage," Henrietta said, wrapping a shawl around her shoulders.

"Oh, Hen, maybe you should take Stan with you," Elsie suggested.

"No, I've got Jack. I'll be okay with him," she said practically and pushed an image of the lurking Virgil from her mind. "He'll go with me. I'll try to get back as soon as I can," Henrietta said, hurrying out and closing the door noiselessly behind her.

Neither Jack nor Henrietta said anything as they made their way through the darkened house and out the East Doors to the path along the lake. Jack seemed tense and agitated, but grateful that she was accompanying him. It wasn't until the cottage was in sight that he finally slowed his pace. He looked back at her now, giving her a strange smile as they made their way up to the door. Henrietta was surprised that there was no lamp burning.

"You didn't leave her in the dark, did you?" Henrietta asked, concerned.

Jack didn't respond, however, but pushed open the unlocked door with more force than Henrietta thought necessary and allowed her to pass through first.

"Helen?" Henrietta called out as she stepped into the kitchen. The room was dark, and there was no sound at all from the bedroom at the back. Oh, God! thought Henrietta, fearing that they were too late. "Helen?" she called again. "I'm here now! Jack," she said turning toward him, "light a lamp, would you?"

Something about the way he was looking at her, though, caused her to stop short. He was grinning at her in a way he hadn't ever before, and in the shadows, his face looked distorted and cruel. "Jack?" she asked, truly concerned. "What's wrong?"

But even as she asked, an unnamed dread began to stretch its icy fingers through her chest. Something wasn't right here, and she felt the beginnings of panic.

"Jack, now, is it?" he said. "Not Fletcher, the servant?" he asked, taking a step toward her.

"What are you doing?" Henrietta asked anxiously. "Where's Helen?" she said, glancing toward the bedroom.

Jack laughed. "Oh, she's back there, all right. A bit worse for wear, but I suppose she'll live."

Henrietta's mind exploded in fright. She gave him a last furtive look before hurrying back to the bedroom and then let out a little gasp when she saw Helen, bound and gagged in a chair at the foot of the bed, her chin to her chest. Henrietta ran to her and dropped to her knees beside her. "Oh, Helen! Helen!" she shouted, pressing her hand to the old woman's forehead, but she appeared to be unconscious. "You brute!" Henrietta said, standing up and turning back to face Jack, who was casually leaning against the bedroom doorway now and holding an old kerosene lamp which grotesquely illuminated his face. "Why have you done this? Let her go! Have you lost your mind?" she shouted.

Jack merely grinned at her. "Don't think so, *Miss*."

Panicking, Henrietta made a move to push past him, but he swiftly grabbed her wrist. "Hold on, sister," he said, his polite manner of speaking gone now. "Not so fast."

"Let go of me!" Henrietta said, attempting to wrench herself free, but he only gripped her all the harder, causing her to cry out in pain. "You're hurting me!" she cried.

"Then stop struggling!" he said, releasing her but giving her a little shove toward the bed. "Sit down! This might take a while," he growled, putting the lamp down on the bedside table and looking out the window.

"How dare you!" Henrietta tried to say boldly, but she felt sick from fear, her mind racing. "What are you trying to do?"

Jack looked away from the window now and back down at her. "No need to play lady of the manor now, sister. All that's over. You know, at first I thought you were all right and I actually felt a little bad about what we planned to do with you, but after the last few days, I changed my mind. You're as bad as the rest of them. All high and mighty. Don't forget; I know where you live, where you're from, and you ain't so special, doll."

"Do you honestly think I care what you think of me?" Henrietta managed to say and stood up warily. "You've got to at least let Helen go . . ." she said, moving toward the old woman now. "She hasn't done anything. At least take off her gag; she can't breathe like that!"

Jack quickly reached out and pushed her back down onto the bed. "Leave her. She can breathe." He stood over her now, breathing heavily himself, and Henrietta felt a paralyzing fear just as she had felt when she was trapped at the Marlowe. It was all coming back to her now. Where was Clive?

"Please," she whimpered. "What do you want?"

Jack suddenly plunged his knee onto the bed beside her and, grabbing her by the shoulders, thrust her onto her back and kissed her roughly. She squirmed uselessly to get away, terror filling her. "I'll tell you what I want," he said, his face very close to hers now, his powerful arms pinning her shoulders to the bed. "Admit you thought of me!" he hissed, so that she could feel his spittle on her face. "Just once. Admit you thought of me."

Henrietta turned her head away, tears coming to her eyes. "No!" she said, hoarsely.

Jack continued to pin her there, staring at her, breathing heavily as if trying to decide what to do next. "Bitch," he said under his breath, finally. Miraculously, then, he released her with a shove and stood up. "I'm to deliver you undamaged, however, so I'll leave it. I'm sure Howard's had a taste by now, though," he said, looking at her with disgust.

Henrietta quickly sat up and moved as far as she could away from where he still stood by the bed. She struggled to remain in control, to not break down. She had to think rationally. "What do you mean, 'deliver'?" she forced herself to ask, her voice more shaky than she would have liked.

"That's what this is all about, doll. It's been a setup from the beginning. You didn't think Neptune'd forget, did you?" He smiled when he saw the look of horror cross her face.

"You . . . you work for Neptune? But he's . . . he's in jail," Henrietta said almost frantically, her stomach churning so badly that she felt in danger of being sick.

"*Was* in jail, you mean," Jack laughed. "You didn't really believe jail could actually hold Neptune, did you? He has his ways. He's got men everywhere. More than fucking Moretti, that's for sure. We're taking over, see? And Moretti can go fuck himself. Neptune's going to take over, and I'm coming up with him," he added fiercely.

Henrietta swallowed hard, wondering desperately who Moretti was.

"All I had to do was knock off some broads. Make it look like Moretti's gang did it." He let out a hollow laugh and licked his lips. "Easy enough. Nothin' to it," he grinned, turning to look back out the little window.

"But . . . but what does that have to do with me?" Henrietta finally asked, trying to speak calmly and fighting to keep her teeth from chattering.

"God, you're dumb," Jack said, turning his attention back to her. "It's got everything to do with it, see? Now that you've caught his attention, he ain't never gonna let you go."

Henrietta just stared at him, afraid to say anything more.

"Let's just say, there's gonna be a jailbreak tonight," he said condescendingly. "Neptune's making his escape, and you're going with him."

"What do you mean?" she whispered. "Where are you taking me?"

"You're goin' on a little journey, you are. Little town on the Mississippi they call 'Sin City.' Neptune's got a hideout there. Good place to lie low. He'll have you with him for a while. You'll be his entertainment, shall we say, till he gets tired of you," he said with a ragged grin as he looked her body over one more time.

Desperately Henrietta fought the urge to give in to utter panic. "What have you done with Clive?" she asked, forcing her voice to be steady.

"Oh, him? He's walking into a trap right now. Don't worry about him. No more knight in shining armor, though, so you can forget about that."

"Jack, listen to me," she said, feeling a desperate urge now to help Clive, wherever he was, despite the danger she herself was obviously in. "You . . . you don't have to do this," she begged, trying to bargain. "I . . . I can pay you. Whatever you want."

"You don't have any money," he scoffed. "Not yet, anyway."

"Then . . . take my ring!" she offered desperately, holding up the back of her hand to show him. "It must be worth thousands and thousands," she said eagerly.

He paused as if considering it for one fleeting moment before he turned away and looked out the window again. "Not worth it. Not worth it to have the mob on me for the rest of my life, which would turn out to be a very short one before they bumped me off. No chance, sister."

Helen moaned then, and Henrietta instinctively stood to go to her, but Jack pushed her back. "I ain't gonna tell you again; stay put! Once more and I'll have to tie you."

"But what does Helen possibly have to do with this? Why torture her this way?" Henrietta exclaimed, looking over at Helen. She was still unconscious, it seemed, which was probably a good thing, but Henrietta worried how long she could remain that way.

"She doesn't have anythin' to do with it. She was just in the way," he said with a shrug.

"What do you mean?" Henrietta asked, shocked.

"What I mean is that I needed this cottage for the rendezvous. It has a perfect view of the lake so that I can see the signal when they approach."

"I'm to be taken by . . . by boat?" Henrietta asked incredulously.

"Why else would I be standin' here? I'm waiting for the signal. It should be any time now."

Henrietta's stomach knotted in despair. "Why . . . why not just take one of the cars?" she asked.

"Too easy to trace, and too hard to get around McCreanney. I saw that right away. He's too erratic of a sleeper, and then there's the idiot Virgil to contend with."

"But . . . why not wait at the boathouse, why tie up Helen? With the flu, she could die, you know! Do you really want that on your head?"

Jack laughed a deep, guttural laugh. "You don't appear to be listenin', doll. You think I haven't killed anyone before? I just told you I've killed loads of women. And, anyway, she doesn't have the flu, the old bag. I just said that to get you down here."

Henrietta's throat constricted at the mention of the women

apparently murdered at his hand. She was finding it hard to make sense of everything he was saying.

"Besides," he went on now, "the boathouse is too close to the house and the garage. Too risky. I couldn't take the chance that you might scream. But I see you're not the screamin' type. You might be, though, when Neptune gets his hands on you. Lots of women scream then," he added, grinning at her.

He looked out the window again, his agitation clearly growing. "Come on!" he said to whomever he was waiting for. "Where are they? It's getting fucking late!" he muttered to himself.

"You took Helen's ring, didn't you?" Henrietta said, still trying to piece it all together and to keep him talking. She was hoping to buy time, but to what end?

"Yeah, I did, so what?"

"So . . . what does it have to do with all of this?"

"Nothing! Don't you get it? This isn't a Sherlock Holmes novel. It's not complicated! I was snoopin' around the cottage, scoping out the place, when I saw the ring on the ground just outside her window," he said, nodding toward the kitchen. "Picked it up and took it into town to sell it. Thought I could make a bit of extra dough. How did I know the dope, Virgil, would wander in and buy it?"

"But . . . why did you go along with me, making me think it was some sort of big mystery?"

"To get you to trust me. Worked, didn't it?" he grinned, and she felt sick again as she remembered dancing with him.

"So it was you all this time lurking around the cottage, not Virgil . . ."

"That's right, doll. You're catchin' on, now. The ole bat's too blind to tell us apart. It was easy then to make everyone suspect him," he laughed.

Henrietta felt nauseous as she remembered Helen's description of the lurking man—tall, blond. How had they not realized it was Fletcher, not Virgil? She winced as another thought occurred to her.

"How . . . how did you know that I'd be here—in Winnetka—so far from the city?"

"I told you. Neptune's reach goes far," he said with a haunted look. "He has eyes everywhere. Knows everything about everyone. He put me on the case right away. I even had to steal some stuff, had to make it look like the old chauffer did it so he'd get fired. Then I could slip in." He looked proud as he said it, eager to tell the tale now. "No one thought you'd be up here so soon, though. Neptune was hopin' to pick you up while you were still in the city. But when he heard you were already up here, he decided not to take any chances and wanted the trap sprung sooner than later. He's arrangin' things at his end, and I'm arrangin' this side. It made it easier that she's a daft old bird," he said, inclining his head toward Helen.

"So there was really nothing to the whole missing-ring story besides a cheap robbery on your part?" Henrietta felt her anger rising. "What about the scratches?"

Jack laughed and pulled out a long stiletto knife. "Yeah," he grinned, almost maniacally. "I carved up the sill. Part of the fun, ain't it? Scaring the old bat to death. Didn't think of it till I heard Edna telling ole Virg about how Helen was afraid, thought that someone stole her two-bit ring. It was just a bit of fun, waiting for the signal."

"You're deranged!" Henrietta sputtered.

Jack looked like he was about to respond when something seemed to catch his eye. "Fuck! There it is!" he said, taking a flashlight out of his coat pocket and flashing it three times in rapid succession out the window. "Come on! Get up!" he said, roughly grabbing her by the arm and pulling her.

"No! I'm not going with you!" Henrietta said vehemently, trying to pull away from him.

Jack responded by lurching forward and grabbing her wrists before she could even think what to do. Dropping the knife on the bed, he deftly took some rope out of his pocket with one hand and began winding it around her wrists. "Oh, yes you are," he hissed.

Henrietta debated screaming, but she feared being gagged, so she kept silent, instead pleading with him again. “Please, Jack. Don’t! Don’t do this! Clive can protect you from Neptune . . . he’ll pay you! I know he will! How much do you want?”

Jack pushed her in front of him as if she hadn’t said anything. “No one can protect anyone from Neptune,” he said grimly as she stumbled outside into the night air. Knife back in hand, he prodded her toward the dock, where a boat, even now, was sliding up.

Chapter 17

Clive raced down Highway 41 toward the city. He hoped he could get there before Moretti could change his mind. Moretti was the ringleader of the gang he was currently after for the suspected murder of one Elizabeth Harding, whom they had found a few months ago lying in an alley off Canal Street. At the time, Clive's main case had been tracking Neptune to the Marlowe with Henrietta, and he had suspected at first that the two cases might have been connected, that perhaps Elizabeth Harding was one of Neptune's cast-off girls. But as time had gone on, any connection he had originally tried to forge hadn't held up, as new evidence had appeared, implicating Moretti's gang instead. There seemed to be a pattern emerging to the new crimes: always a young girl, usually with no friends or family, not brutally assaulted as was Neptune's predilection, but always killed with some sort of stiletto type of knife in the neck just behind the ear. Moretti's gang was known for carrying stiletto knives, and Elizabeth Harding had been found stabbed in just such a way.

But why? Moretti's turf was usually the track, gambling, and booze money; normally, from what Clive knew, Moretti didn't like to dirty his hands with unprovoked murder. They had suspected his gang of various knock-offs over the years but had never had enough evidence to convict. But this was something different, this new pattern of stabbing young girls. It *looked* like Moretti's work, but it didn't add up. Could it be a frame-up? Clive wondered. Someone trying to snuff out Moretti, perhaps? A grab for power now that Capone was behind bars? When Capone had gone down, everyone mistakenly believed that crime in the city would finally drop off, but in reality, it had actually increased as rival gangs like Moretti's or Neptune's or even Capone's lieutenants—the Outfit, they were called—wrestled to fill the power vacuum. Could it be Neptune trying to get rid of Moretti? Normally they stuck to their own turfs, but maybe something had changed.

Clive gripped the steering wheel tighter, cursing the fact that his concentration had suffered lately with the distraction of Henrietta and the problems at Highbury. He couldn't help but remember Neptune's warning as Clive was arresting him a couple of months ago that he would get the mob to come after him.

At the time, Clive hadn't been afraid of the threat per se, but it definitely now left him with a distinct feeling of unease. He wanted this case to be solved, for more reasons than one, especially if he really were to resign as he had told his father he would. Perhaps this should be his last case, he pondered, but it was a difficult one to crack.

Moretti and his gang had eluded them for months, constantly leading them on wild-goose chases so that Clive had begun to suspect an informant. He had tried to get his own man inside the gang, but he hadn't been successful, having stopped in this particular line of pursuit when his last man, one Frank Kuhle, had turned up in the river. The chief had been furious, of course, that there had been yet another death associated with this case and blamed Clive, which Clive accepted willingly and with much more regret, almost angst, then would normally be expected. He hadn't given the man enough cover, nor had he given him enough information, he saw, though in truth, he hadn't possessed much more than what he had related. Still, he had wanted to keep some information close to his chest, and maybe that had cost Kuhle his life. It was always a fine line between giving away too much information to the plant or not enough, but

Clive had taken Kuhle's death hard for some reason and fully blamed himself.

And now, now that he was miles away from the city, a mysterious call had come through from Moretti himself, apparently, which Clancy had passed along to him. He had just gotten to sleep, having stayed up awhile reading to take his mind off Henrietta and the fierce debate inside his head as to whether or not he should go back to her room, when Billings had faintly knocked at his bedroom door, saying that there was an urgent telephone call for him from the Chicago police. A very sleepy Billings, dressed in his pajamas and robe, had dutifully led him to the library and had then taken himself back off to bed.

"Inspector Howard speaking," Clive had said wearily, standing there in his own robe and slippers, one hand in his pocket of his dressing gown. It was Clancy, relaying Moretti's message that he was willing to talk, for a price. Clive usually never gave in to such demands for payment, but after listening to Clancy's information, he had instructed Clancy to play along, taking down the location of the rendezvous point on a piece of stray paper on his father's desk, and telling Clancy to meet him there with plenty of backup discreetly on hand. A nervous-sounding Clancy had gotten off the telephone, then, and Clive had hastily dressed and dashed down to the stables, where, by a stroke of luck, Fletcher had been unwittingly wandering about, doing God only knew what. Whatever the reason, he had luckily been on hand to quickly fetch the keys for the Alfa Romeo for him without Clive having to go through the trouble of waking someone up or having to search for the keys himself in the little cabinet McCreanney had erected in the garage to house them all. He had also told Fletcher, as he spun off down the driveway, to tell Henrietta or his parents in the morning that he had had to leave on police business.

"Damn it!" he said out loud now, pounding his fist on the steering wheel as he sped along. Why had Moretti decided to make a move *now*, when he was so far away? It was almost as if they knew of his movements . . .

There was something he was missing, he thought, as he passed the few lone cars on the highway. He ran through the conversation with Clancy one more time in his mind. Why had Moretti wanted to meet downtown at the Water Tower? That seemed a strange place for a rendezvous, too public. But maybe that's what they were banking on. Clancy had sounded strange, though. Not his usual self. Perhaps he had been sleeping on the job; God knows he had caught him often enough. No, thought Clive, it was something else . . . He seemed flustered, almost cryptic, but why? Had the chief been standing there? Certainly not, Clive reasoned. At almost two in the morning, the chief would be nowhere but in bed beside his wife unless there was some sort of city emergency. Clancy had said something strange, though, when Clive had asked him if he were all right. Something like "Oh, yes, boss, everything's tiptop here; you know, just like when all the planets are in line . . ." his voice had trailed off then, and Clive had heard a noise as if Clancy had dropped the receiver. He had gotten back on the line, however, and had urged Clive to hurry and that he would have the men ready with arrows fletched. Another noise and what sounded like a grunt before Clancy had said a hasty goodbye and then hung up. Clive sighed. He hated to demote a man, as it was lousy for the overall morale amongst the men, but what could he do? Clancy was horribly incompetent. He had proved that over and over again. If he didn't do something about him, Clive realized, he himself would be the one to look weak. And yet, if he were resigning soon, anyway, maybe he should leave it to his replacement to sort out.

He glanced impatiently at his pocket watch, hoping he would make it in time. He was still only about halfway there. Having Fletcher handy had at least shaved off a few minutes, he thought gratefully, and his mind drifted, then, to Fletcher himself. Though he tried to like the man as if to prove something to Henrietta, there was something sneaky there, something he didn't like. For instance, what had he been doing wandering around the stables at this time of night, anyway? Originally, he had chastised himself for his quick judgment of Fletcher, thinking that it had merely been childish jealousy on his part in regard to Henrietta, but he couldn't shake the feeling as time went on that there was something else to it. Something in the back of his mind that he was forgetting . . . but what? He felt he knew Fletcher in some way, but how? He tried to shift his attention back to Moretti, but it kept wandering instead to Fletcher . . .

As he drove alone in the night, farther and farther from Highbury and closer and closer to the city, the pieces to the puzzle continued to swirl incomprehensibly around in his mind until, finally, a chilling revelation suddenly came to him. The pieces began to fall quickly downward, then, to form themselves into an obvious picture, which Clive finally recognized, to his horror, before the last piece even fell into place. He knew now.

How could he have been so stupid? he despaired, pulling the car over to the side of the road, a thin sheen of sweat covering his body as he did so. Clancy had been trying to give him a message in his own idiotic, cryptic way, but, Clive had to admit, it had worked. It was obvious now what he had meant! *The planets are in line* was of course a reference to Neptune. Neptune was somehow involved, and that could only mean that Henrietta was in extreme danger now that he was miles away from her. Not only that, but the *arrows fletched* was a reference, of course, to Fletcher. He knew it! he admonished himself, banging on the steering wheel again.

Madly, he spun the car around, turning it back northward, as he tried to desperately think of what to do. He had passed a lonely roadside bar not too far back, he remembered. He would head back there and use their telephone to call the house and alert them, make sure Henrietta was safe.

As he pushed the car as fast as it would possibly go, causing it to vibrate horribly, he tried to place Fletcher in all this. After racking his brain over and over, it finally came to him that he had heard the name when he was just a junior officer sitting in on an interrogation of Neptune, the *false* Neptune, as it had turned out. They had picked him up on suspicion of running a prostitution ring, but they had eventually had to let him go as they had not had enough evidence to hold him. Clive had been standing guard when Neptune was allowed his telephone call. It was all coming back to him now. He had heard Neptune tell whomever he was speaking to to send *Fletcher* to pick him up . . . So that was it! Fletcher was one of Neptune's pawns, and he had left Henrietta unprotected with him! he realized with a deep groan.

He felt a mad rush of desperate anger as he pulled up to the Three Gables Inn and dashed inside, flashing his badge and demanding to use the telephone. The bartender, a slight, balding man with wisps of hair trailing across his bald spot, hurriedly set the big black telephone on top of the bar for him, his few tired, inebriated customers curiously watching the show unfold through squinted eyes on what had been, up until now, an uneventful evening.

Clive waited impatiently for the number to go through, but instead of hearing a ringing on the other side, the operator came back on and informed him that there was trouble on that line and did he wish to make a different call?

"What do you mean trouble on the line?" Clive almost shouted.

"Just what I said, sir. It appears that line has been temporarily disconnected. We can send a repairman out tomorrow, but there's nothing more to be done tonight yet. Do you wish me to connect you with another number?" she asked with more than a slight hint of annoyance.

Clive hung up then and rubbed his forehead with his hand in agony. Fletcher had obviously cut the line. A burning-hot fear filled his heart as he realized he could never make it back to Highbury in time to save Henrietta from whatever Fletcher's instructions were. He had already been gone too long.

Chapter 18

"Why'd you let her go?" Stan asked irritably as he and Elsie made their way through the squeaky gate at the end of the garden, Elsie wincing at its rusty cry, hoping it wouldn't wake anyone.

"I've already told you, Stanley," Elsie whispered. "You know what she's like; she said she'd only be gone a little while."

That had been over an hour ago, when Elsie, alternately lying on the bed and then pacing around Henrietta's room, carefully watching the clock until exactly one hour had passed (the amount of time she had decided early on that she would wait), had finally in desperation decided to wake up Stanley. He had been flustered and bleary-eyed when he had come to the door, Elsie having had to repeatedly knock, each time a bit louder, and had mistook her presence outside his room in the middle of the night as being suggestive of something else entirely.

"Elsie!" he had said, surprised. "I didn't think . . . I don't know . . ." he spluttered, mentally chalking her erratic behavior up to that stupid officer's attentions earlier in the night. He had obviously corrupted Elsie's better virtues. "You should go back to your room, Elsie, though I'm . . . well, flattered, I suppose . . ."

"Stanley! Can I come in? Quick!" she said, looking up and down the hall and pushing in past him, much to his extreme shock.

"Elsie! You're not dressed!" he said, turning away from her. "You've obviously been stirred up into a fit of passion by that . . . that officer-what's-his-name. But we can't be foolin' around like this! What would your mother think? What would *my* mother think? This is just what she was afraid of, me coming here and—"

"Stanley!" Elsie hissed, interrupting him. "It's Henrietta! She went out about an hour ago, and she isn't back yet. I'm worried . . . it's probably nothing, but I . . . I'm afraid."

At the mention of Henrietta possibly being in distress, Stan spun back around and listened to the exceedingly limited amount of information Elsie had to relate, a sense of doom quickly overcoming him. He instructed Elsie to go back to her room and get changed, while he hurriedly pulled on his own trousers and shirt. They met back in the hallway a few minutes later and had crept down the stairway, Elsie clutching his arm as they went. Elsie told him about the message that she was to deliver to Clive should he turn up, that Henrietta had gone to a cottage to help an ill servant. Neither of them had any idea where to find this said cottage or even how to get out of the house. The massive front doors in the foyer near the bottom of the grand staircase were bolted shut, and they guessed that opening them would rouse the house.

"There must be a different way out," said Stan, as he led them through the dark hallways until they found themselves eventually near the kitchen. Elsie was the first to spot the back door, but as they hurried across to it, they froze in fear as a noise sounded nearby on the back stairwell. Stan peered into the darkness lit only by the moonlight streaming in through the windows and saw a man emerge, who, upon spotting Elsie and Stan, seemed startled as well.

"Who are you?" the man asked with a frown.

"Who are *you*?" Stan asked, Elsie still holding onto his arm.

"Name's Virgil. I work in the gardens . . . usually."

"Well, we're . . . guests," Stan tried to say manfully.

"You don't look like guests," Virgil said, unconvinced.

"Hey! Listen here! We're guests of Henrietta," Stan added, forgetting to address her as "Miss Von Harmon."

"Well, that explains it, then. She's the creepin' type, too."

"She's my sister!" Elsie said.

"That don't change anything," he said plainly, as if her comment was meaningless. "She creeps about here and there, she does."

"Listen, bud. Have you seen her?" Stan asked, impatient.

"Tonight? Yeah . . . she was in the big room."

"No, I mean, now."

"Creepin' about, you mean?" he added with a sly grin.

"Yes," Stan said with exasperation. "Well, no! Come on; we're in a hurry! Have you seen her or not? She said she was going to some cottage to check on some woman named Helen. Where would we find that?"

"I wouldn't bother. Helen's a daft old bat; Henrietta's always down there. Don't know why. She's mesmerized by her, she is. But then again, some say she's a witch . . ."

"Helen?"

"Course, Helen." Virgil paused. "You didn't think I meant Henrietta, did you? Or did you?" He looked toward the back door as if considering something. "Nah, you don't want to be messin' around the cottage after dark anyways; I've seen strange creatures circlin' round there at night."

Elsie's grip tightened on Stan's arm so much that he cried out in pain. "Elsie!" he said, turning to her. "He's just trying to scare us!"

He turned back toward Virgil now. "Are you going to tell us or not? Otherwise, I might have to mention to the Howards how we saw a gardener creeping around the house in the dark."

"Oh, all right," Virgil said, shifting uneasily. "I was just havin' a little fun," he said with a scowl. "You go out the back," he said, pointing his thumb toward the back door. "Down the end of the gardens. Go through the gate and follow the path down to the lake until you see the boathouse, and then it's just beyond that. You'll find it, unless you're as stupid as you look."

"Listen, mack!" Stan said, taking a threatening step toward him, but Elsie pulled him back.

"Stanley! Come on! Leave him!" she said and pulled him toward the back door, which they managed, thankfully, to open without a noise.

Having pushed through the gate now, the path was easy enough to follow in the bright moonlight, which lit up the whole terraced yard in a strange ghostly way.

"I hope this Helen is okay," Elsie said, trudging behind Stan. "She must be bad off if Henrietta hasn't come back yet."

"I'm sure she is. Henrietta probably just fell asleep there," Stan said unconvincingly. "You know how irresponsible she is."

"Stanley! That isn't quite fair, and you know it!"

"For all we know, she's already been there and gone."

"Gone?"

"You know, gone off with Howard somewhere."

"Stanley! What's gotten into you tonight? You seem all . . . flustered, like."

Stan paused in his marching and quickly turned around to face her, surprising Elsie in his suddenness. "Well, maybe I'm not so sure where I stand," he said, gesturing back toward the massive house. "I go looking for your brother half the night, and when I come back you're in the arms of some officer, dancing about without a care in the world as to where I might be . . . lost, if you must know," he said, looking away.

"Stanley!" Elsie said, biting back a smile. "You're jealous!"

"Course I'm not jealous, Elsie, but, well, a man can only take so much."

"That was just for fun! I was merely being polite," she explained.

"It looked like more than good manners to me, Els," he said, seriously. "You couldn't stop looking at him all night."

Elsie looked away and then back at him. "You might kiss me, you know, sometimes," she said shyly, looking down at the ground. "We're almost engaged . . ."

"Elsie!" he said, astonished. "Is that what you want?"

"Oh, forget it," Elsie said, embarrassed now. "Come on, we'd better get going."

They'd reached the beginnings of the beach now, and what looked like a small hut loomed up in front of them.

"Is this the cottage, do you think?" Elsie asked, puzzled.

"Didn't he say there was a boathouse first?"

"What's a boathouse, anyway?" Elsie asked, peering down at the water. "The water's so black, isn't it?"

"Well, seeing as it's right by the water, this must be the boathouse," Stan reasoned. "Look, the path keeps going . . ."

"Did you hear that?" Elsie asked, stopping and straining to listen. They were both silent, but all they heard was the lap of waves. "I think someone's there," Elsie said.

Stan seemed unsure. "You stay here, and I'll run up the path and see if I see the cottage, okay?"

Elsie nodded, still looking out at the water. Stan disappeared, then, and Elsie took a step closer to the boathouse, peering into the shadows cast by the moonglow. Her stomach lurched when she thought she saw a woman . . .

"Henrietta?" Elsie called. "Is that you?"

"Easy, now," hissed Jack in Henrietta's ear. "No sudden moves." They were standing in the shadows of the boathouse, Jack having forced her down here. The small motorboat sat moored behind them, carrying a fat man in an ill-fitting jacket and with a scar running across his face where his left eye had been. He had cut the motor a ways out to prevent any noise and had rowed the last little bit. Fletcher had timed it right, getting Henrietta down to the dock just as the boat was pulling up. He had been about to thrust Henrietta into it when they had heard voices—a man and a woman, it sounded like—coming down the path, and he had instead retreated against the side of the building, pulling Henrietta with him. He put his hand roughly over her mouth and held the blade of his long, thin knife at her throat. Breathing heavily, he watched what was happening.

The man had run off, but the woman was coming toward them now. "That's you're sister, isn't it?" Jack whispered, and Henrietta nodded. "Tell her you're fine and to go back," Jack hissed. "No funny stuff," he said, removing his smelly hand slowly from her mouth.

"Hen?" Elsie called out again.

"Elsie!" Henrietta called out to her, trying to keep her voice from cracking. "It's me!"

"What are you doing down there? I thought you were with Helen, you said."

"Don't! Don't come down, Els! I'm . . . I'm with Clive, you see . . ." she shouted to her.

"Oh!" Elsie said, halting. "I . . . I'm sorry!" she called out hesitantly.

Just then, however, Stan came hurrying back down the path, having found the cottage dark and quiet. He had knocked a couple of times, but no one had come to the door and he felt it wrong to just walk in. Irritated, he decided to return to Elsie and, taking a deep breath, had turned and quickly strode back. Coming from the opposite direction now and seeing the boathouse at a new angle, he could swear he saw the figure of a man standing behind what looked like . . . could it be? . . . Henrietta?

"Hey!" he shouted. "What are you doing?"

Startled, Jack turned suddenly toward Stan now, still gripping Henrietta as he did so and flashing his knife, gleaming brightly as the moon reflected off it. Simultaneously, the man in the boat started the motor, and it purred loudly. Stan took a few slow steps toward them.

"Stay where you are, or she gets it!" Jack shouted almost hysterically over the noise of the boat engine.

Elsie screamed.

"Shut up, you bitch, or I swear to God I'll cut her!" Jack said, quickly turning now toward Elsie.

Stan took advantage of the few seconds that Jack's attention was diverted with Elsie to rush forward to at least get himself closer to Jack and a terrified-looking Henrietta.

Caught off guard, Jack instinctively moved backward, still clutching Henrietta, while Elsie clamped her hand over her own mouth and sank to her knees to prevent any more sound from escaping.

"Let her go," Stan tried to say bravely.

"Fletcher!" called the man in the boat. "Hear that? Sirens! Cops are on the way."

Jack looked desperately at the boat. The whine of the sirens was getting closer.

"I'm going, Fletcher! Now or never," grunted the man in the boat, pushing off now from the dock.

"Get out of my way, kid, or I'll cut her!" Jack snarled.

"No! Let her go!"

In the same instant that the man in the boat put the throttle all the way down, Henrietta attempted to twist away from Jack's grip, and partially, at least, succeeded.

Jack, holding Henrietta only by the wrist now as she strained against him, looked piteously at the boat as it pulled away and then at Stan, who was tentatively coming toward him. Desperate, Jack let go of Henrietta and made a dash for the woods, a startled Stan taking several seconds to understand what had just happened before taking off after him.

For a short time Jack seemed to follow the path to the cottage, Stan gaining on him as he did. Once at the cottage, however, Jack slipped around the back and went into the woods beyond, Stan finding it harder to follow now. There was no more path, for one thing, just broken foliage where Jack had torn through it, and there was no moonlight showing through the thick growth, either. Still, Stan kept going, desperate to catch this villain, not being able in the moment to comprehend exactly why, whether it had to do simply with the thrill of the chase or if it was to somehow prove himself to Henrietta. (Or shouldn't he have said Elsie?) Or was it to prove himself to Inspector Howard, finally once and for all, that he wasn't the pipsqueak, as he so annoyingly called him. Bravely he continued running, trying his best to gain on Jack, his heart nearly bursting in his chest as he ran. Only occasionally did he stumble on a fallen branch or a root, the foliage as he rushed through it scratching him and at times even ripping his skin. Still he raced on, faster now, convinced that he saw Jack just ahead . . .

Nothing could have prepared him, however, for what came next. One moment he was running full tilt, and the next, he was stopped dead in his tracks when two pairs of strong arms, appearing out of nowhere, grabbed him and threw him to the ground.

"Ow!" Stan said, his head hitting the ground hard. A boot held his head to the dirt, his arms were wrenched behind his back, and a pair of handcuffs were clamped on his wrists.

"Gotcha!" said a gruff voice.

"Hey!" Stan tried to say into the dirt, but all he got was kick in the ribs.

"Shut up!"

There was movement all around then as Stan perceived what seemed to be cops appearing seemingly out of nowhere. Didn't they realize that Fletcher was getting away? he thought desperately, unless they had caught him, too . . .

Clive ran up then, holding out his badge and nodding toward the cops resting their boots on the captive.

"Get him up!" Clive ordered them with a shout and drew back his arm to sink a punch into Stan's gut as he stood limply between the two cops holding him up, when Clive, suddenly recognizing him now despite the darkness of the woods, stopped in midair and let out a loud groan. "This isn't him," he said, dropping his fist disgustedly and turning his head away. "This is the pipsqueak."

Chapter 19

The next couple of days at Highbury proved to be quite a knot of confusion in need of careful unraveling. Naturally the whole house had been woken that night when the Winnetka police had arrived in full force at Highbury. Not being able to get through to anyone at the house via telephone, Clive had quickly called the Winnetka police from the Three Gables Inn and informed them of the situation. He had also called the chief in the city and reported what was happening and that he suspected Clancy was being held somewhere against his will. Clive had driven at high speed, then, to Highbury, arriving at the scene well after the police, but, as fate would have it, just as they were mistakenly nabbing Stan, Fletcher having apparently slipped past them.

Stan was understandably angry at first, but he softened considerably after being praised profusely by Henrietta and Elsie for his brave actions by the boathouse, which, really, they said, had truly saved Henrietta from being thrown into the boat and hauled away, and even by Inspector Howard, who sincerely begged his pardon for the mix-up and who admitted that Stan had done a fine job. This moment in the spotlight, plus the extra devotion from Elsie, seemed to eventually ease his ruffled feathers. "Just so long as no harm came to Henrietta," he said, sheepishly, though Elsie caught the emotion in his voice and stored it away to be thought about later.

If she were honest with herself, there was a part of her that had been questioning Stan's true feelings ever since they had begun courting, just shortly after Henrietta had thrown him over, in fact. Elsie hadn't ever minded taking Henrietta's hand-me-downs, so long as the castoffs, as it were, fit her just as well or better, which, up until now, she had been convinced of. But now, after last night, a mirror of sorts had been thrust in front of her in which she was forced to judge whether the fit was suitable or not, and she wasn't so sure anymore. Why had Stanley lurched to save Henrietta and not her? she could not stop wondering, for example. She told herself not to be silly, that of course he had to try to save Henrietta first—Jack had had her by the throat with a knife! Of course that made sense! The mirror, though, Elsie was realizing upon closer inspection, appeared to contain a crack, a tiny shard of which had found its way inside her, creating the smallest sliver of a doubt. It had perhaps always been there, but Elsie was unfortunately conscious of it now, and she desperately hoped it would not grow into something bigger as time went on. She loved Stanley, after all! But more than once the next day, she had to admit, and even on the long drive home, disturbing visions of Lt. Barnes-Smith and his charming smile had appeared before her eyes, confusing the issue all the more.

After the police had found Elsie and Henrietta by the boathouse, Henrietta had hurriedly directed them up to the cottage to check on Helen, where they had rescued her, just barely alive. Helen had accordingly been rushed to the hospital and was still there now, critically ill.

Henrietta had also related to Clive and the police all that Jack had told her in the cottage, how it had all been a setup, and how they were to rendezvous with Neptune in a small town on the Mississippi, though Clive was sure that to chase them there now would be futile.

The setup had gone beyond Fletcher posing as the chauffer to capture Henrietta, however. In truth, it had also been Neptune's gang members who had led Clancy to believe that he was indeed rendezvousing with Moretti.

In order for the plan of capturing Henrietta to work, Neptune had needed Clive out of the way, so they had staged the fake call to Clancy to lure Clive back to the city. It had been child's play to capture the unwitting Clancy, holding him at an abandoned loft on Pearson, where they commanded a perfect view of the Water Tower, the rendezvous point with Clive. When Clive had failed to show after two hours, however, they had, as they'd previously been instructed, abandoned the plan and had Clancy beaten and driven to a remote woods near Joliet, where he was dumped and left for dead. Some kids had found him in the morning, though, and he had then been taken to the hospital, where, the chief related to Clive via telephone the next day, Clancy had been able, despite his rather serious injuries, to confirm that Neptune had had a two-pronged plan. Not only was he to break out of jail and escape with Henrietta, the object of desire in his warped mind, but he would also at the same time muscle out Moretti for control of the Chicago underworld. He had hoped to frame Moretti by using nameless, faceless volunteers, such as Jack Fletcher, to kill young women around the city with stiletto knives and dump them.

Clive's heart constricted at the thought of how close they had come to abducting Henrietta. Worse was the knowledge that his nemesis was now at large again, and in a near fit of anxiety, Clive vowed to keep Henrietta safe at all costs. But how? His parents had been quite ruffled by the night's events and of course took advantage of the situation to point out that the sooner Clive was done with this nasty business, the better. Clive was privately inclined to agree, but how could he give up now that Neptune was free? That being said, Clive knew that whether he was an inspector or not, Neptune wouldn't rest until he had Henrietta, and, as this whole episode had proven, Henrietta's being at Highbury did not necessarily protect her.

Neptune's fingers, as Jack had chillingly relayed to Henrietta in the cottage, did indeed reach far.

Upsetting as all this police business was, Mrs. Howard could not afford to dwell upon it for too long; after all, there was much to be discussed regarding how the party had gone and what steps needed to be taken toward their next big undertaking, the wedding itself. She was impatient to have everything back to normal and the whole unpleasant business put behind them, but she managed to nevertheless maintain a respectable somberness all the next day.

With perfect tact, then, and just the right amount of pleasantry, considering the situation, she bid her houseguests goodbye the next morning and apologized to them for the disturbing events of the evening. She had very much enjoyed meeting Henrietta's family, she had told them, and she sent her love to Mrs. Von Harmon with hopes that they would meet very soon.

Eugene had not said much when told about what had happened the night before, except to sullenly mutter that he should have been woken, as Henrietta's brother, but Stan had replied that he hadn't really thought anything much would have come from their moonlight search for Henrietta. If he had, he said diplomatically, he surely would have. Eugene had looked unconvinced but had not bothered to reply with anything more. Instead, he went back to smoking his cigarette, limply leaning against one of the large columns holding up the stone portico under which the party stood to say their goodbyes.

Henrietta squeezed Elsie's hand and kissed her, telling her she would see her soon at home, whenever that might be. And Stan, too, had kissed her briefly on the cheek and told her to take care of herself and had warned Clive likewise to watch out for her.

"That's my department now, old boy," Clive said with forced confidence, though his insides were churning, and he gripped Stan's hand with unusual firmness before the three of them piled into the old truck, Stan, of course, in the driver's set. As he watched them roll slowly down the lane, Clive couldn't help but feel that Stan's words held a degree of well-deserved admonishment, conscious of the fact that he had twice now put Henrietta in fatal danger.

Their guests having finally departed, Mrs. Howard telephoned the hospital to again check on Helen's condition and to see what could be done for her, but so far she had not regained consciousness. As Antonia hung up the receiver with a sigh, she told Alcott that she supposed the two of them would have to go and see her later in the day, that it was the only decent thing to do, really.

Mr. Howard had responded with an absent, "Quite so, quite so," just as Arthur, a junior footman obliged to take James's place for the day and clearly sensitive to this elevated duty, delivered the tea with only mildly shaking hands. The four of them exhaustedly sat down, each brooding on their own thoughts, Henrietta not being able to stop thinking about poor Helen and the dreadful events of the past evening, discreetly wiping tears every so often.

Mrs. Howard, for her part, tried to brighten the mood by informing them that the Exleys were quite taken with Henrietta, and with Elsie, actually, and had already issued an invitation to them to come to dinner next week. "And," she said waggishly, looking at Mr. Howard over her cup of tea, "tell them what old Exley told you, Alcott."

Mr. Howard shuffled uncomfortably in his chair. "Really, my dear. Perhaps now is not the time."

"Nonsense! We need something to take our minds off this dreadful business. I insist! Come now, let's hear it."

Mr. Howard cleared his throat and said somewhat begrudgingly, "It's just that Exley's quite distressed to discover that his daughter and eight grandchildren are living in . . ." (He was about to say *squalor*, but he stopped himself in time.) ". . . reduced conditions, shall we say, and is insisting on providing for them."

"Oh, no!" Henrietta said, sitting upright now. "Ma . . . Mother . . . would never allow that."

"Be that as it may, those were Exley's words to me, my dear. And

I daresay, he won't be thwarted this time in taking responsibility for them," Mr. Howard said matter-of-factly.

Henrietta sank back in her chair, wondering what all this would mean for them. She knew Ma would hate it, maybe even refuse help for herself, but surely she would let the boys be educated at least?

"And there's something else, Alcott," Mrs. Howard said delicately, swirling more sugar into her tea. "Apparently, there's been another incident of theft, Billings tells me."

Mr. Howard grunted. "Not again. What is it this time?"

Henrietta braced herself for what she felt sure was going to be an accusation against Edna regarding the hairpin she had given her. She had seen her wearing it the other day and had meant to inform Mrs. Howard, but it had been such a terribly busy day that she had forgotten . . .

"A set of the Fabergé eggs, I'm told."

Henrietta breathed an unexpected sigh of relief but was intrigued all the same.

"Not the ones that we brought back from St. Petersburg on our honeymoon?" Mr. Howard said, disturbed.

"I'm afraid so, my dear."

"That's it, Antonia! I won't be dissuaded this time; we've got to get the police involved."

"The problem, darling, is that I'm not sure when they were taken. Billings said that the contents of that particular curio cabinet have not been dusted in several months, so it very well could have been the work of Fritz."

"Actually," interjected Henrietta, glad to have something to contribute, "I'm pretty sure that Jack . . . I mean Fletcher, was responsible for all those thefts. He told me so in the cottage," she said, hesitantly looking over at Clive. She had no wish to further disturb him by bringing up yet again her encounter with Fetcher in the cottage. His mood ever since had been very dark. "He had to find a reason to get Fritz fired, so he staged a bunch of thefts so that he could get himself the job."

"I say! This is a bit out of order," grumbled Mr. Howard. "I'll have words with Billings."

"But what I don't understand is how he managed it when he wasn't even an employee here yet," Henrietta mused, taking a thoughtful sip of her tea. "He must have had help," she said, her eyes narrowing now. "Someone like Virgil, maybe . . ."

"Henrietta," Clive warned, finally breaking his silence, "we've already been through this with Virgil . . ."

"Yes," she said hurriedly before he put a premature end to her theory, "but Elsie told me that when she and Stan came looking for me, they saw Virgil coming down the servant's stairway into the kitchen last night."

"Whatever was he doing up there?" Mrs. Howard asked indignantly.

"Are they sure that it was him?" Clive asked skeptically, his head still resting on his fist, propped along the back of the settee where he sat across from Henrietta.

"Well," Henrietta said, a bit annoyed at Clive's tone, "they asked him his name, and he said Virgil, so maybe that's a clue."

Virgil was forthwith summoned to the library before an irritated Clive and a somewhat-puzzled Mr. Howard only, Clive *insisting* that Henrietta not be part of the interview. Upon being ushered into the room, Virgil had sullenly removed his hat and was offered a chair, which he refused.

"Sit!" Clive commanded, generating a look of concern, but no comment, from his father.

Shooting daggers at Clive with his eyes, Virgil then took the chair offered, but with exaggerated slowness. "Yes? Sir?" Virgil added with disgust.

Clive cleared his throat and cut out any preamble. "You were spotted last night in the house. Coming down from the maids' quarters, to be exact. Is this true?"

Virgil paused, looking from one to the other and shifting slightly in his chair. "Yeah. It's true."

"I say!" blustered Mr. Howard.

"For what purpose?" Clive asked crisply.

Virgil shrugged.

"Listen, Higgins. Are you aware that another theft from this house was discovered last night?" Clive asked him evenly as he leaned casually against the desk, his arms crossed in front of him.

Virgil shook his head but held Clive's eye.

"Are you aware that it has come to light that Jack Fletcher was working with someone inside this house before he was hired on here, to steal various items and to make it look like it was the work of Fritz?"

Virgil's eyes flickered apprehensively, but he didn't say anything.

"Now are you, or are you not, going to tell us what you were doing in the house last night?"

Still Virgil remained silent, looking down at the ground.

"Right!" Clive said, banging his hand on his father's desk. "I'm turning you over to the local police," he said, reaching for his father's telephone. "Let's see how you like doing time."

"Okay! Stop! I . . . I didn't do it," he said with slow deliberation, though he fitfully twisted his cap in his hands.

"Well?" Clive said expectantly, still holding the receiver in his hand.

"Promise you won't dismiss her if I tell you?" he asked pleadingly, looking up into Clive's eyes. "Promise you won't blame her," he begged.

"Blame who?" Mr. Howard asked, confused.

"Spit it out, Higgins."

"I . . . I *was* in the house, but I didn't steal anythin'! I . . . I snuck up to the maids' wing. I wanted to see Edna."

"You what?!" Mr. Howard sputtered, but Clive gestured for him to let Virgil continue.

"Did she let you in?" Clive asked.

Virgil looked at him as if assessing whether or not he could trust him before admitting, "Yeah. She let me in."

"Do you realize that's grounds for dismissal? For both of you?" Mr. Howard butted in.

"You promised!"

"I did *not* promise, actually," said Clive. "But I will do what I can. If you cooperate, that is."

"That or you'll beat my face to a pulp again?" Virgil said bitterly, his temper flaring up.

Mr. Howard looked sharply at Clive but did not say anything.

"How long were you with her?" Clive asked bluntly, again ignoring his father's critical gaze.

"Not long. She gives me a kiss or two then says I have to go. Says we could get into too much trouble. So you see, she shouldn' be blamed for it."

"Were you working with Fletcher?"

"No."

"The truth."

"No!" he said more vehemently. "I hated him!"

"Why?"

"I knew he was up to no good. Knew it from the first minute. Somethin' about him. I keep myself to myself, but when he started getting overly friendly, first with Kitty and then Edna, I just saw red all the time. I was lookin' for a chance to trip him up, but he was always too smooth, always covering his tracks, always scootin' off to town or sneakin', using Mr. McCreanney's telephone."

Clive quickly wondered if this was how he had kept in touch with Neptune's gang. "Go on."

"I don't mind sayin' I might have tried to hurt him if I got the chance," Virgil admitted. "Not kill him, like, but I did want to hurt him," he said angrily, and Clive began to feel a drop of respect for Virgil, having felt similarly himself where Fletcher was concerned.

Clive thought for a moment. "And this Kitty. He was friendly with her?"

"Yeah."

"Perhaps we should summon her as well," Clive said, glancing over at his father.

"Can't," Virgil said before Mr. Howard could even agree.

"Why not?" Clive asked.

"She quit. A few days ago."

"Any idea why?"

"Don't know."

"Take a guess," Clive said, annoyed.

"Mighta been 'cause of him. Always after her, he was. Edna says he got too familiar. Took advantage," he said, looking Clive straight in the eye. "Wanted her to do stuff she didn' want to do. Some men are like that, ya see." Clive got the unmistakable feeling he was trying to imply something and had the urge to thrash him again. Manfully, however, he contained his emotion and merely stared at him, his fury obvious.

"Get out, Higgins," Clive muttered finally, dropping his gaze as he said it.

Virgil stood up unsteadily but did not yet leave the room. He stood there wavering until Clive finally looked over at him again.

"I . . . I want my money back."

"What money?"

"The money I spent on the ring. That or the ring. It's mine, and you've no right to keep it."

"What's all this about a ring, Clive?" Mr. Howard asked, bewildered.

"I'll explain it later, Father," Clive said, looking coolly at Virgil, considering. He stood up, then, and drew out his wallet, placing a ten-dollar bill in Virgil's outstretched hand. "I'll keep the ring for now," he said to Virgil, who merely tightened his fist around the money. "You can keep the change."

"Suit yourself," he said with a scowl as he slunk off out of the library.

Henrietta spent most of the afternoon in her room sleeping after the night's ordeal, trying in her own mind to put what had happened into perspective. Earlier in the day, when they had all sat having tea, she had been intrigued by the discussion of the thefts and was particularly hurt when Clive then forbade—yes, *forbade* her!—to be part of Virgil's questioning. It was *her* theory! Clive's behavior was really too much to be endured, and she had accordingly gone upstairs to lie down, where she had lain, fuming about it, until she had finally drifted off, exhausted.

When she awoke, she did not feel particularly rested, however, but she dutifully changed and did her own hair for dinner, which turned out to be a quiet affair all around. Henrietta did not have much of an appetite and, in truth, spent much of the dinner still sulking about the Virgil interview. Mrs. Howard had insisted that the whole sordid business not be discussed at dinner, so Henrietta was not able to ask about the outcome of the interview, nor was Clive able to share that after a careful search of the woods, a long stiletto knife had indeed been found. Clive had since given it to the Winnetka police, who were trying even now to obtain fingerprints from it.

After dinner, Clive had the obligatory glass of port with his father while the ladies waited in the drawing room, Henrietta's mind still a confused turmoil of thoughts and emotions regarding the whole of last night, all the while having to endure Mrs. Howard drone on about the various gowns worn at the engagement party and who had said what to whom. Henrietta found it absolutely incredible that Antonia chose to dwell only on the minutiae, the social mores of the evening's party, as if what had happened with Fletcher was a minor inconvenience, like James's procuring the flu.

After what seemed like ages, Clive appeared, looking distressed, and asked if Henrietta might care to join him on the terrace. Mrs. Howard, not getting much out of Henrietta in the way of conversation anyway, thought this an excellent idea. Henrietta apathetically declined at first, but after continued urging on the part of Clive, she agreed to follow him out.

The air was unbearably warm, though no heat lightning appeared on the horizon this evening to fool them. Likewise, Henrietta could not make out the sound of the waves tonight through the steady buzz of the cicadas that must have come to life just this week. Still, their droning hum had a similar hypnotic effect as she stood with her back to Clive, looking out in the direction of the lake. She shuddered as she recalled once again the image of Helen tied up in the dark. Her mind jumped then to an image of Jack leaning over her, roughly forcing a kiss from her, and remembered how her heart had beaten so fast that she had felt in danger of it stopping altogether. It reminded her of what had happened at the Marlowe, though all that ever came back to her regarding that night were vague images and feelings of terror. Absently, now, she took the glass of brandy Clive was holding out to her.

"Was it very terrible, darling?" he asked delicately, mistaking the real cause of her silent aloofness during the whole of the evening. Besides the moments that he held her outside the boathouse while she sobbed into his chest after he had made his way back to her following the frantic chase after Fletcher and the mistaken capture of Dubowski, they had not had any time to discuss what had happened, to make sense of it with each other.

Henrietta didn't answer right away. Her pent-up emotions were hovering very near the surface, and she could feel the tears welling up at his tender expression of concern for her, but she was still so very hurt and was determined to stay angry with him. He had dared to forbid her . . . after he had told her at the Burgess Club that she was his superior! Obviously he had been disingenuous—again.

Clearly she was a bad judge of character all round, or too trusting at any rate, she had thought bitterly that afternoon as she lay on the big empty bed in her room. She always seemed to believe in the wrong man, first Larry and then Jack. Perhaps she was wrong about Clive as well . . . After all, hadn't their life together, their initial acquaintance, started out with a deception? He had tricked her at the Promenade, dancing with her, not revealing that he was a policeman sniffing out clues. And then again by not telling her about his privileged life on the North Shore. Ma was right, he had not exactly been honest, and she was more the fool. But hadn't she herself once told Ma that *sometimes lying is necessary*? Oh, she didn't know what to believe anymore! Certainly, she couldn't trust her own powers of judgment. She wiped a small tear from the corner of her eye, which dangerously threatened to spill over and slide down her cheek. After the Burgess Club, she had been determined to put all of her misgivings behind her, but the episode with Jack had unsettled her profoundly.

"Henrietta," Clive said, suddenly drawing her close. "Look at me," he said, gently placing two fingers under her chin and lifting her face to him. "You can trust me," he said slowly, shockingly reading her mind, her fears. The fact that he could so accurately sense what was in her heart, that he knew her so well, left her feeling exposed and raw and caused a well of emotion to erupt within, the sobs coming now without check.

"Oh, Clive," she cried, her shoulders shaking as he wrapped his strong arms around her.

"I'm not the villain. Honest," he whispered. "And yet I'm hardly the hero either," he said, softly rubbing her back. "All I know is that we need to trust each other, completely . . . always. Never hold anything back."

"But you *don't* trust me! You wouldn't let me be a part of Virgil's questioning, you wouldn't tell me about your case in the city, about Sophia, anything . . ." It was all tumbling out now. "You said that as your wife I'm your superior . . . but I'm not, am I? I knew it sounded too good to be true." She began crying again.

"Henrietta," he said urgently. "I did mean it. As the person, *the first person*, I'm utterly giving all of myself to—my whole heart, my very soul—you *are* my superior. You absolutely must be in order for me to do this, and yet," he said, quietly, but firmly, "I am bound to protect you in all things and so must therefore sometimes act as yours. Surely you must see that? I would be remiss if I did not."

He was staring at her with such a fierce intensity now, and she felt weak gazing up at him. All of her confusion and doubt seemed to melt away. She felt almost sick with love for him, and she longed for him to kiss her in this moment. He sensed it, too, and breathing very hard, his face so very close to hers, he softly caressed her lips with his. It excited her beyond words, and she leaned into him, pressing her body against his and kissing him hard in return, an electric shock running through her as she did so.

Clive drew back, trying to steady himself, and rested his forehead against hers. "I never want any Fletchers or Sophias or . . . memories . . . to come between us," he said hoarsely. "I'll never doubt you again, about anything."

"No, don't say that," she said, putting her hand hesitantly on his chest. "This has been all my fault. I was so stupid as to trust someone like Jack."

Clive sighed, still holding her. "I should have believed you from the very beginning that there was something amiss here. And I should have trusted my instinct with Fletcher. I suppressed my suspicions, however, because I thought it was merely jealousy, and I didn't want to appear so uncouth as to give in to such feelings."

"It's ridiculous that you would be jealous of Jack," she murmured.

"I know that now," he said regretfully. He slid his arms from around her, and he walked aimlessly toward the fence surrounding the terrace, leaning his hands against the uneven stones as he looked out over the property. "I was wrong. And I didn't want you in the room when I was questioning Virgil because . . . because . . . oh, I don't know. I was afraid that if he *was* somehow involved in the larger case, he would know you knew and it would put you in even greater danger."

"But Fletcher already knows I know. So . . ."

"Yes, I wasn't thinking clearly," he said, rubbing his eyes. "I'm losing my touch, I think, Henrietta," he continued tacitly, not looking at her. "I put myself up as your protector, and twice now I've put you in harm's way . . ."

"Clive . . ." she said, seeking to stop him.

"No, let me finish. I did the same to a man I enlisted to go undercover in a gang I suspected of murdering young girls. He was a bit on the shady side—most of them have to be to take that sort of job—and I didn't completely trust him. I gave him some information on the leader, Moretti, and sent him in, but it wasn't enough information and he was double-crossed. He ended up dead. His name was Frank Kuhle. If I had told him who we suspected the squealer was ahead of time, he might still be alive. I'm responsible for that man's death," he said, his voice cracking a bit. "I couldn't keep Catherine safe, or my child, or even most of the men in my platoon." Here his increasingly elevated voice caught a bit. "Slaughtered like helpless animals, they were," he said bitterly, slamming his hand down now on the rocks of the fence.

"Ow!" he said, wincing in pain. He had torn the skin, and he reactively drew his fist up to his mouth to catch the blood that was beginning to ooze now from the wound.

Seeing his injury, Henrietta went to him, instinctively slipping back into the role that she had learned to play at home, that of the mother "hen" to all of her siblings when Ma, worn-down and weary, was unable to rise so many times from her prison by the fire. She took his injured fist in her hand and wrapped it with her handkerchief, gingerly tying it into place. Clive watched her, his eyes fraught with anguish.

"Clive," she said soothingly. "You weren't to know. You did what you thought was right in each situation. Catherine's death was not your fault. You know that. There was nothing you could have done. And you couldn't have saved your men. You were following orders, I'm sure. You did your duty."

He looked at her now with such longing, almost despair, and she was shocked to see his eyes filling with tears. He turned his head away, ashamed, but she drew him close and held him. "Oh, Clive. It wasn't your fault," she said softly, fully understanding now as she hadn't been able to quite before that with this man, and this man only, she was becoming the woman she was always meant to be. The days of self-doubt and petulance were truly over now. This man loved her, needed her, wanted her, and she wanted nothing more than to be with him. She saw now that they *were* equal, if only in their need for each other, a perfect compliment despite age or class.

"I'm sorry," Clive said as he pulled back, clearing his throat and looking away again, clearly embarrassed.

"Don't be sorry," she said gently, squeezing his arm slightly. "Please."

He attempted a smile. "Perhaps it's best that I'm leaving the force."

"Don't say that!" she answered quickly. "It will be a while until your father retires, and you're a fine detective, and you know it. You can't let what's happened affect you. Think of all the cases you have solved. And you *did* catch Neptune—it's not your fault that he escaped."

"I hate the fact that Neptune's still out there!" he said fiercely. "I hate that you're still in danger as long as he walks free!"

"I admit, I don't understand his obsession with me, his relentless pursuit . . ." she said with a shudder.

"I've seen similar cases. He's mad, crazed in the head. But I *will* catch him, for good this time. I swear to you, Henrietta, I *will* catch him."

She offered him a smile. "I know you will. Nothing will happen as long as I'm with you. I'm quite safe, I'm sure."

"Do you really feel that way? Truly?" he asked her fervently.

"Of course, I do," she answered. "More than I have with anyone, even my own father. You'll protect me; I know you will. And I'll take care of you," she said, brushing his hair back off his forehead, her soft touch causing his eyes to close briefly in the comfort of it.

"God damn it, Henrietta," he said, pulling her to himself suddenly and holding her so tight she could feel his hard chest next to hers. "I love you so very much. I *need* you," he groaned. "I couldn't bear it if I lost you now."

"I love you, too, Clive," she whispered in his ear. "I want to be your wife . . . your lover." She hesitated and then went on. "I want you to show me how to please you," she whispered.

Clive momentarily stiffened at her words, trembling as she tentatively kissed his neck. A perfect flood of feeling then erupted from him. Madly he kissed her as a man starving—her neck, her lips, her cheeks, and back to her lips again. His hands traveled across her back and then lower as he almost roughly pressed her to him so that she felt his hardened state just as the tip of his tongue parted her lips.

Henrietta thought she would explode with passion. She so badly wanted to be with him. She returned his kisses as she had never before and felt in danger of crossing some sort of line beyond which there was no return.

"When can we be married, Clive?" she asked desperately as he kissed her neck. "Please say soon."

"Whenever you wish," he said hoarsely.

"Fall? October, maybe?"

Clive paused in his lovemaking, breathing heavily, to consider. "That soon? Mother would be beside herself," he said, releasing his grip on her just a fraction.

Henrietta let out a small laugh.

Clive pulled back a little more. "Do you really wish to wed in the fall when everything's dead and dying? Don't you want to be a spring bride?" Clive asked, intrigued. "Most women seem to, anyway."

"Well, you should know by now that I'm not most women," she grinned.

"True enough."

"And besides, I don't see the fall that way, as a time of dying, I mean," Henrietta responded thoughtfully. "Just a retreat. And I've always found the fall so beautiful. It's always been my favorite time of year. And we're not dying—not just yet, anyway, I don't believe."

"Then October it shall be," he said with a smile and looked at her tenderly. "We'll go to Europe for our honeymoon. Leave this place; leave everything behind," he said, taking her hand and kissing her fingers. "No villains, no mothers, no pipsqueaks. Just you and me."

"Oh, Clive! I don't know! That's so far away!"

"Exactly," he grinned. "Say yes," he said, seeing her hesitation. "Please. It will be lovely. Haven't you ever wanted to see London? Paris?"

She smiled in spite of herself. "Do you really mean it, Clive?"

"Of course I do," he said.

"Well, it does sound rather wonderful," she said, her eyes glowing with excitement.

"Then it's settled," he said happily. He looked back toward the house and sighed. "I suppose we should go in and tell them."

"Do we have to?"

"Unfortunately, yes." He smiled and held out his hand to her. "Thank you, Henrietta," he said, his heart full of love for her, as he lifted her hand to his lips again. She returned his smile and let him lead her inside.

As expected, Mrs. Howard had not been overly excited by their announcement that they were significantly advancing the date of the nuptials. She had naturally assumed that she had at least ten or twelve months to plan the extravaganza and was nearly irate, to say the least, that she now had barely three! Relentlessly, she tried to make them see reason, but in the end she finally accepted that they were resolute in their decision, though, in truth, Henrietta found herself on more than one occasion almost giving in to Mrs. Howard's pleas, only to be shored up in her resolve by Clive's firm adamancy regarding the decision. Mrs. Howard sadly accepted defeat, knowing from experience when it was useless to go up against Clive's stubbornness, but did not, all the same, give up honorably and continued throughout the evening to punish them by throwing out barbs of guilt, loud sighs, and fretful pacing. Julia would have to be called in to help, she had finally said with exasperation, to which Clive had calmly responded that Julia would be thrilled to be asked. In the end, Mrs. Howard had excused herself with a headache and had retired to her room, and Henrietta couldn't help feel guilty for the distress they were causing her.

"Nonsense," Clive had said to her. "She loves it, really. She'll rise to the task in the morning with full vigor; watch and see."

As it turned out, Clive had been right in his prediction that his mother would soon set herself to her new task with speed and alacrity. Within days, she did indeed telephone Julia, as well as several other people, and began scheduling appointments with caterers, musicians, stationers, and her seamstress. Henrietta took all of it in stride, knowing that it all had to be born in order to be with Clive in the end as his wife, and actually began to enjoy the preparations despite herself, particularly because it brought her in closer contact with Julia, whom she was liking more and more. Julia was scheduled to arrive this afternoon for tea, as a matter of fact, and Henrietta was rather looking forward to it.

She had risen late, however, and was just coming down the stairs when she saw Billings, who informed her that a letter had come for her. He held it out to her on the little silver salver, and when she took it, he bowed and made his way down the hallway without further comment or disparaging facial expressions. He seemed to have finally, albeit begrudgingly, accepted her as one of the family.

Carefully, Henrietta examined the letter in her hands as she made her way into the breakfast room, which was already deserted by now, everyone else having risen much earlier. The letter was from Elsie again, and she braced herself accordingly. She hoped it was merely a thank-you, but Henrietta was almost certain that if Elsie *were* to have written a thank-you at all, it would have been most probably addressed to Mr. and Mrs. Howard, not to her. Likewise, Henrietta supposed that Elsie would not write to *her* unless she had something urgent or disastrous to relate. With a timorous fluttering of her hands, then, she quickly opened it and proceeded to read.

Dearest Hen,

I hope you are recovering from our strange night at Highbury and that you suffered no lasting injuries. I trust that Clive is helping you just as Stanley is helping me. He is most attentive, for which I am grateful, though he does find the need to speak about the ordeal over and over in a somewhat obsessive manner. Ma was surprisingly willing to hear about the evening, though she had several choice things to say when I tried to tell her how Mr. Exley and co. were really very kind to us. She has not said much about it since, but seems to be in one of her sulks now. I wish you were here to talk with her, as you could tell it all so much better, but I know you are dreadfully busy. I was careful, by the way, not to mention to Ma any of the unpleasant business about what went on in the cottage and by the boathouse, as I don't wish her to worry or form a bad opinion about you, though, I must admit, I sometimes do myself worry and pray that you are quite safe. Let us hope that Eugene does not relate any of it, but, thus far, that seems unlikely.

In fact, the real purpose of this letter is regrettably regarding Eugene once again. I will try to explain it as best I can. The truth is that I felt terribly guilty when I returned home after enjoying such luxury while Ma was here alone. I don't begrudge going, and I am, by the way, ever so grateful, if I haven't mentioned it already, for a lovely evening. The party part anyway. It was the best night of my life. Anyway, I did feel guilty, and to make it up to poor Ma, I decided to give the whole place a good clean. It turns out that just as I was stripping the boys' bed, a sock fell out from under the mattress. While, as you know, this would normally not be anything unusual, the fact that it made a loud clunk as it fell to the ground made me wonder. Obviously there was something in it, so I put my hand in, thinking it might be rocks that Herbie collected again, though I've told him time and again not to ruin his socks that way. But it wasn't any rocks, Hen. Instead it was what looks like two golden eggs, painted beautiful colors with jewels fastened all over. They are so exceedingly beautiful, like nothing I've ever seen before, except perhaps at the Howards' house, and that's when I began to wonder if perhaps . . .

So you see my dilemma, dearest Hen. For now, I stuffed them back under the mattress so that Eugene wouldn't know that I had discovered his theft, as surely it must be. He has no money that I know of to have purchased such things of beauty, which leads me to the obvious conclusion. I am horrified that they may have come from Highbury. Please advise as soon as possible what I should do, if anything.

Your beloved sister,
Elsie

Henrietta's shoulders drooped as she held her head in her hands, her stomach knotting. How could he? After all that Clive had done for him, for her? It was too much! What was she to do with this boy? How could she face Clive and bring up the whole miserable story once again, after they had put it all behind them out on the terrace? How could she tell him that she had been wrong after all, that it was not Virgil or Fletcher or Kitty who had pilfered the Fabergée eggs, but her own brother? Slowly she paced the room, wondering what to do. Clive assumed that it had been the work of Jack. Would it matter so very much if the truth did not come out? she thought, twisting her hands together nervously. What difference would it make now? Is that what Eugene had been up to during his long absence the night of the engagement party? Virgil must not know the truth either, or he surely would have squealed. His dislike for both her and Clive was obvious.

She sat down in a chair to think but just as quickly stood up, anxious, and walked to the long mirror hanging above the sideboard where the cold remains of breakfast still sat out for her perusal. She stood in front of it, gazing at her own image but not seeing it. And what about Eugene's story regarding the stolen goods and Fr. Finnegan? Had that all been a lie, too? What had really gone on in the rectory? If she told Clive the truth, would she be jeopardizing the job he had promised Eugene or, worse, the help that the Exleys had hinted at? She felt sick to her stomach and groaned. What was she to do? She and Clive had pledged no more secrets, no more half-truths, only honesty. She had told him that she trusted him, and she did, but how could she explain this? Did it really matter, now, since it was all said and done, neatly explained? Perhaps she should just throw the letter away, or better yet burn it upstairs in her room. She paused for several minutes, considering.

Taking a deep breath, then, she slipped the letter into her pocket and left the room, knowing in her heart what she had to do.

Acknowledgments

What a long, strange journey it is to get a book published, even a second one. And though I've been told not to compare one's book to something more personal—say, a baby—it's hard not to.

This book, like most second children, was naturally conceived and birthed in the distracted wake of the first one, which has its pluses and minuses. Mostly pluses, I would say, as this second one, *A Ring of Truth* (aptly named), has not been overly subjected to the nervous frettings of a first-time parent. Much of the near-paralyzing worry that gripped me every step of the way with my first book was blessedly absent this time around, allowing this one to breathe and grow with much more latitude. And being less preoccupied with the process, I was able to indulge the writing more, and I hope that shows. Everyone's a better parent the second time around, all the usual mistakes having already been made, and I think this experience is no exception. I hope you enjoy reading it as much as I did writing it.

And as much as conceiving and writing are quite private endeavors, publishing and promoting certainly are not. I again thank my publisher, Brooke Warner, for taking me on and for her amazing insight and navigational abilities. I have a deep respect for her and what she is building. She calls us trailblazers, but, in truth, it is she that leads us forth. I would also like to thank my project manager at She Writes Press, Lauren Wise, for her ability to maintain calm at any given moment and for her extreme expertise.

And on the promotional side of things, I'd like to thank Crystal Patriarche and her fabulous team at Booksparks, who taught me, more than anything else, to see the publishing landscape through a wide-angle lens. It has been invaluable.

And thanks to my core readers, who unfortunately have to slog through the first drafts, bereft, as they are, of the finishing polish. Thank you for the sacrifice of your time and for your excellent feedback: Otto, Marcy, Liz, Amy, Margaret, Kari, Jason, Carmi, Sue, Wally, Hilarie, and Justine. And a special thanks goes out to Rebecca Cartwright, who was a reader in a very different sense, and whose services and insight were essential.

Also I'd like to thank all of you, known to me and unknown, who graciously read *A Girl Like You* and took the time to comment or even to pass it along to a friend. It is amazing to get e-mails from strangers (or friends, for that matter!) telling me how much they liked the book. Thanks for that little slice of heaven. I hope you keep on.

And, lastly, as usual, I'd like to thank my husband, Phil, who is a reader of mine, of course, but thankfully so much more. "You to me are everything, the sweetest song that I can sing." Thank you, my love.

About The Author

© Ciliento Photography

Michelle Cox holds a B.A. in English literature from Mundelein College, Chicago, and is the author of the award-winning, *A Girl Like You*, the first in the Henrietta and Inspector Howard series. She is known for her wildly popular blog, "How to Get Your Book Published in 7,000 Easy Steps—A Practical Guide" as well as her charming "Novel Notes of Local Lore"—a blog dedicated to Chicago's forgotten residents. Michelle lives with her husband and three children in the Chicago suburbs.

SELECTED TITLES FROM SHE WRITES PRESS

She Writes Press is an independent publishing company founded to serve women writers everywhere. Visit us at www.shewritespress.com.

A Girl Like You: A Henrietta and Inspector Howard Novel by Michelle Cox
$16.95, 978-1-63152-016-7
When the floor matron at the dance hall where Henrietta works as a taxi dancer turns up dead, aloof Inspector Clive Howard appears on the scene—and convinces Henrietta to go undercover for him, plunging her into Chicago's gritty underworld.

The Great Bravura by Jill Dearman
$16.95, 978-1-63152-989-4
Who killed Susie—or did she actually disappear? The Great Bravura, a dashing lesbian magician living in a fantastical and noirish 1947 New York City, must solve this mystery—before she goes to the electric chair.

Just the Facts by Ellen Sherman
$16.95, 978-1-63152-993-1
The seventies come alive in this poignant and humorous story of a fearful rookie reporter at a small-town newspaper who uncovers a big-time scandal.

Water On the Moon by Jean P. Moore
$16.95, 978-1-938314-61-2
When her home is destroyed in a freak accident, Lidia Raven, a divorced mother of two, is plunged into a mystery that involves her entire family.

Murder Under The Bridge: A Palestine Mystery by Kate Raphael
$16.95, 978-1-63152-960-3
Rania, a Palestinian police detective with a young son, meets cheeky Jewish-American feminist Chloe at an Israeli checkpoint—and soon becomes embroiled in a murder case that implicates the highest echelons of the Israeli military.

The Black Velvet Coat by Jill G. Hall
$16.95, 978-1-63152-009-9
When the current owner of a black velvet coat—a San Francisco artist in search of inspiration—and the original owner, a 1960s heiress who fled her affluent life fifty years earlier, cross paths, their lives are forever changed . . . for the better.

CPSIA information can be obtained
at www.ICGtesting.com
Printed in the USA
BVHW080526221218
536219BV00002B/184/P